the WITNESSES

D0168329

OTHER BOOKS AND AUDIO BOOKS
BY STEPHANIE BLACK

The Believer

Fool Me Twice

Methods of Madness

Cold As Ice

Rearview Mirror

Shadowed

Stephanie BLACK

the WITNESSES

A NOVEL

Covenant Communications, Inc.

To my children—Amelia, Shauna, Stephen, Jared, and Julia—
with the hope that they will always "stand as witnesses of God at
all times and in all things and in all places" (Mosiah 18:9)

Cover image *Office Skyscraper in the Sun* © PPAMPicture.

Cover design copyright © 2013 by Covenant Communications, Inc.

Published by Covenant Communications, Inc.
American Fork, Utah

Copyright © 2013 by Stephanie Black
All rights reserved. No part of this book may be reproduced in any format or in any medium without the written
permission of the publisher, Covenant Communications, Inc., P.O. Box 416, American Fork, UT 84003.
The views expressed within this work are the sole responsibility of the author and do not necessarily reflect
the position of Covenant Communications, Inc., or any other entity.

This is a work of fiction. The characters, names, incidents, places, and dialogue are either products of
the author's imagination, and are not to be construed as real, or are used fictitiously.

Printed in the United States of America
First Printing: October 2013

19 18 17 16 15 14 13   10 9 8 7 6 5 4 3 2 1

ISBN 978-1-62108-523-2

Acknowledgments

THE PUBLICATION OF THIS BOOK is a dream come true for me, and I'm thrilled both to bring this story to readers who enjoyed *The Believer* and to introduce new readers to these characters. A huge thank you to all the people at Covenant Communications, including managing editor Kathy Gordon, for giving me this opportunity and for all the work involved in the preparation and publication of the book.

Over the years, I've been blessed with three wonderful editors who have believed in this project: Angela Eschler, Kirk Shaw, and Samantha Millburn. I'm grateful to all of you; your support for this book means so much to me. And thank you, Sam, for making it shine with your editorial expertise and for your patience and thoughtfulness. It's an honor and a pleasure to work with you!

Thank you to my test readers: Stan and Amy McConkie, Marshall McConkie, Dianna Hall, Rebecca Hall, Katherine Hall, Bonnie and David Overly, Suzanne Lucas, Kathleen McConkie, Amelia Black, and Shauna Black. If I neglected to list anyone, I apologize—thank you to you, too!

As always, deep thanks goes to my husband, Brian. When he reads or listens to fiction, he usually chooses classics like *Moby Dick* and *War and Peace*, but amidst the Melville and Tolstoy, he always takes time for my books. He has been constantly supportive of my writing and patient with the times in my life when things get crazy with deadlines. Someday I should write a book that includes a white whale, just for him.

Chapter 1

HEART RACING, ALISA KENT SHOVED back the blankets and sat up. Perspiration soaked the old nightgown she wore, and the fabric twisted around her legs. Had it been more than a nightmare?

No. If it had been a reversion, she'd be sprawled on the floor, arms and legs bruised from battering against the dresser or the wall or whatever objects she'd been unable to perceive while trapped in a mindscape of distorted memories and fictitious horrors.

Only a nightmare. But the barrier between dreams and hallucinations was fracturing.

She shoved her fingers through her sweat-dampened hair, fingernails scraping her scalp. Fear squeezed the air from her lungs. She couldn't relapse. Hadn't she caused enough harm without making herself a crushing burden on the people sheltering her?

In the blackness came the soft rhythm of Jill Roshek's breathing. Jill, peacefully asleep. Loyal Jill, who had chosen to die rather than help the Council frame her brother as an anarchist assassin.

Jill deserved peace.

The chilly room made Alisa shiver. She sank back into a pillow that already felt cold and pulled the covers up to her chin, but lying down worsened the sense of airlessness. She sat up and lowered her bare feet to the floor. This basement bedroom had no windows, but there were two narrow windows in the family room down the hall. Fresh air might ease this feeling of suffocation.

They could never risk opening a window during the day, but in the middle of the night, no neighbor would notice the shifting of a pane of glass. Alisa groped for the bathrobe draped over the foot of her bed and slipped it on.

A rustle from Jill's bed froze Alisa in place. She didn't want to awaken Jill or anyone else. The Halbrooks upstairs. Ian Roshek, asleep in the next room. If they knew she was prowling around in the middle of the night, they'd worry about her and report her insomnia to Dr. Lansbury. She didn't want more pills, more needles. She'd had enough of that during her imprisonment.

When she heard nothing but Jill's even breathing, Alisa crept toward the door, hands in front of her to feel her way in the darkness.

The doorknob rattled softly as she turned it. No reaction from Jill. Alisa stepped into the hallway and closed the door behind her.

Warm fingers pressed against her cheek. Alisa gasped, recoiling. Morning sunlight glinted off the row of gold trophies on her bookshelf and threw streaks of light across her quilt.

Anxiety showed in her mother's dark eyes. "Honey, are you sick?"

Alisa was alone, the hallway inky black.

She choked back a moan and shuffled toward the family room. These reversions shouldn't be happening, not this long after Information Extraction. It was the stress of hiding, of being trapped in the middle of Tremont, where any mistake would destroy all of them.

Two months gone, and still no word of how they would escape.

She should confess that the reversions were increasing, but the thought of admitting how damaged she was—how weak . . .

Pray for strength. For an instant, yearning consumed her. God had helped her once when she'd been in agony. Maybe if she asked—

No. How could she again beg for mercy when she had never granted mercy to anyone else?

Get yourself under control. It's your own mind doing this. You're allowing it to happen.

Alisa picked her way across the darkened family room. The carpet was soft beneath her feet, then coarser as she reached the braided rug in the center of the room. Her fingertips brushed the arm of the wicker rocking chair.

Hands gripped her arms, booted feet rapped against tile, a door banged shut. The sting of a needle.

"Lieutenant Kent. Are you a traitor to the government and people of New America?"

Yes.

Her hip slammed the rocking chair. She grabbed the chair to stop its swaying and reeled past it. Her hands hit the wall, and she fumbled to find the edge of the cardboard taped over the window. Fingers trembling, she ripped the tape loose and set the cardboard on the floor. Moonlight punctured the darkness.

Alisa released the latch and tried to slide the window open. It stuck in the track. She yanked at it, bending a fingernail backward. The masked faces of Liberty Cadre operatives loomed over her; fingers dug into her throat. She clawed at the hand, her nails skidding off of a leather glove, and stumbled into the wall in the Halbrooks' basement.

Stop this. Panting, Alisa staggered toward the stairs. The kitchen. She'd open the back door and breathe the freezing air of a March night until her head was clear.

A clock glowed on the stove. Three minutes past one. Shadowy countertops, wooden chairs arranged around a table—everything orderly and quiet. Alisa unlocked the door and pulled it open far enough to allow a blast of wind to hit her face. She inhaled deeply.

Calm down.

Stars sprinkled the limpid sky, now clear after a day of sleet and snow. Alisa relaxed the cramping muscles in her shoulders and focused on the glitter of moonlight reflecting off the icy puddles on the Halbrooks' patio. *Stay in control.*

Teeth chattering, she finally edged the door shut. She'd be fine if she could keep herself relaxed and attuned to her surroundings. *Stay calm.*

"They never thought their own daughter would betray them." At the table, David Garrett closed the contraband book in front of him. He removed his reading glasses and scrutinized her with the keen, affectionate gaze of an almost-uncle. "That's why they didn't run."

Alisa closed her eyes. *Let it fade.*

David grasped her shoulders and drew her into an embrace. His body was cold, his lungs empty, his heartbeat stilled. *My fault.* She struggled against his arms, and scalding pain drowned her, pain at the touch of a button, her own finger on the button, her own voice in her ears: "*Traitor. Anarchist. Religious believer.*"

She couldn't stifle her screams.

* * *

Ian Roshek was out of bed and halfway up the stairs before he fully awoke and registered that he was sprinting toward terrified, pain-wracked cries.

Alisa? Jill? He burst into the kitchen as Nathan Halbrook charged in from the other direction, his wife, Rebecca, at his heels. Nate flicked on the lights.

Alisa lay sprawled between the back door and the table, her body convulsing, her face contorted. Nate and Ian both sprang toward her. Alisa jerked violently, her legs nearly smashing into Nate's ankles. He jumped back.

Ian knelt near her head. "Alisa!"

"She can't hear you, kid; it's a reversion," Nate said.

Rebecca's grandmotherly face was white with fear. "Nate, the neighbors."

Alisa went limp, gasping for air, a dazed expression on her face. Livid scratches marked her pale throat.

"Alisa?" Ian leaned over her. She didn't react.

"Careful." Nate squatted beside him. "She's not all the way out of it yet."

Ian glanced at his sister, standing in the doorway to the basement. "Stay back, Jill."

He lifted Alisa's hand. Blood leaked from under the nail on her right index finger. "Alisa?"

This time she looked directly at him. He sighed in relief. "Are you all right?"

She pulled her hand free and sat up, but she wobbled so badly that she slumped forward, her head nearly touching her knees. Ian gripped her shoulders, steadying her, and Nate ran his plump fingers over her skull.

"She's got a lump here." Nate parted the dark hair above her right ear. "Doesn't look bad though. I hope."

Rebecca shivered. "It's freezing in here."

It *was* freezing, Ian realized, and the wintry smell of wood smoke clung to Alisa's nightclothes. He glanced around for an open window.

"Was she outside?" Rebecca hurried to check the door. "Unlocked," she reported, her voice catching. Ian's heartbeat accelerated to panicky speeds. The police could already be on their way to investigate reports of a disturbance.

Alisa spoke, her voice raspy. "I . . . didn't go outside."

"Did you open the door?" Nate asked.

"I . . . think so." Her hand brushed her scratched throat. "The air—I needed—"

Nate straightened and took two lumbering steps toward Alisa's feet. He bent to check the soles. "She wasn't outside."

"They'd better get downstairs." Rebecca twisted the dead bolt. "If anyone heard . . ."

Alisa pulled away from Ian and started to rise unsteadily to her feet. Ian caught her arm. "Let me help you. You don't want to risk another fall."

"Take her downstairs." Nate plodded over to Rebecca and wrapped his arm around her. His thick white hair was sticking up on one side, and his round face looked wilted and old. "I'll call Daniel."

"*No*," Alisa said. "I'm . . . all right."

"Child, you're not all right. Roshek, stay with her and keep her as quiet as you can. Jill, give him whatever help he needs."

Jill nodded and hurried down the stairs. Ian followed, escorting Alisa to where Jill stood awkwardly in the family room, blonde and petite in pajama pants and a huge sweatshirt that reached her knees. The fear in her blue eyes made Ian desperate to offer some older-brother reassurance, but the closest thing to comfort he could think of was *At least the police aren't here* yet, *right?* which would probably get him slapped.

"Jill, fetch a couple of blankets," he said.

"I'll lie down in my room," Alisa said curtly. "Let go of me."

Ian tightened his fingers on her arm. "You shouldn't be alone."

Jill rushed into the bedroom and returned with a faded quilt, a fleece blanket, and a pillow. Alisa lay on the couch, crumpling against the cushions as if the effort to pretend she didn't need help had devoured the last of her energy. Ian tucked the bedding around her, wishing again that he could think of something comforting to say.

Jill gasped. "The cardboard." She hurried to fix the window covering.

Alisa's face was chalky, and sweaty black hair stuck to her face and neck. Ian pictured the hardwood kitchen floor, the edges of the stone countertops, the heavy table. How hard had she hit her head?

"Alisa." He forced himself to speak calmly. "You do know who you are, where you are, that kind of thing?"

She nodded without looking at him, an answer that might have meant *yes* or *leave me alone*.

"I'll get a washcloth to—" Jill gestured toward the bloodied scratches on Alisa's neck.

Ian tried to give Jill a bracing smile, but the expression felt so phony that he abandoned it. Helplessly, he hitched the quilt higher over Alisa's shoulders and sat on the carpet next to her.

"You'll be fine," he said, wishing he could loosen the knots of panic in his stomach.

Chapter 2

DANIEL LANSBURY'S PHONE RINGING INTERRUPTED him midsentence and provoked raised eyebrows from Councilor Patrick Haines, who was relaxing in a leather club chair across from Daniel.

"Excuse me, sir," Daniel said. "I apologize for the interruption. I'm on call. It must be the Annex."

"One week back at work and already they're hassling you late at night." Haines waved at the phone. "Don't keep the police waiting."

Daniel glanced at the brass filigree hands of the clock on the wall and was startled to see it was past one a.m. He'd been so engrossed in his conversation with Haines that the hours had rocketed by.

The sight of Nathan Halbrook's name on his phone display jolted Daniel. Nate wouldn't call this late for anything but a crisis. Daniel didn't want to take the call in front of Haines, but if he ignored it, saying it wasn't from work after all, Haines might be curious—and then offended when Daniel made improbable excuses to leave, frantic to call Nate back to find out what was wrong.

Mouth dry, Daniel put the phone to his ear. "Lansbury," he said brusquely.

"Dan, sorry to bother you." Nate's voice was matter-of-fact, which meant nothing. As director of the Tremont Euthanasia Center, Nate was accustomed to keeping his cool in emotionally charged situations.

"What's the difficulty?" Daniel asked.

"It's . . . Rebecca." The way Nate paused before saying her name told Daniel it *wasn't* Rebecca. "She's ill. Having some of the same type of trouble she had a few months back. She . . . needs care."

Fingers cold, Daniel held the phone tighter against his ear. Nate was talking about Alisa Kent and the Broc psychosis that had nearly killed her during her incarceration in the Detention Annex.

"Frequency and duration of the episodes?" Daniel asked.

"Um . . . not sure. But the one a few minutes ago was pretty severe. Sorry to bother you, but . . ."

"You did the right thing." Daniel thought fast. Going to the Halbrooks' in the middle of the night was a bad idea. Any insomniac neighbor would be intrigued by a car pulling into Nate's driveway at one in the morning. Though Nate could explain Daniel's visit with the ruse that Rebecca was ill and Daniel was helping out as a doctor and a longtime friend, it was better not to raise curiosity in the first place. But Nate knew the risks of a late-night visit, and if he was still asking Daniel to come, Daniel had better go.

"How is she now?" Daniel asked.

"She's quiet but in a lot of distress. Physically and mentally."

Physically. Alisa must have injured herself. "Is she in immediate danger?"

"I . . . don't think so. We're just concerned."

"All right." Daniel knew Nate couldn't elaborate without saying things that would sound odd if the call was being monitored. "Try to keep her calm. I'll be there as soon as I can."

"Thanks. We owe you."

Daniel disconnected. "I apologize, sir," he said to Haines.

"No need." Haines set his glass of lemon water aside. Since Haines had suffered a heart attack a year and a half ago, Daniel had never seen him drink anything else. "Off to the Annex, then?"

"I'm afraid so," Daniel said, suddenly paranoid that Haines would check up on him to make sure the Detention Annex was truly his destination. *Don't be a fool. Why would he doubt you?* "Thank you for dinner, and for . . . giving me food for thought."

Haines rose to his feet. "We'll be speaking again soon."

Daniel stood. "Yes, sir." But Nate's call had been a slap of reality. Daniel had been living a fantasy tonight as he'd listened to Haines's offer. It could never happen. He didn't want it to happen.

Haines shook Daniel's hand with a grip Daniel would have rated as a five on the pain scale. "Good night, Dr. Lansbury."

"Good night, sir." Daniel was at least six inches taller than Haines, but facing Haines somehow made Daniel's six feet four inches feel short. Strength showed in everything about Patrick Haines—solid features, broad, muscular shoulders, a sonorous bass voice. A man powerful enough to step into Daniel's father's position of Councilor over Internal Defense.

A few minutes ago, Daniel had been admiring Haines's power. Now it scared him.

Shaken and oddly disoriented, Daniel accepted his overcoat from a member of Haines's staff and headed for his car.

* * *

Relief surged through Ian at the faint sound of Daniel Lansbury's voice coming from upstairs. It had been an hour since Nate had called Daniel, one of the longest hours of Ian's life. For the most part, Alisa had remained silent and still. A couple of times, a quick movement or a change of expression signaled another reversion, but these lapses lasted only a second or two. Ian had been ready to think the worst was over when Alisa lurched to the side, nearly falling on top of him in a longer spell that left her in tears and Ian with a bruise swelling around his eye from a swipe of her elbow.

Footsteps descended the stairs. Stiffly, Ian rose to his feet as Alisa pushed back the bedcovers and sat up. Jill leaped from the rocking chair, where she'd been huddled, her face aglow with new confidence.

Daniel strode into the room, followed by Nate. Traces of Nate's usual good humor showed in his expression, probably thanks to the fact that there had been no phone calls from worried neighbors or visits from the police.

Daniel set his briefcase on the floor and peeled off a tweed overcoat. He was wearing an impeccable suit and tie. He always looked distinguished, but Ian hadn't thought even Daniel could look *that* sharp for a two-a.m. crisis.

"Didn't you read the invitation?" Ian asked tiredly. "Tonight's dress code was messy hair, wrinkled flannel, and stubble."

"Missed that part." Daniel gave Ian's bruised eye an appraising look, spared a small smile for Jill, and approached Alisa.

Ian stepped back and stood between Jill and Nate while Daniel examined the bruise on Alisa's head and checked her level of alertness. Alisa's expression was stoic as she answered his questions, but her folded arms were trembling.

"I'm going to go up and sit with Becky," Nate whispered to Ian. "She's pretty rattled by all of this. Tell Dan to call if he needs me."

Ian nodded, his eyes on Alisa as he fought to keep himself from interrupting Daniel with the question he wanted to ask—*Is she all right?*

Finished with his exam, Daniel drew a chair over and sat in front of Alisa. "Did the reversions radically increase in frequency and duration just tonight, or has this been building for a while?"

Alisa looked away from Daniel, her humiliation palpable. Ian caught Jill's eye and tilted his head in the direction of the hallway. Jill nodded and started out of the room. Ian followed her.

Daniel glanced at them. "Jill, go ahead. Ian, you stay."

Ian opened his mouth to tell Daniel this would be easier on Alisa without an audience, but at the grim look on Daniel's face, he walked back toward the couch. Daniel wanted him here to assist in case Alisa started hallucinating again, and Ian didn't want to force him into bluntly saying so. That would make Alisa feel worse.

Ian sat next to Alisa. "You're shivering." He took the quilt and draped it around her shoulders.

She gripped the edges of the quilt and pulled it tight so it enveloped her from neck to knees.

"All right," Daniel said. "Alisa, I asked you if tonight came as a surprise or if the reversions have been building."

"They've been . . . building."

"For how long?"

"Two . . . maybe three weeks."

Daniel loosened his tie with a jerk of his bony hand. "Why didn't you tell me?"

Alisa sat rigid, eyes averted.

"Alisa, look at me."

She obeyed, but the trapped look in her eyes made Ian acutely aware of how intertwined Daniel must be with whatever nightmares had come alive in Alisa's mind. Did she feel she was facing the man who had rescued her or the medical supervisor from her interrogation who had injected her with mind-warping drugs in the first place?

"How frequent have the reversions been?" Daniel asked.

"Up to . . . ten . . . maybe a dozen a day."

Dismay flashed in Daniel's face. "They were brief before tonight?"

"Up to a few seconds . . . nothing this bad."

"Tell me about tonight. How did it start?"

"I . . . woke from a . . . particularly vivid nightmare."

"What was the dream about?"

"Does that matter?"

"It might. Tell me."

"I was . . . at police headquarters, in my office. My . . . parents were with me. I realized—" Her voice went croaky. "Why does this make any difference to—"

"Go on." Daniel spoke gently, and Alisa leaned back against the couch, the stiffness of her pose easing a little.

"Captain Hofstader knew I was a . . . traitor. I heard him coming with Blake Peale, Rae Pulansky, and a few others. My mother was panicking, saying we were going to be arrested. I kept telling her I knew the way out, but I couldn't find the elevators or the stairs . . . I don't remember any more."

"And when you woke up?"

"The reversions started a few minutes later."

"Why did you go upstairs and open the back door?"

"I . . . needed air. I don't know what was wrong." She touched her scratched throat, her expression bewildered. "I felt like I couldn't breathe."

"Anxiety can create that feeling," Daniel said.

"I tried to open the window . . . one of the windows . . . down here. It was stuck."

"How many reversions have you had since you woke up?"

"I don't know."

"More than two?"

She closed her eyes. "Yes."

"More than four?"

"Maybe six or seven."

"All right. Alisa, look at me."

She opened her eyes.

"I need full cooperation from you, including full disclosure of any symptoms you're experiencing. If you're not willing or able to cooperate, then you're a danger both to yourself and to the rest of us, and I'll do whatever is necessary to ensure that an incident like tonight's doesn't happen again. We can't take chances."

"I'll cooperate," she said quietly.

"Good." Daniel lifted his briefcase and opened it. He removed a foil packet about two inches square. "Push your left sleeve up, all the way to the shoulder."

Alisa brought her arms out from under the blanket and pushed up the sleeves of her robe and nightgown.

Daniel tugged exam gloves over his hands and tore open the packet. It contained what looked to Ian like a bloated version of the bandages his mother had applied to skinned knees.

"This is something the Tremont Research Lab has been working on recently," Daniel said. "We've nicknamed it the Broc blocker, a name which is somewhat optimistic considering it's proven useful only in preventing the widely-spaced reversions of stage three. But the good news is that it works without sedating effects."

"Wait a minute," Ian said. "You're saying this blocker stuff is experimental?"

"Administered in a low, controlled dosage, it's safe."

Ian shut his mouth. Challenging Daniel was *not* the best way to calm Alisa's fears.

"This is a transdermal patch," Daniel said. "It will administer a steady dose of the drug over the course of a week." He peeled a strip of translucent paper off the patch and pressed the patch onto Alisa's upper arm, sealing it tightly around the edges. "You shouldn't experience any bothersome side effects, but if you do experience any dizziness, let me know. Don't remove the patch unless it becomes damaged. And keep it dry; cover your arm in plastic wrap before you shower."

He drew Alisa's sleeve down to cover her arm. "If the patch does become damaged, remove it immediately, but don't touch it with your bare hands." Daniel pulled two exam gloves out of his briefcase and tossed them to Ian. "If any gel leaks from the drug reservoir onto her skin, wash it away with soap and water, keep her lying down, and have Nate or Rebecca notify me immediately. This is a very potent drug, and it penetrates the skin rapidly. An overdose is not a good idea."

Ian closed his fist around the thin plastic gloves. "If it's dangerous to even touch this drug, how can it possibly be a good idea to—"

"The patch contains a membrane that controls the rate of release and keeps the drug concentration at therapeutic levels." Daniel stripped off his gloves and tossed them into his briefcase. He put on new gloves and took out a small plastic bag containing a capped syringe.

Ian eyed it warily. "What's that?"

"A small dose of the blocker, highly diluted. Because of the controlled release rate of the patch, it takes time for enough of the drug to enter the bloodstream to start working. This will get her through the next few hours." Daniel tore open an alcohol wipe. "Alisa, your right arm, please."

Alisa pulled her sleeve up. After Daniel finished injecting the drug, he stowed the syringe in his briefcase and removed a plastic medication bottle.

"This will help you sleep," he said, popping the lid off. "Ian, bring her a glass of water."

Ian fetched a cup of water from the bathroom, and Alisa swallowed the pill Daniel gave her.

"All right." Daniel took the cup out of her hand. "Lie down and relax. Ian, stay with her. I need to talk to Nate. I'll be back in a few minutes."

By the time Daniel returned with Nate twenty minutes later, Alisa was asleep. "Nate will stay with her," Daniel said. "Come up to the kitchen."

Ian sat at the kitchen table and watched Daniel heat himself a cup of cider. Ian's head throbbed, and the bruise around his left eye had swollen so badly he couldn't open his eyelid all the way. Gingerly, he probed the bruise.

"Are you all right?" Daniel asked.

"Yeah. Just a headache."

Daniel replaced the canister of powdered cider in the cupboard. "Why didn't you notice she was having problems?"

"She didn't talk about it, Daniel."

"Did you need it spelled out and footnoted like one of your history books? A dozen reversions a day—"

Ian bristled. "She's been spending a lot of time alone, okay?"

"And you didn't wonder why?"

Anger and guilt burned inside Ian. "She's been through a horrific experience. She seemed to want time alone, and I respected that. I didn't know I was supposed to be on the alert for this type of setback. Why didn't you warn us?"

Daniel stirred his cider with loud clinks of his spoon. "She could have gotten every one of us arrested tonight. If she hadn't closed the door before the reversion hit—if she'd gone outside—"

"I *know*." Ian's voice rose. He took a deep breath. "You're right. I failed her. I knew she was still having brief reversions here and there, but I thought she was keeping you updated. I didn't realize things had become so much worse. She did a good job hiding that."

"We can't afford blunders. If any of the Halbrooks' neighbors get the slightest inkling that people are hiding in—"

"Wow, are things really that serious? I guess we'd better cancel the back-yard croquet tournament."

Daniel slapped the spoon into the sink. "Just glance up from your books now and then and notice what's going on around you."

Ian reddened. "Nice suit," he said. "Where were you tonight anyway?"

"That's none of your business."

"It took you long enough to get here."

"I had to go to the lab to get the blocker. Do you think I keep that in my medicine cabinet?" He pulled the pill bottle out of his pocket and tossed it to Ian. "Give her one of these each night at bedtime. Rest is vital to her recovery. During the day, make sure she's not left alone for more than ten minutes at a stretch. She may still be having reversions."

"I thought the blocker was supposed to take care of that."

"It will help, but it may not be enough for her. With the severity of the reversions she's having, she's borderline as a candidate for it."

"You can't give her something stronger?"

Daniel's gray eyes were steady. "How much do you remember about your experiences in the Detention Annex following Information Extraction?"

Ian's hand went automatically to his chest, feeling the scar beneath his pajamas. The Liberty Cadre bullet that had nearly killed him had, ironically, also forced the police to spare him the withdrawal period that usually followed interrogation. They couldn't risk letting the stress of hallucinations kill him before his scheduled public execution. "Uh . . . thanks to the fact that you kept knocking me out, it's pretty much a blank."

"And that's what you were for those two weeks. Pretty much a blank. Insensible. Completely helpless. That's our other option for controlling the hallucinations. Do you think Alisa would choose that?"

"No. But if this blocker is such hot stuff, why didn't you use it on me in the Annex?"

"I told you, it's new." Daniel sat across from him. "Let me explain something. I've dealt with countless patients who have received Broc4 during an interrogation, but I've never dealt with a patient who went through everything Alisa did, nor is there any literature on the subject—except the records kept by my father in his experiments with the drug he used to alter Alisa's confession."

Ian grimaced. Though Daniel spoke with clinical calm, it must hurt him to discuss his terrorist father. At least that's what Jill kept telling Ian; she'd berated him a couple of times for bringing up Marcus Lansbury in front of Daniel. "You . . . have his records?" Ian asked. "I'm surprised he didn't destroy them."

"We have these records because he gave them to the Cadre doctor who worked on Alisa. The blocker patch actually contains the same drug the Cadre used on her. Rapid intravenous administration of the drug created the neurological state that allowed my father to tamper with her subconscious memory, causing her to give false testimony under Broc4. But the same drug administered in a slow, gradual dose has the effect of blocking some of the Broc series' side effects."

Ian stared at Daniel. "That makes no sense. I thought it was *due* to this Cadre drug that she had such an unusually bad experience with Broc4 in the first place."

"It was. Because it targets the same areas of the brain that Broc affects, it interferes with Broc's function, but because of its chemical similarity to the Broc memory stimulants, it also sensitizes the body to them, making initial post-Broc withdrawal much worse. If I'd had my father's notes, I could have tried giving Alisa the blocker during the recovery period, but I don't think it would have done much. If a trickle of water is coming toward you, a sandbag will stop it. If a tsunami is heading your way, that sandbag—along with you and your house—will get washed away. Broc psychosis is a tsunami. Clear?"

"More or less." Three o'clock in the morning was the wrong time to wrap his mind around this. "But are you saying giving her the blocker might help her now, but it's going to make her experience that much worse if she's interrogated again?"

"No matter what I do or don't give her, if she's interrogated again, she's gone. Not that it makes a difference. If we get arrested, we're all dead anyway." Daniel rested his elbows on the table and rubbed his eyes. "I'm doing the best I can for her."

"I know," Ian said. "I'm sorry. I'll quit hassling you. I'm just shaken up."

"So am I." Daniel's demeanor softened. "I didn't mean to blame this on you. If Alisa was deliberately concealing symptoms, it's unfair of me to expect that you'd realize how bad things were."

"I'm sorry I didn't do a better job of keeping an eye on her." Ian slouched in his chair, realizing how tired he was. "You mentioned dizziness as an indication of possible problems. Are there any other symptoms we should watch for with this blocker patch? Any signs she's getting too much of the drug or reacting badly?"

"Disorientation," Daniel said. "Difficulties with perception, including visual and auditory hallucinations."

"Hallucinations! How are we supposed to tell the difference between—"

"Not the memory-based hallucinations she's experiencing now. I'm talking about random images, colors, sounds. But unless you're planning to cut the patch open and spread the drug directly on her skin, she's not going to get an overdose. All right?"

Ian nodded.

"The best thing you can do to help her is to stay with her, keep her calm, and keep her engaged. Without outside interaction, she'll turn her attention inward, and that's not a good idea right now. Questions?"

"No."

"I'll leave her on the blocker for a week, then pull her off of it to see how she's doing. I don't want to leave her on it any longer than necessary." Daniel stood and picked up his coat and briefcase. "I'll check in tomorrow. Put some ice on that bruise."

Ian touched his swollen eyelid. "Do you think Alisa will be better soon? Is this a temporary relapse?"

Daniel's fingers tightened on the handle of his briefcase until his knuckles blanched white. "I don't know."

Chapter 3

"You think I'm wasting my time?" Lieutenant Blake Peale folded his wiry arms and scrutinized Officer Rae Pulansky, who was sitting across the desk from him.

"No, sir," Pulansky said politely. She was always polite. Peale had seen her shatter the spine of a fleeing anarchist with one shot and then address the dying criminal like he was the president's cousin.

"You think Daniel Lansbury is clean, then?" Peale asked.

"I don't know, sir." Pulansky tucked her mousy hair behind her ears.

Peale studied her earnest face. "You think I'm an idiot for going after him when everyone knows Councilor Haines has taken Lansbury under his wing?"

"I think you're taking a huge risk, sir. Dr. Lansbury has the respect of the entire Council."

Peale didn't respond. Pulansky was right. Even though all Peale had done was check ID and phone logs, it was still risky. The Council lauded Daniel Lansbury as the man not only patriotic enough to betray his own father as the leader of the Liberty Cadre but also to dispassionately execute Jill Roshek, the woman he'd loved, along with her brother and that scum Alisa Kent.

"His reputation *is* irreproachable," Pulansky said. "Of course, so was Lieutenant Kent's, so that doesn't prove anything."

"And so was Lansbury's father's," Peale added. "The perfect patriot. That's been Lansbury ever since he came back to work, acting like the whole fiasco with his father and the Rosheks never happened. You really think that after what we made him do at the executions, he's feeling all patriotic and forgiving? He's planning revenge."

"Maybe he's just feeling humbled, sir."

"Humbled?" Peale rolled his eyes. "Do you know Lansbury at *all*?"

"Do you think he knows it was your suggestion to assign him to the executions?"

"Whitney wouldn't have told him, but he might suspect. And even if he doesn't know it, he hates my guts."

"He might, sir."

Peale figured that was her tactful way of saying, *You did mock him about the executions and make it as miserable for him and the prisoners as you could.* "He's an arrogant jerk."

"Do you think he may be targeting you?"

"It's not just about me. We're all in the crosshairs, and I'm not going to sit here and wait for him to pull the trigger. I'm taking the first shot."

"Maybe he's not after revenge."

Peale snorted. "He's Zero's kid, Rae."

"I'm not sure he's like his father. He *did* turn Councilor Lansbury in."

"Yeah, but why? Marcus Lansbury kept his son squashed under his thumb. Maybe Daniel grabbed the chance to get rid of him so he could inherit his wealth and maybe his power—" Peale stopped. *Was* Marcus Lansbury out of the picture?

"His father's never been found," Peale said abruptly.

"Do you think Dr. Lansbury is in contact with his father?"

"I don't know. It's possible." Peale looked out the glass wall behind Pulansky. Sleet pounded against the building. He'd been thrilled to get assigned to this office on the twentieth floor of police headquarters, but the view of downtown Tremont wasn't much to brag about when it was storming. Even the majestic columns of the Executive Council Building and the lavish architecture of the Tremont Mansion looked blurry and boring.

"Sir, if anything, Dr. Lansbury would be in danger from his father," Pulansky said.

"Zero Lansbury won't kill his only kid."

"It's difficult to imagine them working together."

"Depends on what they both want." Peale pictured the angular face and iron-gray eyes of the former Councilor over Internal Defense and tried to imagine him side by side with his son. It wasn't hard; Daniel looked just like his father—a cowardly, spoiled version of his father. "I don't think

Zero would have trouble coming up with a way to pressure his son. He's lost his shot at getting himself to the presidency, but if he can get his son there, a son he's controlling . . ."

Pulansky furrowed her brow and sat quietly, like a teacher's pet pondering the multiplication tables.

"You think this is off target," Peale said.

"It's far-fetched, sir. But Zero is not a person to underestimate. Maybe he *has* found a way to manipulate his son." Pulansky unhooked her computer from her belt. "There's one new item of interest in Dr. Lansbury's phone log. At 0113 hours, he received a call from the home of Nathan Halbrook."

"Halbrook, huh?" A call from Nathan Halbrook wasn't interesting on its own; there were records of interaction between Lansbury and Halbrook since Lansbury's childhood. But one a.m.?

Halbrook. Councilor Spencer Brannigan's brother-in-law. Halbrook had never been in trouble, but rumor labeled him a malcontent prone to get in the way of the police officers assigned to provide security at the Tremont Euthanasia Center. The police left him alone because of his family connections, but Halbrook's attitude had stalled his career long ago. As the brother-in-law of a Council member, he should have done a lot better than a job directing the local death mill.

A prime candidate for getting involved in something illegal?

Brannigan's brother-in-law. Peale drummed his fingers on his desk, excitement growing. "Contacts between Halbrook and Lansbury have increased dramatically in the last few months."

Pulansky regarded Peale with meek brown eyes. "Mr. Halbrook is a lifetime friend. Doesn't it make sense that he would be in more frequent contact, supporting Dr. Lansbury? Like the rest of the nation, he assumes Dr. Lansbury's parents were assassinated by Ian Roshek a few months ago."

"Maybe true, maybe not. Lansbury might have defied orders and told Halbrook the truth." Peale hadn't dared eavesdrop on Lansbury's calls; that was pushing too far at this point. And he hadn't dared plant any transmitters on Lansbury's property because of the danger that Lansbury's security guards were still sweeping for bugs like they had when his father was around.

Peale tilted back in his chair, his eyes on the row of awards hanging on the wall of his office. "We could bug Halbrook's house."

Pulansky raised her eyebrows. "That's risky, sir. If we get caught, will anyone back us?"

"Nope. But if we find enough dirt, we'll make someone happy."

"Dirt on Dr. Lansbury, sir? Or dirt that could be used to taint Councilor Brannigan?"

Smart kid. "Who do you think might want dirt on Brannigan?"

"Colonel McLaughlin, sir?"

Peale grinned. It was no secret that Colonel Glenna McLaughlin, the new head of the Tremont Police Service, didn't like Brannigan and his drive to restrict police powers via a new written charter of government. McLaughlin didn't dare go after Brannigan directly, especially considering the rumors that President Ryce was backing Brannigan's reforms. But if someone gave her the information that let her bring Brannigan down, she'd be very grateful. And she'd offer big rewards.

Like promoting Peale to head of the Sedition and Treason Division?

"Sir, you just mentioned the possibility that Dr. Lansbury is involved with his father's anarchist activities, and now you're suggesting the possibility that Dr. Lansbury is involved in illegal activities with Nathan Halbrook or even Councilor Brannigan. The odds that Marcus Lansbury and Spencer Brannigan would be involved in any criminal activity together are—"

"About as good as the odds of me becoming a professional ballerina. Yeah, I know. I'm not suggesting there's garbage going on that involves Zero Lansbury and Brannigan both. But don't you get it? Daniel Lansbury is corrupt, and he wants to make us—and the Council—pay. The Lansburys think the world ought to lick their shoes, and Daniel is just like his dad. He's working against us, maybe with Brannigan, the so-called reformer, maybe with his father."

"Sir . . . are you *sure* this is wise?"

"You think I'm on a vendetta, don't you?"

"I know you dislike Dr. Lansbury."

"I wouldn't waste my time on him if I didn't think he was a real threat. And if we can discredit Brannigan in the process of bringing Lansbury down, McLaughlin will be thrilled. Or if we can hand her the fugitive Marcus Lansbury, she'll be thrilled. We can't lose."

"Unless we're caught before we have any evidence."

"There are risks, Pulansky. If you don't want to take them, don't. I can't order you to help me on this."

Pulansky looked troubled. Peale knew what she was thinking. It was one thing to pursue Daniel Lansbury, but if they were caught not only investigating Lansbury but also messing with the brother-in-law of a Council member, they'd get booted out of the Sedition and Treason Division, and their careers would be over.

It was worth the risk. He'd started with nothing and fought his whole life to get this far. If he could gain McLaughlin's favor, he'd win much greater power. He'd be an idiot to turn his back on that opportunity.

"We're good at what we do, Rae," Peale said. "We aren't going to get caught."

"I'm in, sir," Pulansky said.

"Fine." Peale was pleased. "How about the ID logs from the last couple of days? Anything interesting?"

"At 0149 hours, Dr. Lansbury scanned his ID at the west entrance of the Tremont Research Laboratory."

"The lab, eh? Half an hour after the call from Halbrook."

"At 0224 hours, he scanned his ID at the same door."

"Leaving the lab," Peale mused. As a researcher, Lansbury might have some experiment going that had to be checked in the middle of the night. That scientific stuff was a closed book to Peale. But it intrigued him that the trip to the lab had followed so promptly after Halbrook's call.

"Halbrook doesn't have anything to do with the lab, does he?" Peale asked.

"Not that I know of. And this is Dr. Lansbury's first middle-of-the-night visit to the lab."

"Who lives at the Halbrooks' house?"

She typed rapidly on her computer. "Only Nathan Halbrook and his wife."

"I want you to get the rundown on the Halbrooks' schedules. Find a time when they're both gone. We'll go in, plant a few bugs, and see what turns up."

* * *

Daniel dove into the pool, startling himself with a skin-freezing rush of water. He surfaced and swam a few laps before stopping next to Spencer Brannigan, who was treading water near the ladder.

"You make me feel like an old man," Brannigan said. "I couldn't swim that fast if sharks were chasing me."

"I'm trying to warm myself up," Daniel said. "How cold do you keep this water?"

"Cold enough to be invigorating."

"You're invigorating me into hypothermia." Daniel started another lap, stretching his muscles, pushing himself as hard as he could. When his chest was aching and his limbs were rubber, he stopped and rested at the shallow end of the pool. Overhead, wet snowflakes spattered against the glass roof. Despite the vigorous exercise, Daniel still felt cold.

Brannigan finished his last lap and joined Daniel. "I appreciate your dropping by tonight. But I assume you didn't come to exercise with me. You could swim at home."

"Where we actually heat the water." *We?* Who was he talking about? He was alone. His parents were gone, on the run.

"Come to the spa, then, if you're going to complain so much." Brannigan climbed out of the pool and dripped his way toward the hot tub.

"How is the progress on the Constitutional Drive?" Daniel asked. He knew he was stalling, reluctant to bring up the reason for his visit.

"Ruth Lin is getting closer to supporting us," Brannigan said.

"Excellent." Daniel stepped into the spa and winced. After the chill of the pool, the spa felt hot enough to cook him. "If you get Councilor Lin, that gives you your majority."

"Yes," Brannigan said, but he sounded grim. "Remember, this is only a beginning. Even if we do win this vote, we've only won approval to select a committee to draft a written constitution. Then the committee must be approved—that will be an ugly fight . . . and all of this before a single word is written."

"Still, it's fantastic progress. A few years ago, they would have laughed you out of the Executive Building for suggesting this."

Brannigan scratched his head, rumpling his wet gray-streaked hair. "It's your father we have to thank for this willingness to entertain thoughts of change. Members of the Council are finally realizing that unlimited power can work against them as well as for them. If your father had gained control with nothing to check his power, we would all have been vulnerable."

Daniel didn't want to talk about his father. "Is President Ryce still backing you?"

"By her silence, yes. She has yet to make any open statement in favor of a written constitution, but by not opposing me, she's given approval for me to proceed."

They sat in the roiling water in silence until Brannigan finally said, "I assume you've come to ask me if I've made any progress on getting you and your friends to the United States."

"Yes," Daniel admitted.

"I haven't. I'm sorry. It's not for lack of trying."

Familiar panic jabbed Daniel. When working out his scheme to fake the executions, he'd been so focused on saving the lives of Jill, Ian, and Alisa that he hadn't given more than minimal thought to what he'd do with three presumed-dead criminals afterward. Brannigan's discovery of his treason, followed by an unexpected offer to help them, had been a bonus, but now Brannigan was failing him.

"Not even I can get around the new security regulations," Brannigan said. "These come from President Ryce and are enforced by the Presidential Guard. Ostensibly she's trying to ensure that your father and any of his remaining Liberty Cadre cohorts can't escape New America, but since it's likely your father escaped to the US before the regulations were put in place, I suspect they're aimed at the rest of us. A reminder of her strength. We can't come and go without her permission. And if we can't meet foreign leaders in person, it reduces the chance that we'll make international connections we might use against her. I'm as trapped as you are."

"I don't understand what she's doing. On the one hand, she's tacitly approving radical alterations in our system of government—alterations that could limit her power. On the other hand, she's flaunting her control over all of you."

"Amanda Ryce is proficient at contradictions these days," Brannigan said sourly. "And it's unwise to challenge her."

"There's no chance she'll change her mind about letting you take a group of doctors to the US to get updated on the latest cancer treatments?"

"I tried every persuasion I could think of to convince her of the benefits of the trip, but the only research she's interested in is the research going on at our own lab. And I hate to tell you this, but President Ryce's forbidding me to go is only part of the problem. The United States wouldn't let me in even if Ryce gave permission."

Daniel gaped at Brannigan. "I thought a nonpolitical mission with humanitarian goals—"

"Not anymore. Not after the uncooperative way we dealt with them over the dissolution of the Cadre, giving them paltry bits of information and refusing to identify Zero. The Cadre has committed crimes in the

US—no major operations, but they've caused enough problems that the US feels entitled to details about them. Along with the rest of the government, I am persona non grata on US soil."

Daniel pressed the heels of his hands against his eyes. It had sounded easy when Brannigan had first suggested it—concealing the fugitives aboard Brannigan's plane when, in his capacity as Councilor over Health Services, he took a medical team to the US. And if that wasn't possible, Daniel had thought Brannigan could arrange to get them fake ID chips and fake travel passes. Disguised, they could have crossed the border. But now, no civilian travel passes were being issued at all. And attempting to run the border nets would be suicide.

"I know your friends must be under terrible strain." Brannigan's face was red from the heat of the water. "I want them out of here as much as you do, for Nate and Rebecca's safety, as well as theirs."

"Alisa Kent may be relapsing," Daniel said.

Brannigan's usually mild gaze sharpened. "You mean Broc psychosis?"

"Not full-blown—at least not yet. But the severity of the reversions has increased markedly over the last couple of weeks. Three nights ago, she had a major breakdown." Daniel described what had occurred.

The horror in Brannigan's eyes rekindled Daniel's guilt. His sloppiness in monitoring Alisa had put Brannigan at risk. "Why is this happening now, so far removed from her interrogations?" Brannigan asked.

"I don't know. But Alisa was already carrying more psychological baggage than she could handle even before her brain became a chemical disaster area. Now add the stress of waiting and her constant fear of getting arrested again. Is it any wonder she's crumbling? She needs out, and soon."

"If I could do anything, I would. It's my life on the line as well as all of yours." A chilly thread edged Brannigan's tone. "Have you tried urging Councilor Haines to get the president to soften her policies?"

Daniel avoided Brannigan's gaze. "Why would Councilor Haines listen to anything I say?"

"Don't be modest. With Nadia Sears still missing, it's not hard to fathom why Councilor Haines has been talking to you."

Discomfort at Brannigan's words magnified Daniel's queasiness from the heat of the water. He lifted himself up and sat on the edge of the spa. "The offer is meaningless. I won't be here. I'm leaving as soon as we can get across the border."

"It's an attractive offer," Brannigan said. "Far more attractive, apparently, than my offer to make you part of the Constitutional Drive."

Even with the copious amounts of steam he was inhaling, Daniel's throat felt dry. "I'm not taking Councilor Haines's offer seriously. If I had any intention of remaining in New America, I'd be working with you."

"There's no reason you *have* to flee with your friends. I know you love Jill, but you'd be leaving a lot behind here. Haines is regarded as the most likely successor to President Ryce. If you link yourself to him—"

"The only reason I began working with Councilor Haines was in the hope that I could glean information that would help us with our escape plans."

"Have you told him you're not interested in what he's offering?"

"It didn't seem wise to do that yet."

"To be frank, I wonder why he's interested in *you*. I have a hard time picturing Haines and you seeing eye to eye on many issues. You know if the clinical trials on the blocker patch turn out as expected, he'll start pushing for random I-X checkups on citizens not accused of any crimes."

"I know. Like I said, I'm not planning to follow through with this."

"The James Tremont Birthday Commemoration is less than a month away. Rumor has it that Councilor Haines will make the announcement at that celebration."

"Nothing is confirmed."

"I wonder if you're trying to live in two worlds, Daniel. If you're leaving New America with your friends, you're leaving. Quit playing with Haines."

"I *want* to leave," Daniel said shortly. "But I don't seem to be going anywhere. Why should I risk spurning Councilor Haines and making him my enemy? I have enough problems right now."

"You're creating more and bigger problems if you imagine you can lead Haines to think you support him and then pull out at the last instant before you have to publicly commit yourself to policies you despise."

Daniel watched the steam wafting from the foaming surface of the water and tried to think of a response.

Chapter 4

"JILL, I'M BEGGING YOU. I'LL crawl if you want. I'll grovel."

"You're groveling now, Ian." Jill didn't look up from the sketchpad on her lap.

"Give it a try." Ian flapped the scissors in his hand. "I don't care if it turns out crooked."

Jill checked the photograph on the couch cushion next to her and continued sketching.

"Jill." Ian grasped a handful of his hair and stretched it toward the basement ceiling. "Look at this."

Jill squinted at his hair. She selected a pencil from the box and held it up. "Definitely burnt umber." She set the pencil down. "And for your eyes . . . if I mix green and orange, I can make hazel—"

"*Jill.* I don't want you to draw me. I want a haircut."

"I don't know anything about cutting hair."

"Who cares? Look how long this is. You could braid it."

"I'll braid it, then," Jill said. "I know how to do *that.*"

"Come on. I haven't had a haircut for—" Ian stopped to calculate. "It was before your solo concert in December. It's been almost four months! I look ridiculous."

"You do look goofy. I never realized your hair was so wavy."

"Help me, then. I don't care what you do to it. Just make it shorter."

"Those aren't even haircutting scissors."

"So?" Ian looked at the fabric scissors he was brandishing. "They cut, don't they?"

"Let me finish this sketch first."

Ian groaned. He turned toward Alisa, who was sitting in an armchair, her body enveloped in one of Nate's cardigan sweaters that looked big enough for three of her. "Alisa, help me out, will you? Tell Jill I look like . . . like one of those shaggy dogs where you can't see the eyes for the fur."

"We've already established that you look ridiculous," Alisa said dryly. "The question is whether or not Jill can improve on that."

Ian laughed, pleased to get more than a monosyllable out of her. Daniel had removed the blocker patch three days ago, and she'd been fine until last night, when a brief reversion had caught her off guard. This morning there had been another short lapse, and she'd burrowed into silence, fear shadowing her eyes.

"How about this, Jilly," Ian said. "You cut my hair, and I'll finish your sketch for you."

"Oh, funny. I want it to *look* like Daniel, thanks."

"Why? The guy's got a big enough ego without you drawing adoring pictures of him so he can hang them over his fireplace."

Jill slapped her sketchpad onto the couch. "Fine, give me those scissors. I'll give you a haircut you'll—"

Alisa twitched forward in her seat. Ian leaped toward her. Over the past week and half, he'd become adept at monitoring her out of the corner of his eye.

Alisa shook her head and sank back. "I'm all right," she murmured, but she still looked like she was straining to listen to something. From overhead, Ian heard the faint thud of the back door closing.

"Must be Rebecca." Ian checked the clock. Twelve thirty. Rebecca was never home in the early afternoon on Wednesdays. She met her grown daughters for lunch at that time. And why hadn't she come in through the garage? They hadn't heard the rumble of the garage door.

Feet trod overhead, accompanied by the murmur of voices. Ian crept to the bottom of the stairs and listened. Two voices, one female, one male. He couldn't make out most of the words, but the male didn't speak with the cheerful cadence of Nate's speech or the smoothness of Daniel's.

"Rebecca didn't warn us anyone was coming over," Jill whispered. "She always warns us."

"Maybe this was unexpected." Alisa rose to her feet, clutching the oversized sweater around her. Ian knew they were all thinking the same thing—why would Rebecca risk bringing a guest home with Alisa in such an unpredictable state?

"Maybe it was something she couldn't get out of," Ian whispered, walking to stand next to Alisa. "They'll probably just be here for a few minutes."

Jill fidgeted with her pencil. "I hope they hurry."

The swish of the door opening at the top of the stairs made them all jump. For an instant, Ian thought he must have misheard and the male voice *did* belong to Nate, but a calm female voice—not Rebecca's—called out, "Basement, sir. Do you want one down there?"

"Yeah, hang on a second," came the response.

Ian grabbed Alisa by the wrist and rushed toward the hallway, Jill following them, their feet muffled against the carpet. Ian charged through the first doorway—Jill's and Alisa's room—and looked frantically around the darkened bedroom for the best place to hide.

The closet. Jill slid the door open, and the three of them crowded inside, ducking beneath the rod and shoving their way between hanging clothes. Ian eased the closet door shut, and they hunched against the back wall. The closet was shallow and long, and there was ample room for the three of them to sit but nowhere for them to conceal themselves should someone slide the door open. Feet poking out beneath hanging clothes would instantly give them away.

Ian listened to the muted thumps of footsteps descending the stairs. Who *were* these intruders? The voices had sounded familiar, but the torrents of adrenaline soaking his brain made it impossible to place them in memory.

Alisa shifted, leaning closer to him. "Peale," she whispered.

Peale. Lieutenant Blake Peale. Ian was astounded he hadn't identified Peale's voice the instant he'd heard it, the voice that had mocked him relentlessly in the Detention Annex and taunted him at his execution with the news of Jill's death. And that mellow female voice—Pulansky, Peale's sidekick.

"Good place for a meeting." Peale's voice came from the family room.

Ian did a frantic mental inventory of the items he and the women had left in view. Jill's sketchpad with the half-finished picture of Daniel—no, she'd had that in her hands along with her colored pencils and Daniel's photograph when she'd jumped into the closet. A hardbound copy of James Tremont's *Treatise on Security* was sitting open on an end table where Ian had abandoned it when he'd tried to persuade Jill to give him a haircut. Nate had borrowed the book for Ian from Spencer Brannigan, and Brannigan's name was written in the front, but that shouldn't be of interest to Peale. Why *shouldn't* Nate borrow a book from his brother-in-law? And the lights were on, but they went on automatically whenever the upstairs door opened.

"Look at this, sir."

Footsteps moved across the room. "Taped up." Peale sounded triumphant.

"It could be for insulation," Pulansky said.

"I doubt it. Halbrook could afford better weatherproofing than tape and cardboard. This is meant to block light."

Alisa's breathing came in uneven spurts, and Ian could feel her trembling. If a reversion hit now—even a split-second one—if she jerked suddenly and kicked the closet door or cried out—

He pulled Alisa's head close to him and whispered, "Turn and put your legs on Jill's lap." He leaned across Alisa and whispered to Jill, "Brace her legs."

Alisa turned obediently so her legs were toward Jill. The rustle of clothing and the scrape of a hanger on the rod were thunderous in Ian's ears, though he knew such quiet sounds wouldn't penetrate to the family room. He crossed Alisa's wrists and gripped them with his right hand. With his left arm, he drew her tightly against him and clamped his hand over her mouth.

"Sorry," he whispered in her ear.

"Here, sir?" Pulansky's voice was still coming from the family room.

"Yeah, fine." There was a thump, like a table being turned on its side. Ian felt sick to his stomach. If they were searching the place, then within minutes, Peale or Pulansky would slide the closet door open and discover three ex-corpses cowering behind a rack of clothes. Ian wondered if he could lunge out of the closet and attack the officer before a gun stopped him, but he was so entangled with Alisa that it would take him multiple seconds to rise to his feet.

Another thud. Peale's voice. "Let's have a look back there."

Ian closed his eyes and prayed desperately that Peale and Pulansky would not feel the need to check the closet.

A switch clicked, and light appeared in the sliver of space beneath the door. Ian buried his face in Alisa's hair and tightened his grip on her. Even the slightest noise now could draw attention to the closet. *Please don't let her have a reversion.*

Footsteps entered the room. Ian held his breath.

The light clicked off, and the footsteps faded into the hallway.

Ian sagged with relief and heard Jill gasp for air. She too must have been holding her breath.

More footsteps in the hall. A few words Ian didn't catch, then Peale's voice. "Let's get out of here."

Retreating footsteps. A thump as the door at the top of the stairs swung shut.

Ian sat paralyzed until Alisa twisted in his arms, trying to free herself. He released her and fumbled in the blackness for the edge of the closet door.

His sweaty shirt sticking to his skin, Ian stepped out of the closet, followed by Alisa and Jill. He drew a breath to ask Alisa if she was all right, but she held up her hand and shook her head urgently. She snatched the sketchpad and pencils out of Jill's hands, flipped to a fresh page and scrawled, *They planted transmitters.*

Transmitters. They hadn't been here to search. They'd been here to bug the place. Ian took the pencil from Alisa's hand and wrote, *Will they hear us moving around?*

She took the pencil. *No. The transmitters are voice activated.*

Alisa led the way into the family room. She looked quickly around, approached the cocktail table, and tipped it onto its side. A button-sized metal object clung to the underside of the table. Carefully, Alisa tilted the table back into position.

Deactivate it! Ian wrote on the sketchpad and held it up.

Alisa shook her head and came to take the pencil. *Peale can check remotely to see if it's functioning. If we turn it off now, he'll return to see what the problem is.*

Ian glanced at Jill. She looked dazed. He squeezed her shoulder before taking the pencil and writing, *Do you think they bugged the upstairs as well?*

Alisa nodded.

We've got to get out of here, Ian scribbled.

And go where? Alisa jabbed at the paper so hard the tip snapped off the pencil.

Ian fought burgeoning panic. They had no car. Walking through Tremont . . . Jill might manage that without getting spotted, but his and Alisa's faces had been all over the news.

They should be safe here for a short period. If Peale was planting bugs, he suspected *something* was going on at the Halbrooks', but he didn't yet know what. As long as the transmitters didn't pick up any suspicious talk—

Ian took a fresh pencil out of the box. *We need to warn Rebecca. One of us should go upstairs and catch her the instant she walks in the door.*

Jill pointed to herself, eyebrows raised in a question. Ian nodded.

Now? Jill mouthed, and Ian nodded again. He tore a sheet off of the sketchpad and handed it to Jill, along with a pencil. Rebecca wasn't due home for another couple of hours, but it would be best to go upstairs early in case her schedule changed. Jill tiptoed toward the stairs.

Ian wrote on the sketchpad. *Do you think they planted bugs in any other rooms down here?*

Alisa shook her head. She took the pencil and started to write something, but her handwriting skewed all over the place, and she lowered the pencil before she produced anything legible. Ian curled his arm around her shoulders and led her along the hallway into the room farthest from the family room—a storage area filled with half-finished craft projects, a dusty sewing machine, sports equipment, and a box of dress-up clothes that Rebecca must have saved for her grandchildren to use.

Ian tossed a couple of leaky beanbag chairs on the floor. Alisa sank down on one of them. Ian settled next to her and leaned against the box behind him. There was nothing to do now but wait in silence for the Halbrooks to return and hope nothing happened in the meantime to bring Peale and Pulansky back.

You okay? he mouthed to Alisa.

She nodded—a dishonest answer to a stupid question.

Chapter 5

AFTER TWO MONTHS OF NEVER leaving the Halbrooks' house, Ian was relieved to be somewhere else, though this room wasn't his favorite venue. Mahogany furniture, burgundy leather, an intricate oriental rug that probably cost more than Ian had made in a year as a history professor—he could understand why Daniel had decided to make use of his father's elegant study, but Ian disliked revisiting the spot where he'd sought Marcus Lansbury's help in stopping the Liberty Cadre and learned Marcus himself was Cadre leader Zero. Not a good memory.

At least Daniel didn't sit in the throne-like chair behind the desk but settled on the couch near the marble fireplace and gestured for Jill to sit beside him. She came toward him but with a hesitation Ian had never seen her display where Daniel was concerned.

"You've—gone back to work?" she asked.

Ian glanced at Daniel and started in surprise. Daniel wore the blue uniform of Detention Annex medical supervisors. Ian had seen him in that uniform so many times during his imprisonment that tonight he hadn't even registered it.

"I had no choice," Daniel said. "My leave was over."

"Oh." Jill slowly settled on the couch next to Daniel.

"I won't be there long," he said, putting his arm around her.

Nate and Rebecca sat together on a love seat to the right of Daniel, holding hands and looking weary. Alisa sat in a wing chair as far from the others as she could get.

Ian debated before settling in a chair across from Daniel and Jill. He would have preferred to be next to Alisa, but the occasional reversions were probably causing her less stress than his monitoring her like he expected her to go berserk at any moment.

"You can talk freely," Daniel said. "The only other person here is a security guard in his apartment near the front gate."

"I hope he isn't someone your father hired," Nate said. "Somehow, I don't trust his judgment."

"No. Councilor Haines handpicked him—actually, picked two guards; they alternate shifts. I didn't think I needed security, but he was concerned about my father trying to return to the house. These men are top-notch and discreet, which they'd have to be for Haines to trust them with the fact that they're on the lookout for my parents."

"Haines told these guys the truth about your parents?" Ian asked. "I thought the Council didn't want *anyone* to know."

"The Councilor over Internal Defense can share whatever information he wants with whomever he feels needs to know it," Daniel said. "But you don't need to worry that the guard will overhear our conversation. He just monitors the grounds via camera as well as the status of the house security system. Tell me exactly what happened this afternoon. What did Lieutenant Peale and Officer Pulansky say? What precisely did they do?"

Ian gave the report, with Jill adding commentary. Alisa offered nothing; she stared at the portrait of Daniel's grandfather that hung on the wall behind Marcus's desk. Ian wondered if she was spacing out, not noticing what she was looking at, or if she was thinking of the irony that a batch of traitors were gathered in front of Jonathan Lansbury's portrait to discuss how to stay safe until they could escape the nation Jonathan had helped found.

"Someone must have reported something after . . . what happened ten days ago." Nate finally had the guts to voice the obvious.

"Maybe." Daniel gave Alisa a keen glance. Nate's old sweater drooped over her shoulders, and she had shoved her hands up the opposite sleeves as though the room were cold. "But it doesn't really explain things. If someone heard screaming, they'd have reported it immediately, and it would have been investigated immediately. Not ten days later."

Chin down, Rebecca twiddled the strap of her giant purse. "When the police walked through the basement, do you think they could tell people were living there?"

"We're always careful to put everything away, wipe the shower down, keep the beds made, toothbrushes in the drawers, stuff like that," Jill answered. "I don't think just walking through the basement would have made it obvious."

Daniel unbuttoned his collar. "Have you eaten?"

"We forgot about dinner, I'm afraid," Rebecca said.

"A first for me." Nate patted his round stomach.

"I'll get some sandwiches." Daniel stood. "Nate, come help me put dinner together."

Nate rose. Rebecca started to stand as well, but Daniel held up a hand.

"No, you relax. Let Nate work in the kitchen for once."

"I work in the kitchen all the time." Nate trailed Daniel toward the door. "Getting all that food from my plate to my mouth is classed as heavy lifting."

The door closed behind Daniel and Nate. Rebecca opened her bag and pulled out a ball of fluffy white yarn and a baby blanket under construction.

Jill smiled thinly. "I can't believe you can keep your hands steady enough to crochet right now."

Rebecca spread the blanket over her knees. "I'm sure it's easier than keeping your hands steady while playing violin solos in front of thousands of people."

Jill sighed, frustration and loss in her eyes. Ian had seen her frenetically pacing the floor when a weeklong family vacation had forced a hiatus in violin practicing. It was a wonder the last few violinless months hadn't driven her nuts.

Rebecca's crochet hook moved with expert speed. "Nate got me started on crocheting."

"*He* crochets?" Jill asked in astonishment.

Rebecca chuckled. "No. He pestered me to take it up to keep my hands busy. I fidget when I'm bored or nervous, and it drives him crazy. Crocheting is perfect for keeping my hands occupied. And it calms me."

"It calms you?" Ian eyeballed the baby blanket and wondered if Rebecca gave lessons. "Is that for a grandchild?"

"Yes. Catherine—our second daughter—has a baby due in June."

"That's great," Ian said. "How many grandchildren does that make?"

"Six," Rebecca said proudly.

"That's great," Ian said again, thinking this conversation was surreal to the point of bizarreness. The police were breathing down their necks, and they were sitting here talking about crocheting and grandchildren.

Fifteen minutes later, Nate and Daniel returned carrying trays of sandwich fixings. Ian piled roast beef, tomato, and lettuce on whole wheat bread and wolfed the sandwich without returning to his seat. He was assembling his second sandwich when he glanced at Alisa's chair and found it empty.

He scanned the room. Daniel and Nate stood at the desk with sandwiches in hand as Daniel pointed something out on the computer. Jill and Rebecca sat near the fireplace, chatting about Jill's too-brief stint with the Tremont Philharmonic—or rather, Rebecca was chatting, and Jill was struggling to answer politely, her worried gaze constantly straying to Daniel. A plate with an untouched turkey sandwich sat on the table next to Alisa's chair, but she wasn't in the room.

Ian forced his attention back to his food. She couldn't have been gone for more than a minute or two. She'd probably exited in search of a bathroom. He scooped up a handful of potato chips and sat down to eat.

Five minutes. Ten. Ian squirmed in his chair, his appetite waning. If Alisa was all right, he didn't want to make a production out of her absence. It would be more tactful to slip out, check on her, and slip in again.

He set his plate on a lamp table and hurried out of the study, trying to reassure himself as he went. She was probably trying to steal a few private minutes. If he were in her situation, he'd have been climbing the walls under the constant supervision. But the risk of leaving her alone any longer was too high.

He turned the corner and found her standing in the hallway, head lowered and hands braced against the wall as though she was struggling to maintain balance. Ian hurried toward her, his footsteps noiseless on carpet as smooth and thick as ice cream.

"Alisa?"

She jumped slightly and looked at him. The black hair framing her face was wet, along with the cuffs of her sweater and the neckband of her shirt. It looked as though she'd tried to splash water on her face and had ended up half drenching herself.

"Why don't you come get dinner?" Ian suggested. "Then we can ask Daniel to show you somewhere you can rest. It's been a horrible day."

She dropped her hands from the wall but didn't answer.

"You're very pale," Ian said. "Are you dizzy?"

She didn't move.

"You need to eat something." He stepped closer, but she jerked away so abruptly she staggered backward.

Not sure if the gesture was deliberate or the beginning of a reversion, Ian leaped toward her and seized both arms.

"Let *go* of me." She wrenched herself free.

"I'm sorry. You startled me. I thought—" He drew a deep breath. "Come on, let's go eat. You can't stay—" He cut himself off. A discourse on how it was unsafe to leave her alone for too long would only make her less willing to submit to the scrutiny of five pairs of worried eyes.

They stood for a moment, facing each other. Ian hunted for something to say that would ease the tension but could think of nothing.

"How can I help you?" he asked finally. "What would make things easier for you?"

"What would make me *sane*, you mean?"

"You're not crazy."

She pushed wet hair back from her face. "What would *you* call it when the smallest noise will cost the lives of Jill, Dr. Lansbury, the Halbrooks, Councilor Brannigan, you, and me—and I can't trust myself to keep silent?"

"Look, that's not your fault."

"It's my fault Peale showed up in the first place."

"We don't know that."

"I'm creating problems for all of you."

"*You* are creating problems? *You* didn't pump Broc4 into your blood-stream. You didn't volunteer to let the Cadre mess with your mind."

"That was months ago. If I were strong enough—"

"That's the issue right there. You think your struggles mean you're a failure, so you hide them until they get so big they eat you alive."

Sadness and exhaustion showed in her eyes. "I'm cooperating with Dr. Lansbury."

"The fact that Daniel bullied you into keeping him updated on your health isn't the point. Try trusting us as friends."

"I've done nothing to earn that friendship. I've done nothing in my life except hurt a lot of people. Including *you*."

"Did you? I've forgotten. All I remember is you risking your life to release a religious believer when you should have sent him to prison."

She broke eye contact, head bowing, posture sagging, hands reaching again for the solidity of the wall.

"Alisa, we care about you," he said. "You know God cares about you. You felt His love when you were a prisoner."

"The fact that He was willing to show love even to me says much for His character and nothing for mine."

"You had the faith to ask for His help. That says something."

She didn't respond.

"Alisa—"

"Everything all right?" Daniel spoke from behind Ian, catching him by surprise.

"I think so," Ian said. Alisa straightened up and nodded.

"More reversions?" Daniel asked.

"No," she said.

"All right. You'd better have something to eat. Come back to the study."

They followed him, Ian wishing Daniel had waited before interrupting. That was the most candidly Alisa had spoken in weeks.

Daniel sat on the edge of his father's desk. "We don't have many options. The police, for whatever reason, have their eyes on the Halbrooks. Clearly, you can't stay there. We're still working on getting you over the border. The question is what to do with you in the meantime."

"Can they stay with you?" Rebecca asked. "The police wouldn't dare poke around here. You're the Council's darling and Patrick Haines's protégé."

Annoyance flashed in Daniel's face. "I wouldn't put it like that."

"Haines's protégé?" Ian asked, curiosity rising. Daniel shrugged curtly, and Ian dropped the subject, instead mumbling a thank you to Jill as she refilled his water glass.

"Mr. Halbrook is Councilor Brannigan's brother-in-law, but they're still bothering *him*," Jill said.

Nate smiled wearily. "My bad attitude isn't much of a secret, Jill."

Daniel shifted his gaze to Alisa. "You know Lieutenant Peale, Alisa. You worked with him. What's your take on this? Is he after Nate?"

Alisa, who had been staring apathetically at her uneaten dinner, looked startled. Ian glared at Daniel. Didn't he realize Alisa blamed herself for what had happened?

But under Daniel's questioning eyes, the remoteness in Alisa's face changed to contemplation. Ian had the feeling that for the first time, she was truly evaluating the situation instead of snatching all the guilt.

"The police would not investigate Mr. Halbrook based solely on his reputation at the Euthanasia Center," Alisa said. "Since he's under Councilor Brannigan's protection, they wouldn't interfere with him at all unless they suspected he was involved in something big enough that Councilor Brannigan couldn't intercede out of risk to his own reputation or big enough that Councilor Brannigan himself was involved."

"They can't possibly have too much of an idea of what's going on," Ian commented. "From what Peale said, it sounds like they think the Halbrooks might be holding illegal meetings, but that's all. If the police thought they were harboring fugitives, they would have searched the place, which they didn't, obviously, or they would have found us. From what we could hear, they just took a cursory look around, planted transmitters, and left."

"Can we remove the transmitters?" Nate asked.

Alisa shook her head. "Not unless you want the police assuming you're involved in something so sensitive that you regularly sweep your home for listening devices."

"Then what do we do?" Rebecca asked. "We can't ignore them."

"The best course would be for you to leave the transmitters alone and go about your lives," Alisa said. "Take care to say nothing overtly treasonous, but don't guard your speech so closely that Lieutenant Peale realizes you're aware of being monitored. If the transmitters don't turn up any incriminating information, eventually he'll remove them."

"I hope that doesn't take long." Rebecca crocheted so rapidly Ian expected to see the crochet hook glow red hot or the blanket erupt in flames.

Nate reached for the bowl of potato chips. Rebecca scowled at him, and he drew his empty hand back. "*Can* you keep our guests here short-term, Dan?" he asked.

"Risky," Daniel said.

Ian leaned over to pick up a carrot stick he'd dropped on the carpet. "Besides the security guards, how big is your staff?"

"Not big. A two-person housekeeping staff comes in every other morning. A cook, usually gone by noon, unless I'm having guests for dinner. Groundskeepers, twice per week or when it snows. So it's not an army, but there are people in and out on a regular basis."

"Then there's no way we can stay here," Ian said.

"The best thing would be to get you out of Tremont altogether," Daniel said. "We do have one possibility. My family owns a cabin at Merit Lake. It's isolated, with few police officers in the area. We could hide you there temporarily."

Ian knew he should welcome the suggestion, but it made him feel more discouraged. Merit Lake meant fleeing deeper into the interior of New America, nowhere near the border. Relocating there felt like backsliding. Ian wracked his brain for a place they could stay without leaving Tremont, but the effort brought only an all-too-familiar sense of helplessness.

"Sounds like a good idea." Nate's relief was clear. "How do we get them there?"

"I'll drive them," Daniel said.

"How soon can you go?"

"It depends on if I can get someone to cover for me at work. I can take time off from the lab without a problem, but I'm on call at the Annex."

Nate raised his bushy white eyebrows. "You must have at least one day of the weekend free."

"I have Friday off, but I have an obligation that evening that I can't get out of."

"Oh, that's right," Nate said. "That's the big dinner party, isn't it?"

"A . . . dinner party?" Jill had taken off the shoes she'd borrowed from Rebecca and sat curling her toes into the deep pile of the rug. "Maybe you could . . . skip it?"

"I'm obligated to be there. The host is Councilor Haines. If I offend him, we're all in trouble."

Alisa's voice was quiet. "Are you the guest of honor?"

Daniel's expression closed, and Ian wondered what in Alisa's question had provoked defensiveness. "Yes."

"Can't you just ask for time off?" Ian suggested. "You're a celebrity. Wouldn't they be eager to accommodate you?"

"I'm not a celebrity," Daniel snapped. "And it doesn't work that way. Let me see what I can do. If I can work it out, we'll leave on Saturday. I'll stay at the cabin Saturday night and return home on Sunday."

"How long does it take to drive there?" Jill asked.

"About four hours."

Rebecca smoothed the half-finished baby blanket over her knees. "Where will they stay between now and Saturday?"

"They stay here, I guess." Daniel rubbed his forehead. "I don't know what other options we have. I have a guest wing that's closed up right now. They can use that. But they'll have to be very quiet. Very careful."

Ian—and everyone else—avoided looking at Alisa.

"So we'll go home and live our lives for the entertainment of Lieutenant Peale." Nate slapped his thighs. "That does it, Becky. No more treason for us. From now on, we're model citizens."

Rebecca sighed and kept crocheting.

Chapter 6

PRESIDENT AMANDA RYCE PICKED UP the memory card, grasping it like a hawk clutching a rat. "You've read the Preserval report?"

Brannigan imagined Ryce's talons ripping out his throat. "Yes, I reviewed it."

"Well?"

"The lack of progress is unfortunate. But there were no surprises."

"You expected resounding failure?"

Brannigan sat up straighter, but the pillowy leather chair still made him feel like his knees were in his face. "Ma'am, Preserval simply isn't the miracle drug we'd hoped for. It's proving useful in treating certain cases of life-threatening traumatic injury, and I think that's where our focus—"

Ryce cut him off. "The antiaging effect."

"Ma'am, there *is* no antiaging effect. If Preserval is administered in dosages low enough to allow for normal functioning, it has no discernible effect. At higher dosages, it arrests cellular degeneration by inducing temporary biostasis, which means the patient can do no more than lie there. And stasis can only be prolonged for a maximum of eight hours before cells begin to deteriorate. Preserval simply can't prolong the normal lifespan. I'm sorry."

Ryce's blue eyes were ice. Brannigan studied her—thick white hair cropped short, creases around her mouth and eyes. She looked two decades younger than her ninety-four years, but that was due to the vigor of her personality, not a surgeon's scalpel. Ryce had no interest in a youthful façade. It was her aging interior that obsessed her.

"Ma'am, we've hit a dead end." Brannigan winced internally at the inadvertent pun and hoped Ryce hadn't noticed. "Preserval isn't an antiaging drug, and we can't make it one."

"Perhaps the Tremont Research Laboratory needs new blood. Scientists who have not already"—Ryce flipped the memory card to the floor—"given up."

Brannigan bent to pick up the card, fighting the urge to point out that this was the tenth life-extension study and twenty-sixth crop of researchers that had failed her. He slid the card into his pocket. "Maybe it's time to put more of our resources elsewhere."

Ryce's eyes narrowed, but Brannigan held her gaze. "There have been radical advances in cancer treatment in the US, but our people aren't benefitting from them. If we were to—"

The anger in Ryce's face stopped him. "Do you find running Health Services to be too much of a strain, Councilor?"

Brannigan's tongue dried to the consistency of parchment. "No, ma'am."

"More than a few members of my Council opposed your appointment."

"I'm aware of that, ma'am."

"I imagine your position is not as secure as you'd like, especially now that you're suggesting alterations in our system of government."

Brannigan's collar and tie were suffocating him. "I've always been grateful for your support, ma'am."

"Maybe you're tired of my help? You'd prefer to stand on your own?"

"No, ma'am." Brannigan understood the warning. If Ryce spoke out against the Constitutional Drive, not only would that kill any hope of reform, but it would also give Brannigan's enemies permission to attack him—and those attacks might not be limited to verbal fights in the Executive Hall and undercutting his work. Marcus Lansbury had failed by a hairsbreadth when he'd tried to frame Brannigan for anarchist activities and assassinate him. Maybe Brannigan's next opponent would succeed— with Ryce's tacit approval.

Ryce reached for a white china cup and sipped. Brannigan wondered what was in the cup—probably an herbal concoction some expert claimed could reduce cell damage. "If you devote the needed attention to Health Services, you won't suffer the problem of incompetent researchers."

Brannigan boiled with frustration but spoke calmly. "I'll see that changes are made at the lab."

"With a fresh approach, there should soon be significant progress." The anger faded from Ryce's eyes, and Brannigan knew she was convincing herself that a new crop of scientists was all it would take to find her miraculous fountain of youth. Brannigan wondered what Ryce would say if he told her the only miraculous use they'd found for Preserval was in faking executions.

"You're dismissed, Councilor. I expect a report on personnel changes within the week."

Brannigan nodded wearily and exited Ryce's office. Wasted money, wasted time, countless seriously ill citizens euthanized to keep costs down so money remained available for Ryce's pet projects. So many wasted lives, all due to Amanda Ryce's inability to confront her own inescapable mortality.

* * *

Ian swung the cupboard doors open and scanned the boxes stacked on the shelves. "Chess?" he suggested, determined to do something to lighten the bleak atmosphere. "Backgammon?"

Jill shook her head. She was sitting on the carpet, leafing through a stack of music she'd found in the bench of a dusty upright piano. The piano, like the rest of the items in this game room, looked like it hadn't been used since Daniel was a teenager.

Alisa was on the couch, her gaze focused on a TV screen bigger than the floor space in Ian's first apartment. The set was off, and Alisa's fixed stare made Ian increasingly uneasy. He'd suggested switching the TV on, but Alisa had shaken her head curtly.

Last night they'd checked to see how well sound traveled from this unused wing of the house into areas where housekeeping staff might pass and had found that only voices raised to near shouting would penetrate. Still, if even soft television noise would make Alisa edgier, it was better to leave the set off.

Ian paced past the covered pool table. He nudged aside the fabric blinds on the window far enough to allow him to look out at Lake Serena. It was a sunny, windless morning, and the lake shimmered green. What he wouldn't give to be able to go for a walk around—

"Don't touch the window!" Jill's whisper startled him.

"I'm not touching the window."

"You're messing with the blinds."

"The window faces the lake, and the groundskeepers aren't here today. Who's going to see—"

"Get *away* from it. You know what Daniel said about the security system."

"I'm not opening the window, all right? I'm not going to set off the alarm."

"You're taking chances." Jill flipped angrily to a new page of music. "Why don't you sit down and quit fidgeting?"

Ian's irritation grew. "Why don't you quit being so paranoid?"

Jill's cheeks flushed pink. She pushed a stray curl behind her ear and glared down at the music in her lap.

"Look . . . I'm sorry, Jilly," Ian said. "I'll stay away from the window if it bothers you."

A tear dripped onto the music. "I'm sorry. I shouldn't have snapped at you."

Jill's tears unsettled Ian. During the two months at the Halbrooks', she'd been the optimistic one, relentlessly upbeat, joking about their confinement, confident Daniel and Councilor Brannigan would soon succeed in sneaking them over the border. Ian fished for something cheery to say but only came up with, "You okay?"

"No." Jill wiped the teardrop off the music with her thumb. "I . . . don't know how Daniel can go back to work."

Ian sat next to Jill on the carpet. "Yeah, that was a shock."

"How can he . . . I thought that now he . . . doesn't approve of what the police are doing."

Revulsion twitched in Ian's gut. "I thought the same."

"He's torturing people." More tears spilled down Jill's face. "That's what it amounts to. Giving prisoners that drug for interrogation. And if it goes wrong, people could end up dead."

"Did you get a chance to talk to him about it?"

"I asked him about it last night after the rest of you were in bed, but he just repeated that he doesn't have a choice and it's temporary."

At which point you dropped the subject and apologized for nagging him, Ian added silently. Jill hated confrontation.

Jill wiped her eyes on her sleeve. "I just never thought he'd do this."

"Neither did I." Ian had never realized what a leap he'd taken in assuming Daniel's decision to break with the government in the matter of their executions meant Daniel wanted nothing more to do with the life he'd formerly led. Daniel had said at the time that he thought Ian's faith in God might be founded in reality.

Might be.

But he'd never declared any kind of faith himself.

Jill's voice quavered. "Doesn't he think what he's doing is . . . wrong?"

"Wrong in what sense?" Ian asked grimly. "It's not against the laws of New America. Wrong as in unpleasant? Or wrong as in morally wrong, in violation of eternal law?"

Jill groaned. "No philosophy lectures now, please. What does it matter?"

"It matters a lot. If Daniel thinks this is just some nasty but required business he has to take care of in order to keep from raising suspicion while he plans our escape, that's how he can justify going back. It makes no difference to the prisoners he's dealing with. If it weren't Daniel holding the needle, it would be someone else."

"Ian!"

"I didn't say I agreed with that. I'm trying to figure out what Daniel is thinking."

"He doesn't get it." Jill spoke softly. "Neither do you, really."

"Are you kidding? I—"

"Oh, I know you think he should quit, that it's breaking moral laws, or however you said it. But you don't really know what it's *like*; you had only a small taste of it. Getting trapped inside your mind, reliving the worst things that have ever happened to you, along with the worst you've ever worried or imagined *could* happen to you or people you love—everything mixed up. Even after you come out of it, you can't totally get rid of it. Those experiences are in your brain like real memories. How can Daniel do this? He can't possibly need the money. Is a job at the Detention Annex a life sentence?"

"He holds top clearance." Alisa spoke, surprising Ian. He thought she'd been ignoring the conversation. "His position is regarded as vital to national security. Were he to attempt to resign, it would stir up questions."

Jill dug her fingertips into the carpet. "What . . . would they do to him if he quit?"

Alisa hesitated. "I'm not sure. I've never known anyone at his level to try. At the least, he would undergo intensive questioning. His resignation would be considered a warning sign for weakened patriotism."

"Would they screen him?" Ian asked, thinking of the preliminary interrogation Alisa had put him through when she'd ordered his arrest. "Or even send him for Information Extraction?"

"I don't know," Alisa said. "But he's in a very precarious spot because he holds classified information about the true nature of the Liberty Cadre."

"Yeah, but I thought the Council adores him," Ian protested. "Couldn't Councilor Haines help him quit the Annex without repercussions?"

"Help him destroy his reputation by quitting one of the most vital jobs in New America? I don't think you've grasped the significance of the fact that Councilor Haines is hosting a dinner in Dr. Lansbury's honor."

"I haven't," Ian said. "Help me out."

Alisa opened her mouth to speak then glanced at Jill and said nothing.

"You're not going to tell us?" Ian asked.

"I have only theories. Maybe speculation wouldn't be helpful."

Ian realized why Alisa had hedged. Sitting cross-legged on the floor, blonde tendrils escaping the short ponytail at the back of her neck and cheeks blotched from tears, Jill appeared about sixteen and as delicate as tissue paper.

"Please tell me what you think." Jill set the stack of music aside. "If you don't, I'll make up things to worry about, and that'll be worse."

Ian grinned. Jill was a lot tougher than she looked. "You're right," he said. "Come on, Alisa."

Alisa looked back at the blank TV screen. "You are, of course, aware that Nadia Sears, a Council Assistant to the Department of Internal Defense, has been missing for a month."

"Yes," Ian said. Reports of Sears's disappearance had been all over the news, along with hysteria over the possibility that she'd been targeted by a new anarchist group rising to take the place of the defunct Liberty Cadre.

"Whatever happened to Sears, Internal Defense will proceed on the assumption that she won't be returning," Alisa said. "That leaves a vacancy in the Council Assistants."

Ian frowned. "Are you suggesting Haines is thinking of nominating Daniel for that position?"

"Councilor Haines has little patience for socializing, and he never does anything without a solid purpose. He wouldn't throw a party to praise Dr. Lansbury for his heroic service to New America or some such fuzzy goal."

"How do you know so much about him?" Ian asked.

"I worked as an intern in his office when I was in graduate school."

Jill's brow wrinkled. "You . . . worked for Councilor Haines?" Her tone was apologetic; she probably feared she was prying. Ian realized that despite two months of living nearly on top of each other, he could count on his fingers the number of times he'd heard Jill and Alisa exchange more than a few words.

"I was studying political science," Alisa explained. "This was before I . . . decided on a career with the police. I will say, though, that Haines's interest in Dr. Lansbury surprises me. Dr. Lansbury is young and inexperienced, and Haines is not a patient man."

"Maybe he *isn't* interested in nominating Daniel," Ian said.

"The evidence indicates that he is. Haines is ruthless, very different from Dr. Lansbury, but maybe that's why he chose him. Dr. Lansbury is a sympathetic figure, attractive to the public, and a compassionate man. Maybe Haines plans to use him to encourage the people to be more receptive to restrictions and policies that would stir anger coming from Haines."

"Sounds like a fun job," Ian said dryly. "Shilling for Internal Defense."

"I imagine Dr. Lansbury is now under double the pressure to continue serving at the Annex," Alisa added. "Not only would it raise dangerous suspicion in the police if he quit, but such an unpatriotic act would make a fool of Councilor Haines. And Haines would retaliate."

"You know all about the police," Jill said. "If *you* were in Daniel's position, would you go back to work?"

Alisa didn't answer. The veiled look on her face made it impossible to tell what she was thinking.

Jill blushed. "I'm so sorry. I didn't mean to—"

"The answer to your question is no. There is nothing that could induce me to go back."

"Even if it . . . would be very dangerous to quit?"

"The consequences wouldn't change my decision. I've done enough to offend God. I won't add to those crimes." Alisa rose to her feet. "Excuse me." She walked out of the game room.

Jill moaned and pressed her forehead to the carpet. "I'm an idiot. I should have left her alone."

"No, you shouldn't have. She needs to talk."

Jill lifted her face from the floor. "Will you go check on her?"

"I'll give her a few minutes. Then I will."

Jill sighed, her gaze on the door Alisa had closed behind her. "I don't even know if I believe in God."

"Have you thought about the things we've talked about?"

"Yes. A lot. But I just . . . I don't know. Maybe it would help if I could read that Book of Mormon."

"Yeah, I wouldn't mind reading it again myself." Frustration grated on Ian. The book he had treasured for those too-short months must have been incinerated long ago, and there was no hope of getting another copy until they got to the US.

If they got to the US.

The thought brought jolting awareness. Until that moment, Ian hadn't realized how fiercely he'd been clinging to the conviction that everything was going to work out. He'd been sure if God had gotten them this far, He'd take them the rest of the way.

But that had been Ian's assumption. Not God's promise.

"I *want* to believe the things you say are true," Jill said. "I . . . want to know Mom and Dad still exist, somewhere—" She inhaled a trembling breath. "I guess I'm afraid I'm trying to convince myself of something because I *want* to believe it."

"It's possible to know for certain." Ian tried to block the fear out of his mind.

"I know that's what you say, but . . . oh, I don't know."

"Jill—"

"I tried to pray," she interrupted.

"You did? You never told me that."

"There was nothing to tell. I just . . . well . . . nothing happened."

"You didn't . . . experience anything?" Ian tried not to sound dismayed. "Feel anything?"

"Well, I felt silly. But I guess that's not what you mean."

Ian looked blankly at the stack of music on the floor and tried to remember a story from the Book of Mormon that illustrated how even fervent prayers were not always answered immediately. The only stories that came to mind were rapid, immediate answers like those given to King Lamoni and his father.

Along with stories of believers thrown into prison, thrown into pits of fire, slaughtered with swords.

What made him think God had safety and freedom in mind for them?

Jill ran a fingernail along the edge of a piece of music. "If Daniel is planning to come with us when we escape, why would he let Councilor Haines think he's interested in being an Assistant? If we're stuck here for too long, he'll end up having to actually take the job. How could he stand working in . . ."

"We'll probably be gone before he'd have to . . ." Ian let the words crumble away, too weary to think of something optimistic to say when doubts weighed on him like gravity had tripled. "I don't know, Jill," he said.

Chapter 7

PEALE GRUNTED. "NOTHING. ZIP." HE slapped his computer shut.

"The transmitters have only been in place for two days, sir," Pulansky said. "Dr. Lansbury hasn't even visited the Halbrooks during that time."

Peale picked up the remaining chunk of sandwich from his desk. He'd been hoping Nathan Halbrook might say something to his wife that hinted at illegal activities, but the computer hadn't flagged a single statement as potentially criminal. "For a guy with a reputation for griping, Halbrook's sure been proper. Did you have a chance to listen to any of the raw recording?"

"Yes, sir. Some of it."

Peale swallowed the last mouthful of his lunch. "Find anything interesting?"

"No. But that *is* interesting. Neither Halbrook nor his wife has had much to say at all, and no conversation went deeper than a discussion of the weather or spaghetti versus pork chops for dinner. They were continually superficial and continually polite."

Peale sat up straighter in his chair. "You're saying you think they're aware of being monitored."

"It's instinct, sir. I could easily be wrong."

"Yeah, okay." Peale excitedly waved Pulansky's disclaimer aside. She was rarely wrong, especially not on something intuitive. "If Halbrook is careful enough that he sweeps for transmitters, this is big. We're on the right track."

Pulansky nodded.

"Lansbury's heading for his posh cabin at Merit Lake this weekend," Peale said. "He's supposed to be on call, but Dunlap's covering for him."

"I know Dr. Dunlap wasn't eager to help him," Pulansky said. "He just recovered from the flu and didn't want to take on extra work. But apparently Dr. Lansbury was very anxious to leave Tremont because he agreed to cover Dunlap's next two on-call weekends in exchange for this one off."

"Where'd you hear that?"

"I overheard Dr. Dunlap and Dr. Lansbury speaking about it, sir."

Peale grinned. Pulansky was a pro at eavesdropping, so bland and quiet that people ignored her.

"Did he tell Dunlap why he's going to the cabin?"

"No, sir. He was very vague about his plans. He said only that he had to go out of town for personal reasons. He didn't say anything about Merit Lake."

This answer pleased Peale. The more elusive Lansbury was, the more likely his plans involved something illegal. "Here's the message he sent to the maintenance service." Peale opened his computer, hit a couple of buttons, and pushed it toward Pulansky.

Pulansky read it. "It's interesting that he doesn't want housekeeping services after the initial preparations. But a demand for total privacy can't be unusual up there."

"I did a search on a bunch of old messages from people with cabins at Merit Lake. It's not a common request but not unheard of." Peale tapped his fingers on the desk. "Have you heard if Lansbury is taking anyone with him?"

"No, sir. But the Halbrooks have mentioned a granddaughter's birthday party they're attending this Saturday here in Tremont, and Nathan Halbrook is scheduled to be at the Euth Center on Sunday."

"I'm surprised Lansbury hasn't snared a cute girlfriend by now. Maybe being forced to kill the last one put him off of dating." Peale tilted back in his chair. "We know he's on shift at the Annex Monday morning at eight. He's probably planning to leave the cabin on Sunday evening."

"Very likely."

"Brannigan's not heading up to his cabin," Peale said. "I already verified that."

"Were you able to find out who else is using their cabins at the government resort this weekend?"

"Yeah," Peale said. "No one. It's not exactly the time of year for it."

"Dr. Lansbury hasn't listed any authorized guests?"

"Nope. If he's meeting with someone, they either already have access to the resort and don't need approval, or they're traveling with him. Or they know how to get in there *without* approval."

"You're thinking of his father."

"It's a long shot. But Lansbury's up to something. He's not driving all the way to the mountains to go hiking in slush."

"We can't get into the resort without authorization."

"I know. I'll work it out." It was time to tell Colonel McLaughlin what they were doing. Glenna McLaughlin's override could get them into the resort and into the Lansbury cabin and erase any record of their having been there. That wouldn't have been the case when Marcus Lansbury owned it, but now that the cabin no longer belonged to a member of the Supreme Executive Council, it wasn't off-limits to the police.

Involving McLaughlin would boost things up a level, both increasing their resources and making things more dangerous. If they did get caught before they found evidence, McLaughlin would cover her tracks, deny all knowledge, and make sure Peale and Pulansky couldn't implicate her. Instead of getting fired, they'd probably get shot.

So don't get caught, Peale told himself. But if Halbrook and Lansbury knew about the transmitters at the Halbrook home, they knew someone suspected them. Peale would have to be twice as careful as before.

"We can't plant bugs," he said. "The cabin for sure has antisurveillance measures in place. But we'll get up there Sunday morning and keep an eye on the cabin until Lansbury leaves. Then we'll get in the cabin before housekeeping does and do fingerprint scans on places that would have fresh prints from this visit—faucets, tables, the kind of items housekeeping would have polished up right before he arrived."

He sat up straight and thudded his boots to the floor. "I want to know who he's meeting up there."

* * *

When the door closed behind the last of his departing guests, Councilor Patrick Haines sloshed water into a glass and drank several gulps to moisten his throat. Too much gabbing, too much maneuvering and manipulating. Too little accomplished. The dinner party had been not only an annoyance but also an embarrassment. Daniel Lansbury wasn't ready for such a prominent post. It was time to say so.

Haines thumped up the stairs and into his library. He closed the door and faced the man sitting behind Haines's desk.

"Your son didn't distinguish himself tonight," Haines said.

Marcus Lansbury shrugged, but his steel-gray eyes sliced like scalpels. "He wasn't at his best."

Haines sat opposite Marcus. He would have preferred to stand and stretch muscles that had grown restless after hours at the dinner table, but if he stood and Marcus sat at his desk, Haines would look like an underling reporting to his boss.

"He's not fit for the post," Haines said. "He's too young."

"He's thirty-two." Marcus opened and closed the velvet box in his hands. "I was thirty-one when I became head of the Tremont Research Laboratory. Thirty-eight when I became Counselor over Internal Defense."

"He lacks your drive. If he's as ambitious as you think, why was he fool enough to rat you out to Brannigan and the police when he learned you were running the Cadre? If he'd kept his mouth shut, he could have followed you to the top."

"He acted out of rebellion, the product of association with a Garrett follower." Marcus's face hardened. "If not for Roshek's influence, Daniel would have recognized that the Cadre was not what it appeared but was a tool I wielded to strengthen—and save—New America."

The Cadre was a group of gullible thugs you manipulated to weaken your enemies, trick the people, and build your power, Haines thought. Why couldn't Marcus state facts instead of glopping everything with rhetoric? "No matter who influenced him, it was still his choice to turn you in."

"The guilt is Roshek's."

Haines shrugged. Lucky for Ian Roshek that he was already dead. And while Marcus might blame the history professor, Haines was certain Marcus would inflict significant penalties on Daniel as well. If one of Haines's children had disrupted two decades of planning and driven Haines underground, Haines would have shot that child without a twinge of remorse. But if Marcus preferred a subtler revenge, that was his business. And Daniel was his only child.

"I don't think Daniel wants the nomination," Haines said. "You watched what went on tonight. He was lackluster. Distracted. Where was that charm he usually spreads around? If he can't be bothered to make a good showing when I've gathered four members of the Council, the head of the Tremont Police Service—"

"What the current government thinks of Daniel is irrelevant. It's not necessary for him to woo anyone with his charisma."

Haines couldn't endure sitting any longer. He rose and paced the perimeter of the library. Marcus remained comfortably in Haines's desk chair. Haines wanted to tell him to get out of it but knew he'd amuse Marcus if he bristled with territorial instincts over a chair.

"I don't understand why you want me to push this right now," Haines said. "By the time I announce his appointment, you'll be in Ryce's place anyway. Why not wait until then?"

"You don't want him as an Assistant? Is that the problem?"

"He's a young idiot."

"I'm surprised you don't see his potential. I saw *yours*. And now look at you. Councilor over Internal Defense."

The muscles cramped in Haines's jaw. Without the subtle, secret machinations that Marcus could work like no other man Haines had ever met, Haines would be nothing more than an ambitious Council Clerk.

"Continue working with Daniel," Marcus said. "This is necessary preparation for Daniel's benefit. I'm sure you'd prefer not to fail my son."

"Whatever you want." He'd sworn his loyalty to Marcus twenty-two years ago. To break that oath now would be fatal.

"Daniel's inexperience won't be a detriment," Marcus said. "He'll be well advised."

And on the world's shortest leash. "Whatever you want," Haines said again and pointed brusquely at the velvet box in Marcus's hand. "Is that the kind they're going to use?"

"Yes." Marcus opened the box and turned it toward Haines to display the interior, where a depression in the velvet awaited Amanda Ryce's medallion. Marcus peeled back a corner of the velvet to expose the plastic mechanism underneath. "When her toadies open the boxes to drool over her generosity, they'll receive a gift worthy of Amanda Ryce."

Haines grunted. It was too much to expect that Marcus would compliment him on how deftly he'd gotten the correct personnel in place at the mint. It hadn't been easy to work that fast without drawing attention. The James Tremont Birthday Commemoration was only a couple of weeks away.

"The mint delivered the prototype medallion to Ryce today, and she's ordered fifty more," Marcus said. "Her own hubris will be the means of her destruction. Poetic, isn't it?"

"Those inoculations had better work." Haines wasn't in the mood to watch Marcus pat himself on the back.

Marcus chuckled. "I take care of people who are loyal to me, Patrick. You're safe. As to Daniel, set your mind at ease. When the time is right, he'll present himself with all the intelligence and force of character necessary to make him a successful leader. He's a Lansbury. It's in his blood. He won't make a fool of you."

"He's made a fool of *you* before." Haines shoved the words at Marcus, wanting to knock that patronizing expression off his face. *In his blood?* The fact that Marcus's father had been one of the founders of New America didn't mean Marcus's son was worth anything. "Maybe this time you'd better not be so sure of your control over him."

Marcus only smiled—a smile that made Haines wonder if Daniel would prefer a bullet to the glorious future his father had planned for him.

Chapter 8

As DANIEL TURNED ONTO THE road that led to the cabin, relief engulfed him. A drive that should have taken four hours had taken seven, thanks to the snow, slush, and rain of an April storm and Daniel's extremely cautious driving. Even a minor accident could have been a disastrous problem with three fugitives hidden in the back of his truck. Now, Jill and the others could finally find respite at the cabin while Daniel tried to figure out what to do next.

He still didn't know why the police were investigating the Halbrooks. He knew from Haines that the police didn't love Brannigan; maybe they were hoping to use Nate against him. In any case, it was safer to keep the fugitives away from Tremont. The police would have no reason to investigate here.

Daniel rolled his shoulders, stretching spots where muscles were knotted or aching. He could only stay at the cabin until tomorrow afternoon, and it would probably be several weeks before he could return. He didn't like the idea of being separated from Jill when things weren't going well between them.

Not that Jill would admit that things weren't going well. She chatted with him like everything was fine, but the way she avoided eye contact— the plastic smiles—the tensing in her shoulders when he put his arm around her . . . And the last couple of times he'd kissed her, she'd pulled back quickly, excusing her skittishness by joking that Ian might walk in on them.

Though she hadn't mentioned it after that first night they'd discussed it, Daniel knew she was still upset over his return to work. Did she think he *wanted* to go back? Daniel had tried to explain to both Jill and Ian that he *didn't* want to, but a façade of flawless patriotism was vital to keeping them safe. After Peale's visit, it should have been easy for them to see why he needed to avoid the kind of attention Nate's questionable attitude had apparently drawn, but from Jill's continuing phoniness and Ian's unusual silence, Daniel knew neither of them got it.

How had his life ended up in such a quagmire? It was unreal how simple everything had seemed last autumn when he'd approached the young violinist with the dimple and sapphire eyes to praise the string quartet's performance. Jill had been so appealing—unpretentious, funny, kind, intelligent. Within two dates, he was in love with her, but they'd had—what?—a month before the trouble began? A month before he'd found out her brother was a wavering patriot with an arrest record? Then, a couple of weeks before his naïve efforts to fix Ian's patriotism had collided with the revelation that Ian was far more than wavering; he was a traitor, a religious believer? Then the shattering knowledge that Jill had been arrested for trying to conceal Ian's crimes. It was over. He'd lost her forever.

Until Ian had shown up, begging for Daniel's help to stop the Liberty Cadre, catapulting Daniel onto a path he'd never thought he'd take.

He didn't regret refusing to join his father in Cadre atrocities. He didn't regret defying orders and saving Jill, Ian, and Alisa; the Council's cold-blooded attempt to sacrifice them to conceal the embarrassing fact that the Cadre was run by one of their own people had been a vicious, unjust ruling. But he'd still feel better right now if Jill would wrap her arms around him, touch her lips to his with gentle trust, and whisper that she knew he was doing his best for them.

The driveway curved toward the garage, and Daniel brushed his forearm past the scanner on the dashboard to transmit the information from his ID chip to the security system. The scanner beeped approval. Daniel reached for the button that would open the garage door, but before he touched it, he hit the brakes so hard he jolted forward in his seat.

A blue jeep was parked on the gravel area at the side of the house.

That jeep didn't belong to housekeeping or maintenance. Their vehicles were green and marked with the resort logo.

It was impossible to tell if there were lights on inside the cabin. All the windows, including the skylights, were treated so passersby saw only opaque panels.

Daniel opened the garage, parked the truck, and walked outside to inspect the jeep. He wiped away a patch of slushy snow on the windshield and peered inside. A clean, empty interior with no hints of the driver's identity. He tugged at the handle on the driver's door. Locked.

Sleet lashed his face. Daniel hastened back into the shelter of the garage. There was probably a harmless explanation for the jeep's being there—anyone with threatening intentions wouldn't have left it parked in the open—but he'd better inspect the house before he let the Rosheks and Alisa go inside.

Daniel opened the door that led to the house. The hallway light flickered on. He took a few cautious steps into the cabin.

All was quiet.

The jeep probably *did* belong to housekeeping. Maybe the engine had died, and they'd had to leave it here. That seemed unlikely, but Daniel couldn't think of a better explanation. They'd probably left him a message about it.

The great room was peaceful and spotless, from the freshly polished oak floor to the basket of wine, chocolates, and coffee sitting on the kitchen counter. Moving briskly now, Daniel hung up his wet coat and checked both his personal phone and the cabin line. No messages, and no note on the counter.

He toured the cabin, entering each bedroom and bathroom and checking the deck and hot tub. Everything looked clean, ready, and undisturbed.

Finishing up in the master bedroom, Daniel slid the closet door shut, feeling ridiculous at how tense he was. He'd call the resort office and ask about the jeep, but he ought to hurry. The Rosheks and Alisa must be stiff, freezing, and carsick after seven hours of riding beneath a camping shell in the unheated bed of a pickup truck.

He reentered the great room, and shock knocked his coordination askew. Gaping at the woman standing near the stone fireplace, he tried to move toward her but struck the arm of the couch.

"Daniel." His mother rushed to meet him. Her arms went around him and, unable to think, he clung to her, his arms all but crushing her slim body.

"Oh, honey." Jocelyn finally pulled back and looked up into his face, her cheeks streaked with tears.

Daniel swiped trembling fingers across his wet eyes. "Dad—"

"He's not here."

"You just arrived?" Daniel gestured at the rain-soaked coat she'd draped over the back of a chair.

She offered a quivery smile. "When I heard you coming up the driveway, I got out of my car and hid behind the cabin. I was afraid if I confronted you before you went inside, you wouldn't let me in."

"Have you been staying here?"

"No, of course not. We never use the cabin. That would be too risky. I came here to see you."

The realization that Jocelyn had tracked him alarmed Daniel. "How did you know I was coming here?"

She smiled. "Daniel . . . you're going to have to forgive me for this, but I've been doing a little prying into your calendar and your messages. I promise I haven't been reading anything private. I just set my program to flag anything related to appointments outside of work or travel. I've been desperate to see you but didn't dare come to the house in Tremont, so I was hoping to catch you somewhere else."

"How did you get access to my messages?"

"That type of thing isn't difficult for your father."

Daniel was always careful not to say anything risky in electronic communications, knowing the police could monitor them, but it still troubled him to find out his parents had hacked into his accounts.

"Where are you staying?" he asked.

"I'd better not say, hon." She linked her arm through Daniel's and led him to the couch. Gray showed at the roots of her hair. It looked wrong on her, and Daniel felt childish for finding it disconcerting. Of course she was old enough that, beneath her always-perfect blonde coloring, she'd gone gray.

"You look tired," Jocelyn said.

"It was a long trip from Tremont," Daniel said stupidly. "The roads were bad."

"Not that kind of tired. It's deeper than that." She patted his hand, her eyes again filling with tears.

The love evident on her face filled Daniel with warmth, like relief from pain. He'd spent the past months fearing she despised him for what he'd done to the family. "Mother, I never wanted—I'm sorry that—"

"Stop." Jocelyn touched his cheek. "We don't blame you for anything."

"I doubt Dad would say that."

"You'd had such a bad time, with the shock of Jill's arrest." Jocelyn ran a firm hand over his hair, reminding Daniel of her standing at the door when he was leaving for elementary school and sending him back for a comb if he tried to skip that step. "Your father laid too much on you too quickly at a time when you were already under terrible stress. It's no wonder you panicked."

"It wasn't panic," Daniel said, but he found himself thinking back on the terrible night when he'd learned his father was the head of the Liberty Cadre. The horror, the maelstrom of conflicting loyalties.

Had he panicked?

Jocelyn spoke soothingly. "Your father was so proud of what he was doing for New America that he forgot what it would sound like to someone who hadn't been working with him all along."

"He murdered hundreds of people. He murdered his own brother! And the bombing at Newbold Bay—he murdered children!"

"He's fighting a war to preserve an entire nation. He wouldn't allow a single death if it weren't absolutely necessary. He loves New America, honey, and he feels the responsibility to carry on his father's legacy. He'd give anything to keep the nation strong." She touched Daniel's sleeve. "I'm so sorry for what you've been through. It must have been awful for you."

Layers of emotion shifted inside Daniel, straining, cracking. "Are you—doing all right?"

"Of course. Your father was always aware of the possibility that he'd have to go underground temporarily, so he prepared for it."

How had his mother entered the resort? She would have needed authorization—a fake ID chip, a disguise, a phony listing as someone's guest? Or someone to sneak her in the way he had Jill and the others? Plainly, his parents still had some influential connections.

"Dad . . . knows I'm here?"

"Of course he knows. He just doesn't know *I'm* here." She smiled mischievously. "And as long as I get back tonight, he'll never know."

Was his father monitoring him in ways other than checking messages and calendar items? Could he possibly know about Jill and the Rosheks?

So cold he felt numb, Daniel searched his mother's expression for any hint that she knew about the three fugitives hiding in the truck in the garage. He saw only the smile that enthralled even his father and led him to give her whatever she wanted.

"It means the world to me to see you again," she said. "How are things going now?"

"Fine . . . going well." Daniel's lips stuck together, and his dry tongue stuck to his teeth. Surely his father didn't know what he'd done at the executions, or he'd have taken action before now.

"How is work?" Jocelyn's warm hand rested on his arm. "It must be different working under Nicholas Whitney."

Daniel swallowed. "Yes, Captain Whitney is very different from Captain Hofstader. Very thorough and cautious. Much more acquainted with the details of investigations. Hofstader preferred to leave everything to his lieutenants."

"We hear good reports of you," Jocelyn said.

Daniel didn't ask where they were getting their information. His mother wouldn't tell him. "If you've been checking my calendar, you know I've been meeting with Councilor Haines. He's planning to nominate me as an Assistant to Internal Defense."

Jocelyn's face lit with delight. "Oh, Daniel! What marvelous news!" She kissed his cheek.

"Thanks." Daniel couldn't stop himself from grinning. Jocelyn's radiant pride was a welcome change from Jill's anxious, phony smiles and Ian's wordless condemnation.

"Tell me all about it." Jocelyn leaned back on the couch. "I want every detail."

Daniel started by briefly summarizing the story of the first time Haines had called him in, but Jocelyn asked so many questions that soon Daniel found himself giving line by line recitations of every meeting he'd had with Haines. It wasn't until he reached the point of reporting on Haines's dinner party that he glanced at the clock and realized over an hour had passed since he'd arrived at the cabin. The Rosheks and Alisa were still in the back of the truck, waiting silently—and miserably—for him to give them clearance to emerge.

"Daniel?"

Daniel realized he'd dropped his report midsentence. "Sorry. Lost my train of thought. To be honest, Mother, the party didn't go well. I was tired and wasn't in the mood for schmoozing. I think Councilor Haines was disappointed."

"Oh, honey, I'm sure it went better than you think."

"I doubt that." Daniel felt strangely irritable at the knowledge that his lack of sociability at the party hadn't sprung from tiredness but from the pressure he'd been feeling from Jill, from Ian, even from Spencer Brannigan.

"You'd better get some rest," Jocelyn said. "You've been on the road all day."

"I'm all right," Daniel said quickly. "I've told you what I've been up to, but you haven't said anything about what you and Dad have been doing."

"We'll save that for later. I can't stay much longer. Daniel . . . I know your father would like to see you sometime."

Daniel felt jumbled fear, half familiar, half new and razor sharp. "Mother. He must be furious—must hate—"

"He loves you. He *was* angry, of course. But he knows it wasn't your fault—it was the fault of that sad, messed-up Roshek boy who pulled you off course. And he recognizes his own mistakes in pressuring you like he did. Besides, it was only a temporary setback. He succeeds at anything he wants."

"Where *is* he?"

"Off meeting with some of his people. Endless meetings! Some things never change. He's nowhere near here, if that's what you're asking." Jocelyn rose gracefully to her feet. Daniel rose as well, his legs so weak that they shook.

Jocelyn hugged him tightly. "I love you," she murmured.

"I love you too. How far do you have to drive? The roads—"

"Don't nag, kiddo." Jocelyn drew back, eyes sparkling with tears. "I was born and raised in Tremont. Do you think I don't know how to drive in this weather?" She picked up her coat. "Take care, Daniel. I'll be in touch soon."

Daniel followed her to the garage, his heartbeat so loud he was surprised she didn't turn around to ask him what was wrong. If she heard any voices or movement from the truck, Daniel had no idea what he'd do.

All was silent in the garage. Jocelyn walked past the truck without glancing at it and out the side door to the jeep she'd left parked at the side of the house.

Daniel stood in the garage and watched her drive away. Rain hammered against the driveway.

With a growing feeling of resentment he didn't want to analyze, Daniel closed the garage door and went to open the back of the truck.

* * *

Still sleepless at two a.m., Ian lay in bed and listened to Daniel pacing around the great room. It didn't take a lot of thought to figure out that Daniel's insomnia had to do with whatever had happened when they had first arrived at the cabin. He had excused the lengthy wait by saying a maintenance team had been at the cabin working to correct an electrical problem—an explanation Ian would have believed if Daniel hadn't looked pale, rattled, and dead set on not meeting anyone's eyes.

Ian rolled out of bed. He'd go talk to Daniel now. Maybe without Jill and Alisa there, Daniel would be more forthcoming. And it would be a private time to mention their concerns about Daniel's involvement with Councilor Haines.

Ian edged the door open and padded along the chilly hardwood floor of the hallway.

In the great room, the flames in the cavernous stone fireplace provided the only illumination. Blackness filled the corners of the room and flooded the high, timbered ceiling.

Daniel stood near the fireplace. He turned as Ian entered. "What's wrong?"

Ian settled onto a couch. There was no point in sidling into this conversation by starting off with a neutral topic. Daniel would never believe he'd come creeping out at two in the morning to discuss baseball statistics.

"What really happened tonight?" Ian asked.

"I told you. There was a problem with—"

"Give me a break."

Daniel looked down at Ian, firelight shifting across the sharp angles of his face. "If there's anything you need to know, I'll tell you. Go back to bed."

Ian nearly shot back that they weren't in the Annex anymore and Daniel could drop the medical supervisor persona, but with an effort, he said calmly, "We're in this together. I don't think it's a good time to be keeping secrets."

"There's nothing you can do to help. Go to bed."

Anger, fueled by weeks of frustration, scorched Ian. He gritted his teeth, fighting not to say something he'd regret.

Daniel turned away. His voice was level but rough around the edges, as if he was feigning compassion he didn't feel. "Do you need something to help you sleep?"

"Yes," Ian said. "The truth."

"I'm doing everything I can—risking my *life*—to protect you. The least you can do is trust me."

This was ridiculous. He could spend the rest of the night trying to chip through Daniel's defensiveness, or he could blast directly to the core of the matter. "Even if we do find a way out of here, are you still planning to come with us?"

Daniel swung around to confront him, fury in his face. "When did I ever say my plans had changed?"

"When did you ever tell us you were back at work? When did you ever tell us Councilor Haines was planning to nominate you as a Council Assistant to the Department of Internal Defense?"

"Who told you that?"

"We figured it out."

"What good would it have done to tell you?" Daniel's voice was a snarl, a tone Ian had never expected to hear from eloquent, cultured Daniel Lansbury.

"You're losing Jill," Ian said. "It's tearing her up seeing you turn back to what you were."

"To what I *was*? What *was* I? The person who had the guts and the brains to save your lives? I'm doing what's necessary to keep us safe. I'd hope Jill would have the maturity to see that."

"The maturity!" The last scraps of Ian's patience burned to charcoal. The age difference between Daniel and Jill—was it eight years? Ten?— had never been an issue for Jill, but Ian suspected she'd feel differently if she overheard Daniel's condescending reference to maturity. "You know what you need, Daniel? You need a taste of what it's like to get your mind turned inside out by that drug you keep shooting into your prisoners. Maybe then you'd know why Jill's upset with you."

"Will you open your eyes? *You* may want to play martyr, but I don't. If you're delusional enough to think your God can do a better job of protecting us, get Him to *do* something. Otherwise, leave me alone."

Daniel stalked out of the room, leaving the word *delusional* pounding in Ian's head.

Chapter 9

THE PAIN IN HER HIPS and knees made Amanda Ryce stumble on the edge of the carpet. She caught herself, leaning heavily on her cane, glad no one had been in her office to witness her clumsiness.

She'd noticed the glance her secretary had exchanged with one of her Presidential Guard as Ryce had strutted past, her cane striking the floor like she wanted to punch holes in the marble. They thought she was too senile to notice the message in the slight arching of eyebrows: *Old Amanda off on another rampage.* She should have them arrested.

Ten years ago, she would have done it, but now it seemed like too much trouble. Getting rid of them would involve selecting new people, testing loyalty, searching for the right mix of strengths that would benefit her and vulnerabilities she could use to control them. At ninety-four, she was too old to give herself weeks of work just to penalize staff members for a smirk.

Cautiously flexing her aching knees, she settled into the chair behind her desk, her temper cooling beneath the chill of fear.

At the end of February, a Council Assistant had vanished. Now, this morning, Ryce had received word that Councilor Richard Montoya was gone.

The police, from Colonel McLaughlin on down, were frantically investigating Montoya's disappearance, questioning his family, taking every member of his staff in for screenings, and sending anyone with questionable readings straight to Information Extraction. But Ryce had a feeling that as in the disappearance of Assistant Nadia Sears, the police would find nothing.

Were they dead at the hands of anarchists? The government had received no threats or claims of responsibility. Since the dissolution of the Liberty Cadre, no significant anarchist group had announced its presence at all. The remaining scum fighting against national stability were scattered and petty, operating solo or in minor groups—religious believers, intellectuals who felt brilliant for reveling in illegal sources of information, vandals who thought throwing rocks through windows at a Neighborhood Security Watch Headquarters made them rebellious heroes. None of them would have the skill to take out two high-government officials.

Had Montoya and Sears been murdered by rivals in unrelated incidents? Possibly. So far, the police had discovered no strong connection between the two of them, beyond their powerful government positions. But the timing was too coincidental.

Had they fled because they were anarchists themselves and feared discovery? Were they involved in a conspiracy that was disintegrating—or could they even be remnants of the Cadre? Ryce wanted to think they couldn't have left New America, sneaking past the new border restrictions she'd put in place, but no border was impenetrable.

No matter how she interpreted their disappearances, she had an enemy operating in Tremont. If someone was targeting the government, ultimately, they would target her. Enemies—and alleged friends—all wanted her power.

Someday, even if she conquered every enemy, she'd still lose everything.

She glared at the portrait of James Tremont hanging on the wall of her office. Tremont had built New America, but now he had nothing. He *was* nothing. He didn't exist.

How many years did she have left? Already, she could see her dismissal in the greedy faces of young Council Assistants. She was ancient, almost gone. Their ambitions were raging, their futures ahead of them. And she'd be in the ground.

She opened her center desk drawer and took out the black velvet box she'd received from the mint on Friday. She opened the box and set it on the desk in front of her.

The medallion had turned out beautifully. Pleased with the design, she'd ordered the mint to strike fifty more medallions for her to present to the Council and the Assistants at the James Tremont Birthday Commemoration.

She cradled the weight of the gold in her hand and examined her image stamped into the metal. Many would think her arrogant for presenting a gift that celebrated her own thirty years in office on an occasion meant to honor James Tremont, but she'd distributed enough trinkets to honor Tremont. New America was hers now.

But for how long?

Ryce clapped the box shut. Montoya was probably dead. Yesterday he'd been alive, vigorous and powerful. Now he was nothing.

She used to fantasize that she could arrange for her own death to coincide with the deaths of everyone in New America. Then, at the moment her heart stopped, she'd have the comfort of knowing she was leaving nothing behind, for there would *be* nothing here.

But that was useless. The slaughter of ten million people, even if she could arrange it, wouldn't end the world. The United States would simply swarm into the desolate New American territory and reclaim the portion of their northeast coast they'd allowed James Tremont to partition off forty-six years ago in order to avoid a civil war. A new population would grow, people who knew nothing of Amanda Ryce and cared nothing for the power she had once wielded. There would be no comfort for her at the moment of death. Only rage.

Only terror.

Ryce set the velvet box on her desk, opened a drawer, and took out the memory card that contained a recording of Ian Roshek's execution.

She held the card in her palm, a fragment of black plastic against her wrinkled skin. It would have been easy to save Roshek's life if she'd wanted to. The Council had been wavering on the matter, hammered by Spencer Brannigan's protests, uncomfortable under the realization that Roshek was chiefly responsible for thwarting Marcus Lansbury's takeover. If she had spoken against the plan, others would have followed.

Roshek was a young man. He could have had another seventy years of life, or more.

She'd stolen that from him.

She tucked the card into the computer port and hit the button to lower the video screen from the ceiling. The menu flashed on the screen. Ryce skipped the interviews, the commentary, the Neighborhood Security Watch Representatives beaming with excitement as they took their seats in the spectators' gallery. When she'd informed the police she wanted an unedited version of the executions, they'd dressed up the recording with hours of glitzy preexecution nonsense, presumably thinking she'd revel in the blathering of people who had no idea what was really going on, along with the lies of people who did. She hadn't reprimanded them for these obnoxious embellishments, not wanting to make it *too* obvious that only one part of the records interested her.

Roshek's death.

She'd already watched the recording once, and it had annoyed her so severely that she'd thrown the card into a drawer, angry that she'd been curious enough to review his death and promising herself she wouldn't do it again. But she couldn't stop thinking about it.

Ryce zoomed in so she could study Roshek's face as he was escorted into the termination room. He looked haggard—not surprising since he'd spent the previous weeks recovering from a near-fatal gunshot wound.

But his eyes were calm.

She watched his expression change as the police escorted Lieutenant Alisa Kent into the room. The flare of pain as he looked at Kent—the way he shifted in the officers' grasp, leaning toward her. Then a small smile, a raised eyebrow, a hint of dry humor.

A smile. Ryce closed her eyes and let the recording run. Lieutenant Blake Peale's voice was a harsh whisper as he taunted Roshek about his sister, making it sound as though she were still alive but scheduled for execution. Roshek's voice, rough with shock and anger. *I never violated your orders; I never talked. She doesn't know the truth. She's no threat.*

The scuffle. Roshek pleading for his sister's life, his voice cutting off when they gagged him.

His sister's life. Why not his own? Why not a surge of venom toward the people assembled to watch him die? The altered version of the execution that had been broadcast to the nation had superbly represented Roshek as a vindictive maniac, his pleas for his sister replaced by computer-generated curses and threats against the government. But in reality, Roshek had shown no hatred. If not for Peale's artful taunts, he would have submitted docilely to death. He'd been ready to climb voluntarily onto the gurney before Peale had carried out his orders to create drama for the viewers.

She opened her eyes and hit mute before her speech began. She didn't want to hear the tiresome grandiloquence her speechwriters had produced for the occasion. She played with the controls, settling on a close-up of Roshek's face. His spasm of rage had passed. If it hadn't been for the tape covering his mouth, he'd have appeared as relaxed as a child sprawled on the grass on a June afternoon. And he'd remained that way through the execution sequence. Tranquil, unafraid as he'd died.

She imagined herself into the scene as the executioner, with different weapons than a gentle needle and merciful drugs, Roshek screaming. She couldn't have made him fear death, but she could have made him plead for it.

Ryce reached to turn off the screen but changed her mind, returned to the menu, and switched camera angles so she could watch Alisa Kent. Ryce hadn't bothered to review the unedited version of Kent's death. Kent's brain had been too scrambled from her brush with Broc psychosis for her attitude to interest Ryce. But maybe there would be *some* satisfaction in watching Kent's broken mind struggle to cope with oncoming death.

Ryce watched the screen intently as Daniel Lansbury inserted the needle into Kent's arm. Kent's eyes were opaque and her face blank. Ryce felt frustration stir. There was no satisfaction in watching Kent confront death with trancelike impassivity . . . ah. Her hands were balled. Ryce zoomed in on Kent's white fingers and found what she sought. A tremor.

She zoomed out and watched the Lansbury boy step aside. She studied the tension in Kent's limbs and the movement in her throat as she swallowed. *Good.* Kent's mind might have been in ruins, but she still had the sense to be afraid at the prospect of obliteration . . . Ryce leaned forward, frowning.

Kent's hands had loosened, her fingers partially uncurling. The muscles in her arms slackened, and her shoulders dipped a little as her body relaxed against the gurney. Ryce jabbed at the controls, zooming in on Kent's face. She no longer looked stoic. She looked peaceful.

Like Roshek. With the tube in her arm, her death only minutes away, she was *calm*.

Ryce's heart pounded furiously. Calm? Or skilled at hiding her feelings?

She chose a new camera angle and focused on the monitor displaying Kent's vital signs. The readouts meant little to her. But a fast heartbeat followed by a slower one would signal that Kent's earlier fear had faded— wouldn't it?

Ryce backtracked and watched the jagged lines on the monitor. The insertion of the tube . . . thirty seconds later, Kent's heart rate began to drop, declining until it was half of what it had been before . . . a third . . .

That wasn't normal, was it? Was she going into shock? If she were on her feet, she'd have fainted. Ryce would have enjoyed seeing Kent crumple, overwhelmed by terror.

Ryce backtracked and switched to Roshek's monitor. A rapid heartbeat, a gradual slowing, then a precipitous drop like Kent's.

She skipped to the point of death for Roshek, then Kent. Their heart rates were slow, their faces free of anxiety.

Was it shock? In both of them, in such a similar pattern? She didn't have medical training; she couldn't tell if—

Ryce touched the controls, selecting a new angle. Lansbury's expressionless face filled the screen.

Daniel Lansbury. Assigned to perform the executions as a test of his patriotism. There had been questions about Lansbury despite the way he'd rejected his father's attempt to recruit him into the Cadre.

How thoroughly *had* he obeyed orders? In criminal executions, the executioner was not permitted to administer any antianxiety medication before the start of the execution sequence. Death via lethal injection was benevolent enough without cushioning criminals in foggy serenity prior to their losing consciousness. They *should* be terrified; they'd earned it. But perhaps Lansbury had defied that order in an effort to make the deaths less stressful. It would have been a foolish move, but perhaps it was the only defiance Lansbury had had the guts to offer.

Ryce surveyed the screen. She had paused the recording with Lansbury's mouth open as he prepared to declare Kent dead.

Fury made her want to reach for the image of Lansbury and break his neck. Ever since the execution, Roshek's calm had mocked her. Had it all been a sham? Had his apparent calm at the moment of death been the result, not of courage or of the comfort of his religious delusions but of the numbing effects of a sedative? Maybe Lansbury had even doped him before he'd walked into the execution room, taking the edge off of his apprehension, then doped him more heavily when he'd stuck the needle in his arm.

Ryce touched the button to retract the video screen into the ceiling. If Lansbury *had* defied orders in making things easier on Roshek and Kent, there was no question he would have done the same for his sweetheart Jill Roshek.

She didn't have a copy of Jill's execution, but she'd get one—discreetly. She didn't want to tip off the Council to what she was doing in case she turned out to be wrong. Her enemies would delight in exposing her as an obsessed and paranoid old hag.

If Jill's execution showed the same odd pattern, Ryce would give the recordings to Dr. Kelleher and see if he confirmed her theory. If Kelleher concurred, she'd order Daniel Lansbury arrested and put through Information

Extraction. If Lansbury had defied orders in seeing to the comfort of three condemned criminals, he might be guilty of more.

No . . . she wouldn't immediately order his arrest. She wouldn't involve the police at first, not until she'd had the pleasure of confronting Lansbury herself. Maybe Roshek had escaped much of the terror that should have attended his death. But that terror, tenfold, would be there in Lansbury's eyes when she personally confronted him with evidence of his treachery.

* * *

The clock on Ian's nightstand read nine thirty-four, but from the silence beyond the door of his room, he figured he wasn't the only one who'd slept in.

Instead of getting up, he stayed under the plush pile of blankets on the king-sized bed and stared at the ceiling slanting high above him. Rain pounded on the skylight and grayness filled the room, dulling bright blues and greens and dimming polished wood.

Last night's confrontation pressed against his chest, stone heavy. He'd heard harsher words from Daniel in the past but not since Daniel's break with the government.

If you're delusional enough to think your God can do a better job of protecting us, get Him to do something.

Delusional. Had Daniel returned to that view of him?

Your God. Was Daniel distancing himself from Ian's beliefs, edging back toward the familiarity of what he'd believed up until a few months ago—that religion was dangerous rebellion, anarchy mutated by insanity, rightfully banned to protect national security? Whatever respect Daniel had gained for Ian's faith had apparently withered under the fact that if there was a God, He didn't seem remotely interested in getting them to safety anytime soon.

So they hid at the cabin for how long? A week? A month? An isolated cabin, a restricted area—those factors would help keep them safe but didn't guarantee no one would get suspicious. If someone did come nosing around, they were stuck. They had no car, no way to escape. What if Alisa's condition worsened? Daniel had said he'd leave a blocker patch just in case, but that would help her for only a week.

If Ian could just know that things would work out, that God hadn't forgotten them, he could be patient. But this uncertainty was ripping his sanity into confetti.

He pushed the covers back, climbed out of bed, and knelt on the floor. The rug chilled his knees, and he thought of Jill, praying and experiencing nothing beyond an embarrassed sense that she was talking to the ceiling.

Jill's prayer *must* have been sincere. She'd give anything for the assurance that God had made it possible for her to be reunited with her parents. Why hadn't He answered her?

Was she now wondering if her brother was crazy to think God had answered *him*?

How hard would it have been for God to—

Okay, settle down. Ian drew a steadying breath and interlocked his fingers. There was something in the Book of Mormon about listening to God instead of trying to tell Him what to do . . . what was the quote? Words he'd studied used to come smoothly to mind, and now if they came at all, they were garbled. He felt suddenly awkward on his knees, self-conscious, even though the door was closed.

Stop it. After everything that's happened, how can you doubt? It's a miracle that you're alive.

Miracles. Fire from heaven encircling and protecting two believers. The walls of a prison crumbling, allowing two believers to walk free. Two thousand young warriors preserved in battle while thousands died around them. Was it too much to ask God to open the way so four people could slip to freedom?

Feeling both cranky and ashamed, Ian closed his eyes. *Thank You for preserving our lives. I'm not asking for an immediate miracle. I just need some hope.*

Without meaning to, he opened his eyes and stared at the rain spattering against the skylight. Why did he think there was any hope to be had?

All right. Fine. If God had a reason for not opening the way, then ultimately, everything would still work out for the best.

Is that so? What could possibly be "best" about getting arrested again? What could be "best" about Alisa ending up with Broc psychosis so her own mind tortures her to death? Or about Jill suffering through a second round of interrogation—

He cut the complaints short and closed his eyes. *I'm sorry. But we're all losing our minds. If it's not time for us to get out of here, please send us some comfort . . . Send us anything.*

He waited, sweat sticking his palms together.

Just let me know we're not forgotten.

A knock at the door sent him springing to his feet. "Yeah?" he said gruffly.

"I'm sorry." It was Jill. "Did I wake you?"

"No, I was up." Ian trudged to the door and swung it open.

Jill tried for a cheerful smile, but reddened eyes in a wan face made it clear she hadn't slept any better than Ian. "Did Daniel tell you he was going somewhere this morning?"

"No. He's not here?"

"No. And he didn't leave a note."

"Maybe he went for groceries."

"Housekeeping took care of that."

Ian pushed his fingers through his shaggy hair. "Maybe he went for a walk."

"A walk! It's—"

"Pouring rain," Ian finished. "How long has he been gone?"

"I don't know. I got up at nine, and he wasn't here. At first I thought he was sleeping in, but the truck's gone."

"Look, he probably had to run an errand and didn't want to wake us up to tell us he was leaving. He'll be back soon." Ian started to shut the door.

"Don't take too long," Jill whispered. "Alisa looks stressed, and it's no wonder after—"

"She's awake?" What was he doing sleeping in when he should have been keeping an eye on her? He all but mowed over Jill as he hurried out of the bedroom.

"Wait, I didn't mean you need to . . ." Jill's voice trailed off as he headed into the great room.

Alisa was standing at the sliding door that led to the deck, facing out toward rounded, snow-frosted mountains.

"Are you all right?" he asked.

She turned. Her hair was damp, and for a panicked moment, Ian wondered if she'd been outside. No, her clothes were dry. "No significant problems," she said.

Ian looked at the pink lines on her throat, traces of the healed scratches she'd inflicted on herself during her breakdown at Nate's. "No problems, or none you want to talk about?"

"Two reversions. Both less than a second in duration. I'm fine."

"Two! Over how long of a period?"

"One last night and one this morning. They were only flashes. It was nothing that—"

"Why didn't you *tell* me? What are you doing standing there checking out the scenery?"

Alisa shot a questioning glance at Jill. "These types of reversions pass so quickly they generally don't present a danger. You know that. If we were in more sensitive circumstances, I would have immediately—"

"What do you mean they 'generally' aren't dangerous? Are you having a lot of these short ones?"

Blood began to redden her cheeks. "Dr. Lansbury remains fully apprised of the situation. I'll inform him of these latest incidents when he returns."

"Well, *great*. In the meantime, would you mind letting *us* in on what's going on with you?"

Jill stepped between Ian and Alisa, her face scarlet. "What's *wrong* with you, Ian? Quit hassling her and come have breakfast. I think you're running low on blood sugar."

Jill's embarrassment finally pierced Ian's awareness. *I'm losing it.*

Over Jill's shoulder, Alisa studied him with a drill-to-the-bone expression. He was abruptly conscious that he was standing there unshaven, disheveled, dressed in a T-shirt and a pair of Daniel's old sweatpants.

The faint sound of a door opening made Jill sigh with relief. They waited in silence until Daniel emerged from the hallway leading to the garage.

"Hello," Jill said awkwardly. "We were wondering where you were."

"Running a few errands." Daniel wasn't wearing a coat—he'd probably hung it on the rack near the door—but his shoes were dry and no spatters of rain dampened the legs of his jeans. "By the way, has anyone seen my watch?"

"Your watch?" Jill asked.

"I can't remember where I put it. I thought I took it off in my room, but I don't see it there."

"Check between the couch cushions," Jill suggested.

"What kind of errands were you running?" Ian asked.

"I don't see how that's your business." Daniel walked past Ian into the kitchen area.

"Maybe it's not my business. I was just curious to see if you could improve on last night's story."

Daniel stopped midstride and pivoted to face Ian. "The visitor who met me here last night was my mother. And no, I didn't know she was going to be here. Satisfied?"

The words jarred Ian like he'd stepped off a curb he hadn't seen coming. Daniel's mother! He'd assumed Daniel's parents were far away, probably in the United States. If his mother had been here, what about—

"No," Daniel said flatly, reading Ian's unasked question. "My mother wouldn't say where he is, but she did say he's off on his own business, nowhere near here. She just wanted to see me and didn't dare come to the house in Tremont. Now do you understand why I didn't feel like talking about it?"

"I'm sorry." Ian couldn't imagine what it must have felt like for Daniel to see the mother he'd driven into hiding. He glanced at Alisa. The blood had drained from her face, and he wondered if she was imagining an impossible encounter between her and the mother she'd betrayed, ultimately to her death.

"Did . . . you go see her again this morning?" Jill asked.

"No. She's not at the lake anymore. I went for a drive. I needed time to think." Daniel headed toward the refrigerator.

"How did she know we were here?" Ian tried his best not to make the question sound like he was drawing his sword for a rematch.

"I don't know." Daniel swung the refrigerator open. "I'm not interested in discussing this further."

Ian's sympathy began to vaporize. Even if it hurt Daniel to discuss it, this wasn't a subject they could ignore. "If your parents are still around and keeping tabs on you, they could have discovered—"

"Don't be so paranoid." Daniel poured milk into a glass. "She learned I was coming to the cabin because she's accessed my calendar and messages, which is not dangerous because I'd never put anything incriminating there. She hasn't been skulking around my Tremont house or the Halbrooks'."

"The fact that your parents are monitoring you at all *is* dangerous," Ian said. "It's not a good idea to underestimate your father."

"If he knew you were alive, he would have killed you weeks ago."

Jill flinched. Daniel either didn't notice or didn't want to apologize for how callous his words sounded.

"Maybe he didn't learn about us until we went to your Tremont house," Ian said.

"My parents can't get close to the house—that's why my mother approached me here. Even if they could defeat the security system—which I ordered redone after they left—my guards would see them. And the place isn't bugged. After what happened at Nate's, I had my men sweep for transmitters. They found nothing." Daniel jammed two slices of bread into the toaster. "If my father did know you were here at the cabin, why would my mother have come, knowing that would tip us off? He'd have acted without warning."

"What if once you leave, your parents show up, thinking this is a good place to hide?"

"My mother came here to see *me*. After I'm gone, she won't come. They aren't using the cabin."

"How can you be sure of that?" Ian asked.

"She told me."

Ian goggled at Daniel. "And you trusted her? We can't stay here."

"She's not going to come back."

"Will you get real? Your mother's on the run with a terrorist mastermind. Don't you think it's possible she didn't tell you the whole truth?"

Daniel stabbed a knife into the butter like he wished he could thrust it between Ian's ribs. "Do you think I'd leave you here if I thought it wasn't safe?"

"I think things would be a lot easier for you and Councilor Haines if we were out of the way."

Jill gasped. "Ian!"

The fury in Daniel's face chilled and hardened into ice. "No one's forcing you to accept my help. If you think you can do better on your own, go ahead and walk out the door. See how long you can stay alive." Carrying his breakfast, Daniel strode out of the room.

Chapter 10

IAN TRIED REPEATEDLY TO SIT down and read, but he couldn't focus. In the hallway that led to the garage, Daniel and Jill were talking as Daniel prepared to head back to Tremont. Their voices were too quiet for Ian to eavesdrop, but he guessed Jill was peacemaking, trying to relieve some of the tension that had strangled them all day as he and Daniel had avoided each other. Was she suppressing her own anguish over his return to work in an effort to ease friction in the group? Probably.

Jill entered the great room alone and smiled halfheartedly at Ian. "He's on his way. I wish the weather weren't so awful. That's a long drive, and he looks tired. Really tired and almost . . . out of it. I wonder if he's getting sick."

Ian glanced out the sliding doors to where rain had turned to snow. Heavy white flakes fell steadily in the twilight, coating leafless trees.

"He found his watch, at least," Jill remarked.

"Uh . . . fantastic. I've been worried about that."

Jill sighed. "I'm going downstairs to play that keyboard. It's not a violin, but at least it's music, right?" She hurried out of the room, and Ian suspected it wasn't music time she wanted but private time to cry.

Should he try to comfort her? He had no idea how.

Ian abandoned his book and started exploring Daniel's cabin, examining each room, opening drawers and closets, even looking under beds. Daniel would be furious if he knew of Ian's prying, but even if he did find out, Ian didn't care what he thought. Daniel was acting like a fool.

"Exactly what are you searching for?" Alisa asked as Ian rooted through a utensil drawer in the kitchen.

Ian looked past the counters to where Alisa sat on the couch, an embroidery hoop in her hands. "I don't know."

"If you're looking for evidence that Councilor Lansbury has been at the cabin recently, you're wasting your time." Alisa poked her needle through the fabric. "He's not that careless."

"He's messed up pretty big in the past." Ian examined a spatula for no reason whatsoever. "He might do it again."

"You need to get some rest," Alisa said.

Ian dropped the spatula in the tray and slammed the drawer. "Daniel's on his way to Tremont to hobnob with Councilor Haines, Zero could walk in on us at any time, and we're supposed to relax and accept that? What are we supposed to do if Zero shows up? 'Hey, Councilor, good to see you. Sorry about thwarting your life's work, corrupting your son, and making you a fugitive. If you put that gun down, we can shake hands—'"

"We're not safe in Tremont either."

"Then let's figure out somewhere we *can* be safe. Why are we *sitting* here?"

"Do you have any suggestions as to where we could go?"

No. He had no suggestions, and the thought made him so angry that he wanted to start smashing the Lansburys' crystal goblets. He hadn't had a single productive idea to offer anyone since the moment he'd awakened at Nate's following the faked executions, amazed to be alive. He'd wracked his brain a thousand times trying to think of a way to get them to safety, but all thoughts ended in a dreary nothing.

Like this morning's prayer.

"Ian." Alisa gestured toward the cushion next to her. "Come sit down."

This quiet invitation quelled his anger. He'd never known Alisa to reach out like this, and he couldn't imagine responding to her with hostility. He shuffled across the room and slumped on the couch. "You think I'm going nuts, don't you?"

Alisa focused on the embroidery in her hands. "I'm hardly in a position to judge anyone else's sanity."

Ian watched her skillful fingers directing the needle through the cloth as she embroidered the leaf on a sprig of lilac. She had found the embroidery kit in the game room at Daniel's, presumably a long-abandoned project of Jocelyn's. Ian had an incongruous memory of Alisa as a police officer, cold authority in her voice and hatred in her eyes. It was hard to link that memory with the woman sitting next to him, peacefully doing needlework Ian associated with the Victorian era.

"I didn't know you knew how to embroider," he said.

"I've never done it before. But the instructions weren't difficult, and there isn't a wide selection of activities at the moment."

"You have a knack for it." Ian's words made him aware of how erratic his emotions must appear—one moment shouting about Zero, the next complimenting Alisa's skill at handicrafts. He leaned his head against the back of the couch and stared at the vaulted ceiling.

"What's wrong?" Alisa asked.

"What's *wrong?* Why don't you ask what's *right?* That would be a shorter list."

"I'm not referring to our situation. I'm referring to a change in you. Something you're holding back."

Under her gaze, Ian felt as guilty and vulnerable as he had when he'd faced her in the interrogation room. "Give me a break, all right? Everything's a mess. The police are watching us. Zero's on the prowl. Sorry if I don't look happy."

She studied him, waiting. Ian could only hold eye contact for a couple of seconds before he looked away. What could he say to her? That he had prayed for reassurance and received none? That Jill had prayed and felt nothing? That he was becoming increasingly certain they were either going to end up back in the Detention Annex or dead at Zero's hands?

No. The last thing he wanted to do was dump his doubts on Alisa.

"Ian," she said softly.

"I'm *fine.* You have enough to worry about."

"It's thoughtful of you to ease my burden by hiding your difficulties until they create problems for all of us."

He looked at her and saw the crooked near-smile on her face. She was mocking herself more than him.

"You really do think I'm losing it," he said.

"I think you're working under a great deal of stress."

"Yeah, well, it doesn't help that the guy who claims to be helping us is acting like an arrogant idiot."

"You and Dr. Lansbury are both working toward the same goal." Alisa meticulously divided a piece of embroidery floss. "I don't think that's changed. His involvement with Councilor Haines is troubling but easy to understand. I imagine Dr. Lansbury went along with him on the assumption that we would leave New America before anything came of Haines's interest in him—flattered, perhaps, that Haines would consider him for such an influential position or not wanting to create trouble by rejecting him. He may have even thought getting close to Haines might give him access to information that would make our escape easier."

She slipped the floss through the eye of the needle. "I suspect Dr. Lansbury is now in deeper than he intended, but sarcasm and personal attacks are the least helpful way of encouraging him to reevaluate his actions."

Ian grimaced. "All right, okay, I get it." Suggesting it would be convenient for Daniel if Zero did away with them had been far out of line. "But Daniel hasn't been running short on nasty comments lately either."

"Do you feel that justifies your actions?"

"Look, I'm just saying—"

"I thought God declared anger and contention to be tactics of His enemy, not tactics He favored Himself."

Ian felt an uncomfortable shadow of recognition: "*He that hath the spirit of contention is not of me, but is of the devil, who is the father of contention—*" He slumped lower on the couch, eyes closing. "You win. And how do you remember that so well? You only read the Book of Mormon once, and extremely quickly at that."

"I have an excellent memory." She put a slight edge on the word *memory*. "And the subject of contention is also one David Garrett discussed with me when he—before he was arrested."

Ian's eyelids sprang open, and he sat up straight. It had been a long time since he'd heard Alisa mention Garrett, the neighbor who had given her parents the Book of Mormon. "What did he say?"

Her eyes darkened with a look of pain that had become as familiar to Ian as the contours of her face—smooth lines left sharp by too much weight lost during her imprisonment. "He spoke of peace. Of the unity God desires us to have as families and as a nation, as opposed to an ethos of fear and hatred." She moistened her lips. "He was trying to show me an alternative to what I believed was the only way to maintain national stability."

She made a rapid stitch, but even Ian could tell it was too long and would have to be removed. Alisa slid the needle off the thread and looked at her marred creation. "Confronting the fact that you have been avidly supporting what is, at best, a terrible mistake is a difficult challenge. It's something *you* dealt with over the course of many years, but even then, when you came to the point of accepting truth that would radically change your life, you were still afraid. Is that correct?"

"That's right, yeah."

"Consider how such awareness feels when it comes abruptly, linked to deeply painful experiences. Maybe then you might feel more patient when Dr. Lansbury struggles to put the remnants of his former life behind him."

Ian looked into her eyes and saw compassion—and sadness. "I've been a jerk. Thanks for the wake-up." He owed Daniel an apology, but it would be a couple of weeks before he could give it—assuming they weren't imprisoned or dead by then. What a self-centered idiot he'd been to sit glowering as Daniel had driven away.

"May I ask you something?" Ian said. "You don't have to answer it if you don't want to."

Her fingers tightened around the embroidery hoop. "Ask your question."

"Was David Garrett afraid?"

Anguish flickered in her eyes, but compassion remained. "Yes and no. He's human. When he surrendered, he knew what he was facing. But he was certain God wanted him to return to New America—specifically, wanted him to come share his faith with me. That certainty gave him a great deal of courage."

Certainty. Lucky him. Afraid Alisa would know what he was thinking, Ian averted his eyes and scanned the kitchen. Maybe he could change the subject to what was for dinner.

"Do you think God has abandoned us?" Alisa asked.

"No."

Alisa said nothing, but out of the corner of his eye, Ian could see her still watching him—knowing he had more to say, deftly leaving an uncomfortable silence for him to fill.

He caved. "I'm just having trouble accepting that what I want might not be what He wants. Pretty weak faith, huh?"

"You've already proven that in moments of crisis, you have the faith to do whatever God requires of you, no matter what the consequences. It seems that what is required of you now is the patience to wait for His aims to become clear—and the humility to acknowledge that you are reliant upon others for help. For you, I think those are more difficult battles."

Somehow, this rational analysis of his turmoil calmed much of it. "You're remarkable, you know that?"

She raised her black eyebrows. "I'm far more frightened than you are."

"I doubt that. But you *are* far more perceptive. Let me ask you this— and don't take it as an attack on Daniel. *Do* you think his parents know about us?"

"That depends on Councilor Lansbury's plans. If he stayed in New America, he did so for a reason. He doesn't think in small terms, so whatever his intentions, they'll have nationwide repercussions."

Ian winced at the thought of Zero's ordering new atrocities.

"If he intends for Dr. Lansbury to be part of whatever he's planning, it's possible he's keeping close enough tabs on him to have discovered us. If, on the other hand, he wants nothing to do with his son and spares Dr. Lansbury's life only for his mother's sake, it's likely he doesn't know about us. In any case, Dr. Lansbury is right that if his father intended to attack us here, it's unlikely his mother would have shown up and put us on guard—" A distant thud made them both jump.

"What was that?" Ian leaped to his feet.

"I don't know. Is Jill—"

"I thought she was downstairs playing the keyboard." But the thud hadn't come from the lower level. It had come from the direction of the utility room and the garage.

Ian hurried in that direction. He checked the utility room, but nothing seemed out of place. Maybe something had fallen over in the garage. He couldn't open the door without first deactivating the security system, and it wasn't wise to—

Alisa rushed up behind him. "The security system is off," she whispered.

"*Off?* But Daniel said he'd arm it remotely as he drove away—"

"The readout shows the garage door is open." Alisa grabbed three coats from among the parkas and ski jackets that hung on the rack and sprinted toward the stairs that led to the lower level.

Cursing a garage door that opened so quietly he'd barely heard it when he was *in* the garage, Ian followed. It couldn't be Daniel returning. He'd been emphatic that he'd always message first to warn them. And Daniel had changed the security settings so housekeeping and maintenance couldn't enter. If it wasn't Daniel and it wasn't a worker from the resort—

They burst into the room where Jill sat at the keyboard, her back to them, earphones on. Ian ripped the earphones off, and Jill twisted around on the bench.

"*What—*"

"Someone's here," Ian whispered. "We need to get out."

Alisa flung a coat at Jill, threw one to Ian, and yanked the door open.

Wet snowflakes splattered Ian's face as he charged onto the snow-covered patio. To his horror, security lights flared, highlighting the patio.

"Get away from the house," Alisa whispered. "Not toward the lake—the trees, that way—"

The three of them skidded across the patio and sprinted across the lawn, heading for trees Ian could see only as a dark blur.

Chapter 11

ARMS HELD OUT IN FRONT of him, Ian plunged into the forest. A branch whipped his forehead. He lifted an arm to protect his face, and a root caught the toe of his shoe. He stumbled.

"Slow down," Alisa hissed. "We just need to get out of sight. If they come after us, we'll hear them."

Ian doubted he'd hear anyone over the din of his crazed heartbeat unless they announced themselves with a trumpet fanfare, but he switched to a trudge, feeling his way through the trees. Clouds blocked the moonlight, and the forest was so dark that even after his eyes had adjusted, he could still see only the dimmest hints of what surrounded them. After stumbling over another obstacle—a decomposing log?—grating his left palm on the bark of a tree, and nearly being blinded by the branch of a sapling, Ian paused and turned toward the dark shapes of Alisa and Jill.

"You both okay?" he whispered.

Alisa and Jill huddled around him.

"Do you think whoever it is *will* come after us?" Jill whispered.

"Who knows?" Ian couldn't imagine Jocelyn Lansbury chasing them into the forest, but it wasn't hard to imagine Marcus with a flashlight in one hand and a gun in the other.

"Whoever it is didn't know we were there," Alisa said. "If they wanted to surprise us, they wouldn't have been so clumsy as to alert us to their arrival."

"Good point," Ian said. Maybe Daniel *had* been right about his parents not knowing they were alive. But he'd been wrong about their not using the cabin—unless the visitor was someone else. But who? Peale? If he was investigating the Halbrooks, was he suspicious of Daniel as well? But Daniel had said even the police couldn't get into the resort without authorization.

"They'll know *someone* was there," Jill said. "We left the lights on and our stuff around."

"And three sets of footsteps leading into the forest," Ian added. "Let's hope the snow covers them soon."

Alisa's fingers were a pale blur in the darkness as she pulled up the hood of her coat. "We should head toward the road."

"Why?" Ian asked.

"If we cross the road and position ourselves on the hill opposite the cabin, we'll be able to see if the visitors leave. When they realize someone is staying there, maybe they'll leave quickly."

Another good point. Even if Daniel's father *was* there, if he didn't realize the cabin's guests were three fugitives—at least one of whom he'd like to murder—why *would* he chase them? He was a fugitive too.

"Follow me." Alisa pushed past Ian. The ground beneath their feet sloped gently upward, then turned into a steeper angle as they headed toward the road.

Jill yelped and slammed into the back of Ian, grabbing his coat to catch herself. He stumbled, nearly crashing into Alisa.

"Sorry," Jill whispered. "I tripped. My feet are numb."

"Yeah, mine too." This was crazy. They had coats, but beyond that, they weren't dressed for the weather. Snow had spilled into the too-big running shoes Ian had borrowed from Nate, soaking his socks. He tried to remember what shoes Jill and Alisa were wearing. Nothing appropriate for hiking in snow, anyway. If the visitors did stay in the cabin overnight—or longer—where would they go? They were in a mountain resort with cabins spaced miles apart and protected by security systems. If only there were some way to get in touch with Daniel—but Daniel would be halfway to Tremont by now. There would be no public phones in this resort, and even if they did find one, it would take an ID chip to operate it.

The flat surface of the road finally showed between trees.

"No tire tracks," Alisa murmured. "They must have come from the other direction."

Ian squinted at the road. How could she see so well in the dark? He was barely able to confirm that there was a road at all.

Alisa edged out of the trees, paused, then moved swiftly across the road. Ian hurried after her, his feet so numb he felt like he was balancing on wooden blocks.

"I wanted to spend some time outside, but this isn't what I had in mind," Jill said as they resumed their inch-by-inch slog through the trees.

Alisa stopped abruptly.

"What—" Ian began.

"*Shh.*" Alisa grabbed his arm. He stood, trying to keep his teeth from chattering, wondering what she was listening for when a crunch and snap of branches sent a wave of adrenaline through his body.

Should they flee and risk making noise that would give them away, or should they crouch here, hoping that in the darkness their pursuer wouldn't find them?

Alisa gripped the back of his neck and pulled his head down so she could whisper in his ear. "They're moving away."

Ian searched for the beam of a flashlight and saw only the exterior lights of the Lansbury cabin, visible through the trees. He focused all of his attention on listening and heard what Alisa heard—rustling footsteps but progressively fainter.

They stood motionless. With no idea who else might be out here or what was going on, Ian didn't want to risk moving just to bumble into greater danger. He stood with his ungloved hands tucked under his arms and snow coating his hair, trying to figure out where they could go. Jill and Alisa apparently agreed with the strategy of waiting and getting frostbite; no one spoke or moved.

A mechanical hum sounded in the distance. He peered at the road through the trees and saw headlights approaching on the snowy road Alisa had pointed out as being free of tire tracks. If it was Zero, he wasn't leaving the way he'd come. A small car sped past.

"I don't get it," Jill whispered. "Were they looking for us?"

"If so, they were doing a poor job of it." Alisa sounded puzzled. Ian was equally confused. The footsteps hadn't come from behind them, as from someone following their trail, but from farther up the mountainside. Had their "pursuer" been there first—and then departed when they approached?

"I'm freezing." Jill's teeth chattered. "We can't stay here."

"Yeah, I know." Ian stared at the lights around the Lansbury cabin. That car hadn't come from the cabin. How many people were involved in . . . whatever was happening? "No matter what, we—" He squinted at a bright patch on the cabin. "Wait. The garage door is still open. Why wouldn't they have closed it?"

"I don't know." Alisa started down the hill.

"No—don't get closer—" Ian leaped too quickly after Alisa and smacked into an icy branch. Wincing, he licked blood off his lip and ducked under the branch.

"Alisa, we can't go back there. Whoever drove away didn't come from the cabin. Someone's still there." He dove forward and caught her arm. "Stop."

"I need to check something. I won't get too close." She tugged her arm out of his grip and resumed her trek down the mountain.

Behind Ian, Jill gasped.

He whirled around. "You all right?"

"Just—twisted my foot—there are a lot of rocks under the snow, and my shoes—it's nothing; I'm all right."

Ian resumed picking his way down the mountain. Alisa was too far ahead. In the dark, he could no longer see her at all. He didn't dare call to her, so he increased his pace. He didn't know what she had in mind, but—

His foot slipped on a rock, and his left leg shot out from under him. He crashed to the ground, pain ripping along the side of his calf.

"Ian!" Jill whispered frantically.

"I'm all right." He tried to stand, but something had snagged the leg of his pants. Fumbling in the darkness, he tried to free himself from a hard, sharp object—a broken branch with fragments of wood projecting upward. When he'd fallen, the branch must have torn the leg of his pants and scraped the side of his calf. How bad was he hurt? He probed tentatively at his leg. Wet warmth tingled his icy fingers.

"Ian?" Alisa had retraced her steps and was leaning over him.

"I'm all right. Just slipped."

Jill and Alisa grasped his arms and heaved him to his feet. He clenched his teeth, restraining a groan.

"You're injured," Alisa said.

"It's nothing," Ian mumbled. "Scraped my leg." He shrugged off the supporting hands and took a tentative step. The pain brought a storm of nausea, but his leg held his weight.

"I'm all right," he said, swallowing. "Let's go on."

It was only ten or fifteen yards farther to the road, but with every step, Ian doubted he'd make it. The pain was dizzying, his leg shook, and he stumbled over every rock or branch he passed. Jill finally drew up beside him and gripped his arm.

"You are such a liar," she whispered. "How bad is it?"

"Not bad," he lied. From the heat streaming down his calf, he knew he was bleeding heavily. Was he leaving a trail of blood in the snow? He ought to bandage his leg, but with what?

Ahead of them, Alisa had reached the edge of the road, the silhouette of her hood faintly visible between the trees. She stood still for a moment, then came back toward them.

"There is one vehicle in the garage," she reported. "It looks like Dr. Lansbury's truck."

"Daniel's truck!" Jill exclaimed. "Wait a minute. Could *he* have been the person you heard in the garage?"

Wind gusted. Ian grimaced, blinking snow out of his eyes. "He said he'd always send a message before coming back."

"Maybe he couldn't for some reason," Jill said.

"Some reason like his father holding a gun to his head?"

"It's useless to speculate until we've confirmed that it *is* his truck," Alisa said. "It's impossible to be certain at this distance. I'll go to the house, investigate, and return to tell you what I find."

Ian figured crisis trumped tact and spoke bluntly. "No, you *won't*. You're doing a lot better, but it's still a lousy idea to send you into a situation where any uncontrolled noise or movement—"

"I'll go," Jill said.

"No *way*, Jilly. You could smack right into Zero. I'll go. You two stay here."

"You can hardly walk." Jill's voice was taut with fear, but her words were steady. "If something goes wrong, you couldn't run. I'll cross the road far from the house and approach from the side. I'll be careful."

"*No*," Ian said. "I can do it. My leg is fine—"

"No, it isn't," Jill fired back. "You're limping like crazy."

"You're not going."

"We have to find out if Daniel is there. I'm the best person to check things out, and you know it."

"She's right," Alisa said. "Let her go. Dr. Lansbury may need our help. And if we can't return to the cabin, our chances of finding shelter tonight are almost nonexistent."

"This is crazy." Ian tried to sound firm, but he felt so queasy that he was going to lose this argument by throwing up while Jill ran off. He drew deep breaths of cold air, struggling to quiet the nausea. "Why did they . . . leave the garage door open anyway? It could . . . all be a trap."

"That doesn't make sense," Jill snapped. "Do you think Daniel's dad left the door open to lure us back to the cabin? If he'd wanted to trap us, he'd have been smart enough to sneak up on us in the first place. I don't think he knows we were there."

"Jill, it's *too risky*. We have no idea what—"

"Stop treating me like a child. You'd do it yourself without blinking, but somehow it's too risky for me? Do *you* know anything about sneaking up on a cabin that I don't?"

"That's not the point. The danger—"

"We're wasting time," Alisa warned. "Jill, don't try to enter the cabin. Just get close enough to verify that it is Dr. Lansbury's truck and check around the property for any other vehicles. Then come out onto the road and head in this direction. We'll watch for you. Once we've determined whether or not he's there, we can decide what to do next."

"I'll be right back." Jill darted between the trees. Ian leaped after her, but pain blasted through his leg, and he staggered, knees nearly buckling. "Jill—"

"Let her go." Alisa seized his arm, whether to hold him back or hold him up, he didn't know.

"Too—dangerous—"

"You can't protect her. In our current situation, that's impossible. Let her do what's necessary."

Ian closed his eyes. *Please keep her safe. Don't let anyone hurt—*

But his attempt at a prayer sank into the scalding helplessness he'd felt when he'd watched Jill being arrested and could do nothing to save her.

* * *

Heart thudding, Jill inched through the darkness. Despite Ian's injured leg, she had half expected to hear his crashing footsteps pursuing her and his furious whisper ordering her to stay away from the Lansbury cabin.

The longer she shuffled alone in the forest, the more she wished she *would* hear Ian calling her.

Her feet were numb, and her hands ached with cold. What if she met Daniel's father?

Run. What else can you do?

But maybe he wasn't there. Maybe Daniel had decided to return. Maybe on the drive he'd pondered what she'd said before he left—that even if his quitting his job at the Detention Annex put them in greater danger, they were all willing to risk it. He'd probably tried to contact them to tell them he was returning to the cabin, but coverage had been poor and the message hadn't gone through. If she could get to the cabin and confirm—a branch caught her hair, and she tore it loose, wincing as numerous strands ripped from her scalp.

Shouldn't the lights of the cabin be visible through the trees by now? She'd tried to walk parallel to the road, just far enough into the forest to be invisible if anyone drove by. She decided to head up to the road to get her bearings. The darkness was disorienting.

She started up the slope that led to the road, but the crack of branches coming from somewhere to the right of her made her gasp. Marcus Lansbury—or a hungry bear—

Stop scaring yourself. It's Ian.

No, it isn't. He would have called your name.

Branches rustled. More footsteps coming toward her.

How could someone have found her so quickly—but she couldn't see a flashlight—it had to be an animal—

Get to the road. Out in the open, there was a chance Ian and Alisa might see her and come to her aid. She didn't dare yell. Someone at the cabin might hear her, or her shriek might spook the animal into attacking.

She scrabbled up the hill, the soles of her tennis shoes skidding on rocks. Branches lashed her face; bushes snagged her clothes. Her pursuer was closing in on her—no, curving farther to the right, *passing* her. It must be something harmless, like a deer.

Could you be any more jumpy? Stop and listen a little more carefully before you freak out over a deer. She stood motionless and waited for the snap of branches to fade. The animal was heading toward the road.

Wind shook the trees. Clumps of snow pattered onto her hair. Shivering, she waited.

At the edge of the trees, silhouetted by the relative lightness of the snowy road behind it, a dark outline became visible.

It wasn't an animal. It was a man.

A branch snapped. The shape moved toward her, blending again into the blackness of the forest.

Panicking, Jill gasped in a breath so she could scream but shut her mouth. Her pursuer was probably armed, and if she yelled for help, she'd draw Ian and Alisa out onto the road where they'd be much clearer targets than she.

She threw up one arm to shield her face and held the other out to feel for obstacles as she floundered back down the hill. Something caught her foot, and she fell, banging her knees and scraping her hands. She scrambled to her feet. Behind her, the crunch of footsteps continued, forcing her farther from the road and toward the lake.

How could her pursuer see her? When she looked over her shoulder, she saw only blackness. Should she throw herself to the ground and wait, hoping that in the darkness he'd miss her? He didn't have a flashlight; he must be following the sound of her footsteps.

Jill's hand struck the trunk of a tree. She swished her fingers across it; it was wide. She stepped to the other side of it and crouched low, a hand over her mouth to mute her gasping breaths.

The footsteps continued toward her. Light-headed from her effort to breathe silently, Jill tried to ward off panic. *Don't move. He can't possibly see you. He's following the noise you make.*

Closer. Jill gritted her teeth. *Stay quiet. Let him walk past you.*

A hand grasped her shoulder.

Jill screamed. Striking blindly to knock her pursuer away, she launched into the darkness, but within a few steps, she tripped. Tears made icy streaks on her face as she fought her way to her feet. He *could* see her—did he have night-vision equipment?

Footsteps behind her. Splashing water against the shore ahead of her. She would end up pinned between her pursuer and the lake. She lurched to the side, trying to move parallel to the lake. Underbrush tangled around her legs, and she flailed, trying to keep her balance. *Help me. Help me.* The words repeated in her head. Did God hear them? *Help me. Please.*

She struggled out of the brush, and her shin struck something—a broken tree limb? She tried to climb over it, but wood cracked beneath her feet, throwing her forward. One hand hit the trunk of a tree; the other missed, twisting her body around the tree. Bark grazed the side of her head.

For an instant, she held on to the trunk, catching her balance, then stepped away. Her feet were so numb she couldn't feel rocks or roots, and the flat soles of her shoes gave no traction. She slowed—slow was better than tripping—but her toe struck something hard, and she fell.

Jill gave up trying to walk and began crawling. She could no longer tell which direction she was going. The slosh of the lake and the rustle of branches surrounded her. Within seconds, her pursuer would overtake her. She wanted to scream again, but gasping sobs consumed her breath.

Please help me. I can't outrun him. I can't see where I'm going. I don't even know where I am—

Thoughts penetrated the blur of panic, brightening her mind with such clarity that it startled her. She knew exactly where she was. She needed to turn to her right, go forward about twenty steps until she reached the beach, then turn left and run along the beach until she reached the Lansbury dock. From the dock, she should run up the hill and go into the house.

But I can't see where I'm—

She *could* see. Outlines of trees became clear. Bushes and rocks became distinctive lumps.

Heat flooded her limbs. She sprang forward, pushing branches aside, weaving between trees, jumping over rocks. The lake rippled black through gaps in the trees. Her heartbeat pulsed in her ears, muffling the sounds of her pursuer. She didn't look back.

The beach. With speed she'd never thought she could muster even under the best of circumstances, Jill sprinted along the narrow strip that separated the forest from the water.

The sight of the dock jutting into the lake made her want to shout with joy. When she'd nearly reached the dock, she wheeled to the left and raced up the snow-covered lawn.

A figure approached her from the direction of the cabin. For a terrified instant, Jill hesitated, thinking her pursuer had beaten her there, but when the person called her name, relief propelled her toward him.

Daniel reached for her with an uncoordinated jerk of his arms. "Are you—all right?"

"Someone—chasing me—we need to get inside." She started toward the house. Daniel kept veering to one side or the other, and when he tried to open the door, he fumbled with the handle. Jill reached past him and yanked the door open, shooting a glance over her shoulder. No sign of her pursuer. She pushed Daniel into the cabin and locked the door behind them.

The warmth and light of the room enveloped Jill and made her instantly conscious of Ian and Alisa waiting in the cold. "Ian and Alisa are across the road. We need to—"

"You're . . . hurt." Daniel touched her face.

Jill put her hands to her cheeks, but her fingers were too cold to explore the marks left by countless branches. "We thought you were on your way to Tremont. Why did you—" She stared at Daniel. A bruise swelled on his left cheekbone, along with a crimson patch of scraped skin.

"It's your father, isn't it? He attacked you and came after—" At the rage contorting Daniel's face, she stopped. "What—"

"What did Ian . . . do . . . to you?" His voice was strange. Halting, slurred.

"What did *Ian* do?" Confused, Jill took a step back. "Daniel, who hurt you? *Is your father here*? Is anyone else inside the house?"

"*No.* I told you he wouldn't . . . come here . . ."

That blow to the face must have left Daniel dazed. "We need to get Ian and Alisa. They're—"

"He's *insane.* Now he's endangering *you.*"

"Your father?"

Contempt hardened Daniel's bleary eyes. "Is that what Ian told you? His excuse for . . ." He gripped both of her hands and turned them upward. Jill glanced at her filthy, bloodied palms.

"I fell a few times. We need to get Ian and Alisa. *Now.* Whoever was chasing me might decide to go after them, but if we take the truck, we'll beat him there."

"Why did you . . . go outside?"

"Ian and Alisa heard someone—I'll explain later. Come *on.*" She pulled her hands out of his grasp.

"Ian doesn't need rescuing." Daniel brushed his fingers across his eyes.

"*Daniel*! What's the matter with—" This was a waste of time. Daniel was too dazed to understand what was happening and too woozy to drive. "Give me the keys to your truck."

"Let me show you something I found in your brother's room." Daniel wobbled toward the stairs.

She followed him. "The *keys,* Daniel. Where are they?"

Daniel ignored her. In the great room, he went to the table next to the couch and picked up a small plastic bag. He held it out to her.

A blocker patch, cut in half, was inside the bag. "I don't understand," Jill said.

"Talk to your brother about it."

"I *will*—after we go *get* him. Give me the—"

"Jill." Ian spoke from behind her.

Jill spun around.

Ian and Alisa stood in the hallway leading from the garage. "Anyone else here?" Ian asked.

"*What* are you doing—Daniel says no, but he's hurt, not thinking straight, so we'd better—"

"There's no one here," Daniel said coldly, sounding more clearheaded.

Ian moved toward her. He was scratched, bedraggled, and limping badly. "Are you okay?"

"Yes," Jill said.

"There are fresh footprints coming from the dock up the hill. They meet up with footprints coming from the house."

"Those are mine and Daniel's." Jill's surprise at Ian and Alisa's arrival turned to jubilant relief. "What are you doing here? And did you check the garage? I didn't have time to—"

"There's only Daniel's truck in the garage, and there are no tracks in the driveway."

"The snow might have covered—"

"Not completely," Ian cut her off. "And there are no wet tire tracks in the garage or vehicles parked elsewhere on the property. What are you doing inside? You were supposed to—"

"It's a long story." Jill smiled, joy and gratitude swelling inside her. How could she explain what had happened in the woods?

"We thought we heard a scream. And you look like you had a rough time of it."

"You could use some first aid yourself. But first we'd better close the garage and arm the security system. There's someone—"

"I'll do it." Alisa turned toward the garage.

Daniel tossed the bag containing the mutilated blocker patch at Ian's feet. "The danger isn't outside, Jill," he said.

Chapter 12

Ian sank into a chair and watched Alisa pick up the bag. "I don't understand," he said.

"Don't you?" Daniel said stonily.

"Used on you?" Alisa asked.

"Yes." Daniel's hand shook as he lifted another bag from the table next to the couch. He held it up, and Ian recognized Daniel's steel-and-gold watch inside. "Take a look."

Alisa set the patch on the table and used one of Jill's sketching pencils to reach into the bag and take the watch by the band. She held it near the lamp and turned the watch so the interior of the band was toward the light.

"See anything?" Daniel sat heavily on the couch.

"Traces, where it dried between the segments," Alisa said.

"Wait a minute." Bewildered by the accusatory look Daniel was giving him, Ian tried to sort out the situation. "You're saying someone cut the patch open and spread that drug on your watch?"

Jill's eyes widened. "This evening," she said. "You found your watch not too long before you left. I remember you had a funny look on your face while we were talking. Like you were having trouble seeing."

"That's when I started to feel it." Daniel rubbed his forehead. "I thought I was just tired. Stressed."

"Hold on," Ian said. "If someone spread that stuff all over your watch, wouldn't you have noticed the instant you put it on?"

"A thin layer, already dry or nearly dry? And it *must* have been mostly dry, or the effects would have hit me a lot quicker and harder than they did. I didn't get dizzy until I was in the garage, looking for my keys."

"Looking for your keys?" Alisa asked.

"I'd left them in the truck, but I couldn't find them. When I started feeling dizzy, I tried to come back inside, but I didn't make it."

"You never left for Tremont?" Jill asked. "You were out in the garage the whole time?"

"Yes. My mind was . . . I couldn't remember where I was . . . didn't know what was happening. When I'd try to stand, I'd fall."

"It's *you* we heard out there." Ian thought of the thud that had alerted them to the presence of an intruder. "We thought it might be—"

"Don't start with some spiteful attempt to blame this on my father. Why would he do this to me?"

"Revenge," Jill said tentatively.

"He's better at revenge than this. This was the work of your compassionate brother, fantasizing that he's making a point."

"*What?*" Ian swiped away the melted snow dripping down his forehead. "What point?"

"That I shouldn't be back at the Annex messing with people's minds. With no Broc4 around, I suppose the best you could do was sentence me to a few hours on the garage floor."

"This is *ridiculous*. How would I even *think* of something like that? I'm not a doctor—"

"You grilled me about the Broc blocker when I used it to treat Alisa. I told you the dangers of an overdose. And last night, you told me that if I had any idea how it felt to lose control of my mind—"

"We were all unhappy about your going back to work, but none of us would *ever* hurt you to make a point," Jill interrupted fiercely. "I can't believe you'd blame—"

"'You know what you need, Daniel?'" Daniel quoted caustically. "'You need a taste of what it's like to get your mind turned inside out by that drug you keep shooting into your prisoners.'"

Ian was acutely conscious of Alisa standing by the lamp table, her dark hair tangled, a bloodred scratch across her cheek, her gaze steady as she waited for his response. "Okay, I said that. I'm sorry. But I didn't mean it as a threat."

Jill came to stand next to Ian's chair. "Ian wouldn't harm you."

"Look at *you*." Daniel gestured at Jill's scraped hands. "You're a mess. He could have gotten all of you killed out there tonight."

"He wasn't the one who chased me on my way back to the cabin," Jill retorted.

Ian clutched her arm but quickly let go, afraid she might be bruised under her sleeve. "Someone was chasing you? Is that why you screamed?"

"Yes. I have no idea who it was. I just saw a shadow and heard—"

"I don't think anyone was chasing you," Daniel said. "It's dark. You were out there in the middle of the trees. Wind sounds, lake sounds—it's no wonder you got spooked."

Jill looked stung. "It wasn't imagination. Someone grabbed my shoulder."

Guilt and horror mashed Ian's heart to paste. The doubt on Daniel's face made it plain he was still dismissing Jill's report, assuming she'd been bumped by a branch and had imagined it to be a human hand.

"We all heard someone," Ian said roughly. "On the hill across from your house. We heard him—or her—walking through the trees and then saw a car driving away. We assumed whoever it was had left, but maybe we were wrong. Maybe they went after Jill. Or maybe there was more than one person out there."

"Who?" Daniel asked. "A werewolf and a ghoul? If you thought there was any real danger, you wouldn't have dragged Jill and Alisa out there as part of the pretense that my father is stalking you."

"We all saw the car," Jill said. "We didn't imagine—"

"There are other cabins in this resort," Daniel snapped. "It's not my private road."

Ian struggled to keep his temper in check, but the pain in his leg and the miserable burning in his rewarming toes and fingers made him angrier at Daniel's obstinacy.

"It was considerate of you to take my keys to make sure I didn't crash and kill myself while you were teaching me a lesson," Daniel said. "But next time, find a better place than your closet to hide them."

"How can you be stupid enough to—" Ian's gaze caught Alisa's, and their conversation of earlier that evening sprang to mind. *"He that hath the spirit of contention—"*

Struggling to gather the mangled pieces of his self-control, Ian said, "I didn't put your keys there or the patch or whatever other 'evidence' you found. But someone did, and that means someone has been in the cabin since we've been here. The most likely candidates are your parents. You know your mother has access to the cabin."

"When she met me here, she waited outside until *I* had deactivated the security system. You are completely irrational. You're suggesting my parents could enter, get the blocker patch, do their dirty work, then leave the patch and keys in your room and slip out again—all unseen—yet when my father wants to murder Jill, he has to go chasing her through a dark forest? Why didn't he shoot all of you in your sleep?"

Ian couldn't argue this any longer. His leg was aflame, cold sweat soaked his shirt, and if he had to listen to more attacks on his character and his sanity while Zero closed in on them, he'd break Daniel's jaw.

He rose to his feet and limped toward the hallway.

"Wait!" Jill cried. "Don't go off alone. Whoever did this to Daniel can bypass the security system—"

"They won't go after me tonight. That would make it impossible for Daniel to keep blaming me." He limped into his bedroom, closed the door, and started toward the bathroom, avoiding the rug in the center of the room. Hot blood ran down his leg, and bleeding on the carpet seemed like a bad idea—he'd probably already left stains on the rug in the great room.

He stepped into the bathtub and sat on the edge. The dark pants he wore didn't show any blood, but it trickled down one side of his shoe, mingling with melting snow. He eased the shoe off and peeled off his blood-soaked sock. How seriously *had* he gashed himself? Gingerly, he pulled up the leg of his pants. The sight of torn skin and dripping blood brought a new rush of nausea. Pressing his shoulder hard against the tiled wall to steady himself, he dabbed at his calf with a towel, trying to clear away blood so he could assess the damage.

A strip of skin an inch wide and maybe four inches long flapped loose. Splinters of wood and bits of leaves stuck to raw flesh.

Feeling sicker, Ian stripped off his other shoe and sock and turned on the tap. The lukewarm water burned his feet, and blood dyed the accumulating water pink.

He inhaled, fighting dizziness. *Get a grip. You've been hurt a lot worse than this.* He reduced the flow of water to a trickle and edged his injured leg under the stream. When the water touched his lacerated flesh, a shock raced up his nerves. He jerked his leg back.

Take it easy. You have to clean it out. Ian forced his leg back under the stream. He prodded reluctantly at the flap of skin with his fingertip and turned his leg more fully toward the running water. Again, pain made him yank his leg back.

He rested against the wall, eyes closed. Yes, he'd been hurt much worse than this, but he hadn't had to do anything about it except lie there and bleed. Peeling back chunks of flesh and hosing out the debris trapped beneath was more than an ex-college professor had signed up for.

The sickness intensified. He needed to lie down. He clawed a new towel down from the rack and wrapped it around his leg. Bracing his hand against the wall, he stepped out of the bathtub, but dizziness pushed him to his hands and knees on the bath mat. He flopped to the side and rested his face against the soft mat.

Should he yell for Daniel to step in and rescue him? Daniel *would* help—Ian couldn't imagine him ignoring an injured person, even a nut he thought had viciously attacked him.

The thought stirred more nausea. How had Ian forgotten everything he liked and respected in Daniel and focused only on Daniel's flaws, feeding the conflict between them until Daniel was ready to blame him for that attack? Ian already owed Daniel his life, and what had he given back? He'd gone from being useless to actively making things worse, and the thought of receiving Daniel's help again was so repugnant that Ian lay there, silent, struggling to breathe steadily, hoping he wasn't going to vomit, and trying to think of a way he could deal with this without assistance.

So lie here on the bathroom floor and wallow in pride.

Pride.

Was that his problem?

He reached for the edge of the bathtub and pulled himself to a sitting position. Blinking and straining to focus, he realized Daniel was standing in the bathroom with Alisa and Jill behind him. Over the gush of running water and the buzzing in his head, he hadn't heard footsteps or doors opening.

"You left a trail of blood," Daniel said.

"Sorry," Ian mumbled, blearily aware of how ridiculous the apology sounded. Daniel wasn't berating him for contaminating the hardwood.

Daniel squatted next to him and peeled back the towel Ian had bunched around the wound. "What happened?"

"Slipped . . . landed wrong on a broken branch."

"You should have told me. I thought you'd just twisted your ankle." Daniel's fingers pressed against his wrist, checking his pulse. "Alisa, in the master bedroom closet on a shelf on the right, there's a black briefcase. Bring it to me."

Alisa turned toward the door. She looked shaken, Ian thought, but why wouldn't she? A lunatic attacking people and dripping blood through the house would rattle anyone. He wanted to ask her if she was all right, but before he could speak the question, she was gone.

"You need to get out of those wet clothes," Daniel said. "And you need to lie down. What kind of a fool are you to try to handle this on your own?"

Ian didn't try to answer. Detailing his foolishness would take a lot more energy than he had.

* * *

The nightgown and robe were brilliant turquoise, a color Alisa knew would once have flattered her. Now the blue looked clownishly bright against the gray of her skin. She stared at the image in the mirror: a haggard, disheveled woman incongruously clad in Jocelyn Lansbury's silk nightclothes.

Alisa moistened a washcloth under the tap and wiped at the blood that had dried in a deep scratch across her cheek. At one time, that scratch would have evoked fears of a scar, but now the thought was ludicrous. What did it matter?

She wiped another scratch, scrubbing with savage pressure. How could she have encouraged Jill to go alone to investigate the cabin? How could she have sent her to what could have—*should* have—been her death? Unarmed and running blind, Jill should have been easy prey.

Easy prey for Marcus Lansbury. If it hadn't been Lansbury in the woods, it had been someone operating on his orders. Probably someone instructed to make Jill's death look accidental.

Daniel claimed it made no sense to say his father had assaulted him with the drug from the blocker patch, and it *didn't* make sense if all Marcus wanted was revenge.

But what if he wanted his son's loyalty back?

The visit from Daniel's mother, followed by the attack on him, had answered the question as to whether or not Marcus knew about the fugitives. He knew, but he was moving carefully, unraveling Daniel's loyalty to his friends so when Marcus destroyed them, he'd gain not a furious son blaming him for their loss but a penitent son ready for a new start.

Was Marcus responsible for Councilor Haines's interest in Daniel as well? Possibly. She didn't know of a link between Haines and Marcus Lansbury; Haines had not served as one of Marcus's Assistants but rather as an Assistant to National Defense, drawn from that department to take over Internal Defense when the Council had wanted a fresh start there. But Marcus and Haines might have an unknown connection. Haines had gained power very quickly—maybe Marcus's expertise in secret dealings was part of the reason for his success.

Alisa rinsed the washcloth and swabbed her face and neck. Dried blood still clung to her cheek. Blood was so sticky. Sticky on her hands. Jill lay curled on the floor, eyes blank, blood spreading toward Alisa's bare feet. Fingers squeezed Alisa's arm.

"At least *she* didn't get stuck in prison before getting murdered. If I'd known you were offering choices, I'd have taken that one."

Alisa stared into Callie's shy, teasing eyes and battled the urge to answer the sister she knew wasn't there.

Callie leaned against Alisa's arm. "Kill me fast, 'kay, Ali?"

Alisa jerked away from her. *What are you doing? Don't move. You'll hurt yourself.*

The hallucination vanished.

Her hip aching—she must have slammed it against the sink—Alisa reached to pick up the washcloth she'd dropped. Tears made her vision murky. She couldn't panic. She couldn't relapse. She rinsed the cloth, wiped her eyes, and shoved her thoughts back toward tonight's problems. If Marcus was working to regain his son's loyalty, he wouldn't risk that goal by acting too soon. They were safe for the moment.

She draped the washcloth over the towel rack and walked into the bedroom. A few hours of rest would—

Fear whipped through her. She stood paralyzed, waiting for the image to disappear.

He was still there, sitting in the chair by the bed. A chiseled face, much like Daniel's but carved with stronger lines. Silver hair instead of light brown. Cold amusement in his smile.

Stay calm. This isn't real.

Marcus rose to his feet and walked toward her.

It's not real. You were thinking about him, fearing him. You created this.

She felt the cool touch of Marcus's fingers, tilting her chin back so she was looking into his face.

"Lieutenant Alisa Kent." His voice had barely any volume, but each word was sculpted from stone. "You can't even decide whether or not to scream. Your senses are useless. One of the finest officers in the Tremont Police Service, now a psychotic wreck." He slipped his hand into his pocket. "Are you glad, Lieutenant, that you threw away your sanity to save a religious lunatic?"

Terror built inside of her. The reversions were coming quickly and getting longer.

Marcus drew his hand from his pocket and unfurled his fingers to display a filled hypodermic syringe.

"Broc4," he said. "You know it will happen sooner or later. You'll be arrested. They'll put you through Information Extraction. Even the lowest dose would be enough to destroy what's left of your mind."

Alisa stared at the syringe in his hand. *It's not real. He's not here.*

But how can you be sure? Someone slipped into the cabin to tamper with the blocker patch. Why couldn't he be here now?

Her bruised hip still hurt, and the scratches on her face still stung. Wasn't that evidence she was lucid? She inhaled, preparing to shout, but held the cry back. *The pain doesn't prove anything; you could imagine it into the reversion. If he were really here, he'd have surprised you in your sleep, not given you ample time to sound an alarm.*

"Scream if you want to," Marcus said. "I'm sure Daniel would be delighted to top off a miserable evening by nursing you through another breakdown. Aren't you tired of being a burden?" He pulled the cap off the needle. "Tired of dreading the inevitable?"

His left hand closed around her arm.

His right hand brought the needle forward.

Chapter 13

A SCREAM TORE OUT OF Alisa's dry throat. This was not a reversion—he was *here*. She twisted, knocking Marcus's hands away, and she felt herself falling, terror drowning her.

He seized her shoulder. She screamed again, throwing herself to the side and swinging her arm up to break his grip.

"*Alisa.*" Daniel Lansbury's voice. She froze. Daniel leaning over her . . . Jill rushing through the doorway, nearly tripping over the trailing hem of her nightgown . . .

"Alisa, can you hear me?" Daniel asked.

She nodded, feeling his fingers moving over her skull, checking for injury.

Ian limped into the room, his face ashen. "Is she all right?"

Alisa sat up and looked frantically around. That sliding door opened onto the deck—was there a chance—

Daniel helped her to her feet. He started to lead her toward the bed, but she pulled away.

"I . . . have to . . . check—"

"You need to lie down." He caught her arm, his grip tighter. "Jill, turn down the covers."

Jill hurried to ready the bed. Alisa wanted to protest, but her head spun, and her knees were crumbling. Why did she feel so woozy? She *must* have hit her head. She felt herself sinking into the softness of the mattress, then pinned under the weight of the blankets Jill drew over her.

"Alisa." Ian knelt by the bed. "What happened? Was it something besides a reversion?"

"I don't . . . I don't know. It seemed—he was—but I don't—"

"Was someone here?" Ian asked.

"Don't play with her mind," Daniel said angrily. "How many and how long, Alisa?"

"Two . . . the first only a few seconds. The second . . . maybe a minute or a minute and a half."

Daniel's expression was weary and bitter. "With the blocker gone, there's not much I can do for you."

"What about the sleeping pills?" Jill asked.

"If she's having reversions that lengthy, the sleeping pills alone would only make her more agitated and disoriented." His tone was pitiless. Even when she'd been a prisoner under his care in the Annex, she'd never heard him sound so harsh.

"Daniel, we'll take care of her," Ian said. "Go get some rest."

"Suit yourself." He exited and banged the door shut behind him.

Alisa looked desperately around the room. Besides the sliding door, the only other entrances were from the hallway—Marcus couldn't have risked entering or exiting that way—and the bathroom. There were no outside doors or windows in the bathroom, and no other windows in the bedroom.

Ian leaned closer. "I don't want to make this harder for you. But could you describe what happened? I've never seen you have trouble coming back to reality after a reversion ends."

Humiliation flickered and faded into exhaustion. "It happened all the time in the Annex."

"But not since then," Ian said. "Is that right?"

"Tonight was . . . much worse than it's been."

"Not surprising," Ian said gently, but his gaze followed hers to the sliding door. He limped to the door.

"Don't open it!" Jill said. "You'll set off the alarm."

"I don't need to open it." He flipped the light switch next to the door and looked out.

Adrenaline jolted Alisa's heart. If there was physical evidence that he'd been here—

Ian flicked the switch off. "No footprints in the snow."

Too confused to know if she was relieved or dismayed, Alisa said, "It was just a reversion. He couldn't have exited without being seen."

"Marcus Lansbury?" Ian asked.

She nodded.

He searched her face, his eyes troubled. "Could you describe the reversion for me?"

Jill folded her arms and stepped between Ian and the bed. "I doubt she wants to talk about it."

"I'm sorry," Ian said. "I just want to make sure . . . well, let me put it this way. Were there any elements in the reversion that logically couldn't have happened?"

"Stop hounding her!" Jill said. "She needs to rest."

Jill's effort to defend her made Alisa's eyes burn. She'd always thought Jill was afraid of her—intimidated by her fractured mind, repulsed by her crimes. "It's all right," Alisa murmured. Briefly, she described the hallucination, concluding with, "There were no illogical elements except there was no time for him to leave, even if he could have left unseen by the rest of you."

"What do you mean?" Ian asked.

Alisa struggled to brush the fear off the memories so she could see details accurately. "One instant I was fighting with him, then it was Dr. Lansbury. Had it been a real occurrence, Councilor Lansbury would have had to exit the room before his son entered."

"I'm going to look around anyway," Ian said. "Can't hurt."

Jill frowned. "He couldn't have gone out the hallway door without Daniel seeing him. He was sitting on the couch that faces the hallway—I know because I was in the kitchen getting a drink and talking to him."

"Maybe there's another way out," Ian said. "A way to exit quickly."

Jill tugged the covers up higher so they reached Alisa's chin. "Do you need more blankets? There are some in the closet."

"I'm fine." Cocooned in warmth, Alisa watched as Ian checked the outside door a second time. He walked the perimeter of the room, investigated the walk-in closet, peered under the bed, and finally disappeared into the bathroom. He returned a few moments later, moving slowly, grimacing with each step.

"There's no other way in or out of here," he said. "I'm sorry I dug for details."

Jill ran her fingers through her tousled hair and picked out a twig and a fragment of leaf. "How's your leg, Ian? You look awful."

"It hurts, but Daniel did a good job patching it together." Ian glanced at the armchair. "I'll stay in here tonight in case Alisa has any more trouble."

"Me too," Jill said. "We'd better stay together."

"Take the recliner, then," Ian said. "I'm fine with the floor."

"I . . . just want to go talk to Daniel for a minute. To see if I can . . . help calm things down." Jill was trying to sound matter-of-fact, but she wasn't good at hiding anxiety. "Then I'll come back."

Alisa sat up. "Ian, go with her," she said sharply.

Jill bit her lip. "That's okay. I'd better talk to him alone."

"If she's looking to make a peace treaty, it won't happen with me there." Ian rested his hand on Alisa's shoulder. "It's all right."

"We can't afford to be careless!" Alisa couldn't level her voice; it sounded jumpy and screechy. "If he'd caught up with Callie in the forest, he would have killed her. You can't assume—"

"Not Callie," Ian said quietly, pressing her back to her pillow. "Jill. You need to rest."

Alisa's breath caught, and tears broke loose. Why had she said Callie's name? That cursed reversion was still distorting her thoughts. The faces mixed in her mind; Jill, blue-eyed and blonde; Callie, with her long brown ponytail and soft autumn-colored eyes.

So brave. So vulnerable.

Jill slipped out of the room and closed the door behind her.

Ian stroked Alisa's hair, his fingers gentle. "Take it easy. Try to rest."

She let her heavy eyelids close. It *was* completely irrational to think Marcus was lying in wait to pounce on Jill the instant she left the room. He wouldn't risk doing anything to Jill that Daniel would be able to blame on him.

Irrational. More evidence of her madness.

"Can I get you anything?" Ian asked. "Would you like some water?"

Madness? Or manipulation?

Abruptly, she sat up.

Ian's jaw tightened with worry. "Alisa, please. Lie down."

She couldn't obey. Beneath the deadening certainty that Marcus had attacked her only in her mind, instinct bumped her awareness.

"Alisa." Ian gripped both her hands. "With what's happened tonight, it's clear Daniel's parents—"

"I know. They're trying to turn Dr. Lansbury against us."

"Yes, and they're doing great. But if they attack us here, Daniel will realize—"

"I know."

"They aren't going to mess up their progress by coming back here tonight."

Alisa pulled her hands free and lowered her feet to the floor.

"Wait. You're not going anywhere."

"I won't leave the room."

"What are you doing?"

"The same thing you did. Please. It will . . . ease my mind."

"If you keep this up, you'll win yourself another reversion," Ian said, but he didn't try to stop her as she stood. She headed toward the sliding door, with Ian limping beside her.

* * *

Daniel was sitting in the great room, staring into the fire. He didn't acknowledge Jill's entrance, so she stood studying the straightness of his posture, the long fingers resting on the arm of the chair, the elegant handsomeness of his profile.

The rock-hard expression.

She couldn't picture herself sharing with him the story of the miraculous assistance she'd received in the forest. He'd reject it as her imagination. Or insanity.

"Are you okay?" she asked.

Daniel finally turned to look at her, revealing the livid bruise on the other side of his face. "Fine." He looked back toward the flames rippling inside the stone fireplace.

Jill sat on the couch. She wasn't sure what to say next, but she couldn't stand the tense silence. "Alisa's still having a hard time."

"More reversions?"

"No. But she's agitated and confused. It was a very realistic reversion, and she's having trouble accepting that it didn't happen."

"I'm not sure what you expect me to do for her."

"I'm not asking you to do anything for her. I thought you'd be interested in a report." Bad topic. She needed something that might mollify Daniel and make him willing to consider that he was wrong about who had attacked him.

"Thank you for fixing up Ian's leg tonight," she said.

Daniel met her eyes, but his expression was so guarded she couldn't perceive what he was thinking. She suspected he was waiting for her to defend Ian. No point to that. She'd already tried. Daniel would figure it out himself as soon as he stopped being stubborn.

"Did Alisa tell you what the reversion was about?" he asked.

Hearing him return to this subject comforted Jill a little. Even through his anger, he wasn't any better at ignoring Alisa's suffering than he'd been at ignoring Ian's. He'd probably been out here engaged in a fist fight with his compassion, trying to knock out the impulse to go check on her. "Yes. Your father."

"She thinks he actually confronted her?"

"Well . . . not really. It was all logical until one instant she's struggling with him and the next instant he's gone and you're there. There was no time for him to sneak out. But I understand why she'd—" At the surprised look on Daniel's face, she stopped. "What?"

Daniel shrugged. "She was unconscious when I went in there. It wasn't until a few seconds later when you were coming in that she woke up and started fighting."

Jill's nerves tingled. "She doesn't remember losing consciousness."

Daniel rose to his feet and came toward her. His expression had softened, and some of Jill's anxiety ebbed—which left room for her to notice she was chilled and aching, with her palms and knees smarting like someone had attacked them with a cheese grater.

"I'll go check on her," Daniel said as he headed down the hallway toward Alisa's room.

* * *

Alisa moved around the room, running her fingers along the walls and checking behind furniture. She repeated the process in the walk-in closet, trailing her fingers along the wall, searching for any seams that shouldn't have been there.

"Alisa." Ian hovered at her elbow as she inspected the closet. She'd tried twice to get him to sit down and take the stress off his injured leg, but he wouldn't leave her side. "I don't think—"

At the click of a doorknob turning, Ian limped to the closet door. Alisa heard Daniel's voice. "What's going on?"

Ian exited the closet and muttered something in reply that Alisa couldn't make out.

Urgency colored with panic drove Alisa. Her time was up. Rapidly, she worked her fingers along the edges of the nearly empty shoe rack, searching, prodding.

"Alisa." Daniel stood in the closet doorway, Ian behind him. "I told you to rest. You need to do that. You are endangering—"

The wall yielded beneath her fingers, and she heard a click. A panel swung outward. Behind the wall, Alisa saw a narrow passage, illuminated by lights set in the ceiling.

She looked at Daniel. With one long-legged step, he was at her side.

"Did you know anything about this?" she whispered, but she already knew the answer from the shock on his face.

"Does that lead outside?" Ian whispered. "Or to somewhere else in the house?"

Alisa's triumph morphed instantly to terror. Considering the wide spacing of the cabins in this resort and the conspicuousness of any cars on the road, it was unlikely Marcus would have risked a lot of exiting and entering the cabin. He had been here since before they'd arrived.

And he was here now.

Chapter 14

"WE'RE IN TROUBLE," IAN WHISPERED, unable in his fear to think up anything beyond a statement of the obvious. "Do you think he knows we opened the panel?"

"I don't know." The determination in Alisa's expression was gone. She looked like she was counting down the seconds to her execution. "But it still doesn't make sense. Even if he could get in and out this way, I should have seen him leave."

"Are you *sure* you were alert the whole time?" Ian asked.

"Yes—no—I got very dizzy for a moment—"

"He might have knocked you out for a few seconds," Ian whispered.

Daniel stood like a statue, a slack-jawed, baffled look on his face.

Ian pushed past him and eased the panel shut. "Let's get out of here."

"The keys are on the table next to the couch." Jill spoke from the closet doorway, her face snow white but her voice controlled. "I'll get them." She sped out of the room.

Gripping Alisa's arm, Ian followed Jill as rapidly as his limping gait would allow. Daniel trailed after them, saying nothing.

Jill snatched the keys, and they raced toward the garage. Ian half expected Daniel to wrench the keys from Jill's hand and declare they weren't in danger and weren't going anywhere, but Daniel deactivated the security system, followed them into the garage, and climbed into the driver's seat of the truck. Ian gestured Alisa and Jill into the extended cab to ride with Daniel and climbed in after them; they could transfer to the back in a few miles, once they were sure Daniel wouldn't lock them in the bed of the truck and head back into the house.

Jill tossed the keys to Daniel, and he backed the truck out of the garage.

* * *

Peale glowered as he sped along the freeway. He would have liked to vent his frustration in an eruption of cursing, but Pulansky's presence in the passenger seat kept his lips glued shut. He could rage if he wanted, and she would listen courteously, but he'd feel like a fool for foaming at the mouth while she remained calm. Anger was futile anyway. They couldn't get into the Lansbury cabin now. The only thing they could do was return to Tremont, analyze what little evidence they'd been able to collect, and hope it wasn't completely useless.

Hours wasted in a primitive stakeout and in the end, they hadn't been able to collect so much as a fingerprint. He glanced at Pulansky. Her expression was placid, but she kept folding and refolding the ski mask she held in her lap. Good. She *was* frustrated. Rae Pulansky's fidgeting was the equivalent of anyone else's pacing and swearing.

"What's your take on this?" Peale asked.

"I'm still figuring that out, sir."

Peale couldn't figure it out himself. Early in the evening, the garage door had opened. They'd caught a glimpse of Lansbury climbing into his truck. Then he'd climbed *out* of the truck and turned in the direction of the house, moving out of their line of vision.

For two hours, nothing. The garage door had remained open, but Lansbury hadn't driven away. Then, without warning, they'd seen three figures scurrying out of the forest and across the road toward the hill where Peale and Pulansky were hiding.

Close one.

But the situation didn't make much sense. If Daniel Lansbury's anti-surveillance measures were thorough enough to reveal Peale and Pulansky on the hill opposite the Lansbury cabin, why hadn't the people coming after them been sly about it instead of blundering across the road where Peale could see them? They'd scared Peale away, but didn't they want to know who the spies were, to catch them? Maybe not. Lansbury's people were probably cowards, afraid of direct confrontation. At least Peale knew they couldn't get any information from the car he was driving—the license plate was fake, and there was no other identifying information on the vehicle.

"Maybe Lansbury kicked his friends out after a fight and them heading toward us was coincidence," Peale said.

"Maybe, sir. But why would they come up the hill?"

"Take another look at those pictures. See if you can pick up anything else."

Pulansky pulled the camera off her belt and tapped the buttons. "I'm not an expert at this," she muttered. "Three people, one smaller with light hair—probably a woman. One taller, broad through the shoulders, darker hair—probably a man. The other . . . I can't tell. He or she is wearing a bulky coat with a hood covering the head. There are several partial shots of the faces, but they're too blurry and incomplete for the Central Identity Network to make a match."

"What's the matter with you? You're better than this. You'd have to *try* to be incompetent not to get any good shots of the faces."

"I'm sorry, sir. I'm not accustomed to photographing moving targets through a night-vision camera when tree branches keep getting in the way and we're in the process of retreating."

Peale swore. If Pulansky was getting sarcastic, they *had* hit a low. He couldn't assign any experts at headquarters to identify the people in the photographs. It would be far too risky to involve anyone in the police. He'd have to find outside help.

Peale increased their speed. Maybe none of this would turn out to be evidence he could use against Lansbury or that Colonel McLaughlin could use to discredit Spencer Brannigan, but after Peale had wasted a day sitting on a stump, peering through binoculars at the Lansbury cabin, he wasn't going to quit until he'd wrung every clue from those photographs.

* * *

Ryce waited on the couch in her private office, watching the clock and steeping tea bag after tea bag from the dozens of varieties the herbalist had brought her, dumping each cup in the trash as the taste displeased her and trying a new blend. At last, the chime signaled a visitor, and Sean Kelleher's ID showed up on the screen over the door. Ryce touched the button to unlock the door.

"Good evening." Kelleher closed the door behind him and tugged off a woolen ski cap, leaving his curly, gray-streaked hair a mess. He was still wearing his coat—no surprise to Ryce. Kelleher always brushed away offers of assistance from her staff.

Ryce gestured him to the couch. "Come."

He removed his coat, draped it over the arm of the couch, and sat, leaning his wide shoulders against the brocade cushions. "What can I do for you?"

"I have a special project for you, Dr. Kelleher."

"Yes?" He looked dubiously at the collection of tea bags on the table next to her, and she knew he was making a mental note to grill her about the contents of the tea bags and from whom she had purchased them.

She pulled a memory card out of the pocket of her suit jacket. "This contains video records of the executions of three anarchists. I want you to review them."

"*Execution* records?" He pushed up the sleeves of the thick wool pullover he wore. He always found her office too warm. "I'm an expert on keeping people alive, Madam President, not killing them."

She handed him the card. "I want to know if the executioner did anything illegal to ease the distress of the prisoners, either before or during the termination sequence."

Kelleher set the card on his thigh as though not sure he wanted to claim it definitively enough to put it in his pocket. "Administration of anxiety-reducing medication you mean?"

"Yes."

"The bodies haven't yet been cremated?"

"They have. The executions took place two months ago. I'm not asking you to run blood tests on ashes. I just want you to review the records and tell me what you see."

"I'll need to know exactly what drugs the Euthanasia Center administered during the termination sequence, in what doses, and in what order."

"I'll see that you get that information."

He scrutinized her, his eyes wary. "Why are *you* asking *me* to look into this?"

She knew what worried him. Kelleher figured if she was involved in what should have been a matter for the police and the Euthanasia Center, the situation must include political intrigue. He hated getting ensnared in any brand of power struggle.

"I'm asking because I want to know," she said. "This has nothing to do with a plot against a rival or any other political nonsense. And I don't want anyone learning I'm interested in this."

He kept studying her. "Who is the executioner?"

"Daniel Lansbury," she said.

"Lansbury! Three anarchist executions . . . Then you're talking about that Cadre assassin Roshek and the Newbold Bay bomber. Alisa Kent. Who's the third one?"

"Jill Roshek. Ian Roshek's sister."

"I don't remember hearing about her."

"Her execution wasn't publicized. Did you watch Roshek's and Kent's executions?"

"No."

"You're the only person in the nation who didn't. Which isn't surprising, considering how hard you try to ignore anything going on outside of your hospital wing."

"I don't find death entertaining."

She almost smiled. Only Kelleher was blunt enough to not even pretend to revel in watching anarchists become corpses.

Kelleher sat tapping one finger against the card. "What makes you think Daniel Lansbury might have done something to ease the distress of Cadre killers? Roshek murdered his parents!"

He sounded edgy again. He thought she was skidding into paranoia, fantasizing hints of treason into Lansbury's faultless behavior. "There's more to the story than was released to the public."

"What's the rest of the story?"

"Do you want the entire tale? Or just my assurance that Lansbury had good reason for sympathizing with the prisoners?"

He gave her an incredulous look, as though she'd suggested he take her assurance that she was feeling energetic rather than running tests for thyroid function. "The more information I have, the better I can evaluate this."

"Very well." He was always candid with her, and he expected her to be candid with him—which was why she trusted him. She'd trusted his grandfather. She'd trusted his father. The day Sean Kelleher abandoned his family tradition of candor, she'd fire him. She could never trust a personal physician who was so afraid of her that he neither asked what he needed to know nor told her what *she* needed to know for fear of offending her.

"Would you like tea?" she asked. "It's a lengthy tale."

"No, thanks."

She sipped from her cup. "Roshek and Kent were traitors, but they were not Cadre."

"What does that mean?"

"It means we lied, and Lansbury wasn't happy about it. Here is the history. Dr. Roshek was arrested at the University of Tremont last fall when he tried to protect a girl accused of reading contraband literature from a mob determined to make an example of her. The arresting officer was Lieutenant Alisa Kent. When she put him through a preliminary screening, sensor readings made it clear he was guilty of reading and believing religious literature. But Kent released him instead of sending him for Information Extraction."

"Why?"

"Her own family had been believers. As a teenager, she discovered their treason and turned them in, along with her neighbor, David Garrett. Garrett escaped; her family was arrested and eventually executed for their delusions. Garrett's return to Tremont last year and his execution finally cracked Kent's patriotism. When she realized Roshek was another believer, she let him go and tried to join his illegal meetings. Unfortunately for her, the Cadre noticed."

She set her cup on the table and picked up the empty cup Kelleher had declined to use. "They came after her, trying to recruit her." Ryce poured steaming water into the cup and added a different tea bag. "She and Roshek rejected the Cadre's offer, but the Cadre decided to use Kent anyway. They drugged her and conditioned her mind—unknown to her—so that under Information Extraction, she would give false information."

Kelleher's brow furrowed. "They were able to tamper with a Broc-induced confession? How?"

"I don't know the science involved. But the false information identified Kent as the Newbold Bay bomber and gave clues that would allow the police to conclude that Cadre leader Zero was Spencer Brannigan."

"Brannigan!"

Ryce picked up her original cup and sipped, hoping it would taste better this time. "When the police learned of Kent's and Roshek's treason, Kent didn't bother to run. She inadvertently played into the Cadre's hands by surrendering. Roshek *did* start to run, but when he heard news reports that Kent was the Newbold Bay bomber, he knew it wasn't true. He was determined that she not be falsely accused but knew the police wouldn't listen to him."

Ryce forced down another sip. Were *all* of these blends an acquired taste? "He thought Daniel Lansbury—who was involved with Roshek's sister—"

"*Wait.* Lansbury was involved with—" Kelleher stopped, apparently realizing he'd interrupted her. "I apologize—"

Ryce ignored him. "Roshek thought he might be able to convince Lansbury that Kent was not the Newbold Bay bomber and Lansbury could use his credibility to carry the story to the police. Already puzzled by Kent's extreme reaction to the administration of Broc4, Lansbury was ready to believe there was a problem, but he doubted the police would listen to him either—his credibility had been damaged by his association with the Rosheks. So in an effort to ensure that the police took Roshek's report seriously, he first took Roshek to his father."

"Ah." Kelleher brightened, clearly assuming he had *finally* hit a section of the story that didn't flummox him. "So that's how Roshek was able to assassinate Councilor Lansbury."

Ryce sighed. "He didn't assassinate him. Marcus Lansbury revealed that *he* was Zero, the leader of the Liberty Cadre."

"*What?*"

"Councilor Lansbury attempted to recruit Daniel and kill Roshek. But Daniel freed Roshek, and they went to warn Brannigan that he was being framed and targeted for assassination. One of Brannigan's security guards was a Cadre man. He attempted to kill Brannigan. Roshek jumped in the line of fire and saved Brannigan's life. Marcus and his wife fled."

Ryce had never imagined that Kelleher could gawk like that, looking blindsided and flabbergasted. "How did a man like Marcus Lansbury end up running the Cadre?"

"The Cadre was actually a very clever idea. The scum who carried out Cadre atrocities had no idea who they were working for or that Councilor Lansbury was using them to frighten the nation into rejecting all forms of anarchy while conditioning the people to venerate him as the leader who could keep them safe. He intended to force me to resign, so weakened and humiliated by Brannigan's downfall that I would have had no choice."

"Where is he now?"

"Recent intelligence reports indicate he might be in the United States, but we don't know for certain."

"Huh. How did Roshek end up getting blamed for—"

"It was a touchy, messy situation," she interrupted curtly. "We certainly couldn't tell the nation that the Councilor over Internal Defense was the head of the Liberty Cadre. But we needed to explain why Marcus and

Jocelyn Lansbury were gone, and we needed to reassure the people that we'd defeated the Cadre, which included giving them public villains to hate. Roshek was already involved, so we used him. And since Kent had already 'confessed' to the bombing at Newbold Bay, why not let that stand? As for the Roshek girl, they tried to get her to denounce her brother to add credibility to the charade, but she refused, so they executed her as well."

Kelleher was still gawking, the distaste stark in his face. Ryce dumped the disgusting brew in the trash can and reached for the second cup. "Stop looking so appalled. Anarchists are all the same at heart. What did it matter if we played with the details of their crimes? It was a practical solution to a volatile situation."

"After all of that, how did Lansbury end up assigned to the executions?"

Ryce lifted the tea bag from the cup and dropped it in the trash. "A test of his loyalty. He *had* been friends with traitors—and romantically involved with one of them. Well? Is that adequate evidence that it is not irrational for me to question Lansbury's actions before and during the executions?"

Kelleher shoved the memory card into his pocket. "Setting aside the history, what specifically prompted you to think Lansbury did something wrong?"

"Watch the records, and you tell me," she said and took a tiny sip.

He frowned at the cup in her hand. "What are you drinking? I want to see an ingredients list."

Chapter 15

ALL WAS PEACEFUL IN THE guest wing of Daniel's house when Jill arose late Monday morning. Ian and Alisa were still asleep, and no wonder. It had been a long, miserable night. The residual effects of the blocker and the lateness of the hour had left Daniel so fatigued that he'd had to stop several times on the drive back to Tremont so he could nap. Jill wasn't sure how many hours the trip had taken, but she still felt a motion-sick yearning to walk everywhere she went for the rest of her life. No more trucks.

She was grateful for the quiet of the game room. A growling stomach had coaxed her out of her room in search of food—they'd missed dinner last night—but she didn't feel like company. She needed time to think. She took a container of yogurt from the nearly empty fridge and was reaching for an apple when Daniel's voice behind her made her start.

"How are you feeling?"

She fixed a smile on her face and turned around, feeling silly standing there in a bathrobe with a cup of yogurt in her hand. Daniel looked exhausted, and the bruise on the side of his face had spread into the hollow under his eye.

"Oh, just a little sore," she said. "You?"

"Same."

"Are you on your way to work?" she asked, even though he wasn't in uniform.

A bleak twinge of discouragement showed in his face. "They don't expect me in today. I called in sick last night."

"Oh." She'd never before wanted to escape from Daniel's company, but right now she didn't feel like talking to him. They hadn't exchanged more than a few required words since rushing out of the cabin last night, and Jill had no idea what to expect from him.

"Are the others awake?" Daniel asked.

"I haven't seen them. Or heard anything." Jill opened a drawer and selected a spoon.

Daniel watched her as she opened the yogurt and settled at the table. "You're angry with me," he said.

"No, of course not." She didn't know *what* she was feeling, but she wasn't angry.

"Jill. You have every right to be upset."

She stirred the yogurt. If she told him that in the middle of the stress and terror of last night, she'd experienced the most amazing, most significant moment of her life, he would think . . . what?

Blood heated her cheeks. Would Daniel even give *her* the credit for imagining she'd received an answer to her prayer? Or would he say Ian had planted that idea in her mind, with the implication that she didn't have enough intelligence or willpower to resist Ian's brainwashing?

"Jill—"

"Did you get any sleep? You must be exhausted after driving all night."

"Jill."

"I'm not angry, really." She tried to sound upbeat, but the cheer sounded weak and fake.

"Jill, it's all right if—"

"Do you think Ian is crazy?" The question escaped before she'd given herself permission to ask it.

Daniel drew a deep breath and let it out. "Forget everything I said last night. I was out of my mind."

"I'm not just talking about last night. He said you called him delusional, Daniel."

Daniel's fingers curled around the back of a chair. "Jill . . ."

"You didn't used to think he was crazy. Right after you rescued us, you said you thought what he believed might be true. Are you back to thinking—"

Polished gentleness settled over Daniel's expression, and Jill knew he was about to say something soothing about how she shouldn't read so much into words spoken in the heat of an argument. But before he opened his mouth, his eyes dulled and he said hollowly, "I don't know what I think. I don't know. I'm sorry. I know that's not the answer you wanted."

Jill pushed her uneaten yogurt aside. "I wanted the truth."

"That's the truth." He pulled the chair out and sat down across from her. "I don't know what I think."

He looked so gaunt. Worn down, physically and mentally. Had she ever tried to understand how painful turning against his father had been for him? How turning against the Council had pulverized his life? How weary he must be from carrying the responsibility of protecting three fugitives?

"Maybe it would help if you figured out what you think," she said softly.

"I don't have time to worry about that right now. Do you have any idea how precarious—"

"Give me a *little* credit for intelligence." Jill tried futilely to put some humor into her tone.

"I apologize. I didn't mean—"

She reached across the table and touched his hand. "Don't worry about it. But I'm saying our situation is why you can't afford *not* to figure out where you stand. Take this weekend, for example. One minute we're all allies. Then something goes wrong, and you're accusing—" She stopped. "I'm sorry. I'm just worried."

"Worried. You mean you don't trust me."

"I didn't say that." Jill fought the temptation to backpedal and start on a harmless subject. "But so much is . . . pulling at you. There's . . . well . . . Councilor Haines. Your parents. If you haven't made up your mind what you believe and we seem like nothing but a burden . . . Do you see what I'm getting at?"

"You seem very sure of yourself," Daniel said coolly. "I take it you've figured all this out?"

Jill pushed her bare feet against the carpet, wishing she could stop herself from trembling. She'd thought she didn't want to tell Daniel what had happened in the forest, but she felt a sudden desire to share it with him. "I don't have everything figured out. I'm just starting to learn. But . . . when I was in the forest last night—" Her mouth went so dry she had to stop and swallow. Daniel watched her in silence, his gaze somber.

She told him what had happened, forgetting her uneasiness as she felt again the joy that had amazed her last night when she realized God was listening to her.

"I know you're thinking my mind just—*created* these thoughts and abilities in a moment of stress. But it wasn't that way. This wasn't something that came from inside of me. This was completely beyond my capability.

And it wasn't just what I was able to do in escaping. It was what I *knew*. What I felt." She smiled at Daniel. "How could I have imagined my way out of a dark forest when a moment earlier I was tripping over everything around me and smacking into trees?"

Lines deepened between Daniel's eyebrows. Cold dismay dripped over Jill. He didn't believe her. There was nothing she could say that would make him understand.

"It's okay." She played with the handle of the spoon sticking out of the yogurt. "I didn't expect you to believe me."

"I never said I didn't believe you." Daniel rested his elbows on the table and slouched forward. "A few months ago, it did seem possible that—I *was* almost ready to . . . After witnessing your brother's courage, the way he was willing to turn himself in if that's what it took to stop the Liberty Cadre . . . watching him tackle that assassin, take that bullet meant for Councilor Brannigan . . ." Daniel massaged his bloodshot eyes. "I admit, I got curious. And things seemed to come together so miraculously. Faking executions in front of a national audience, including the highest officials in the government, and getting away with it? How could that be *anything* but a miracle?"

Jill nodded, heart jumping.

"I just never imagined it would turn out like *this*. This whole situation has become an ugly joke. The new security restrictions that even Councilor Brannigan can't circumvent . . . the police bugging Nate's house . . . now my parents . . . we're not safe at the cabin, we're not safe here at the house, we're not safe *anywhere*, and we can't get over the border. I *want* to believe God helped you last night, but if He can do that, why hasn't He gotten us out of here?"

"I don't know," Jill said. "Maybe that's not . . . what He wants to happen."

* * *

If Ian added all the scraps of sleep he'd accumulated in the past twenty-four hours, he figured the sum would equal a solid catnap. His leg hurt, and his mind kept dissecting events from the night before, but the worst discomfort boiled over from the remorse simmering inside him.

Sitting on his bed, he watched the late-morning sun highlighting the edges of the curtains. He'd already had two more months' worth of mornings than he'd thought he'd ever experience. How could he have been so ungrateful? In his heart, he'd accused God of forgetting them. But God wasn't the one who'd done the forgetting.

Thinking of the incredible story Jill had shared with them on the drive back to Tremont, he remembered with shame how irritated he'd been when God hadn't seemed to answer Jill's first prayer. Why hadn't he mustered the faith to wait, knowing God was listening to her and would answer her in His time?

I'm sorry.

He sat for a long time, resting his forehead on his hands. God wasn't the only one from whom he needed to ask forgiveness. He needed to talk to Daniel.

Ian headed toward the door, putting as little weight on his injured leg as possible. As he passed the mirror above the dresser, his appearance made him want to laugh. He had no comb, no razor, no clothes to substitute for the sweatpants and T-shirt he'd slept in. All the personal items Nate and Daniel had provided for him had been abandoned at the cabin. He couldn't even get dressed without asking Daniel for help.

If he was genuinely sorry for his pride and lack of faith, he'd quit resenting Daniel's help and start thanking him for it.

He limped along the hallway. In the doorway of the game room, he paused. Jill and Daniel sat at the table in the kitchenette. Daniel's back was to him, but the intensity in Jill's face made Ian feel he was interrupting a private conversation. He started to retreat, but Jill beckoned him in.

"Good morning," she said. "If it *is* still morning. And that is by far the worst bedhead I've ever seen on you. Your hair is all over the place."

Ian groaned and put his hands on his head. "Hey, I begged you for a haircut, and you turned me down."

"I'd be willing to try it now, if you can hunt up some scissors. I can't imagine how I could make it look worse."

Daniel glanced over his shoulder at Ian. "There's a haircutting kit in my mother's bathroom closet. She always cut my father's hair. I'll find it for you."

"Thanks," Ian said, relieved at the lack of hostility.

"How's your leg?" Daniel asked.

"Fine."

"Fine, as in you're too stubborn to admit how much it hurts?"

"Uh . . . yep."

"You ought to stay off of it as much as you can and keep it elevated. Did you take those painkillers I gave you?"

"Yes."

"Sit down and let me have a look at it." Daniel stood.

Ian limped toward the couch. "Is Alisa up?"

"We haven't seen her yet," Jill said.

Deciding he'd go check on her as soon as Daniel finished with him, Ian sat on the couch, propped his leg on the cushions, and carefully pulled up the leg of his sweatpants.

Daniel lifted the bandage and examined the wound. "It looks fine, but I'm going to give you an antibiotic as a precaution. I wasn't too clear in the head when I fixed you up last night."

"Thanks for your help," Ian said. "Once again, I owe you. I'm . . . sorry for the way I've been treating you. I'd never harm you, and I'm sorry I gave you the impression that I would." Out of the corner of his eye, he saw Jill sitting motionless, apparently afraid to breathe for fear of interrupting him. "I know I've made things harder for you at a time when you didn't need any more stress," Ian continued. "I'm sorry."

"I'll get you some clothes." Daniel turned toward the door. "I assume you'd like to get dressed." He exited the game room, leaving Ian wondering if his apology had been accepted, rejected, or ignored as the ramblings of a crazy man.

He glanced at Jill. She had a brooding expression on her face.

"One of these days he's going to run out of clothes to lend us," Ian said tiredly.

Chapter 16

AFTER FORAGING IN HIS PARENTS' closets to find clothes for the fugitives and handing over the haircutting kit, Daniel trudged into an empty bedroom in the guest wing. Leaving the door ajar so he could still hear faint voices from the game room, he lifted the dustcover off a chair and sat down. He desperately needed solitude right now, but he didn't want to move too far away from Jill and the others—though he'd have to leave soon anyway. He had an appointment with Brannigan at one o'clock.

He shouldn't have brought them to the house last night, but where else could they go? The police were monitoring Nate's. If Daniel had tried to take them to Brannigan's home, he'd have had to deal with Brannigan's security service or call Brannigan beforehand to arrange for them to enter the house without questions from his guards. He couldn't have risked a call like that.

So here they waited at the house, sitting ducks with a new security system that was a pathetic waste of circuit boards and sensors. After what had happened at the cabin, it was clear that if his father wanted in, he'd come in.

His parents were waiting for him.

His mother's tender persuasions—his father's cold-blooded actions—all to the same end. They wanted to reclaim his devotion and erase the evidence of his mistakes.

Daniel lowered his head into his hands. Given how viciously his father must hate Ian for triggering the events that had destroyed Marcus's attempt to murder and maneuver his way to the presidency, Daniel had convinced himself that if his father knew the Rosheks were alive, he'd take immediate revenge. Therefore, his lack of action meant he didn't know.

Why, even now, was he so easy for his father to manipulate?

It was clear now what his father had been aiming for up at the cabin. The first step to reclaiming Daniel's loyalty was to show him a reconciliation was possible—hence, Jocelyn's visit. The second step was to convince him that his friends were burdens he regretted taking on. Marcus had obviously been monitoring them closely enough to know there was friction between Daniel and Ian, and Ian himself had inadvertently given Marcus an idea for how to cement Daniel's belief that he was a liability.

Once Daniel came to believe Ian was dangerous, the widening rupture between him and his friends would make the rest simple. Last night, Marcus must have been delighted when Jill and the others had fled into the forest, creating an ideal opportunity for an "accident." If Jill had drowned in the lake or ended up with her head smashed in by a rock, Daniel would have blamed Ian for taking her into the woods, and Ian would have blamed himself for not taking care of her. Ian was already under colossal stress. Would Daniel have questioned it if a few days later, Ian was dead, an apparent suicide? As for Alisa—last night's seeming relapse had set the stage for when Daniel found her at the bottom of the stairs with a fatal head trauma or any other accident that could happen when she was caught in a lengthy reversion. His father could be patient in exacting his revenge if it meant he could destroy the Rosheks and Alisa in such a way that Daniel couldn't blame him for their deaths—where, in fact, the strain of disintegrating relationships would make the deaths as much a relief as a tragedy.

And Daniel had willingly cooperated, *wanting* to be angry at Ian and the others.

The thought of Jill stumbling through the forest in the darkness with someone—his father or a Cadre flunky—in pursuit now scorched Daniel with fury and terror. But when Jill had told them, he'd labeled it her imagination, wanting to justify his own view of what was going on. Could he be any more despicable?

What of the things Jill had told him this morning about praying and receiving help? Jill's experience in the forest had affected her the way Ian's reading and praying had affected him. She was a believer.

Ian's laughter came from the game room, followed by Jill's voice, indignantly protesting her inexperience. How could the Rosheks focus on anything as mundane as a haircut, let alone find it funny? But then again, what else could they do? Sit and debate whether the police or Marcus Lansbury would get to them first?

Or whether Daniel was going to betray them?

Jill's warning: *So much is pulling at you. If you haven't made up your mind what you believe and we seem like nothing but a burden—*

Discouragement shrouded Daniel and intensified the aching in his bruised cheekbone. Did Jill even love him anymore? He didn't want to explore that question, but he feared the answer already stood in plain sight.

And tomorrow—what? He had to be back at work, but he couldn't leave the fugitives here alone for long. Brannigan might be able to find them some sort of refuge, a place Daniel's father wouldn't know about. Brannigan wouldn't be pleased at being drawn deeper into this situation, but there was nowhere else Daniel could turn.

Back at work. Why couldn't Jill and Ian let go of that? They knew how dangerous it would be for him to quit.

He knew what Ian would do in his situation: he'd quit and let the consequences come. But Ian would act with the conviction that what he was doing at the Annex offended God, and loyalty to God was worth more than life.

Daniel rubbed the tight muscles in his shoulders. *Was* he offending God by returning to the Annex? Was that why nothing was working out for them? But he'd only been back at the Annex for four weeks. Their efforts to escape New America had stalled before that.

If he quit, would God step in to help them? Trusting in supernatural help felt like trusting that if he flung himself off a building, gravity would reverse itself to save him.

How could it possibly be wrong to do what was necessary to save their lives? Keeping up a front of untarnished patriotism was the only rational option.

So you trust only in yourself, even though you know this situation is so far out of your control that it could explode at any moment.

The thought sounded so much like something Ian would say that it made Daniel want to punch him, even though he didn't remember Ian ever making that statement. Ian—and now Jill—were willing to trust God, even if He offered no guarantees of their safety.

That was insane.

But hadn't Daniel once done the same thing?

No. He'd never claimed to follow God. He'd just known he could no longer support the lies, the cruelty—

Why not? If it was necessary to your survival, why couldn't you perform the executions? Was it because of Jill? If she dumps you now, was it all a mistake?

His mind looped back to Jill's experience in the forest. How could he know *what* had happened? The fact that *she* believed God had helped her proved nothing. Under stress, the mind could—

"Dr. Lansbury."

Daniel jumped in his chair, adrenaline splashing through his veins like hot pepper sauce. Alisa stood in the doorway.

"I'm sorry," she said. "I didn't mean to disturb you."

Daniel felt foolish. "You didn't disturb me."

The dark circles under Alisa's eyes made her appear ill, and the scratches stood out on her pale face like claw marks. "Ian said you wanted to see me."

"Yes." He checked his watch. "Did you just wake up?"

"About half an hour ago."

"Any reversions?"

"No."

"Did you sleep well?"

"Off and on."

Brief, cagey answers. The way she always reacted to his questions about her health. After all this time, didn't she trust him to help her?

Her eyes met his, and a jolt shot from Daniel's chest to his feet. For an instant, he was back at the Annex, standing over Alisa, a syringe of Broc4 in his hand. Already exhausted from her first interrogation, Alisa was sobbing, struggling in a vain effort to elude the needle, pleading with him.

It hadn't even crossed his mind to question what he was doing.

"Is that all?" She took a half step into the hallway.

He swallowed to moisten his dry throat. Why *should* she trust him after what he'd done to her?

I didn't have a choice. And she was better off with me than she would have been with any other medical supervisor. Anyone else would have given up on her and let her die. I saved her.

I saved her?

Like Jill saved herself in the forest?

He'd never been able to explain why Alisa had pulled out of what had looked like an unstoppable fall into lethal Broc psychosis.

"Dr. Lansbury?" Her gaze jumped from his face to the paintings on the walls, the bed, the carpet, the dust cover he'd dropped on the floor. His silence was not what she expected of him, and he could tell she was trying to determine whether or not her brain was misshaping reality.

"Take it easy today," he ordered inanely, as if she'd been planning a ski trip or a 10K run. "And I'd prefer that you stay with the others." Another pointless remark; he'd been giving her that advice for two weeks.

She nodded and turned to leave.

"Wait," he said.

She turned expectantly, and he realized he had no idea what to say to her. He drew a steadying breath, but he still felt so sick he was trembling. "Alisa, we're not in the Annex anymore. My name is Daniel."

Surprise glimmered in her eyes, followed by a searching of his face that made Daniel want to hide. "As you wish."

He waved dismissal and watched her walk away, remembering her moving through the corridors at headquarters, intent on police business. She'd always had a rapid, graceful gait, and until now, he hadn't noticed how that had changed. Now she walked with careful, deliberate steps. Her fingertips lingered on the doorframe as she passed through it, testing its solidity.

Daniel felt again an urge to call her back, to say—what?

He didn't know.

* * *

"What makes you think I can help you now?" Brannigan's expression was stony as he faced Daniel across the table in the corner of his study. "Do you think anything has changed since you ran to me a couple of weeks ago? You're the one who dreamed up this harebrained scheme to save your friends' lives. You created the problem. You fix it."

Daniel gulped water. Mouthfuls of pasta kept lodging in his throat. "I'm only asking if you can think of a place where I could take them. Anywhere *I* could come up with is a place my father would think to look."

"In all of your panicking, has it occurred to you that not one of you has actually *seen* your father?"

"Alisa—"

"You know better than I do that Alisa Kent is not a reliable witness at this time. You have no proof he was there last night or that he's even in New

America. In fact, the police have recently discovered new evidence that he's in the United States."

A strip of roasted pepper fell off Daniel's fork and landed in his lap. "They didn't tell me that."

"Keeping you informed is not their top priority. But I'm surprised Councilor Haines didn't tell you."

Daniel *was* surprised—and annoyed—that Haines hadn't mentioned it. "What was this evidence?"

Brannigan impaled a chunk of chicken on his fork. "Captain Whitney had a computer expert recheck the border records of the people who crossed legally into the US the night your father disappeared. The expert found someone who might have been your father. The person was disguised, but the height and facial features are a possible match."

"*Recheck*? Let me get this straight. Captain Whitney looked at the records four months ago when Dad ran, and he found nothing. Now, he tries them again and voilà—there he is!"

Brannigan shot him a glacial look. "If you mock Captain Whitney like that to his face, I'm amazed he hasn't arrested you yet. Apparently, the travel pass and the video record had been deleted, but the expert was able to retrieve them. And I'm not taking it at face value. I'm only saying it's possible he did leave. Our agents in the US have gathered some tips that indicate he's operating there."

"The borders are sealed so tightly that not even members of the Council can get through," Daniel said. "I don't think my parents could come and go now, and I *know* my mother is here. He wouldn't go to the US and leave her behind. He could never endure being away from her for long."

"If circumstances required it, I think your father could handle a temporary separation. I'm not saying you're wrong. I'm trying to get you to evaluate all possibilities. You don't want to think your friends could harm you, but consider all factors. They're under tremendous strain."

Doubt snaked into Daniel's mind but slipped back out again at the vivid memory of Ian, chalky with pain and soaked in sweat as Daniel cleaned and sealed the laceration on his leg. The scene had evoked unsettling memories of Ian's recovery from the Cadre bullet that had ripped through his chest, but it wasn't only Ian's pain that had stirred memories. It was the frustration and discouragement in his face—hints of the way he'd looked when struggling to accept that his reward for stopping the Liberty

Cadre was to be labeled a Cadre assassin and publicly executed—and that even if he *could* tell the nation the truth, no one would believe him.

No. Ian hadn't been the one who'd assaulted Daniel with the Broc blocker.

"I'm not going to argue about it," Daniel said. "The fact is that I can't keep them at the cabin, I can't keep them at Nate's, and I can't keep them at my house. Is there even the slightest hope that President Ryce might soften her stance on travel—"

"I can't ask President Ryce for anything right now," Brannigan snapped. "She's a hairsbreadth away from turning on me and withdrawing her support from the constitutional vote."

"She's *what*? Why?"

"What else? Preserval. The final report is in: Preserval is completely ineffective at extending the lifespan. She's hounding me for an elixir of life, and I'm failing her."

A gust of wind threw rain against the windows. "She must know it's not your fault. She ought to be used to the failure of her life-extension projects by now."

"Whether or not it's my fault, she blames me. Ryce is a shrewd woman on every topic but this one. She's obsessed. And she's pursuing more than scientific research. Last time I was in her office, she quoted some wild theory—who knows where she picked it up—about consciousness lingering in inanimate objects. Next thing you know, she'll have Health Services setting aside funds to mummify her and build a pyramid." Brannigan shrugged angrily. "Forget I said any of this. But I'm frustrated. Ryce is frustrated. I can't ask her for anything right now. Why don't you see if Patrick Haines can lean on her?"

Daniel focused on the book-lined walls of Brannigan's study. He must own more hardbound books than the rest of Tremont's population combined.

"Be candid with me," Brannigan said. "Why are you involved with Haines? Are you feeding your ego? You don't plan to accept the position of Council Assistant to Internal Defense, but you like knowing it's yours for the taking? You think you can strut around with Haines, collecting admiration and envy, and then bail out unscathed?"

"I don't think that, sir."

"Sir? You sound so humble. Whatever happened to that charming Lansbury arrogance?"

Daniel flushed. He'd never experienced such cutting sarcasm from Brannigan.

"Indulging in a few daydreams about a meteoric rise to the presidency?" Brannigan asked.

Daniel kept his tone even. "Maybe I liked the thought that this was something my father hadn't arranged for me. This was Councilor Haines coming to *me*—not my father mapping out my future and strong-arming everyone into going along with his plans. Maybe I was worth something on my own after all."

The anger in Brannigan's face abated. "I can sympathize with that. But do you realize Haines doesn't want *you* at all? He wants a Daniel Lansbury who doesn't exist—the golden patriot who'll kill the woman he loves if we give the word. Not the man who made fools of the Council and the entire Tremont Police Service by faking executions on national television."

Shame sliced through Daniel. Somehow, he'd never thought of it in that light.

"You're a wreck," Brannigan said. "And I'm not talking about that nasty bruise on your face. You've aged ten years in the last few months. You're losing weight, which you can't afford, and you look like you haven't slept all week."

"Councilor—"

"I don't have time for this. There are only three weeks left until the Council will vote on whether or not to draft a new written constitution. Do you understand what that means, to have a document establishing laws that are out of the reach of greed and ambition?"

"I understand the importance of what you're doing."

"I don't think you do. Your focus is on escaping New America. Why should you care what happens to it after you're gone?"

Daniel felt six inches tall. "I do care. I'm just not in a position to do anything about it."

Fire ignited in Brannigan's eyes. "You could have been a powerful voice in the reform drive, but you threw it away to save three people who'd be better off dead."

"Ian Roshek saved your life."

"With your help. I'm grateful to both of you. But do you understand what will happen if the police figure out your perfidy and we're both arrested? I'm seen as the linchpin for reform. If I'm discredited—something your father tried to accomplish—then the Constitutional Drive will collapse. Those who hoard power will be stronger than ever. That's what your selfish focus on your own needs may cost us."

Brannigan's words conjured familiar shame. Different voice, different context, same message: *You're weak, selfish, unpatriotic.* "I never intended to draw you into this. You chose to become involved. If you thought my saving the Rosheks and Kent was such a mistake, why didn't you turn me in when you first figured out what I'd done?"

"Sometimes I wish I had." Brannigan dropped his fork onto his nearly full plate and rose to his feet. "The cost of protecting you may be higher than any of us can afford."

Chapter 17

"You missed a few right here." Ian fluffed stray hairs over the top of his left ear. Jill snipped off the stragglers.

"Anywhere else?" she asked.

"Nope. Looks great." He handed her the mirror and stiffly lowered his injured leg from the ottoman where he'd rested it during the haircut. "Thanks, Jilly. I love you."

Jill circled him. "I cut it too short right here—" She touched the crown of his head. "It's sticking up—"

"It's fine." Ian ran his fingers through his hair. "Ah, I feel much better."

"I never thought you cared that much about how you looked."

"I don't. I was feeling sorry for those of you who had to look at me."

"Yeah, I'll bet." A mischievous look sparkled through the tiredness in Jill's eyes. She glanced toward where Alisa was napping in an easy chair. "I can see how that might concern you."

Ian felt a rush of blood to his face. "That's not what I meant."

Jill smiled and wiped the haircutting scissors on a towel. Ian wanted to defend himself further, but he wasn't sure if Alisa was truly asleep or just resting, and he didn't want to draw her attention to the conversation.

"You're so cute when you blush," Jill whispered as she packed the clippers back in their case. She unsnapped the cape that had protected Ian's clothes. "It still amazes me that Daniel's mother cut his dad's hair," she said at normal volume.

"No kidding," Ian said, glaring at her. Later, when they were alone, he'd correct Jill's teasing assumption. He sneaked a glance at Alisa. She slept with her head turned to the side, black hair falling across the graceful lines of her cheekbone and jaw.

Jill slipped the faded instruction manual into its slot and clicked the haircutting kit shut. "Jocelyn is so elegant that it's hard to imagine her doing, well . . . regular work."

"Maybe it was a carryover from their poverty-stricken student days."

"Be serious. Daniel's grandfather was President Tremont's best friend. When you have *that* kind of connection, your kids don't do the student apartment thing."

Ian grinned. "Maybe not."

"It's sweet, though, that he wanted her to cut his hair instead of going to some expensive barber. He totally doted on her."

"I can see why," Ian said, remembering when he'd met Jocelyn Lansbury. Besides being beautiful, she exuded charm that made everyone around her feel important, admired, and brilliant.

"Daniel said she could get his dad to do anything she wanted." The spark in Jill's eyes died out, and Ian knew what she was thinking: *What if she's asked him to bring her son back to her?*

"This time, she's not going to get what she wants." Ian stretched to his feet. His leg throbbed as he rested his weight on it, but he circled the room a couple of times, glad for the chance to restore circulation to the lower half of his body.

"We need a vacuum," Jill said, brushing hair off the front of her shirt.

The door to the game room opened, and Daniel walked in. He was carrying his suit coat, his tie was loose, and the sleeves of his white shirt were unbuttoned as though he'd intended to roll them up but had forgotten to finish. The lack of energy in his bruised face made it clear nothing had happened at Brannigan's to give him hope.

"That was quick," Ian said. He glanced at the clock on the wall, and his eyes bugged. "Or not so quick. I didn't realize how long—"

"I know," Jill interrupted sheepishly. "The only four-hour haircut in history."

Ian kneaded his back muscles with his thumbs. "It'll go faster when you get brave enough to cut more than one hair at a time."

"Oh, ha, ha."

"Well done, Jill," Daniel said mechanically. "It looks good. Ian, would you come with me?"

"Uh—sure. Where—"

"Just down the hall." Daniel led the way out the door.

Ian followed Daniel into an unused bedroom. Daniel turned on the bedside lamp and gestured Ian into the overstuffed chair.

Daniel sat on the edge of the bed. In the light cast by the lamp, shadows gathered beneath his cheekbones and darkened the flesh under his eyes.

"Councilor Brannigan can't help us," Daniel said.

Ian wasn't surprised that Brannigan had no solutions, but the finality in Daniel's voice unnerved him. "He's sorry he ever got mixed up with us traitors, isn't he?"

"He's angry, frustrated, overwhelmed by the job of preparing for the constitutional vote and, frankly, wishes we were all dead."

"Did he say that?"

"Essentially. But he did consent to arrange a doctor's excuse for a week off work for me so I can have some time to figure out what to do."

"Well . . . that's helpful."

"I'm out of ideas," Daniel said. "If I take you to any place I already own—like the cabin—my father will think to look there. I can neither rent nor purchase any new housing without using my ID chip in the transaction, which would doubtless allow my father to track it. Councilor Brannigan can't help. Nate can't help. There's no one else we can turn to. We're never going to survive long enough to escape."

"If we're not dead yet, there's still hope."

"If you fall off a cliff, you don't have to wait until you hit the ground to know your life is over."

"I've known my life was over several times. Twice when I had Cadre thugs pointing guns at me. Once when you stuck a needle in my arm in front of ten million viewers."

Daniel shook his head wearily. "This time there won't be anyone cheating death with a vial of Preserval."

"How can you be sure of that?"

"Who do you think is going to save us?"

"I don't know. But I didn't know last time either. Trust me, I had zero hopes of surviving my execution."

"Do you believe God helped us last time?"

"Yes."

"Do you believe He'll save us this time?"

"I . . . don't know what His plans are."

"So you *don't* have a reason for thinking we'll come out of this alive, beyond wanting it to be so?" The intensity in Daniel's voice made Ian sit up straight and look him in the eyes.

"No," Ian said. "I don't have a reason."

"Nothing?"

"No."

"You've prayed?"

"Countless times. The answer . . . hasn't come yet."

"But you still trust God."

Ian debated what to tell Daniel and decided to be candid. "I've been struggling with this, wondering why things aren't working out. Why would God take us this far and then abandon us? What Jill experienced last night—she said she told you about it—finally made me realize He hasn't forgotten us, but maybe He has something different in mind than we do."

"You mean He never meant for us to escape."

"I don't know. Maybe not. But . . . look at it this way. A few months ago when I freaked Jill out with the news that I was a religious believer and she panicked and ran away from me, I prayed fervently that God would protect her and I'd find her before the police did. The police beat me to her. It wasn't until later that I realized if God *had* given me what I'd asked for that night—if Jill had remained safe and we'd both made it over the border—the consequences . . . I wouldn't have been here to learn that the Cadre had tampered with Alisa's mind, using her to transmit false information to the police. I wouldn't have been here to warn you about it. You wouldn't have taken me to your father, asking for his help; he wouldn't have told you the truth about the Liberty Cadre; you couldn't have made the choice to stop him. His scheme would have succeeded. He'd be in control of New America. Councilor Brannigan would be dead, along with any hope for reform. Alisa would be dead. And you—I guess you'd still be an upstanding citizen with a brilliant future ahead of you." He smiled thinly.

Daniel closed his eyes and bent forward, resting his folded arms on his knees. "If I quit work, that will bring everything crashing down."

Ian couldn't tell if Daniel was switching to a new subject or if he thought Ian's last words implied criticism of the work/Haines situation. "I won't try to tell you what to do about work. It's your decision, and I'm not picking a fight. For once."

"How would *you* resolve our situation? Sit back and trust God to save us if He wants to?"

"We trust God, but we don't sit back. If Councilor Brannigan isn't able to help us, we figure out what to do next. Let's talk to Jill and Alisa and hammer out a plan."

"Are you scared?"

"I'm terrified."

"But you say you trust God."

"I trust that God will help us do whatever He wants us to do, but that doesn't mean I'm not scared at what we might have to go through along the way. I've never been fond of suffering."

The desperation in Daniel's eyes clawed at Ian like a drowning man trying to fight his way to the surface. Ian struggled to keep from sinking into the same panic. "I don't know if this story will interest you," Ian said. "But it might help, and I assume Alisa has never told you about it."

"What is it?"

"When Alisa was a prisoner struggling to recover from Information Extraction, she reached a point where she felt she absolutely couldn't endure more."

"I know what she suffered," Daniel said coldly. "You don't have to—"

Ian held up a hand. "She remembered a story she'd read in the Book of Mormon about a man who'd fought against God, then realized the nature of what he was doing, and suffered agonies of guilt. In torment, he prayed for relief and received it."

"And?"

"She prayed. And she received peace. She didn't immediately break out of the hallucinations, but she received strength so she could endure them."

Daniel rose to his feet and began pacing, his long strides taking him around the room multiple times before he stopped and looked silently at Ian.

Realizing Daniel wasn't going to comment, Ian continued the story. "When she received that strength, she also had a strong feeling that she wasn't going to die. She couldn't imagine how she *could* survive—she was scheduled for a public execution . . ."

"You've made your point." Daniel's composed voice hid whatever he thought of Alisa's experience. "We don't know what's going to happen."

"More than that," Ian said. "Whatever *does* happen, God will give us the strength to get through it, even if—well, never mind the even ifs."

"Thanks for your input. Go back to the game room."

Ian stood. Protesting this brusque dismissal or pointing out that they hadn't made any progress on deciding what to do next wouldn't do any good. From the brittle expression on Daniel's face, Ian knew if he pushed back, the conversation would shatter into angry shards, and the last thing they needed right now was another argument.

* * *

Daniel crumpled into the chair Ian had vacated and closed his eyes, seeing in memory Alisa contorted in agony, her heart straining, her eyes staring sightlessly at the nightmares that had become her only reality. She'd been hallucinating for nearly seventeen hours with no breaks. He'd been certain she was gone. Irreversible Broc psychosis. Then suddenly she was calm. Her vital signs stabilized. Short breaks began to appear between hallucinations. Thus began her astonishing climb to recovery.

Had God done that for her and Daniel had claimed the credit, even *knowing* she'd been beyond his, or anyone's, medical skill?

Her own mind did that for her. She became convinced God was helping her, and the power of that delusion was enough to—

Daniel frowned. *Her own mind? When was the last time you heard of someone able to delude themselves out of the neurochemical train wreck of Broc psychosis?*

What about Jill in the forest? Had God saved her? Or had she credited God with magnified abilities brought on by an adrenaline response to danger?

He rested his head in his hands, despair flooding him. Did he really imagine prayers were heard anywhere outside the believer's skull?

It's insanity.

Had he thrown away his family and his future to take three anarchist lunatics under his wing? If he wanted to be rid of them, his father would take care of that. He'd fix Daniel's mistakes. Free him from this mess.

The thought made Daniel sick.

God . . . I don't know if You exist, and if You do, I don't know how to talk to You, but I can't go on any longer without some assurance that this wasn't a huge mistake. Our options have closed up. I can't get us out of here on my own. No one can help us. If we die, we die, but I can't stand wondering if I'm dying for a mistake.

Tears streamed down his face, and his pulse accelerated. *I can't do this any longer without help. It's beyond me. If You're there, if Ian and Jill and Alisa are right, I'd give anything to know it.*

Anything.

Chapter 18

DINNERTIME PASSED WITH NO SIGN of Daniel, and all that remained in the game room fridge were a cup of yogurt, a couple of slices of ham, and two apples. Remembering the stress in Daniel's face, Ian didn't want to go pester him about food, but by nine o'clock, Ian had devoured the ham, Jill and Alisa had eaten the apples and yogurt, and Ian was so hungry that mental images of mashed potatoes and gravy kept diverting his attention from the history journal he was reading.

Jill and Alisa were sitting on the piano bench discussing some of the old sheet music Jill had found, with Jill softly playing an occasional tune. She had been delighted when Alisa had admitted she'd performed with the prestigious Jameston Singers during high school. Clearly embarrassed by Jill's awe, Alisa had responded to her questions with short—but polite—answers, and Ian had expected the conversation to die quickly. But Jill had pressed on, and Alisa had responded with increasing enthusiasm until the conversation became an animated discussion of choral and instrumental music, solo disasters, and quirky conductors.

Hunger wasn't the only reason Ian was having difficulty focusing on his reading. The new and enjoyable sound of Alisa's laughter was enough to make him forget the letters of the alphabet entirely.

At ten o'clock, Jill dropped another sheet of music onto the pile on the floor and looked at Ian. "I'm starving. Too bad we can't order a pizza."

Ian rose to his feet. "I'm going to go raid the kitchen."

"Are you sure it's a good idea to go into the main part of the house?" Jill asked.

"You know Daniel's housekeeping staff is gone in the evenings, and the security guys aren't inside. And he'd have been sure to tell us if someone was coming over."

"True," Jill conceded, but her eyes were worried. "What do you suppose Daniel is doing?"

"No idea," Ian said. "Thinking, maybe. He has a lot on his mind."

"I wish he'd come talk to us about it."

"I'll be back soon." Ian walked toward the door, trying not to limp too heavily lest Jill feel compelled to do the dinner run for him.

It took Ian a few wrong turns before he found the kitchen, a massive room with black-and-gold marble countertops. In a walk-in freezer, he found a mother lode of frozen dinners, labeled by Daniel's cook. Inspired by Jill's pizza joke, Ian selected four individual-sized pizzas and started back toward the guest wing.

When he reached the door of the game room, he learned that the chatting and piano playing had progressed to singing. He knew little about music, and Jill and Alisa were singing quietly, but even so, he could tell their voices harmonized beautifully. Jill fumbled with a passage on the piano, and her part of the duet ended in rueful laughter while Alisa continued singing. Alisa's voice was lower than Jill's, clear and smooth, and Ian stood in the hallway, unwilling to enter the room for fear of shutting down the recital.

"They sound good." Daniel spoke behind Ian, startling him. "I had no idea Alisa sang."

Ian swallowed, not sure why the singing had made his throat knot. "She has a nice voice, doesn't she?"

Daniel's skin was ashen, and his eyes were bloodshot, but he looked deeply calm.

"Everything all right?" Ian ventured.

"Yes. I'm sorry. I lost track of time. You must be starving."

"Nothing pizza can't fix."

Daniel took the pizzas and opened the door of the game room. "Then let's eat before we all pass out. We have a lot to talk about, but I don't want to do it tonight. There are some preparations I need to make."

* * *

Peale drummed his fingers on the steering wheel and eyed the bus stop in front of the Terrance Apartments. Holly Sutherland's calendar had listed no activities for tonight, no messages or calls had mentioned plans, and her ID record showed she had boarded bus 18 as she did every Tuesday evening after her evening class in graphic design. Unless she'd decided at the last minute to disembark at her boyfriend's house on the way home, she'd be here in three minutes. No, six minutes. The bus was running three minutes late.

Peale disliked having to approach a civilian, but involving anyone at headquarters in this job meant risking that word would leak to Captain Whitney.

The bus rumbled to the curb, and three people exited. In the glow from the streetlight, Peale scanned the passengers and found the girl he sought—a slender black girl with a backpack over her shoulder.

He exited his car and strode along the breezeway toward Holly's apartment. The lightbulb outside her front door was broken, courtesy of Peale. He stood in the darkness and waited.

Holly didn't notice him until she nearly walked into him. She gasped and stepped back.

"Police, Ms. Sutherland." Peale flipped open his badge, angling it so it caught the light from the parking lot.

"What . . . what is this about?"

"Come with me."

Obediently, she walked in step with him toward the parking lot. Peale remained silent. Let her wonder if she was being arrested. Holly's file was clean, but chances were that she—like nearly everyone else—had made a few minor mistakes that were now inflating in her imagination to full-scale acts of treason. A few whispered sarcastic remarks about President Ryce's advanced age or some griping about the intrusiveness of the Watch—few people were so innocent that they didn't sweat when confronted by a police officer.

He opened the front passenger door. "Give me your backpack and get in."

"Sir—what—"

"Get in."

Holly handed him her backpack and climbed inside. Peale rounded the car and slid into the driver's seat. The tinted windows would keep their conversation private, unless someone looked directly into the windshield—unlikely, since he was parked with the front of his car nearly touching the building.

"You're an artist," he said, stowing her backpack next to his feet. "And you're a genius at fixing up antique photographs."

"I—it's a hobby, sir," Holly said tentatively.

"You make money at it?"

She squirmed. "Just a little here and there, to help with school, rent, or whatever."

"You design that website yourself?"

"Yes, sir." Her voice trembled. "It's just a hobby. It's not really a business. I don't even have prices set—people just give me . . . little gifts sometimes."

"You're a pro at restoring even badly damaged photographs."

"I've done some work like that. Water damage, smoke damage. It's a hobby. I'm only a student."

"You do all the work yourself? Or do you have any partners?"

"No partners, sir."

Peale reached behind him and picked up a computer from the backseat. He opened it to display a series of photographs.

"Take a look at these." He passed her the computer. "These were taken with a night-vision camera. There are three people in the photographs. I want pictures I can identify them in. What could you do about that?"

The computer jiggled as she took it in her shaking hands. She clicked through the photographs, head bowed close to the screen. "I could make them a lot clearer, a lot cleaner." Holly zoomed in on the murky sliver of a face nearly obscured by the hood of a coat. "If I did some cleanups, some composites, filled in some blanks . . . but . . . you must have people in the police who could do a lot better job than I can. I'm just an amateur."

"You care about national security, Holly?"

"Yes, sir!"

He almost chuckled at her overacted enthusiasm. "Then do what I ask. If there isn't enough to work from in those photos, use your art skills and do your best to complete the faces. They don't have to be perfect. I just need good enough shots to run through the Central Identity Network."

"I'll do my best, sir." Now she sounded flattered. Time to scare her.

"Don't tell anyone I came to you. Don't tell anyone what you're doing. You'll work solely on that machine I just handed you. It has all of your usual software loaded on it, and it isn't linked to the network. I don't want anyone snooping in your work."

"Yes, sir."

"Don't work on it when anyone can see you. Don't tell your roommates. Don't tell Jake Thorne."

She tensed at the mention of her boyfriend. "I'll keep quiet, sir," she said nervously.

Peale reached over and tipped the computer shut. "Not one word, Holly. Not one hint."

"Yes, sir."

"How's your family doing?"

She gripped the laptop. "They're fine, sir."

"Your brother enjoy his hike at Rory Glen last weekend?"

"He—yes, he did, sir."

He handed her the backpack. "Scraped his knee, didn't he?"

"Not too badly, sir." Her voice was trembling again.

"Not one word, Holly. Tuck that computer in your backpack and go home. I'll meet you here one week from tonight, at the same time."

"Yes, sir." She stuffed the computer in her backpack and scrambled out of the car.

* * *

When Daniel returned home Tuesday night, he instructed Ian, Jill, and Alisa to change into clothes, coats, and shoes that he'd thoroughly examined for listening devices. Ian hurried to cooperate, looking forward to the discussion Daniel hadn't wanted to hold if there was any chance his father could overhear. Daniel drove them to a restaurant parking lot where they transferred into a car he'd borrowed from a friend. He then drove to north Tremont and parked behind the hockey rink.

Ian felt strange sitting in a car in a public parking lot, but in the darkness, there was no reason anyone would notice this ordinary car or the people inside. He assumed Daniel had chosen this spot—rather than a completely deserted area—so the car could blend in rather than stick out if an officer on patrol passed by. There were a couple dozen cars in the lot, enough for camouflage but few enough that they could keep an eye on every car that arrived or left.

Ian picked up a glove from the floor of the car and stuffed it in the cup holder between the front seats. "I'm curious what excuse you gave your friend for—"

"Borrowing his car when I already own several? I said I needed a vehicle no one would recognize. He's tactful enough not to ask questions."

Or too intimidated by the fact that you're a Lansbury, Ian thought.

Daniel rotated partway in his seat so he could look at Jill next to him and Ian and Alisa sitting behind him. "Here's the issue. Clearly, my father is still in New America, and he knows the three of you are alive. The fact that he hasn't made his move yet probably means he's waiting in hopes that he can snare me in the family web before he takes action against you. Anyone disagree with that?"

"It's the most logical explanation," Ian said.

"But sooner or later," Daniel continued, "he's going to—"

Jill sighed. "You don't need to finish that sentence."

Ian grimaced. Marcus Lansbury was a man capable of blowing up a building filled with children just to manipulate the nation into thinking the anarchist threat was so terrible they'd cling to whatever restrictions he wanted to place on them. Ian didn't want to imagine what Marcus had planned for the people who'd corrupted his son and thwarted his takeover.

"There's another issue besides your father," Alisa said. "We've never resolved the question of why the police planted transmitters at the Halbrooks' home, nor have we determined who was on the hill opposite your cabin on Sunday night."

Jill picked up a glove from near her feet and stuck it in the other cup holder. Apparently, she was feeling Ian's fidgety compulsion to organize the scattered winter gear of whoever owned the car. "The person who drove away," she said.

"Yes," Alisa said. "It may have been someone working with Dr. Lansbury's—with Daniel's—father, but it's also possible his father is not the only one interested in him."

"Do you think the police are suspicious of him?" Ian asked. "Not just of bad-attitude Nate?"

"It's possible," Daniel said. "I know Blake Peale would love to nail me for any crime he could find. But it all comes down to the same thing. Where can we take you?"

"It's futile to think we can avoid danger indefinitely if our strategy remains one of simply shifting from hideout to hideout," Alisa said.

"What do you recommend instead?" Daniel asked. "It's not safe to keep you at my house."

"Moving us to a location connected with neither you nor the Halbrooks *would* help reduce the danger from the police." Alisa spoke quietly. "But with an opponent like your father, there's only one route to safety."

In the weak light from a dented light post several yards away, Daniel's face looked bloodless. "Destroy him."

Jill shuddered. "How are we supposed to . . . do that? We don't even know where he is."

"*We* don't necessarily have to kill him," Alisa said.

"We can't turn him over to the police," Ian pointed out. "If he gets arrested, he'll tell them what Daniel's been up to."

A group of teenage boys exited the hockey rink. After they headed toward the bus stop, Alisa said, "I doubt the police will ever be able to put Marcus Lansbury through I-X."

"Do you think he still has contacts in the government who'll be able to rescue him or kill him before the police can question him?" Ian asked.

"It's possible. I'm sure he'll have prepared well for the possibility of arrest. I can't imagine he would allow himself to undergo the . . ." She hesitated. "The experience of Information Extraction. He'd choose death instead."

"A suicide device?" Jill asked.

"The police do their best to circumvent the use of them. But if Marcus Lansbury chooses to employ one, I doubt they'll succeed in stopping him."

"You're right." Daniel rotated in his seat so he was facing the windshield. Ian wondered if Daniel was resting from the awkward pose of looking behind him or if he didn't want eye contact with anyone during this discussion of his father's fate. "He *would* prefer death. But that doesn't mean he wouldn't betray us voluntarily before his death—unless . . . that might depend on my mother. If she hasn't been arrested as well, he'd do anything to avoid hurting her."

"Including hiding your treason?" Ian asked. "Because if he turns you in, he's killing her son?"

"I know it's hard for you to . . . believe someone as ruthless as my father could care that much, but . . . he adores her." Though the tone of Daniel's voice remained level, the words came jerkily.

Ian realized how little he knew of Daniel's relationship with his parents. Jill had said Daniel idolized his mother. And his father? Ian had always viewed Marcus as the enemy, not considering what it meant to Daniel that Marcus was his father—a man Daniel was bound to by blood and a lifetime of experience. A man he respected, admired, feared.

Loved.

"We can't know for sure *what* he'll do if confronted by the police." Daniel broke the silence. "But it's not just to protect ourselves that we need to stop him. Knowing my father, there's a lot more going on with him than stalking us. If he succeeds with whatever he's planning, you aren't the only people who'll die."

"What are our ultimate goals here?" Alisa asked. "To stop your father, yes, to protect the innocent. But not so we can remain in New America in hiding."

Daniel nodded. "The goal is escape. If anyone has any suggestions . . ."

A surprising thought occurred to Ian. "You told us one of the problems with getting to the US is that even if we could get past Ryce's new security restrictions, the US doesn't want to let any New Americans in after the way the government refused to give the US information about the Liberty Cadre. What if we could offer them the head of the Cadre?"

"Catch him." Daniel's gloved hand clenched around the gearshift. "And offer him to the US in exchange for their help in escaping."

"Yes."

Jill laid her hand over Daniel's. "*Could* they help us?"

"They have undercover agents in New America." A tinge of excitement enlivened Alisa's voice. "The police caught one of their operatives a couple of years back, but that agent couldn't tell them where to find his compatriots or what their names were—only that they existed."

"If the police can't find the US spies, how are we supposed to do it?" Jill asked.

"We don't find them," Daniel said. "We let them find us. If Councilor Brannigan can send US leaders the message that we have the head of the Cadre and will hand him over in exchange for assistance in escaping—it's not a bad idea, Ian."

"I don't think even US spies have the ability to turn invisible," Jill said flatly, obviously determined not to let herself get hopeful. "How will they sneak past President Ryce's travel restrictions?"

"They may have means we aren't aware of." Passing headlights made Alisa's dark eyes glitter. "Even if they can't get us across the border immediately, they have the means to hide us more effectively than we can hide on our own."

"Ryce's restrictions can't last forever." The new optimism in Daniel's voice made Ian's excitement grow. "There's grumbling in the Council, and the shipping of goods in and out has become so onerous that the economy is suffering."

"Okay," Jill said. "But why do we keep talking like we have your father locked in the closet and we're trying to decide what to do with him? How are we supposed to catch him without . . . getting killed ourselves? And we have no idea where he is. He probably didn't stay at the cabin."

Daniel probed at the bruise on his face. "I'd guess there are two things that would bring him into open confrontation. The first is if he thinks he's won and I'm ready to go crawling back to him. The second is if he thinks he's lost and there's no point in further delay. But one thing is plain. I need to face him alone."

"You've lost your mind," Ian said. "The safest way to—"

"This *is* the safest way to draw him out. We find a temporary place to hide the three of you. I remain at the house in Tremont. I tell Councilor Haines I'm withdrawing my name from consideration for the position of Council Assistant, and I quit the Annex."

Ian glanced at Jill. In profile, all the evidence he could see of her reaction was one wide eye.

Daniel continued matter-of-factly. "When my father realizes he doesn't know where the three of you have gone *and* he sees me backing away from whatever future he's setting up for me, that may provoke him into showing himself."

"The future *he's* setting up for you—wait a minute," Ian said. "Are you suggesting Haines is working with your father?"

"It would explain why Councilor Haines is so interested in me. It's not as though I'm qualified for the position." Self-contempt roughened the words. "Maybe it isn't Haines who wants me there. Maybe it's Dad who wants me in a key position for whatever he's planning. Maybe he's the one who got Nadia Sears out of the way to open up the post so I could take it. But if Haines *is* working with Dad, it's a good thing for us."

"How?" Ian asked.

"Normally, my offending Haines by rejecting what he's offering would create severe consequences. But if my father is behind Haines . . ."

"Then, for your mother's sake, your dad will tell Haines not to punish you," Ian finished.

"Warped, isn't it? Maybe Dad's interference will save us momentarily." Daniel rested his hand on Jill's shoulder. "I'm sorry for not listening when you tried to talk to me about work. I was too much of a coward to accept that I had a choice, but you were right."

Tears running down her face, Jill tilted toward Daniel, and they embraced—a hug Ian figured would have lasted longer if they hadn't had to lean clumsily to bridge the gap between the front seats.

Daniel drew back and looked at Ian. "I owe you an apology as well. I've said a lot of harsh, unfair things to you lately. I'm sorry."

"Don't worry about it. I earned most of them."

"Alisa—" Daniel's voice caught. After a long moment of silence, Ian realized why Daniel had stopped: this wasn't a straightforward apology for recent conflict.

"Alisa . . . the things I did to you . . . I never thought about—never comprehended . . . I don't even know how to begin to . . . There *is* no way to apologize for—"

"You saved my life," Alisa said. "Which makes you far better at making restitution for your errors than I am at making restitution for mine. Please move on; we need to complete our plans."

"Just know I'll do anything I can to help you."

"I know that. Thank you."

Hope filled Ian. They were making progress. They *would* escape.

"Returning to our original question," Daniel said, "we need a place to hide you where my father won't think to look."

"You can't face him solo," Ian said.

"He won't hurt me."

"About what happened at the cabin—"

Daniel gave a hoarse laugh. "He won't *kill* me."

"Let's get something straight." Ian leaned forward and gripped the back of Daniel's seat. "There is *no way* we're hiding under the bed while you duel Zero. Maybe he won't kill you, but he plays dirty. You can't put yourself in that kind of danger."

"And I won't let him get his hands on you three because I wanted to keep you around as bodyguards. Think about it—if Councilor Haines *is* on his side, that means you're living in a house guarded by a security team handpicked by . . . Zero's sidekick."

Ian groaned. He'd forgotten Haines had arranged for Daniel's guards.

"For once, I may have a few advantages over my dad," Daniel said. "From the way I've been acting lately, I doubt he knows where I stand or what to expect from me. For my mother's sake, he's limited in what he can do to me. *And* he believes I'm weak—I'll betray him behind his back, but I wouldn't have the guts to take him on face-to-face. Maybe . . . for a short period . . . I can surprise him."

Ian shook his head. "We can't leave you alone to—"

"You're not listening to me. Besides my mother, I'm the one person who can safely confront him. You are the person *least* likely to survive a confrontation with him. Do you have any idea how much he must hate you? And even if you're willing to risk yourself to stay here, I don't think you're willing to risk Alisa and Jill. I can deal with him far better on my own than I can if he has a knife at Jill's throat."

"He's right," Alisa said. "We'd be less a help than a liability."

Jill wiped tears off her cheeks. "I don't like this. But it does seem like the smartest strategy."

"Let's brainstorm our options," Daniel said. "All suggestions are welcome, no matter how insane or impractical."

"If those are the criteria," Ian said, "then I have plenty of ideas."

Chapter 19

"I NEED MORE INFORMATION." KELLEHER sat in a chair across from Ryce's desk. "You said you didn't want anyone to know you were investigating this, so I assume you'd like to acquire the information for me in a way that doesn't leave a trail."

Ryce's eagerness transformed into frustration and anger. When Kelleher had asked for an appointment, she'd hoped he would come with answers, not questions. She'd even canceled a meeting this afternoon so she could take private time to watch the recording of Roshek's execution again, reveling in anticipation of Kelleher's report that Roshek's calm was drugged phoniness. Now she felt mocked.

That was not an emotion she wanted to reveal to Kelleher. "You've reviewed the execution records?"

"Yes."

"And?"

"They're odd. But I don't have answers for you yet. I'd like access to some other records for comparison. Are all criminal executions recorded?"

"Yes. I'll see that you have full access to Euth Center information."

"I want to know who was in charge at the Euth Center on the dates of the three executions."

Ryce thought back to the report she'd received before the executions explaining how the police would ensure that information remained secure. "It was the director, Nathan Halbrook. The police didn't want any other Euth Center personnel on site because of the risk of staff coming into contact with prisoners who held classified information about the nature of the Liberty Cadre. Halbrook was not permitted direct contact with the prisoners prior to the executions—he was assigned only to manage the preparation of the facilities and disposal of the bodies."

"Halbrook." Kelleher pursed his lips. "Do you know if there's any connection between Daniel Lansbury and Nathan Halbrook?"

"I don't know. Halbrook is Spencer Brannigan's brother-in-law, and Councilor Brannigan and Lansbury are friends. They may be acquainted. You can find that out yourself if you're discreet."

Kelleher absently rapped his knuckles against the gold-leafed arm of the chair he sat in. "Lansbury works at the Tremont Research Lab as well as at the Detention Annex. Do you know what project he works on at the lab?"

"I believe he's on the Broc series. His work was key to creating the process that allowed the police to decondition Cadre prisoners whose confessions were affected by Marcus Lansbury's tampering. Why?"

"I need access to Lansbury's account at the lab. I want to look at what he's been doing, what he's been studying, what experiments he's been running."

"Why are you wasting my time?" The anger in her voice made her as angry with herself as she was with Kelleher. She hadn't meant to show that degree of emotion at all, and her jump from calm to fury had just told Kelleher she'd been hiding rage all along. "I don't want you to analyze his whole career," she said, controlling her tone. "I just want to know if he did something illegal at the executions. We'll get answers to other questions when we interrogate him."

"I am focusing on the executions," Kelleher said stolidly. "I may know more when I study Lansbury's records."

"You have a theory you're investigating. What is it?"

Kelleher shook his head. "Let me do some research. I need more facts."

Ryce wrangled with her anger. She wanted to press him, but Kelleher hated getting pushed for premature diagnoses, and the best she'd get out of him now were cranky generalities. "Then get your information. I'll see to it that you have full clearance for all lab records for the next seventy-two hours. Come back on Sunday night, and I expect some concrete answers."

"I wasn't at the executions. I didn't study the bodies. The best I can do for you is conjecture."

"I require expert conjecture, then."

Kelleher stood up. "Sunday," he said.

* * *

Every time the driver of the Euthanasia Center supply truck stopped and opened the back of the truck to fill an order, Ian held his cramped body as motionless as he could in the canvas bin where he was hiding. He tried to breathe noiselessly, but with the limited air circulation under the concealing pile of sheets, he felt suffocated. As soon as the driver closed the door, Ian would pop his head out of the bin and see Jill and Alisa coming up for air from the bin next to him.

When Daniel had suggested asking Nate for fresh ideas on where the fugitives could go, Ian had doubted Nate could help, not with the police already watching him. Nate *didn't* know where they could stay, but he did suggest a way to sneak them out of Tremont: stowing them away on the weekly Euth Center supply run. As director of the Tremont Euthanasia Center, Nate had access to the trucks and invoices involved in sending materials to the smaller centers from a central Tremont warehouse. He added a couple of extra bins to the truck scheduled to leave next and layered the bins with linens that were not on the delivery invoices so the driver wouldn't have a reason to touch the bins.

During the day-and-a-half wait for the supply run, which they'd spent hiding in a storage room in the Tremont Euth Center basement, they'd debated where on the seven-city supply run they should exit the truck and try to find a hiding place. At Alisa's suggestion, they'd settled on Jameston, the city where she'd grown up. It was the only city on the delivery route any of them was familiar with, and knowing the area would make it easier to get supplies without being on the streets longer than necessary. Alisa was certain that the fact that she'd lived there as a child made no difference to their safety. They weren't worried someone would recognize her because they'd known her at fourteen; they worried someone would recognize her because her picture had been all over the news a few months ago. That was a problem no matter where they stopped.

They counted stops. Once they reached Jameston, the fifth delivery on the route, they waited for the driver's footsteps and the rattle of dolly wheels to fade, then climbed out of the bins, walked through the still-open truck doors, and exited the underground Euth Center garage, wearing coats and hats Nate had looted from the lost-and-found closet.

Cold rain soaked the streets of Jameston, and Ian gladly hid his face under an umbrella Nate had provided. Even in the darkness, he felt blazingly conspicuous. Walking side by side, Alisa and Jill put distance between themselves and Ian until they turned left and disappeared from sight. Silently praying for their safety, Ian headed toward his assigned destination. He'd rendezvous with Jill and Alisa in two hours.

His leg was hurting badly by the time he reached the sporting goods store a mile and a half from the Euth Center, but he was careful not to limp. He didn't want to give anyone even the smallest reason to pay attention to him. Inside the store, he couldn't hide beneath an umbrella, and though he knew the worst that was likely to happen was someone remarking that he was a dead ringer for that anarchist assassin who got executed a few months back, he still preferred to avoid the subject. Pulling his baseball cap lower over his eyes, he plunged into the brightly lit store.

An hour later, toting the items he had purchased with Daniel's cash, he emerged into the rain and started toward the rendezvous point. He didn't have a hand free for his umbrella, the supplies were heavy and awkward, and fire seared his calf every time his foot hit the ground. He surrendered to the limp, figuring limping was less noticeable than his second choice—crawling.

When he arrived at the spot Alisa had designated—the bus stop in front of a busy movie theater—Alisa and Jill were waiting for him. As he approached, they stood and walked away. He followed them until they passed out of the business district into a residential street. With no one else in sight, Jill slowed her pace until Ian caught up.

"How's your leg?" Jill asked, holding out her umbrella to shield him from the rain. Alisa walked ahead, keeping distance between them.

"It's fine." Ian figured if he hadn't collapsed yet, "fine" still applied. "Did you find us a place to stay?"

"We have a few options. We found a real estate office with one of those touch-screen ads in the window. You know, the screen that flashes up all of the properties one by one in hopes people will stop to look. You can also use it to search for specific types of property, and since it's an ad, it doesn't take an ID to make it work."

"Fantastic." Ian took a step without lifting his injured leg high enough and slammed his toes into the elevated edge of the sidewalk where roots had pushed the concrete slabs up.

"Ian?" Jill dropped a shopping bag on the wet sidewalk and clutched his arm. "Are you okay?"

Teeth clenched, he shifted the weight off his injured leg and waited until he'd lost the compulsion to yell. "Yep. What did you find?"

She picked up the bag, and they resumed walking. "We found four rental properties that fit our criteria. Freestanding homes, no close neighbors, on the market for at least a year. Apparently the rental market is really slow here. One of the properties has been listed for four years."

"Good." The slower the market, the less likely they'd get surprised by a real estate agent with a prospective tenant. If that did happen, there was always the back door, though at the moment, the only agent Ian could outrun was a grandmother who needed knee-replacement surgery.

* * *

They decided on the second house. It was set back from the road and surrounded by trees and scraggly bushes. The house was a blocky ranch style, sided in warped wooden shingles. The paint that hadn't flaked off was orange, and the front steps were rotting away. Ian could easily see why no one had rented it.

"This place is seriously creepy," Jill whispered. They were standing at the back door with Alisa ready to pick the lock, but the door hung so crookedly it didn't latch correctly. A push swung it open.

"Daniel's father would never think to look for us here," Jill said. "I wouldn't look for anything here except mouse droppings. Not that I'm complaining. It looks like a great place to hide."

Ian pulled the flashlight he'd purchased out of the bag and pointed it at the floor. They made a careful inspection of the house and yard. When they found the water was off, they located the shutoff valve in the laundry room, and Ian forced the rusty handle to turn, almost sure that when he did, water would spew from cracks in every pipe.

The pipes shuddered. Jill jokingly opened her umbrella.

At the laundry room sink, Alisa turned the tap. The faucet jerked and sprayed rusty froth. After a moment, the shuddering stopped and mud-brown water flowed into the stained sink.

"Yuck," Jill said. "Let's hope it clears."

Ian swished his hand through the ice-cold stream. "Home sweet home. Jill, you can take the first shower."

* * *

Patrick Haines waved Daniel to a chair and dismissed his staffer. "What's going on? You told my secretary the matter was urgent."

Daniel steeled himself. "Sir, with my deepest apologies, I am withdrawing myself from consideration for the post of Council Assistant to the Department of Internal Defense."

"What are you talking about?"

"Sir, I can't accept the position. I don't want you to nominate me."

Haines slapped his glass onto the table next to him, splashing water onto the wood. "What kind of game have you been playing?"

"I wasn't playing a game, sir." Fear had swamped Daniel the instant he'd made the appointment with Haines, but he had to go through with this. When he'd prayed, he'd known with clarity that he needed to break with Haines no matter what. He *hadn't* felt he should break with Haines only if he was sure Haines wouldn't order him arrested for his disloyalty. "I thought I wanted what you were offering. But I don't have the qualifications for the post."

"I'll judge your qualifications." Haines's face was as hard as kiln-fired clay. "You're an inexperienced young idiot. But do you think I'll let you fumble around unadvised? I'll see to it that you reflect well on the department."

Daniel wanted to fold his arms to hide his shaky hands, but the pose would make him look either defensive or so scared that he'd stuffed his icy hands in his armpits to warm them up. "Sir, I don't want the position."

Haines's biceps bulged against his sleeves. "I'm offering you a chance to become one of the most powerful people in New America."

"I know, sir. I'm sorry."

"Is this some stupid modesty ploy? Are you waiting for me to stroke your ego and tell you what a great leader you'll be? Your name has been submitted to the Council. You're scheduled to attend the Tremont birthday celebration next week."

"I know, sir. But I won't be there."

"What's *wrong* with you?" Haines sized Daniel up as though calculating how much effort it would take for him to rip Daniel apart. "Did that coward Brannigan put you up to this?"

"No, sir." Normally, Daniel would have defended Brannigan from that insult, but now wasn't the time.

"Then what's the issue? Don't give me any silly statements about how you're not worthy."

Daniel knew there was no explanation shrewd Haines would believe except the truth—or as much of it as didn't involve admitting to treason. "Sir, I don't agree with the direction you're taking Internal Defense. I don't agree with your refusal to rein in certain police activities. I emphatically do not agree with the proposed change to allow the police to use Broc4 in random checks on citizens not accused of any crimes. Broc4 is a powerful, dangerous, and sometimes deadly drug. I will not stand up and endorse its use in random security checks."

Haines's square jaw looked so hard that Daniel had a ludicrous thought of himself punching Haines and breaking his knuckles. "A weak and indecisive Lansbury. Your grandfather would have cut your throat for your cowardice."

Sweat trickled down Daniel's back. "I value national security. But you and I don't see eye to eye on how to attain it."

"You're a hypocrite. You're up to your eyeballs in Broc4 every day, both at the Annex and at the lab. You're the last person who ought to be squeamish."

"I'm quitting the Annex." It scared Daniel to say it, but he wanted it to go into his father's ears. He wanted his father to know how completely he was losing his grip on Daniel and to act without thinking. "And I'm asking for a reassignment to a different project at the lab."

"You're quitting the Annex." Haines growled the words.

"It was a mistake to think I could go back. After what happened with my father and the Cadre . . . I can't keep reliving that. I'm quitting. I'm taking a few months off, maybe a few years."

"What happened to your face?"

Daniel touched the bruise on his cheek. "I slipped on some stairs."

"And shook your brain to mush? You need a doctor. Have you told Whitney you're quitting?"

"Not yet."

"Do you think they'll let you walk away? You with your knowledge of the Cadre?"

"I'll never speak of what I know. They know I support the decision to keep silent on my father's activities."

"That'll impress Whitney."

"I'm sorry." Daniel rose to his feet. "But I don't want any of this. I need to live below the radar for a while. I don't want the kind of power my father had."

"Are you trying to make a fool of me?"

"No, sir. I'm sorry for taking your time and attention. I know it's inexcusable." Daniel took a step toward the door, pulse drumming.

"Stop right there." Haines spoke angrily, but when Daniel met his gaze, he saw uncertainty.

Ruthless Patrick Haines was hesitating.

He didn't know how Marcus would respond to Daniel's stubbornness, and he didn't want to make a false move.

Daniel had guessed right. Every word of this confrontation would be repeated to his father, if Marcus wasn't already eavesdropping.

"You are out of your head," Haines said. "I'll give you until Monday to get yourself straightened out. Come back Monday night at nine, and if you haven't started making sense by then, you'll regret it."

In that moment, Daniel wanted to hedge by accepting the delayed deadline and thus giving Haines the impression that he might change his mind. But he didn't want to buy time. He wanted to provoke his father as rapidly as possible.

"Sir, I won't be back on Monday. Good night." Daniel walked out the door, expecting a staffer or security guard to intercept him.

No one stopped him. The staffer who had admitted him offered him his coat and showed him to the door. He drove home and parked in his garage.

What would he do if his father did show up? What if his mother accompanied Marcus? Daniel pictured himself trying to take action against his father with his mother watching, and he felt too demoralized to even climb out of the car. He slouched in the driver's seat, wishing he hadn't ignored Ian's insistence that he was foolish to face his parents alone.

Chapter 20

"CHECKMATE." IAN TRIUMPHANTLY PASSED THE chess game to Alisa. She glanced at the screen, gave Ian a brief smile, and set the game aside.

"Congratulations, Ian." Jill looked up from her sketchpad. "It must be refreshing to beat Alisa at a game for a change."

"Funny." Ian stretched out on his sleeping bag, his fingers interwoven behind his neck. "You want to play, Jilly?"

"Not a chance. I stink at chess."

"Have you ever played it?"

"With Dad, when I was a kid. Remember, he tried to teach me, but you kept butting in?"

"Oh yeah." Ian grinned at the memory of Jill and their father sitting at the kitchen table with an old wooden chess set between them—Jill with her chin resting on her crossed arms and a glaze of boredom on her face.

Jill picked up the camping lantern set next to the folded sleeping bag she was sitting on and tried to turn the dial higher. "Is it still light outside?" she asked.

Ian checked the watch Nate had given him, a sports watch with a partially cracked band that one of Nate's sons-in-law had left at his house. It was hard to tell day from night in this back bedroom—Alisa and Jill's sleeping quarters at night and the all-purpose kitchen/family room during the day. The multiple layers of paper bags they had taped over the windows kept it perpetually dark.

"It's almost nine," he said. "It's dark."

"Oops, I missed my chance. I was thinking of sitting under that big window in the living room to get better light for drawing. But at least it's warmer in here. A little bit warmer. Can we turn this back on yet?" She nudged the portable heater with her toes.

"Whenever you want," Ian said. "It depends on how quickly you want us to have to go buy another power source for it."

"Never mind," Jill said. "I don't want to risk going back to the store so soon. I'll wait for summer."

Ian chuckled. He rolled over and braced himself on one elbow so he could look at Alisa. She was sitting with her back against the grimy wall, swathed in the overcoat Halbrook had given her.

"How about another match?" He reached for the chess game. "We could make it two out of three."

She didn't meet his gaze. "No, thank you."

"Don't want to lose again?" he teased, though he knew the tension in her voice had nothing to do with losing the game. Was she okay? He hadn't noticed signs of any reversions, and she was still on the blocker patch Daniel had provided for the trip.

"I need a breath of air." Alisa rose to her feet. The doorknob jiggled as she turned it, sounding ready to break off the door.

"Do you want company?" Ian asked.

She shrugged and walked out of the room.

"That means yes, dolt," Jill whispered as soon as Alisa's footsteps receded.

"I don't know, Jilly," Ian whispered back. "She'd probably like some time alone after being stuck in here with us all day."

"Something's bothering her. Couldn't you tell how distracted she was during the game? Go find out what's wrong!"

Jill was right. Ian stretched to his feet.

He found Alisa standing in the backyard next to the trunk of an oak that would block her from the view of anyone approaching from the vacant lot behind the house—not that Ian could imagine anyone going on a stroll through weeds and mud on a chilly April evening.

"You all right?" he asked.

She drew a deep breath. "We are . . . about two and a half miles away from the house where I grew up."

The hair on Ian's arms prickled. "It must be hard for you to be back here."

"I've been to Jameston on a couple of work-related matters. But I haven't been to my neighborhood. And I didn't view things the . . . same way."

Ian understood what she meant. Coming here as a police officer, she had kept herself armored in the denial that had protected her for over a decade.

"I'm sorry," he said. "We should have chosen a different city to hide in."

"Don't be absurd. Jameston was my suggestion. It was the logical choice." She touched her fingertips to the bark of the tree, her gaze tracking her hand. Ian doubted she could see anything interesting in the bark. She didn't want to look him in the eyes.

"Alisa—"

"I . . . want to go to the house."

The wind ruffled Ian's hair and made him zip his coat to the top. "I'm not sure that's a good idea. How will it help you to see it?"

"I've seen it. I've hallucinated it so many times in so many distorted forms that it would be a relief to see it. To see it as it is *now*."

"I don't think it's going to help you. So you walk past it. You see the neighborhood. But you couldn't go inside. Someone is sure to be living there. You couldn't linger. And I'm afraid of how being back in that setting will affect you. That blocker patch is only good for a few more days, and even then, it can't control everything—"

"This won't cause a setback." Wind whipped Alisa's hair across her eyes. She brushed it back. "Please. It's difficult for me to explain why it matters so much. I just . . . need to go back. I know it wouldn't be wise for me to go alone. I can ask Jill to—"

"No," Ian said firmly. "If you go, I'm going with you."

In the moonlight, he could see the relief on her face. "Your leg—" she began.

"My leg is fine. And it's not too dangerous for us to be seen together. I spent Thursday evening walking around busy stores, and no one glanced at me. At night, no one will notice us. But I'm still not sure this is—"

"What I see will be far better than what I imagine. I think it might help. Please. It doesn't have to be immediately. I know your leg *is* bothering you. But as soon as it's possible—"

Ian buckled. He'd have better luck swimming up Niagara Falls than resisting the pleading in her voice. "If it means that much to you, let's do it. How about tomorrow night?"

"Thank you." He saw her lips move but couldn't hear her over the rustle of branches in the wind. He reached for her hand and held it between his palms, wondering if he'd agreed to a trip that, far from making things better, would only magnify the guilt she couldn't let go.

Chapter 21

THE HOUSE HAD NEVER SEEMED so large or so echoingly empty. The whisper of air from the heating system made Daniel start; the flicker of his own movements reflected in the glossy wood of his desk brought goose bumps.

This afternoon, he'd resigned from his position as a medical supervisor at the Detention Annex. Captain Whitney's reaction had been far milder than Daniel had expected; Whitney had plainly been forewarned and coached by Councilor Haines on how to react. His parting ultimatum was identical to Haines's. Daniel had until Monday night to reconsider his decision.

He slipped his hand into his pocket and fingered the two items he kept with him constantly: a police stun square and a filled hypodermic syringe. Either item would render his father unconscious.

Monday. Would his father wait for that deadline to see what Daniel would do? Or would he come earlier to try to persuade Daniel to cooperate with Haines?

Or was Daniel overestimating his importance to his father?

What if nothing happened? What if Marcus, through Haines, kept the police from arresting Daniel but took no action himself, simply allowing Daniel to hole up in the house and wait?

He'd go mad.

But it wouldn't happen. Marcus had Haines, but he didn't have everyone. If Daniel quit work and broke with Haines, rumors would spread. His reputation would suffer. Haines's reputation would suffer. Curiosity would swell as to why Whitney and Haines had not taken action against Daniel. Someone might start to suspect Marcus's involvement. Marcus couldn't afford that.

Daniel rested his head on his desk and wondered what Jill and the others were doing now. Had they found a safe hiding place? He yearned to follow the trail of the Euth Center delivery truck—to check on the underside of the benches in each of the memorial gardens until he found the coded message they'd planned to write wherever they disembarked, telling Daniel their location. He pictured himself going to their hideout, Jill's welcoming kiss, his sharing the news that he'd captured his father and been contacted by US agents and that they were on their way to escape.

And that he could travel in time, had built a spaceship out of paper plates and shoelaces, and had a new job teaching leprechauns how to invest their gold.

Get a grip. Sarcasm won't help.

The click of the doorknob rotating made Daniel vault to his feet. Jocelyn stepped into the room.

Daniel came out from behind his desk, his palm sweating on the stun square in his pocket. "What are you doing here? Where's Dad?"

Jocelyn shut the door. "He's not with me." She was pale, and the ponytail Daniel used to see her wear when she was exercising or in a hurry was off center, with wisps of hair falling on one side of her face. She reached for him, but Daniel lifted his hands to keep her at arm's length.

"You shouldn't have risked coming," he said. *What risk?* Jocelyn had probably driven right up to the house and overridden the security system while Daniel's guard—chosen by Haines—ignored her.

Tears filled her eyes. "Honey, let's talk. Please. You don't understand what you're doing to yourself. Why did you tell Councilor Haines you don't want the position?"

Daniel listened for any hint of movement outside the study. He didn't trust his mother's assertion that Marcus wasn't here. "How do you know *what* I told him?"

"Oh, stop with the games! We love you. Of course we've been following what you're doing."

"If we're stopping the games, then let's drop the pretense that Dad isn't listening to me right now. I assume he has this whole house bugged."

"No one's listening to us tonight." Jocelyn wiped her eyes. "Your father is away, and I turned off the equipment. I didn't want this recorded."

Daniel hadn't expected her to immediately confirm that they'd been eavesdropping. "How many people are working with you? I assume Dad still has an army of lackeys. Including Patrick Haines."

He expected her to deny that Haines was involved, but she said, "Your father is working for your good. He's trying to open a door for you, to guide you away from some . . . damaging mistakes."

Time to provoke Marcus a little further. "I don't consider saving my friends to be a mistake."

"Sweetheart. You've been through so much. I've felt all along that the Council was unspeakably cruel to punish you like they did. I wanted your father to order his people to stop your assignment to the executions, but things were in such upheaval that it wasn't a good time for him to exercise his influence. But you can't tell me you haven't regretted what you did."

"I'd do the same thing again."

"I don't think so." She stepped close to him, and he didn't stop her as she laid her hand on his cheek. The familiar touch of her fingers muddled Daniel's emotions. In his pocket, he rolled the syringe between his thumb and index finger.

"I know you're angry that we've been keeping an eye on you." She withdrew her hand. "But our only concern was your welfare. I know you don't realize . . ." She hesitated, averting her eyes.

"Realize what?"

"I'm sorry." She drew a tissue from her pocket. "But I've . . . heard the conversation of your friends when you're not around."

Embarrassment and apprehension unsettled Daniel. "I'm not interested."

"You *should* be," she said fiercely. "The vicious way Ian Roshek criticizes you—*mocks* you . . . After what you did for them, they should have been kissing your feet. Instead they . . ."

"They?" Daniel asked. So this was the next ploy in his father's campaign to create a rift between him and his friends. "All of them?"

"Well, Lieutenant Kent doesn't say much, which you probably already know. And Jill tried to defend you at first, but she's so leery of anything she thinks might take your attention away from her that she's had nothing nice to say since you started back at the Annex." Jocelyn's face reddened. "But Ian Roshek—he undermines you and tries to get the women to side with him. I think he hates accepting your help. He's tried to convince the others that they never needed it. He says the most ridiculous things—he thinks some religious magic would have saved their lives if you hadn't."

She touched the bruise on his face, her hand trembling. "And then he *hurt* you and blamed it on your father! I didn't know what had happened until Dad told me the next day, and I was *furious*." Tears streamed down her cheeks, and her sobs broke her voice. "Do you know why . . . Roshek's been . . . nicer to you lately? His injury. He told the others he'd better kiss up to you for a couple of weeks so you wouldn't kill him off with an infection."

Rattled, Daniel didn't know what to do. He'd never seen his mother lose composure and sob. "Mother . . ."

"I'm *sorry*. I know you don't want to hear this, but you *have* to know the character of the people you're protecting."

With no idea what else to do, he wrapped his arms around her. She embraced him, her arms constricting his rib cage, her head pressed against his shoulder. While she cried, Daniel tried to think. He knew he'd been the target of some criticism. He'd earned it. But he also knew his mother was both exaggerating and outright lying.

It scared him to realize that a few days ago he *would* have been ready to believe her report. But now he felt splintered, not by suspicion and anger but by the realization of how completely she was participating in Marcus's efforts to manipulate him.

Why did it hurt as though it were new? He'd already known she sided with Marcus; he'd already known he couldn't trust her.

Jocelyn lifted her cheek from his damp shoulder. "I'm sorry." She wiped her eyes. "Sweetheart, I'm sorry. You made a mistake. Please don't let it destroy you."

Daniel touched the sleeve of her caramel-brown leather jacket. She'd had that jacket for years—for decades, but he hadn't seen it in a long time. She must have stored it somewhere with other clothes ready for retrieval if she and Marcus had to go underground. He could picture her wearing it on the front row at his piano recital. Wearing it as she walked in the door carrying a bag of supplies for his birthday cake, the cakes she always baked herself. Wearing it on a walk on the beach in Newbold Bay as she enthusiastically admired the shells Daniel showed her.

"I'm sorry about my breakdown." She smiled, charm beginning to revive in her tear-blemished face. "Your father would thank you for letting me fall apart here so he didn't get cried on."

Daniel's throat cramped, and his eyes burned.

"You have the ability to be a leader like your father and grandfather. Like James Tremont. I know you're angry at your father, but don't reject what you want because he's involved in bringing it to you."

He shoved a few words out, his voice gravelly. "That's not why I'm rejecting this."

"You're exhausted, I know. How can you think about stepping into a leadership position with so much . . . unfinished business hanging over you?"

Daniel said nothing.

"Honey . . ." Jocelyn smoothed her hand over the wrinkled, tear-wet spot on his shirt as though trying to tidy him up. "I know how trapped you're feeling. You have a problem you can't solve, and we're terrified for you. *Please* let your father help. It would be so much more merciful to end this than to let your friends get arrested again—which they *will*, and so will you if this goes on any longer."

Tell me where they are, and Dad will kill them for you, Daniel translated.

"You wouldn't believe the things that are happening now, Daniel—it's amazing. Your father has great plans for New America, and he wants you at his side. But if you keep fighting him, he can't wait for you. Everything is already moving forward."

Daniel shuddered. *Great plans.* What was his father up to? Images of the bombing at Newbold Bay crowded into his mind. "If Dad values me so much, let him come tell me in person."

Hope radiated from Jocelyn's face. "You want to see him?"

"Yes, I want to see him. I want him to look me in the face and tell me he has more in mind for me than being his puppet, because that's all he's shown me so far."

"I'll talk to him," Jocelyn said. "I'll tell him." She stood on tiptoe and kissed his cheek. "I'll be in touch soon."

"Mother . . . I'm sorry I've hurt you. I never wanted that."

"I know. I love you, Daniel." She slipped out the door.

Daniel didn't make it to a chair. He collapsed on the carpet and sat with his head on his knees, feeling sick to his stomach.

Chapter 22

MOONLIGHT BRIGHTENED THE STREETS, AND wind carried the woodsy smell of bark mulch homeowners had newly spread in flowerbeds and around bushes, eager to fix up their yards after months of snow and ice. Alisa was sweating in her heavy coat, but every time she unzipped it, the wind chilled her.

Ian, walking next to her, glanced over the third time she unzipped and rezipped her coat. "You all right?"

"Yes." She was careful to speak calmly. Ian was jittery about this excursion, and she didn't want to give him additional reasons to worry about her. "It seems mild out here, but when the wind picks up—"

"Yeah, that's spring for you," Ian said.

Spring. Soon the scent of lilacs would sweeten the air, the way they had that night sixteen years ago when she'd returned home from the spring dance unexpectedly early following that ridiculous quarrel with Cliff Coleman.

Ridiculous and petty. A disagreement over the planning of activities for upcoming Founders Week that began casually while they were dancing and escalated into a public quarrel. *"You can't stand to let anyone else have input, can you, Ali? It's all about you, what will make you look the best, what will give you the most glory."*

She'd finally stalked out of the dance, ignoring the friends who had wanted to console her and gossip about the fight. She hadn't wanted anyone to see her cry. The only place to go was home.

Two hours before her family expected her.

Her parents had never imagined she'd leave the dance early. She had attended every school function and stayed until the end, making herself visible, savoring admiration.

Sweat soaked her hands. She peeled off the mismatched gloves Halbrook had dug out of the lost-and-found. She wanted to remove the knit hat but didn't want her dark hair making her more recognizable—not that she thought anyone would give Ian and her more than a cursory glance. Ian was wearing a baseball cap that shadowed his face, and from her police work, she knew people didn't tend to be observant.

They were approaching her neighborhood, passing familiar landmarks. The elementary school surrounded by a chain-link fence. Security lights illuminated the deserted playground equipment.

"Ali, stop pushing. I'm dizzy. Quit, I said!" Callie's brown ponytail flying, her skinny arms wrapping frantically around the bars of the merry-go-round. *"That's too fast!"*

Alisa laughing, wood chips scrunching beneath her tennis shoes as she grabbed the bar and gave the merry-go-round another whirl.

"Stop it! I'll throw up. Stop! I'm telling Mom."

Another spin. Callie's arms slipping from the bar. Callie hurtling off the merry-go-round, crashing against the tree behind her. Callie in a bloodied heap—

Alisa drew a wobbling breath and pulled her gaze from the dull metal of the merry-go-round. *Stop treating your hallucinations like memories. You know it didn't happen like that. She wasn't hurt. Just scared.*

Why did I take pleasure in scaring her?

"Alisa?" Ian touched her arm.

She realized she had slowed her pace and veered too close to the fence. She tried to walk faster, but her legs were rubber.

"Did you go to school there?"

She nodded. If she started breaking down at the sight of the school, Ian would drag her back to their hideout before she even got within sight of her home.

He paused at the gate to the school grounds. It stood ajar. No one had locked it in her day either. "Do you want to go onto the grounds?" he asked.

She looked at him in surprise. She'd expected him to hurry her through this trip with no detours.

He gave her a wry smile. "I'm under orders from Jill. I am to let you go wherever you want and stay as long as you want—within reason."

Alisa slipped her fingers through the links of the fence and clung so hard that the cold metal dug into her flesh. "She said that?"

"She understands why you want to do this. She said in your position, she'd want to do the same thing, that it would help her get memories clear in her mind, even though things would have changed a lot over sixteen years."

Alisa looked through the fence at the merry-go-round, emotions roiling at the thought of Jill's championship. Jill understood the havoc Broc4 could wreak on memories, but she couldn't understand Alisa's guilt. She was too innocent.

"Do you want to walk around the school grounds?" Ian asked again. His voice was gentle.

"No." Alisa kept gripping the fence, the wires hurting her fingers. The swings, Callie in one, Alisa in the other, their feet straining toward the sky. Always, she had to swing higher than Callie, so high that Callie would shout in alarm.

Why had she felt that compulsion to be braver, smarter, prettier, to outdo Callie in every way? Callie had never wanted to compete. She'd just wanted a companion, a friend.

A sister.

Weak and useless. That was how she'd viewed Callie once they'd reached their teen years, and she'd pounded that message into Callie's ears. Every humiliated blush on Callie's face, every glint of tears, every shrinking back from vicious words—each was evidence that Alisa was stronger. Superior.

Regret slashed her chest, slit her heart, punctured her lungs. She couldn't breathe.

"Alisa," Ian said softly. "It would be better to go into the schoolyard. We're too conspicuous standing here on the sidewalk."

"No . . . let's move on." She released the fence and stepped back.

Ian reached out, interlaced his fingers with hers, and resumed walking toward the house.

"Your hands are ice." He drew her hand with his into the pocket of his coat.

At his touch, tears spilled, blurring her vision, crawling in cold streaks down her face. A car drove past. Alisa averted her face from the glow of headlights. Crying on the street. She was a fool.

"Would it help to talk about it?" Ian asked.

She shook her head. Nothing she could say would take them back in time so she could remove the hurt and give Callie the love and respect she'd deserved. Callie was dead, murdered by prison guards.

My fault.

"If you want to spread it out, do this over a couple of nights, we can come back tomorrow or the next night," Ian suggested. "We don't have to do it all at once."

Alisa struggled to master her emotions. It would be monumentally stupid to keep coming back; Ian knew that. He was hoping he could persuade her to leave then talk her into not returning. "Let's finish it," she whispered.

"Are you trying to help yourself or punish yourself?"

She didn't know. Whatever semirational reasons she'd had for doing this were now rubble. She could feel only the relentless compulsion to go home.

They passed the post office. The brick exterior had been gray sixteen years ago. Now it was painted white, but otherwise, it looked the same.

Maplewood Drive. The third house from the corner. Light showed through bent window blinds. The paint was peeling. The rhododendron bushes were overgrown. David would never have let the property get that way.

She tried not to slow her gait as they walked past. People were home there, and she couldn't risk lingering.

The porch swing was gone, the swing where she'd sat to brag about her latest triumphs—until she'd realized that beneath the fatherlike affection David had always shown her and Callie, he'd disapproved of her diamond-hard ambition. She'd grown impatient with his efforts to coax her into greater awareness of others, greater compassion, greater empathy.

She'd pushed him away like she had her parents.

"Is that your house?" Ian asked, and she realized she was digging her fingernails into his hand.

"No." She forced herself to relax her fingers. "That's . . . it was David Garrett's home. It's—changed."

Ian squeezed her hand.

Two more houses. Across the street. Sickness spread from her stomach to her chest. Her legs went feeble, and her heart raced.

Her house was dark, the blinds gaping open. Dead weeds and mud made the yard a wasteland. A sign in the yard advertised it for rent, available immediately. It must have come on the market within the last few months, or she would have seen it when Jill and she checked the older listings for a place to stay.

She started up the front sidewalk. Ian pulled her to a stop. "We'd better not."

Alisa inhaled cold air deep into her lungs. "It's all right. No one's living there." She worked her hand out of his and cut through the weeds to the back of the house.

The wooden patio where her mother had barbecued hamburgers on summer evenings was weathered and warped. Boards creaked under Alisa's feet as she stepped onto it. Ian followed her, all but stepping on her heels.

Most of the paint had worn away from the screen door, and the screen was torn, but it was the same door. She remembered that circular pattern in the metal. The door had never closed correctly, slamming shut the instant you released it. She pulled the door open and let it go. It shut with the same speed she remembered. Ian thrust his arm between the door and the frame in time to keep it from banging loudly.

"Alisa," he hissed.

"I'm sorry. My father meant to fix that." She pulled the screen door open again and pressed her face against the window on the back door. Bands of moonlight illuminated the blue-patterned tile on the kitchen floor. She cupped her hands around her eyes and studied the familiar scrollwork on the empty built-in hutch.

It didn't surprise her that no one lived here. Homes once owned by traitors often maintained a stigma that made them difficult to sell, and it was no surprise that her house had apparently ended up in the control of an indifferent rental company.

If they hadn't ever fixed the back door, they probably hadn't fixed the windows. The one next to the heat pump didn't latch correctly. That was how she'd crept into the house on that last night. She'd eased the window open and hoisted herself inside, planning to sneak into her bedroom unseen. She hadn't wanted her family to see her crying and stick their noses into what was wrong.

"I'm going inside," she said.

Ian reached past her and rattled the doorknob. "Locked," he said. "We didn't bring any tools to—"

"I think I can get in the window by the heat pump." She tried to move past Ian, but he blocked her.

"Wait a minute. This house isn't isolated like that dump where we're staying. We could get caught."

"I can do it quickly."

"Forget it. We're not sneaking in there like burglars. If someone sees us and calls the police, it's over."

"Who could see us?" A fence ringed the backyard, blocking it from the view of surrounding neighbors. "It will be all right."

"I don't like this," Ian said, but he stepped aside.

With Ian trailing her, she hurried to the familiar window. She leaped onto the heat pump, popped the screen out of the window, and handed it to him.

The window stuck, but Alisa jiggled it, and it slid open. She climbed through the opening into the utility room. Ian followed her and swiftly shut the window behind them. "I don't like this," he said again. "Let's keep it quick."

The utility room was freezing and smelled of mildew. She pulled the flashlight from her pocket, but Ian swiped it out of her hand.

"No light. We can't risk it."

Alisa gouged her fingernails into her palms. She had to calm down. She was making poor judgments, putting them at risk.

Spilled soap gritted under her shoes as she walked slowly across the utility room. Whoever had recently moved their appliances out hadn't bothered to sweep up.

When she'd come in after the dance, she'd slipped her shoes off, tiptoed along in her socks, her heart churning with fury at Cliff, her eyes achy from rare tears. If only she hadn't been so stealthy—if only she'd bumped into a laundry basket and knocked it off the counter or jarred the wooden drying rack so it had bumped against the wall—*any* noise that could have penetrated to the living room and alerted her parents that she was home. Anything to give them time to conceal what they were doing.

Soft voices from the living room. Her father. David. She'd had one foot over the threshold of her bedroom when words came clearly to her ears. Words speaking of God, of commandments, of faith.

Treason.

Paralysis. Disbelief. Then she'd crept toward the living room, her feet noiseless, her heart pounding wildly, her shoes still clutched in her hand. She'd listened to David, her father, her mother, Callie. Listened to them read, listened to them talk.

Listened until anger and betrayal built inside her to a numbing rage.

A hand touched her shoulder. She jumped, gasping.

"It's just me," Ian whispered urgently. "Are you all right?"

"Yes."

"Are you having reversions?"

"No."

"Keep this up and you *will*. This whole thing is a rotten idea. Stop punishing yourself. Let's go."

"A few more minutes."

"No. We're leaving now."

Alisa faced him in the darkness. "I don't need your permission to remain."

In the moonlight through the window, she could see him shove his hands into his pockets, plainly fighting the urge to drag her out of there. "I'm begging you to listen to me. You won't find anything here except pain. Show yourself a little mercy and let's go."

"Did I ever show *them* mercy?" Her voice was too loud for the graveyard silence of the house. She lowered it. "Do you know what I was thinking when I betrayed them?"

"Alisa."

"I wasn't thinking of national security. It had nothing to do with patriotism. I just wanted to hurt them. They'd turned against me. They'd shut me out. They were jeopardizing *my* future. I wanted them to pay for it."

She could still see the shock on their faces when she'd stepped into the room, could hear her mother's voice calling her name as she'd fled, her father and David in pursuit, could feel the damp grass soaking her socks as she'd darted between houses until she'd eluded them.

The police had arrested her mother and Callie at home, where they were waiting for her to calm down and return, believing that no matter how angry she was, she'd never turn them in.

Ian's hands closed on her shoulders. "You've punished yourself enough. It's time to focus on forgiveness."

She jerked away from him. "Nothing can bring my family or David Garrett back to life. Nothing can mend the other families I've ripped apart or remove the pain I've inflicted on more people than I can remember. It's absurd to talk of forgiveness."

Information he'd studied intensively saturated his thoughts. "You're an intelligent woman. Do you want to explain how you could read the Book of Mormon and remember it clearly enough to chastise me straight from its pages yet apparently miss the whole point of the book?"

She couldn't stop either her trembling or the tears once again spilling down her face. "You speak of the Son of God and His Atonement for sin."

"Do you believe it's real?"

She couldn't answer, couldn't even seize coherent sentences out of the welter of memories.

"You believed that book enough to draw on what you'd read when you were suffering the worst pain of your life. I think you know God is willing to forgive you—wants to forgive you. But you won't ask for that forgiveness because you've already decided you don't deserve it."

She walked down the hallway, guiding herself with a hand on the wall, and entered the empty living room. Her father and mother had been sitting on the couch underneath the window. Callie had been sitting cross-legged in the easy chair next to the bookcase. David—

"*Alisa.*"

She looked at Ian. The streetlight shone brightly enough through the bare front window that she could see him clearly. His shoulders were hunched with tension, and his arms were tightly folded, but his eyes were calm.

"You'd give anything to repair the damage you've done, but you can't," he said. "So rather than admit this problem is beyond you and put it in the hands of the only person who can free you from this burden, you'd rather stand alone until the pain demolishes you."

Wanting to close the blinds, she headed toward the window but stopped herself. She shouldn't do anything to change the appearance of the house from the street. "I can't ask for relief from this guilt when I've done nothing to earn forgiveness."

"You're doing everything you can. Remember Alma? The one whose story gave you the strength to pray when you were in the Annex?"

She nodded.

"Then you remember Alma did terrible things. Do you think everything he did wrong was set right when he changed his life? Do you think every person he drew away from God, every person who turned to evil because of him—do you think every one of those people instantly regained their faith? Or were there things Alma did that he couldn't fix?"

Shivering, Alisa touched the dusty windowsill. It felt colder in here than outside.

"He did everything he could possibly do to repair the wrongs he'd done, and he did an unbelievable amount of good. But it was only because of this sacrifice made by the Son of God that Alma was able to put his guilt behind him. On his own, he would have remained trapped in agonizing regret, unable to do the incredible good that he did. Does that sound familiar?"

She couldn't answer him. If she opened her mouth, she'd scream uncontrollably like she had that night when she'd finished talking to the police hotline and realized—one minute too late—the consequences of what she'd done.

"Alisa, you can't bring your family back. You can't undo the past. But you *can* move forward like Alma. And don't doubt that God is offering His comfort and peace to anyone you've harmed who'll seek His help. You say things are hopeless because you can't undo the consequences of your actions. He offers blessings that far outweigh whatever anyone has suffered at your hands."

Her knees were about to buckle. She sat down on the matted carpet. It must be the same flooring from sixteen years ago.

Ian knelt next to her. "Alisa—"

"I . . . need to be alone."

"I don't think—"

"Please." Her voice choked. "I'll stay in this room. But I need to be alone. Fifteen minutes. Then I'll leave whenever you say."

"You'll leave?"

"Yes."

Hesitantly, he straightened up. "All right. Fifteen minutes. I'll wait in the utility room. Call if you need me."

He retreated, leaving her alone in this room she had rendered cold and musty and empty. With the comfort of Ian's presence gone, pain consumed her, a raw agony of torn flesh and shattered bone.

Alma.

Tears drenched the hands she pressed over her face. "I'm sorry," she whispered. "I'm sorry. I don't deserve mercy. I don't deserve peace. But please—" She struggled for breath.

Please forgive me.

* * *

His leg aching from the trek to Alisa's house and the climb in the window, Ian sat on the utility room floor, propped his leg on a drawer he'd pulled out from the storage cabinet, and kept checking his watch. At fifteen minutes and twenty seconds, he wanted to be out the window with Alisa and heading back to the hideout where Jill waited, this excruciating trip finally over. But when fifteen minutes had passed and he started out of the utility room, a strong impression stopped him in the doorway.

Wait.

A second attempt, fifteen minutes later, brought the same unmistakable message.

Wait.

He sat on the dirty floor, propped his leg on the upside-down drawer, and waited, eyes closed.

He had no idea how much more time passed before Alisa entered the utility room. She thanked him for his patience and said she was ready to leave. She said nothing of what had taken her so long, and he didn't ask. If she wanted to share it, she would.

On the trip home, she was quiet, walking slowly, holding his arm for support. In the glow of the streetlights, she looked pale and exhausted.

And at peace.

Chapter 23

"WHAT DO YOU HAVE FOR me?" Ryce didn't bother to greet Kelleher or offer him a chair. Every joint hurt tonight, and she had no patience for courtesies. "Did you do your research?"

"Yes." Kelleher dropped his coat on the couch in her office and sat without being invited.

It usually amused her that the only person unimpressed by her power and uninterested in making a good impression on her was a doctor with no political influence and young enough to be her grandson. Tonight, his insolence made her want to see how bold he'd still be if she had one of her Guard break half a dozen bones in his scowling face . . .

"You look grouchy," Ryce said crossly. "Did you fail to find evidence to confirm your mysterious theory?"

"I found what I needed. Here's my report." He drew a memory card out of his pocket and set it on the arm of the couch. "I'll give you the summary. According to what I saw on those three execution records and according to the material Daniel Lansbury was studying at the Tremont Research Laboratory in the weeks immediately prior to the executions— material that had nothing to do with his assignment to the Broc series— it's my guess that at the executions of Ian Roshek, Jill Roshek, and Alisa Kent, Daniel Lansbury broke the law and administered an unauthorized drug to the condemned prisoners."

A sense of vindication exhilarated Ryce, dulling the pain in her spine as she leaned forward. "An antianxiety drug?"

"A tranquilizer or sedative in a dose aimed at reducing anxiety would not cause vital signs to plummet like they did."

She frowned. "Then what was the drug? Could you tell?"

"My guess? Your failed wonder drug, Madame President. Preserval."

Ryce gaped at him. "That makes no sense."

"I backtracked through the history of Lansbury's lab record searches for the past three months. For three weeks prior to the executions, he was all over the Preserval records. That drop in vital signs seen in all three prisoners could result from a slow intravenous infusion of Preserval."

"I don't understand. Why give them Preserval only to kill them?"

"*Did* he kill them?"

Ryce gripped the arms of the chair, winced, and relaxed her hands. "You're suggesting he put them in stasis. That their vital signs were so minimal that the monitors didn't pick them up."

"It's possible."

"But the bodies were cremated."

"By Nathan Halbrook, supposedly. Apparently, the police never bother to attend the cremations of executed prisoners, so there's no reason to assume anyone besides Halbrook witnessed the cremations. And I found out more about Lansbury and Halbrook. They've been friends since Lansbury was a child, and Halbrook's like an uncle to him. Halbrook has a reputation for being a troublemaker who isn't afraid to stand up to the police who keep an eye on the Euth Center. It's not too much of a stretch to think he might have helped Lansbury."

Ryce's thoughts reeled. "You're suggesting Ian Roshek and the others are still alive."

Kelleher's voice went sardonic. "Considering the true circumstances of the executions, it doesn't seem out of the realm of possibility that Lansbury might have found an audacious way to defy the Council."

If what Kelleher suggested was true, the executions had been nothing more than a play. A performance. *Alive.* Roshek, the religious believer whose calm in the face of death had haunted her for months, hacking up her sleep, twisting her mind—

No. After all that, he *hadn't* faced death with calm dignity. He hadn't faced death *at all.*

She laughed.

Kelleher didn't ask why she found Lansbury's treachery amusing. "I've explained everything in my report. It will provide enough evidence for Colonel McLaughlin to order Lansbury and Halbrook arrested."

"Bring it to me."

Kelleher rose and brought her the card. She set it delicately on her desk.

"Will that be all?" Kelleher asked. "I've done what I can. It's in police hands now."

Ryce's tumultuous thoughts settled. "I'm not giving this to the police yet."

"What are you talking about?"

"Think about it. Nathan Halbrook is Spencer Brannigan's brother-in-law. Daniel Lansbury is Spencer Brannigan's close friend. Brannigan fervently protested the decision to execute Roshek as a Cadre assassin."

"You're saying you think Councilor Brannigan is involved?"

"It's a possibility. This is a precarious matter."

Kelleher shrugged testily. "Then leave the police out of it. Let your Guard handle it off the record."

"I will. But first I have a few questions of my own. And a score to settle."

Kelleher's piercing eyes took stock of her. "You'd be better off handing this over to the Presidential Guard immediately."

"Go home, Dr. Kelleher. And thank you. I'd offer to reward you if I didn't already know you are ludicrously uninterested in money or acclaim. I need to make some preparations, but I want you to come back tomorrow night at eight. You will personally deliver a message for me."

"A message." Kelleher scratched his head. "To whom?"

"To Daniel Lansbury," she said.

* * *

Being summoned by President Ryce disconcerted Daniel, but having the message delivered by Ryce's personal physician pushed him into complete bafflement. Ryce couldn't be in the habit of using Sean Kelleher as a messenger, but Kelleher offered no explanations—just the message that President Ryce expected Daniel at the Tremont Mansion immediately and Kelleher would escort him there.

Despite the odd summons, Daniel wasn't worried that his father might be engineering this. Amanda Ryce was one of the few people he couldn't lure into his net. Notwithstanding Marcus's negative opinion of her, Ryce wielded tremendous power. Marcus could offer her no enticement to join him, nor would she be suicidal enough to ally herself with him, knowing he'd never be satisfied until he was in her place.

Dr. Kelleher's involvement made Daniel wonder if this had something to do with Ryce's obsessive search for ways to extend life. It didn't seem possible that she could be aware of Daniel's recent request to switch from the Broc series to another project at the lab, but maybe, coincidentally, she was interested in recruiting Daniel to participate in whatever new project she was pursuing in her efforts to ward off death. Considering how highly Ryce valued this longevity research, maybe she liked to approach potential researchers personally.

The opulence of Ryce's private office left Daniel trying not to stare. Pictures of Ryce in her state office were common, but pictures of her private rooms had never been published. Elaborate plasterwork on the ceiling gleamed with gold leaf. More gold adorned the carved furnishings. Large panels of iridescent opal gleamed on her ebony desk.

Sitting behind her desk, Ryce looked frailer and more wrinkled than Daniel had expected. Had it been that long since he'd seen her in person? It couldn't have been more than a few years since he'd accompanied his parents to some government event or other.

Ryce gestured curtly at a chair facing her desk. "Sit down."

Unsettled at the lack of any greeting—or any courtesy—Daniel sat. When he'd met Ryce on previous occasions, she'd always been brisk but pleasant, with a dry sense of humor.

Kelleher sat next to him. The grim look on Kelleher's face and the way he sat with his hands closed into fists and his spine straight told Daniel that Kelleher did not want to be here. What was wrong?

Ryce impaled Daniel with a gaze that made it painful to hold eye contact. Had he done something to anger her? Haines couldn't have told her about Daniel's withdrawing his name from consideration—Marcus wouldn't have allowed it. Had Captain Whitney told her he'd quit the Annex? That couldn't be something the president would deal with personally.

"You are a traitor, Dr. Lansbury," Ryce said. "In tampering with the executions of three vile criminals and sparing their lives, you have become one of the worst anarchists New America has ever known."

So stunned he wondered if his mind had cracked and dropped him into one of Alisa's hallucinations, Daniel couldn't speak.

"For your sake and the sake of your friends, I recommend that you don't waste my time with denials. Is that clear?"

Daniel nodded mechanically.

"Did the Rosheks and Kent know beforehand that their executions were a sham?"

The urge to deny his crimes rose, but he restrained it. Ryce might not know details, but she knew what he'd done. If he provoked her, she'd make the path to death as miserable as possible for all of them. He didn't want Jill and the others to suffer needlessly for his stubbornness.

"No," Daniel said. "They didn't know anything."

Ryce's eyes narrowed. "You didn't tell them?"

"How could I? They were prisoners in the Annex. I couldn't talk about my plans in that setting."

"You didn't forewarn them in any way? Not even a hint?"

From the way she was scrutinizing him, Daniel feared there was a landmine in the question that he was about to step on, but he didn't know what else to give her besides the truth. "As far as they knew, the executions were the real thing. The crime was mine. They had no part in planning it, and they've already suffered more than enough for—"

Ryce lifted a hand. "Very well. This morning, I ordered three people taken into presidential custody. Do you know what that means?"

Daniel shook his head.

"That means my Presidential Guard is holding them, not the police. There will be no delays in carrying out any of my orders regarding them, and there will be no interference from anyone. Do you understand?"

Daniel nodded, still so deadened by shock that he couldn't make sense of what was happening. Three people in custody—she already had Jill, Ian, and Alisa. How had she found them? How had she discovered his treason? She must be working with his father after all. Why?

"The following people are in my custody at the moment: Catherine Darby, Jennifer Mulcahy, and Rachel Wilkes."

Daniel stared at her. Those were the Halbrooks' daughters.

"Do you know these people?" Ryce asked.

"Yes, but they had no involvement in—"

"Very well. If they are innocent, let's make a trade. Give me your three friends, and I'll release the Halbrook women unharmed."

Confusion and terror spiraled inside of Daniel. Why was Ryce acting as though he'd have a choice in whether or not to betray his friends? Why was she dealing with him at all instead of handing him over to Captain Whitney?

"Make your decision," Ryce said. "I'll get the information from you eventually, of course, but if you don't want three innocent people to die along with you, then I advise you to cooperate with me—*now*."

Rachel, Catherine, Jennifer. He couldn't sacrifice their lives. But why this scheme to force confession when a syringe of Broc4 would do the job effortlessly? Would Ryce feel little triumph defeating him through chemical coercion? He'd have no options, then, no ability to control his words. Maybe she'd enjoy watching him voluntarily condemn his friends. Broc4 would follow.

It was a flourish worthy of Marcus Lansbury. "Is this my father's idea?" He immediately regretted the question. If he was wrong, he'd offend Ryce to suggest she was susceptible to his father's manipulation.

Ryce was silent for a moment. He couldn't tell if she was angry at the question; her expression looked shielded, steely. Battle ready. "Why would you think that?"

"Because . . . he's been breathing down my neck for a couple of weeks."

"He's been in contact with you?"

"Not directly. But my mother has visited me twice."

"Your mother is in Tremont?"

"I don't know if she's in Tremont now. She visited me once here and once at Merit Lake."

"She's discussed your father's whereabouts? We had information indicating he'd gone to the United States."

"She's never been specific about where he is or what he's up to. But he's here."

"What *has* she said?"

Daniel related what he'd learned from his mother, including Councilor Haines's involvement. "You'll have to be careful with Haines. If he realizes he's under suspicion, he'll make sure he's never interrogated."

"Thank you for your counsel. Now, as to our bargain." Ryce leaned toward him, poison seeping from fissures in her formerly inscrutable expression. "Where is Ian Roshek?"

* * *

Jill's knowing grin finally embarrassed Ian into focusing on the book he was supposedly reading instead of letting his gaze stray—as it had repeatedly throughout the morning—to Alisa.

Alisa was leaning against her rolled-up sleeping bag, working on a new embroidery project. She hadn't had much to say about the trip to her house two days ago, but she didn't need to speak for Ian to perceive the change in her.

Alisa had always been beautiful—an unexpected, incongruous beauty on the merciless woman he'd first met, then a familiar beauty always shadowed by pain on the face of a friend. But he'd never observed the breathtaking beauty he saw in her now.

The radiance. The joy.

He realized he was staring again. He lowered his gaze and jammed another few lines of text into his brain, but he couldn't even remember what the book was about.

"What do you think?" Jill turned her sketchpad to display her progress on drawing the budding branch she'd snapped off a tree in the backyard.

Ian glanced fleetingly at the sketchpad. "It's a masterpiece."

Jill spoke sweetly. "Is there something else you'd like me to sketch for you? Something more . . . interesting . . . to you than a branch?"

Heat flared in Ian's face. "Sure, Jilly. Why don't you draw that picturesque old stove in the kitchen? It will be a nice memento for when we get out of here."

"I'd *love* to." Jill picked up her pencil. "But I'm comfortable where I am. Would you like to choose something in this room?"

"How about that charming paper bag taped over the window?" Ian hoped Alisa was too focused on her embroidery to notice and interpret Jill's teasing. He risked a glance at her. She was separating a strand of embroidery floss, not looking up, but the lamplight showed a blush in her cheeks. Her lips curved in a flattened, lopsided shape; she was repressing a smile.

"Never mind," Jill said airily. "I'll stick with branches for now."

Ian couldn't help grinning. That half smile on Alisa's face made him not mind at all being stuck in this dreary, cold house, showering in ice water, and subsisting on crackers and granola bars.

Jill reached for her pencil sharpener and asked, "Is anyone interested in a midmorning snack?"

"I think all of our meals qualify as snacks," Ian said. "How about beef jerky on a cracker?"

"I'd give anything for a steaming bowl of corn chowder and a loaf of fresh-baked—" Jill stopped.

Ian jumped to his feet. He'd heard the noise too—a squeak . . . a rattle.

A door opening?

"*Wait*," Alisa whispered. "It might be nothing. The wind."

Ian stood rigid, fighting an urge to herd them all out the window. Alisa was right. It would be unwise to panic at a slight noise and draw attention to themselves by fleeing the house.

When no other alarming noises followed, he sighed and sank back onto his sleeping bag. "Nothing like a scare to keep things interesting. Pass the crackers, will you, Jilly?"

"Graham or saltine?"

"Surprise me."

Jill reached for the food supplies stacked against the wall. "With the beef jerky, I recommend the—"

"Hello?" a voice called. "Hey, kids? Don't panic! It's Nate Halbrook. Where are you?"

Already on his feet at the first word and hauling Jill toward the window, Ian stopped.

"You just dislocated my shoulder." Jill pulled her arm free and bent to pick up the pencils that had spilled when Ian yanked her to her feet.

"Sorry. All adrenaline and no brains. I hope this is good news." Ian walked to the door and stuck his head into the hallway. Nate's heavy footsteps moved through the living room.

"Back here," Ian called.

Nate appeared at the end of the gloomy hallway. "What a dive you people chose as a hideout." His voice was a thin counterfeit of his usual joviality.

"What's happened?" Ian asked.

"Long story. Are you all together here?"

"Yeah, come in." Ian stepped back. Nate would only have spent hours checking for their coded message and driving to their location for something extremely serious, good or bad. And he didn't sound happy.

"Ladies." Nate nodded at Jill and Alisa, but the lamplight illuminating his face confirmed that this wasn't good news. Nate looked heartsick.

"What's wrong?" Alisa asked.

Nate closed the door. "Maybe you three ought to sit down."

Jill was so pale that Ian feared she would fall, but before he could move toward her, Alisa grasped her elbow and helped her back to her place on the sleeping bag. Ian remained standing, bracing himself for whatever bad news Halbrook was about to deliver.

"Sit down, Roshek. Please. You're making me nervous."

Ian sat next to Jill. Nate stood with his shoulders drooped and head bowed. He picked up the camping lantern from the center of the floor.

"I'm sorry," he said. "I'm so sorry." He switched the lantern off, leaving the room dark.

"Wait a minute," Ian protested. Something hit the floor with a clunk. There was a pop and a hiss and a rush of wind brushed his face. His throat burned and dizziness swooped through him.

"Get out of here!" Alisa cried. "Go! Hold your breath!"

"*Nate*—" Ian staggered to his feet and fell instantly, his knee crushing a box of crackers. He heard a shuffle of movement—Jill—Alisa—

His head hit the dusty wood floor.

Chapter 24

THE THICK PILLOW UNDER HIS head and the fleece blanket covering him gave Ian the foggy thought that the Detention Annex had certainly upgraded their cells since he'd been here a few months ago. The Annex cells didn't used to have wooden doors, ceramic tile floors, and walls painted pristine white.

Or cellmates. Daniel was sitting on a bed across the room, elbows on his knees, face in his hands.

"Daniel," Ian rasped.

Daniel lifted his head. His skin was gray, his expression lifeless.

"What happened?" Cautiously, Ian sat up, gritting his teeth at a pounding headache. This wasn't the Annex. "Where are we?"

"The Tremont Mansion."

"Uh . . . we are?" What were they doing at President Ryce's residence? "How did we end up here?"

"President Ryce figured out what I did at the executions." Daniel's voice was as dead as his expression.

"*Ryce* figured it out?"

"Yes."

"How?"

"No idea. But I . . . told her how to find you."

No wonder Daniel looked so rotten. "I'm sorry, Daniel. She already put you through Information Extraction, didn't she?"

"Not yet." Daniel's eyes were clouded. "I don't know why she hasn't."

"Why are we here? Why aren't we at the Annex?"

"I . . . assume she wants to keep things discreet. Because of Councilor Brannigan's involvement."

"Tell me what happened. Start at the beginning."

Daniel explained in monotone, leaving Ian with a horrified understanding of why Daniel had voluntarily yielded up their location and why Nate had participated in their capture.

"Do you think she's released them yet?" Ian thought miserably of the pictures of the Halbrooks' daughters and their families displayed all over the Halbrooks' house.

"I don't know. I hope she was telling the truth about letting them go." Daniel lifted his hands and let them flop to the bed. "I'm sorry. I didn't know what to do. She was going to get the information anyway, and to sacrifice the lives of three innocent—"

"You did the right thing. She had us. There was no point in fighting it." Ian sank back on his pillow. Sitting up too long made him dizzy.

"Do you know anything about Jill and Alisa?" Daniel asked.

"No. Nate knocked us out at our hideout, and I didn't wake up until now."

"*Nate* was there? She made Nate come after you?"

"Apparently." Ian pressed his fingers against his aching temples. "I wish there were some way to convince the police that Jill and Alisa don't know anything that I don't. They don't need to interrogate all of us. There's no need for the women to suffer."

Daniel gave him a tired look. "Do you think sparing us suffering is a priority?"

Anguish washed over Ian, tossing his emotions like driftwood. *Please, not again.* Jill had already been through this once. And Alisa couldn't endure another interrogation.

"I'm sorry," Daniel said. "In trying to rescue the three of you, I only put you through more torture, and in the end, you'll die anyway. And I sacrificed Councilor Brannigan and Nate and Rebecca . . ."

Ian pictured Rebecca nervously crocheting and chatting about her grandchildren. The Halbrooks knew information that could humiliate the government. They wouldn't receive a prison sentence. They'd both be executed.

Ian felt woozy and cold, and his clothes—a khaki uniform he didn't recognize—were clammy. He tried to reach for the blanket he'd pushed down but couldn't reach the edge of it without sitting up.

"You okay?" Daniel asked.

"Doing as well as you are." Ian closed his eyes. "Just wishing Nate and Rebecca . . . and Councilor Brannigan—"

Ian heard Daniel stand. "This is going to shatter the reform movement." Daniel pulled the blanket up to Ian's shoulders. "That's what Councilor Brannigan feared. You dizzy?"

"Getting better." Ian looked up at Daniel. "If President Ryce is being so careful to keep this secret, maybe it's because she *doesn't* want it to destroy Brannigan's reputation. Maybe they'll cover for him, like they did for your dad."

Daniel returned to the edge of his bed. "They'll cover for him publicly, yes, but the Council will know the truth, and none of them will want to spearhead causes formerly led by a traitor. The reform movement will still die."

"If it does, it's temporary. Brannigan can't be the only person sickened by the problems in New America."

Daniel said nothing.

"Look, we did our best," Ian said. "And I guess the good news is they can't keep us around long. We're too much of an embarrassment. Soon, we'll be fine."

A hint of a smile brought some animation to Daniel's face. "That's the first time I've heard anyone speak of their impending execution as good news."

"Hey, I'm an expert on being executed. It's not as bad as it sounds."

"They'll do it right this time," Daniel said bleakly.

"Good. It's about time they gave the job to somebody competent."

Daniel lay back on his bed as though he'd finally relaxed enough to let exhaustion overtake the misery of guilt. Ian stared at the ceiling, hoping shock and his throbbing headache would dampen his concentration. He didn't want to think clearly right now. Clear thoughts would turn to Alisa and Jill and the fact that he could do nothing to help them, had no idea what was happening to them, couldn't stop Ryce's people from hurting them—

Stay calm. He thought of the peace in Alisa's eyes. They wouldn't endure this alone.

"I can't figure out what's going on," Daniel said. "I understand President Ryce's not wanting word to get out that I faked the executions, but the police can be discreet. Or if she prefers, her Presidential Guard could handle us. Why hasn't she interrogated us? She doesn't even seem to have the Guard assisting her. The only person I've seen besides Ryce is her private physician, Kelleher."

"Her doctor, huh? Maybe she's planning to interrogate us on her own."

"Who came to arrest you?" Daniel asked. "Who was with Nate?"

"I don't know. He was the only person we saw. There could have been half the Presidential Guard there, for all I know. Or no one."

Daniel's forehead creased.

"Could this have anything to do with your father?" Ian asked.

"I don't think so."

Ian shut his eyes. He had no idea how to analyze Ryce's eccentric tactics, but no matter what she was up to, they were dead.

* * *

"May I leave?" Kelleher's brusque question drew Ryce's attention away from the screen she was watching. She'd half forgotten he was there, still slouched in his chair, sulking over the role she'd forced him to play in arresting the prisoners.

"Go," she said. "But I may need you at any time."

Kelleher stood. "Good night."

Ryce nodded absently, her eyes returning to the screen. Both Roshek and Lansbury looked tired and dazed, but their voices were composed as they speculated on her motives for not handing them over to the police or to her Guard. Pain showed when the conversation turned to the fates of their coconspirators, but neither of them looked frightened.

Anger simmered inside Ryce.

"Madame President."

Ryce started. She'd been so intent on her video screen that she hadn't noticed Kelleher lingering.

"I thought you were leaving," she said shortly.

"Are you going to sit here all night watching your prisoners? Or are you going to send them for interrogation and get this over with?"

"How long I monitor them is not your business."

"Why did you let Halbrook go?"

"I didn't let him go. I sent him home, temporarily. Fear for his family will keep him cooperative; a cell is superfluous at the moment. I don't want to bother with him yet."

"Does he know you never actually arrested his daughters?"

"Does that matter? He knows I could do so at any moment and will if he doesn't do what I order."

"Have you ordered Councilor Brannigan's arrest?"

Ryce slapped the button to mute the conversation from Roshek's cell. She couldn't concentrate on it until Kelleher was gone. "You know that will need delicate handling if I'm to avoid destroying myself along with him."

"So delicate that you've done nothing about it. So delicate that you not only won't involve the police, but you also won't even involve the Guard. Do you plan to send me to arrest him like you sent Halbrook and me after Roshek?"

Furious at Kelleher's gall, she said, "I'll involve my Guard when I'm ready. Get out of here. You're overstepping your bounds."

"I'm your doctor. I'm not a police officer. I'm not a trained interrogator—"

"A point you drove home catastrophically while working on Councilor Haines. Your incompetence cost me a lot."

The threat would have worked on anyone else. Kelleher just looked grouchier, and Ryce knew what he was thinking: he *wasn't* a trained interrogator, but he was a brilliant physician, and if he hadn't been able to thwart the vicious allergic reaction to Broc4 that had killed Haines before Ryce could question him, no Detention Annex medical supervisor would have been able to save him either.

"Get out of here," Ryce snapped. "I'll call you when I need you."

Kelleher didn't turn away. "Guarding your physical and mental health is my job. Here's my professional assessment. If you don't stop what you're doing right now, you're going to destroy yourself."

Ryce pushed back her chair and rose to her feet. "Explain."

He approached her desk. His normally ruddy face was even redder than usual. "I know why you were so interested in Roshek's execution that you studied the record until you noticed something was wrong. I know why it bothered you so much when you suspected Daniel Lansbury might have illegally eased the prisoners' distress."

He rested his palms on the surface of her desk and leaned toward her, a disrespectful pose that made Ryce wish she were strong enough to shove husky, middle-aged Kelleher backward. "I know why you were so dismayed when Lansbury insisted the prisoners didn't know in advance that the executions were fake. You can blame Preserval for the fact that Roshek looked so relaxed at the moment of death, but no drug accounts for how calm he was when the police marched him in there."

"Do you have a point?" Ryce asked icily.

"You're frowning at that screen because you're angry that Roshek is calm and rational and refusing to blame Lansbury or anyone else for his situation. That's why you told me to put him with Lansbury, isn't it? You wanted to hear Roshek raging, but he's not doing it. He's not scared of dying. He's upset about his friends and his sister, but he's *ready* to die. He's *joking* about it. You can't stand that. Is that why you're holding him here? Are you hatching ways to break him down until he's something you don't have to envy?"

Rage gushed through her, the concentrated, dynamic fury no one had dared provoke in her for decades. "If you say one more word on this matter, I'll hand you over to my Guard."

"I'm telling you what you need to hear. I've always told you the truth. That's why you trust me. If you can't endure truth anymore, then kill me. Replace me with a doctor who'll lie to you like everyone else does. Good luck on finding someone who isn't for sale when an enemy makes it worth their while to poison you."

She shoved her hand into her pocket and rested her thumb on the button of the transmitter she carried that would summon her Guard in an instant. "*Get out.*"

"Face up to what you're doing. You can't afford this distraction. You have Marcus Lansbury to worry about. If you don't dare involve the police, order your Guard to execute Roshek and his friends. Turn your attention where it needs to be."

The urge to have Kelleher punished for his insolence was overflowing, wearing away her last effort to remind herself that if she got rid of him, she had no idea who would replace him.

Kelleher lifted his hands from her desk and stood up straight. "If you can't let this go, maybe you need to acknowledge that what you want isn't Roshek at your feet sobbing for mercy. What you want is his courage. You won't get that by watching him like he's an animal in a zoo. Bring him up here and talk to him."

Ryce's reluctance disintegrated. She brought the transmitter out of her pocket so Kelleher could see it. She wanted to relish the expression on his face when she pressed the button and he knew he'd destroyed himself.

Kelleher didn't flinch. "I know you kept his book, Amanda," he said.

Chapter 25

As soon as Holly Sutherland settled into the passenger seat and closed the door, Peale asked, "Could you do it?"

She removed the laptop from her backpack. "Yes . . . yes, there was enough to work with."

"You get good shots of the faces?"

"Not—not perfect, sir. I had to fill in some blanks. But good enough, I think."

"Show me."

Holly opened the laptop. "Was this some kind of . . . test or something?"

"What do you mean?"

"I mean . . . you already knew who was in the pictures and wanted to see if I could do this right?"

"What are you talking about? If I knew who was in the pictures, I wouldn't have wasted my time asking you to fix them up."

Holly bit her lip. "According to the time stamp on the photos, these were taken just over a week ago. Is that . . . right?"

"Of course it's right," Peale said irritably. "Quit stalling and show me what you have."

Holly's hands quivered as she passed him the laptop. "The finished composites are at the top. Beneath each photo are thumbnails of the pictures I used to form the composites along with the steps I used to fill in the blanks."

Peale looked at the three pictures lined up on the top of the screen. Astounded, he tipped the screen to give himself a better angle. The likenesses weren't perfect, but the resemblance was unmistakable.

"I'm—I did my best, sir. But it makes no sense, since . . . I recognized two of the people, and they're . . . dead."

No sense is right, Peale thought, nerves prickling. How could this be? He'd witnessed all three of the executions. He'd been there in person, watching poison flow into the prisoners, watching their breathing stop, watching the monitors as jagged heartbeats flattened into death.

This is impossible.

Holly nervously filled the silence. "I'm confident my work is accurate. Could someone have altered the date stamp, sir? To tamper with evidence?"

Three bodies, bloodless and still. Daniel Lansbury declaring them dead.

Lansbury. Peale clicked rapidly on the thumbnail shots beneath each photo, retracing the steps Holly had taken in creating the final pictures. Following her work made it easy to pick out things he'd missed before—the line of Roshek's profile; the dark blur of Kent's hair blowing across her face but still revealing the curves of her mouth; the angle of Jill's chin.

The Rosheks and Alisa Kent were still alive. He had no idea how Lansbury had done it—Lansbury and Halbrook—but somehow, the executions had been a sleight of hand.

Holly fidgeted with the straps of her backpack. Peale clicked the laptop shut, keeping his expression grim despite his elation. Whatever the facts of the situation, they would certainly be kept classified. No way would the Council ever permit news of hero Daniel Lansbury's treason to become public or allow people to learn that three anarchists had lived three months past their "deaths."

Which meant Holly Sutherland had seen some dangerous things. He could kill her now with McLaughlin's approbation. But she was just a hardworking kid, doing what he'd ordered, and she'd given him the information that would blast him to the top.

"You're right, Holly," he said. "Someone's playing with our minds."

"Is it . . . ? Sir, is the Liberty Cadre back? Is this a message from them?"

"Could be. There were a few strays who escaped. Maybe one of them tampered with evidence to taunt us. To let us know he's out there."

Holly nodded, transparently relieved that Peale wasn't blaming her for the "tampered" photographs. "I won't say a word, sir."

"Good," Peale said. "Because if you breathe one word of this to anyone, you're dead and so are they. When we're fighting the anarchists, we can't play games. Is that clear?"

"Yes, sir. I'd never tell anyone."

"If the anarchists had any idea you helped the police, they'd make an example of you."

Holly twisted toward him, panic in her face.

"Keep your mouth shut, and you'll be safe," Peale said. "Got it?"

"Yes, sir. Are you *sure* they won't figure out I helped—"

"Not if you don't talk about it. Get going."

"Thank you, sir." Holly jumped out of the car and rushed toward her apartment building, obviously wanting to get away from him before an anarchist killer spied them together.

Peale set the computer on the seat and gloated. He needed to report to McLaughlin in person before he took any action. Along with Lansbury and Halbrook, there was a significant—*oh yes!*—chance that Spencer Brannigan was involved. Lansbury would have needed a lot of help to pull this off. And Roshek *had* saved Brannigan's life. Maybe Brannigan had decided to return the favor. This was far better than McLaughlin had hoped for.

And Blake Peale would get the credit for discovering it.

* * *

The man who unlocked the cell door was big and broad shouldered, but he didn't look to Ian like someone accustomed to marching prisoners around. He held a gun, but stiffly, and his expression was tense.

"Put this on." The man tossed something to Ian that looked like a black knit hat. "Pull it over your face. All the way."

Clumsily, Ian pulled the mask over his head and was surprised to find he could see through it easily. Evidently, the goal was to conceal his identity from onlookers, not blind him to render him more helpless.

"Lie facedown and put your hands behind you."

Ian did as ordered. The man handcuffed him, fumbling with the shackles with an inexperience that confirmed this wasn't his usual line of work. Ian turned his head toward Daniel, who sat on the other bed watching stoically.

Kelleher, Daniel mouthed.

Ryce's doctor. Were they ready to interrogate him, then? Kelleher pulled him to his feet, and the partly healed gash on his leg ached more sharply than it had in days, as though anticipation of pain amplified existing pain. *Here we go.*

To his surprise, Kelleher escorted him not to an interrogation room but to an office where President Ryce waited, a room so ornate that it struck Ian as absurd. How much gold could be incorporated into the décor of a room before it began to look like an upscale mutation of a pirate's cave?

Ryce looked older than she did in her news photos and television appearances. The skin around her eyes and mouth buckled into creases, and her hands looked fragile, papery skin marked with age spots. How old *was* she, Ian wondered? She'd been with James Tremont before Separation, a core member of his conspiracy, but Ian couldn't remember if she'd been older or younger than Tremont . . . in her late forties or early fifties at the time, maybe, so she was in her nineties now . . . What was wrong with him? He ought to know her age to the month; he'd studied Separation in detail, taught courses—

Kelleher poked him in the shoulder, refocusing his wandering thoughts, and pointed to a chair. Ian sat in the carved wooden chair accented with enough gold to provide wedding rings for half of Tremont. Kelleher chained Ian's ankles to the legs of the chair and peeled off his mask.

"You're dismissed," Ryce said. Her voice was strong, a young voice from an ancient throat. "I'll call you when I need you."

Kelleher exited.

The shackles scraped against the legs of the chair as Ian shifted, trying to make himself more comfortable. He stopped moving, weirdly concerned that damaging the gilded legs of Ryce's furniture would anger her. *And if you don't chip the furniture, maybe you can have a friendly, cheerful conversation.*

"Please, there's no need to hold the Halbrooks' daughters," Ian said. "They had nothing to do with this."

Ryce stood in front of her opal-paneled desk and studied him. "At your execution in January, did you know Daniel Lansbury and Nathan Halbrook were planning to save your life via the administration of Preserval?"

"No. I didn't even know Daniel had been assigned to perform the executions until he was there sticking a needle in my arm."

"What were you thinking, then, when the police brought you into the termination room? What was going through your mind?"

The question puzzled him, but he didn't dare ask Ryce why it mattered. "I guess I just wanted to get through the execution with some dignity."

"Were you angry?"

"By then I was pretty resigned to what was happening . . . until they told me about Jill, anyway. Have you seen the record of the execution— the record they didn't alter, I mean?"

She nodded.

"Then you know what happened. Yes, I was furious that they'd drag Jill into this mess when she didn't even know anything about the cover-up." Ian mustered his courage. "Ma'am, there's nothing Jill or Alisa Kent could tell you that I can't. We've been constantly together since the executions. There's no need to put them through Information Extraction again."

"Are you pleading for their lives?" Ryce's eyes sliced him, analyzed, cut deeper, analyzed again. "Or pleading for their deaths?"

"I'm asking you to spare them further suffering."

"A quick death, then?"

"Yes." It hurt to say it, but a quick death was the best he could ask for them. "It's plain you want to keep this matter as secret as possible. It would be to your advantage to have fewer prisoners to interrogate."

Ryce walked toward Ian and stopped directly in front of him. Close up, her mien was formidable, and Ian could imagine her cutting his throat at that moment if she decided his existence was too embarrassing for her to send him for interrogation.

"When you faced what you thought was your death, were you afraid?" she asked.

From the way his hands were squashed between his back and the chair, with handcuffs gouging his wrists, he realized he'd unconsciously shrunk away from Ryce. He tilted a little forward and flexed his sweaty fingers. "I wasn't eager to die, especially not under those circumstances."

"I realize that. But that wasn't my question. When they marched you into the termination room, when you knew you had maybe an hour left to live, were you frightened?"

Was she taunting him? He could see no cruel humor in her face, but why else would she harp on this? He thought back, trying to remember his feelings at the execution.

"I was nervous," he said. "Death was something I obviously hadn't experienced before. It's a . . . an unsettling feeling, realizing this portion of your life is over and not knowing exactly what to expect next."

"This *portion* of your life," she echoed.

"You know I'm a religious believer."

"Yes?"

"I believe we lived before we were born. I believe life continues after we die."

"Is that what you were thinking as death approached? After Lansbury had prepped you for the termination sequence? When your life was numbered in minutes?"

"It was, yes. At least until the drug Daniel slipped me had me too dozy to think at all. I was thinking about some things I'd studied about death and resurrection."

"Information from contraband material."

"The Book of Mormon . . . yes."

Ryce walked to her desk. She opened a drawer, removed something wrapped in a white plastic sack, and brought it to Ian. She opened the sack and tipped the object onto his lap.

It was a book. The cover, title page, and table of contents had been torn off, but he recognized it instantly.

She tapped the book with one finger. "Where is the material you were pondering immediately prior to your supposed death?"

"I—don't remember what the exact pages were—"

With power that amazed him, she gripped his shoulder and yanked him forward so his chest was pressed against his knees. She reached behind him, and Ian felt the release of the pressure around his wrists.

Ryce slipped the handcuffs into her pocket and stepped back. "Find the information."

With half-numb hands, Ian picked up the book.

* * *

"Good news, sir?" Rae Pulansky settled primly into the passenger seat of the car.

"You won't believe it," Peale said. "You got everything I asked you to bring?"

"It's all ready, sir." Pulansky patted her computer.

"Well done." The information from the investigation would all be impeccably organized, ready for perusal by Colonel McLaughlin. Peale just needed to add the conclusion, the mind-blowing explanation for Lansbury's behavior—and, almost certainly, the key to destroying Spencer Brannigan.

Peale wanted to bounce in his seat like a preschooler waiting to open his birthday present. He'd been keyed up ever since his visit with Holly earlier that evening, and the fact that he'd had to wait until ten o'clock for a private meeting with McLaughlin had almost driven him insane.

"Are you going to tell me what you found out, sir?" Pulansky asked as Peale sped through Tremont.

Peale smirked. "Guess."

"Does it involve Zero himself?" Pulansky graciously entered into the game of twenty questions.

"Better." Peale couldn't stand it anymore. "Pick up that laptop by your feet and open it."

Pulansky complied. "Are these our pictures you asked that student to— *What?*"

"Crazy, right? Somehow, Lansbury and Halbrook faked the executions. I don't know how. That's what we'll find out as soon as we have Lansbury in I-X. I can't wait."

"Sir . . . are you sure these are accurate?" Pulansky sounded troubled, not triumphant. "The girl who worked on these pictures is an amateur."

Peale was annoyed. "A genius amateur, as good as our crew, and yeah, I'm sure. Go back and look at the pictures you took and see how she put them together. It makes sense, Pulansky. I always thought it was strange that a coward like Lansbury had the guts to execute his sweet little girlfriend. Turns out he didn't kill her at all."

"But I don't understand how he could have done this. We were there. We watched the prisoners die."

"You a medical expert?"

"No, sir."

"Me neither. We'll let the experts work that out. All I know is that three traitors are alive and Lansbury is mine. And there's a good chance Brannigan is involved too. This is what McLaughlin's been looking for."

"Maybe we should . . . wait until we're sure. We could go back to the cabin and—"

"Pulansky!" Peale exploded. "What's the matter with you? We've got enough for McLaughlin to order Lansbury's arrest. We'll get what we need with a shot of Broc4, not a trip to the mountains."

Pulansky didn't respond, and Peale's annoyance increased. He'd expected her to applaud, not get cold feet. Out of the corner of his eye, he saw her lift her hand. He glanced at her.

Pulansky aimed her gun at him. "You're about to pass a shopping center on the right, sir. Pull into the parking lot and stop."

"What the—have you gone crazy?"

"The next driveway. Turn. Now."

Peale swerved into the lot and screeched into a parking space. "What's *wrong* with you?"

"Sir, we can't report this to Colonel McLaughlin."

Peale goggled at her meek face. "Did you know about this all along? Are you working with Lansbury?"

"No, sir. Not with Daniel Lansbury, and I know nothing about the Rosheks or Lieutenant Kent or what Dr. Lansbury did at the executions. But I know we can't report this to Colonel McLaughlin."

Disappointment and anger kicked Peale in the ribs. "Zero," he said. "You're working for Lansbury's father, and he doesn't want his son in trouble. You snake."

"I don't want to kill you, sir. You're a valuable officer, and with the changes that are coming in New America, we'll need you. Think about it. You always wanted power. You can have it, if you're willing."

"You sneaky—If you were working for Zero, why did you go along with me in investigating his precious little boy?"

"It's what Zero wanted me to do, sir. That way I could keep him informed at every step."

"Why didn't he shoot me to keep me from figuring out what a coward his son is?"

"I told you. We don't want to hurt you if we don't have to. And if you'd died, Colonel McLaughlin might have encouraged someone else to investigate Councilor Brannigan, which would have led them to check out Daniel anyway. This way was better. Take your stun square, sir. Now."

Fuming, Peale jerked the stun square off his belt.

"Use it on yourself. I need to talk to some people to figure out what to do with you."

He'd seen Pulansky in action. If he balked, she'd shoot him without hesitation. "I never thought you'd be a big enough idiot to turn traitor."

"I won't be considered a traitor when Councilor Lansbury is in charge. Big things are coming, things you'll like. But I don't have time to explain them now." She gestured with the barrel of the gun. "Do it. Or I'll shoot."

So angry that he nearly chose the bullet over the stun square, Peale slapped the unit against his chest and knocked himself unconscious.

Chapter 26

Up until the last few years, Ryce had never had difficulty sleeping, no matter what the circumstances. Even in those thrilling and terrifying days before Separation when she'd worked in secret with James Tremont to overthrow the corrupt United States government, she'd never found it hard to put the challenges of the day aside and settle into restful slumber. Through the failure of their initial ambitions to win control of the United States, through the founding of their own breakaway nation, through the turbulent early years of New America, through the perilous maneuvering that had allowed her to step into the presidency when Tremont died—through it all, she could drop into bed, shut down in minutes, and sleep without waking.

No more. Now she spent part of every night sitting in the chair next to her bed, exhausted but not sleepy, her thoughts shadowed with awareness of her mortality. She hated the hours between midnight and dawn.

Tonight, she'd headed straight for her chair, not even attempting to go to bed. Wild thoughts coiled in her head as she sat with earphones on, listening to her earlier conversation with Roshek. At the beginning, his voice had been tight, his sentences short. He'd thought the only reason the president of New America would dig into his beliefs was to map his vulnerabilities to the end of designing a more exquisitely fitting punishment for him and others like him.

Hadn't that thought been at the back of her mind, her last flicker of justification for what she was doing?

But as her questions had pushed him deeper into his book, his voice had strengthened, his hands had steadied, and the guarded look on his face had opened into an expression of such conviction that Ryce couldn't doubt he truly believed his delusions. He read passage after passage, giving her far more than she'd asked for, speaking of death and resurrection and judgment, repentance and atonement and eternal life, relating stories of believers in days gone by, of nations destroyed when their people fought against God, of nations thriving in peace and prosperity when they obeyed God.

How James Tremont would have hated Roshek. It gave Ryce perverse satisfaction to know she'd sat in Tremont's obnoxiously bejeweled office discussing the book he'd hated above all others—and he could do nothing to stop her. He no longer had the power to punish her for violating the oath they'd made with each other, vowing to fight the corrupting influence of religion.

Too bad for Jim Tremont.

But it had shaken Ryce to find out Kelleher knew she'd kept the book. She should have known he'd sense something amiss when she'd ordered the police to hand over the troublesome propaganda David Garrett had brought when he'd left his refuge in the United States and returned to New America. She should have known he wouldn't be fooled by her insistence that she had the right and responsibility to destroy it personally—or deceived by her charade of burning a fake book consisting of a stack of printed pages cut to the same size and shape as Roshek's book and glued into the book's cover.

She'd told herself she wanted to examine the book privately to better understand this threat to New America. But she'd left it locked in her drawer, repulsed at the thought of reading it, wondering why she'd been foolish enough to keep it, but unable to throw it away.

Why *hadn't* she read it? She'd read a multitude of other philosophies, but she'd always skirted the philosophies of Tremont's worst enemies, not wanting to propel her eccentricity past the point where her supporters would tolerate it.

Kelleher could have effortlessly destroyed her. A hint to her enemies . . . They would have given him anything he wanted in exchange for the information that would bring her down.

Fortunately for Ryce, Kelleher never seemed to want anything except to do his job. She'd never met anyone so determined to avoid political machinations or so uninterested in wealth or power. Either he was an inexplicable anomaly among greedy men and women, or he'd seen too many casualties among the people who fought for gain, including his mother and two of his brothers.

She was beginning to understand Kelleher's cynicism. She'd won the glory she'd sought so many years ago, but what would her victory be worth in the end?

Nothing. She was going to die.

Soon.

When Council Assistant Nadia Sears, followed by Councilor Richard Montoya, had disappeared, Ryce should have known Marcus Lansbury was responsible. She'd let herself be deluded by Colonel McLaughlin's assurances that they'd destroyed the Cadre, that Marcus's secretary, whom they'd arrested and interrogated, had had reasonably complete information about Cadre members and activities. She'd let herself be conned into believing Marcus had fled to the United States because she wanted him gone. But Daniel's information had finally compelled her to recognize what she should have known from the first: Marcus would never leave New America. He regarded it as his inheritance. And he would never settle for anything less than complete control. That meant eliminating her.

He'd worked slowly last time, planning to weaken her and force her out of office. She doubted he'd be so subtle this time. According to Daniel, he was planning something "great" that was already in progress.

For three months, she'd tried to reassure herself that Lansbury could never return from the "dead," but that was self-delusion. Any brainless story about how he'd gone into hiding to protect himself from anarchists but was now back to save the nation would fool a populace that wanted to believe him. And the Council would support whoever had the most power.

Why had she underestimated Marcus?

Because she hadn't wanted to fight him. She hadn't wanted to expend limited energy on another battle, so she'd chosen to fool herself.

She could go to the police and tell them Zero was back and Councilor Haines had been working with him, but for all she knew, she'd be delivering that report to another of Lansbury's conspirators. Lansbury had probably even infiltrated her Guard.

She could order a security sweep, screen everyone at all levels of government, and put anyone with suspicious readings through Information

Extraction—and months from now, when it was all completed, she could go back and start over to catch anyone Marcus had recruited *after* they'd been cleared. Repeat, ad infinitum, trusting no one, paralyzing the functioning of the government. Except the Council would rebel before she could accomplish a mass screening, and Lansbury would order her death.

Then what? She'd always feared annihilation, but if Roshek was correct, it was not oblivion she'd be facing at death but the realization that she'd wasted her life building up a lie.

Which fate was worse?

Kelleher was right, as always. She *was* distracted. Tired and old. She needed fresh counsel, but to seek it was to expose her weakness to a potential enemy. Beyond Kelleher, who did his best to keep himself ignorant of everything going on in the government, there was no one she could fully trust with this issue.

Except, ironically, her prisoners. At the moment, they were the only people she knew to be implacably opposed to Marcus Lansbury. And they had no power to betray her, since she'd never allow them contact with her potential enemies. When she was done with them, she'd execute them privately.

Ryce removed the earphones and dropped them on her bedside table. She rose to her feet, assessed the pain in her hip, and reluctantly picked up her cane.

Slowly, she walked through the empty silence of the house. For the past decade, she hadn't allowed any staff members or even any officers of her Guard to remain in the residential wing overnight. When she was ready to retire, she sealed the steel doors that shut her private quarters off from the rest of the Tremont Mansion, and only her ID chip or the emergency button she carried would open those doors again. Now, the precaution seemed more pathetic than wise—a ritual to ensure that no one could kill her in her sleep but not a ritual that could save her unless she stayed here around the clock.

She stopped in her office to gather the items she needed, then took the elevator to the basement dorm rooms that had housed members of the Presidential Guard before Ryce had evicted them. She'd had the locks on the doors modified so her prisoners couldn't open the doors from the inside.

She drew the handgun out of her pocket, unlocked the third door along the corridor, and switched on the lights.

Alisa Kent sat up, one hand shading her eyes.

"Lie facedown," Ryce said. "Now."

Kent shot Ryce a curious glance before lying prone on the bed. Ryce switched the handgun for the tranquilizer gun she had used on Haines and fired.

The dart stabbed Kent in the side. She flinched but made no effort to remove the dart. Within a few seconds, her body went limp, and her eyes closed.

Ryce entered the room and closed the door behind her. Fingers annoyingly stiff, she plucked the dart from Kent's side and dropped it on the floor, shackled Kent's hands behind her back, and chained her ankles. Finished, she sat on the bed against the opposite wall.

It was a hassle to wait for Kent to awaken, but there had been no other safe way to manage her. Ryce didn't want to involve Kelleher right now, and if she'd tried to talk to Kent while holding her at gunpoint, her hand couldn't have managed the heavy weapon for long. She didn't want to get tackled and disarmed by a former police officer.

Ryce drew the handgun from her pocket, set it on her knees, and waited.

Fifteen minutes later, Kent was awake and struggling to sit up. Too groggy to manage it with her hands manacled behind her, she sank onto her side. "What do . . . you want?"

"Advice," Ryce said.

"Advice?" Kent closed her eyes. "Concerning what?"

"Concerning the most effective way to stop Marcus Lansbury. According to his son, he's here in New America and planning a significant operation. We may assume he's planning to move against the government—and has probably already begun, considering the disappearances of Sears and Montoya."

"Why would you come to me for counsel?"

"You were a top-notch member of the Sedition and Treason Division. Your reputation was impeccable, your work stellar."

Kent opened her eyes but squinted as though still having trouble focusing on Ryce. "Are you . . . that short on advisers you can trust not to betray you to Councilor Lansbury?"

"Maybe I am, Lieutenant. Are you interested in helping me? Or has treason stripped you of any interests except those which promote anarchy?"

"I'll give you any help I can, but I don't know what I can offer. If you've spoken to Daniel Lansbury, I assume he's already told you his suspicions regarding Councilor Haines."

"Patrick Haines is dead."

Kent lay silent, watching Ryce. Ryce had the feeling Kent was attempting to evaluate her as she would have done a suspect in her police days, but traces of tranquilizer and Ryce's expert inscrutability were thwarting her. "How? Did you attempt to question him?"

"I lured him to my office on the pretext of telling him I was appointing Dr. Lansbury to serve as the head of a new life-extension project at the lab, and thus, Lansbury would not be able to serve as his Assistant. He was off his guard; I was able to tranquilize him as I did you. Dr. Kelleher thoroughly scanned him for suicide devices and administered Broc4. An unstoppable allergic reaction killed him before I could ask any questions."

"An allergic reaction?"

"Not something we'd seen before. Councilor Lansbury has apparently developed a way to sensitize someone to Broc4 so the administration of the drug is instantly fatal."

"Given that he's been underground, it's unlikely he's had much opportunity to complete additional research," Kent said. "Which means this isn't new."

"Probably not. Which means he could have done it before for key Cadre members like his secretary, Todd Kinnock, but didn't," Ryce said. "Instead, he let Kinnock think he knew the scope of the Cadre, and then when Lansbury's original plans unraveled, he made no effort to stop us from questioning Kinnock."

"Sacrificing a handful of key people and a few dozen pawns to produce a false sense of security but leaving his most vital supporters safe." A lock of hair fell over Kent's face. She rolled her head, trying to move it out of her eyes. "Which means potentially anyone in your government is with him. If you try to conduct mass screenings, particularly among those at the highest levels, you'll offend and infuriate enough people that you could end up forced out of office. Even people not with Lansbury have secrets they don't want to share."

"I'm aware of that."

Kent tried to sit up again, contorting her body. This time she succeeded. "If you want to defeat Lansbury, it can't be on his terms."

"Explain."

"He thrives on secrecy. His connections are made in secret, his operations are planned in secret. When you try to fight him in secret, you're in his territory, and you're giving him the advantage. If you want to defeat him, force him into the light."

"How do you propose I do that?"

"Tell the nation the truth."

Ryce ran her finger along the barrel of the gun on her lap. "That Marcus Lansbury was the leader of the Liberty Cadre."

"Yes. That he went into hiding when his crimes were exposed. Tell them he was the mastermind behind the bombing at Newbold Bay, along with dozens of other Cadre atrocities. Tell the complete story, including the Council's culpability in hiding his crimes and blaming them on others."

Ryce gave a harsh laugh. "Who are you trying to destroy here, Lieutenant?"

"Turn it to your advantage. You are the one who will no longer manipulate the nation with lies. You are the one willing to stand up and take responsibility for what the government has done."

"You're insane."

"You can't risk trying to gather allies first because you don't know who's working with Lansbury," Kent said. "Rip this open before he can stop you. Not just in New America. Send full reports and documentation to the United States. There are many people here who listen to illegal US broadcasts. Make it so even if your enemies manage to shut down the flow of information here, they still won't be able to silence it. You have the Tremont birthday celebration coming up on Friday. You'll be speaking to the nation. It's a perfect opportunity."

Ryce lifted the gun and her cane and stood up. Time to abandon this nonsense and get some rest. She couldn't fathom what had impelled her to talk to Kent in the first place—a traitor with a mind so damaged it was a wonder she could form sentences.

"If you can convince the people of what Lansbury is, they'll never back him," Kent said. "And once the nation knows the truth, his allies in the government can't risk backing him either. He's lost his power."

"If I tell the people the facts of the situation, they'll never back any of us. You've given me a recipe for chaos."

"Not if you show the people you're willing to change. Don't limit this to a discussion of Lansbury's crimes. I can give you many examples of police deceptions that would infuriate people. Take, for example, the contraband sweep carried out at the University of Tremont last September, where religious literature was planted on students who were then arrested—innocent people sacrificed to spread fear. Those students are still in prison. Release them. Send them back to their families with an apology. Show the nation you are no longer willing to rule through deception."

"Chaos," Ryce said.

"The government has already been moving toward approving the drafting of a written constitution. Tell the people about that. Seek their input. Let Councilor Brannigan speak; he's a convincing voice for reform. If you give people hope, they'll stand with you."

"You've said enough." Ryce wanted to jam the gun against Kent's forehead and watch her beg for mercy. But she *wouldn't* beg. She'd probably wait happily for death.

"You asked for my advice," Kent said. "I'm giving it. Marcus Lansbury shelters himself in the darkness the Council creates. Turn the spotlight on him. On all of you."

Ryce shook her head derisively.

Kent leaned forward, her face radiating the same conviction Ryce had seen in Ian Roshek. "I've told you the most effective way to defeat Marcus Lansbury. If you don't have the courage to tell the nation the truth, then by all means, confront him on his terms. I wish you the best of luck."

* * *

Five sealed white cardboard boxes containing ten medallions each sat on the floor next to Ryce's desk. Each medallion displayed her name and image; each was engraved on the back with the name of a Councilor or Council Assistant. The gifts from the president to the Council were a beloved part of the James Tremont Birthday Commemoration—pens, watches, rings, always some expensive trinket displaying Tremont's name or image or words. This year, Ryce had reveled in the thought of breaking with tradition as she gave not a gift honoring Tremont but a gift honoring herself.

She drew the prototype medallion out of her drawer and studied it. What had once felt like an audacious move now felt like her last move. Her personal copy of the medallion would end up in the National Museum next to a card explaining how she'd been murdered by anarchists less than a week after presenting the medallions to the Council. It was easy to imagine newly appointed President Marcus Lansbury towering next to the display case, denouncing her killers and calling for the nation to eradicate all forms of anarchy.

Turn the spotlight on him—on all of you. Ryce had walked out of Kent's cell wanting to shoot all of her prisoners and be done with it. But silencing Kent wouldn't silence the thoughts now spinning through Ryce's head any more than silencing Roshek would erase his words from her memory.

Kent was suggesting that the only way to defeat Marcus was to destroy the environment in which he thrived. In essence, to tear down the New America James Tremont had built and raise something different in its place.

Naturally. What else would a traitor suggest?

But why *should* she feel obligated to perpetuate what Tremont had started? Beneath all of his high-minded philosophical rhetoric—and he'd excelled at oratory—he'd built New America to feed his own lust for power. She'd sworn to support him in exchange for some of that power, and Tremont had kept his bargain with her. But he'd been dead for thirty years. She was in charge, and if the current political situation no longer served her, why should she keep it?

She had no loyalty to Tremont's memory. He'd hated her the way he'd hated Jonathan Lansbury and the others who'd worked with him, even as they'd labored side by side. He'd needed their strength, but he'd feared that their intelligence and ambition made them dangerous. If he'd recognized how skilled Ryce was at making secret alliances, quietly gaining power while keeping a low profile, he would have killed her like he had several of their colleagues. Not until Tremont was succumbing to cancer and Ryce had a network strong enough to support her had she revealed her quest for the presidency.

Tremont's legacy. What was it worth to her? She'd set New America ablaze herself if it meant she could walk away healthy.

But Marcus would never let her walk away. She'd have to fight him. Did she want to fight on his terms?

Knowledge of her vulnerability ignited burning in her stomach and throat. She despised herself for this sense of inertia that kept her sitting at her desk gawking at her youthful image stamped into gold. No matter what she was going to do, it was time to act.

There was one person who'd have no choice but to help her in whatever way she demanded. She glanced at the clock. Five twenty-two a.m.—the perfect time to jolt Spencer Brannigan out of bed and slap him with the news that she'd discovered his treason.

While she waited for Brannigan to arrive, she'd do some research.

* * *

Dr. Kelleher's hand jiggled Ian to consciousness. President Ryce wanted to talk to him. Yawning, Ian looked at the circles under Kelleher's eyes and wondered sleepily if he would conspire in postponing this meeting if Ian offered to shove Daniel to the floor and let Kelleher use the other cot.

President Ryce, on the other hand, looked manically energetic. Her eyes gleamed, and she fidgeted as Kelleher shackled Ian to the chair, this time leaving his hands free. Kelleher was barely out the door before Ryce thrust the Book of Mormon into Ian's hands and started asking questions again. She wanted more information on the history of the nations recorded in the book—the rise of governments and what had made them strong and stable, the fall of governments and what had preceded their declines, their intrigues and internal power struggles, their political evolutions.

From the depth of her interest, both in this conversation and in the one yesterday, Ian couldn't make himself believe this was merely an intellectual exercise for her or a tutorial on how best to destroy religious believers, but he had no idea what her motives were. He tried to focus on answering her questions without mentally sidetracking himself by obsessing about why she was asking, but that was nearly impossible.

Ryce appeared so immersed in their discussion that a chime from the door seemed to disconcert her. Wrinkled eyelids narrowing, she sat silent for a moment, then smiled and rose to her feet. "Give me the book."

Ian surrendered it.

She stowed it in her desk. "Come in." The door clicked; her invitation had apparently unlocked it.

Spencer Brannigan entered the room, followed by Kelleher. Brannigan's gaze hit Ian. He tried to keep moving forward, but his steps were so ungainly and his face so pale that Ian hoped Kelleher would catch him when he tripped.

"Good morning, Councilor," Ryce said cheerfully. "Please sit down."

Brannigan shuffled to a chair. At a gesture from Ryce, Kelleher sat next to Brannigan.

"I take it you've abandoned your passion for reform within the system," Ryce said.

Brannigan cleared his throat. "Madame President . . . the circumstances . . . I never intended . . ." He looked at Ian.

"I have no idea how she found out," Ian said. "I'm sorry."

Brannigan inhaled and straightened in his chair. "Scandal is something you can't afford at the moment, ma'am."

Ryce laughed. "Appealing to my sense of self-preservation. Your father was my trusted adviser. I'm the one who pushed for your appointment to the Council. Marcus Lansbury tried to destroy me a few months ago by framing you as an anarchist, hoping your downfall would drag me down as well. So to save myself, I should let your treason go unpunished."

"New America is struggling. We need to balance and stabilize the government, and we need to do it in a written charter. I'm not asking you to spare my life. I'm asking you to conceal my treason as you did Lansbury's. Let my death be announced as a heart attack or an accident, then lead the Constitutional Drive yourself. Don't let my mistakes destroy it. Without a course correction in the way we control the allocation of resources—"

"I didn't bring you here to give me your well-worn reform speech. I want you to listen to a radical idea and give me your opinion on it. Dr. Kelleher, go get Lieutenant Kent and bring her up here. I'd like her to be part of this discussion."

Ian's heart jumped. He'd been deeply worried about Alisa. But if she was capable of joining this discussion, clearly she hadn't been through Information Extraction. He tried to keep the gratitude from showing too openly on his face, but Ryce chuckled. "When you bring her in here, sit her next to Dr. Roshek. He looks eager to see her."

* * *

Ian had never participated in a more grueling discussion in his life. It was his background as a historian that interested Ryce now. She mined his knowledge relentlessly, snatching at anything she found relevant to her current situation. At some moments, she seemed intrigued by his analyses of historical events; at other moments, she derided his interpretations with such irritation that Ian felt sure she was on the verge of throwing him and Alisa back in their cells, executing them, and abandoning whatever interest she'd had in Alisa's bold suggestion.

But Ryce's questions kept coming, pounding at Ian, Alisa, and Brannigan in turn as she sought their input. Ryce's strength never seemed to flag, but Ian was exhausted and his words had deteriorated from firm to raspy to croaky by the time she cut the conversation off with the statement that she and Brannigan needed to head over to the Executive Building for the morning Council session.

Ryce instructed Kelleher to escort her out, then return to feed the prisoners and take them back to their cells. She exited her office, her gait steady, her cane abandoned by her desk. Brannigan followed her, looking weary and befuddled.

Alone with Alisa, Ian smiled tiredly at her. She wore an old khaki uniform like his—presumably an old Guard uniform—and socks with a hole in one toe. Her right wrist was handcuffed to the arm of the chair.

"I *would* ask how you're doing," he said hoarsely. "But obviously you're doing fine. Your arguments were brilliant. It took guts for you to suggest that to Ryce."

Alisa smiled. "I can't take credit for the idea. When President Ryce came to talk to me, I had no idea what to say to her. And then . . . it was clear. As to whether or not she'll follow the advice, I have no idea."

"If she weren't seriously considering it, she wouldn't waste"—Ian checked the mother-of-pearl clock on the wall—"three hours talking to us about it. I hope."

"She's been a very pragmatic leader . . . in most things," Alisa said, clearly not wanting to refer directly to Ryce's life-extension fixation while sitting in her office. "If she sees this as the best solution, she may take it."

Ian bent and rubbed his ankles where the shackles chafed his skin. "Alisa, look. I don't know if we're going to have the chance to talk again—"

Kelleher entered the room, carrying a plate of fruit and muffins. Ian fell silent.

After breakfast, Kelleher walked them back to their cells. In Ian's cell, Daniel was still asleep on the other cot. Trying to move quietly, Ian peeled off the mask he'd worn through the hallways and collapsed on his cot.

"When the president is done with her meetings, she wants to talk to you again," Kelleher said.

"Tell her not to hurry," Ian muttered into his pillow.

Chapter 27

AFTER A USELESS DAY SPENT mostly in pacing, Daniel wandered into his father's study on Thursday evening. Somehow, knowing what would transpire soon—what he *hoped* would transpire soon—made him want to stand in the room that, more than any other room in the house, emanated his father's power. The antique rug, the massive mahogany desk, the burgundy leather chairs. The portrait of Daniel's grandfather. Now Jonathan's grandson was poised to help his old rival Amanda Ryce shake up what Jonathan had helped build.

Daniel quashed the urge to unhook the portrait from the wall and shove it in a closet.

The past couple of days had knocked him so violently between despair and hope that he doubted he'd ever feel on an even keel again. He still had no idea how Ryce had discovered his treason. And he'd never imagined she'd commission him to help her stop his father—then send Daniel home.

Not that he was free. Ryce still had Jill, Ian, and Alisa, and she knew Daniel wouldn't make a futile attempt to run, leaving them to pay for his betrayal. The only sense in which she really had to trust him was to trust that he opposed his father, and given how he'd fought Marcus so far, that wasn't much of a gamble for Ryce.

How much did Marcus suspect? He must know Daniel had been escorted to the Tremont Mansion and had stayed there for two days. Ryce was excusing that stay by leaking word that she was considering appointing Daniel to head the team for a new life-extension project at the lab and had brought him to the Mansion to interview and evaluate him. Marcus *might* believe that; it was conceivable that Daniel might have asked Brannigan for help in getting off the hook with Haines, and Brannigan, in his capacity as

Councilor over Health Services, had recommended Daniel to Ryce. But Haines's death was going to make Marcus suspicious. It had already been publicized as a heart attack—not difficult to believe since Haines had had a heart attack a year and a half ago—but Marcus would still be skeptical.

The real question was if Marcus knew Jill and the others were in Ryce's custody. If he did, he knew Ryce had discovered Daniel's and Haines's treason.

No matter what, Ryce had decided that letting Daniel go was the safest choice. If Marcus thought Ryce had imprisoned Daniel and planned to execute him, then, for Jocelyn's sake, Marcus might strike immediately to rescue his son. Ryce needed to buy time. So Daniel was back at home, pacing with the stun square and syringe in his pocket, his plans to capture his father the same as they had been before his arrest, but now under Ryce's direction—and instead of turning Marcus over to the US in exchange for help in escaping, he'd be turning him over to Ryce in exchange for the unknown. Ryce had made no bargains about what would follow for Daniel and the others if this plan succeeded. None of them had asked her—there was no point; she knew they wanted to help her bring Marcus down regardless, and she didn't need to negotiate.

If Marcus did visit him and Daniel did manage to capture him, would Ryce follow through on confessing the truth to the nation? Why would she? Her goal in exposing Marcus's treason and the government's duplicity was to break Marcus's power. If he was dead, she'd won. She wouldn't risk creating upheaval by admitting the government had lied.

Daniel was losing the optimism that had glowed today during the time he'd been working with Ryce. She was an expert at using people. She'd latched on to Daniel and his friends as weapons she could wield in the fight against an enemy. But she was as dangerous as Marcus.

The fact that she wasn't planning to reveal the truth at the Tremont birthday celebration tomorrow troubled him. It was an ideal opportunity, but Ryce insisted it would be disastrous to act too quickly—she needed time to prepare. He understood that, but the longer she waited, the greater the chance that Marcus would move first. At least Marcus was unlikely to suspect what Ryce was planning. He'd never anticipate that she'd risk her own power by spilling the Council's secrets.

If Marcus *did* show up here, Daniel would try to incapacitate him and hold him prisoner, but he would *not* give Marcus to Ryce until after she told the nation the truth.

Unless Ryce was monitoring him so closely that she'd know immediately if he captured Marcus and would come for him. She wouldn't have dared send people to the house to plant bugs lest it tip Marcus off, but Daniel might be carrying some type of injectable bug or tracker on his person. He'd slept heavily that second night—had that been exhaustion, or had he been drugged?

Or was he just paranoid? Yes, but that was necessary in dealing with someone like Ryce. *Be paranoid, then, but don't lose hope.* Maybe Ryce *was* genuinely willing to embrace reform. After all, she hadn't opposed Brannigan's Constitutional Drive.

The room felt eerie. The whole house felt eerie. Daniel interlaced his fingers and bowed his head. The fact that Ryce was even considering telling the nation the truth was a miracle. Additional miracles might come—

A beep from his phone cut off his prayer before it started. Daniel checked the screen and found a text message from Nate.

Hey, Dan. If you have a few minutes tonight, come over. Becky made cookies. If you don't eat them, I will. Save me.

Nate wanted to know what was going on—why Ryce had released Daniel. Daniel had called Nate earlier and given him the "news" that Ryce wanted to appoint him to a new life-extension project, to the end of letting Nate know he was all right. Nate had played along, congratulating him, but Daniel knew he was confused, terrified, clinging to his family, and wondering why he and Rebecca hadn't yet been arrested.

Be right over, Daniel texted back. He headed toward his garage. He couldn't tell Nate and Rebecca what Ryce was up to, but at least he could hint that there was reason for hope.

Trying to figure out what he could safely tell Nate, he settled into the driver's seat and reached for the ignition. A rustle from the backseat startled him, and something slapped against his shoulder. A buzz knocked him into oblivion.

* * *

For a nightmarish period, Daniel thought he was in the Euthanasia Center, prepped for execution. As the mist thinned, some elements of the nightmare faded and others became stark reality. He wasn't in the Euth Center or the Annex. Wooden cabinets and a laminate-topped counter lined one wall. No windows. The bed he lay on and one folding chair were the only furniture.

The door opened.

Daniel stared into his father's face. Marcus appeared as dignified as always, but new coldness chilled his eyes. Ruthlessness formerly kept hidden now showed on the surface.

Daniel yanked futilely at the straps that bound him. When he'd pictured himself confronting his father, he'd never pictured himself flat on his back, helpless. His gaze flicked to the tubing trailing from his arm and the unlabeled bag of clear fluid hanging from a hook on the ceiling. "What are you doing to me?"

"Helping you." Marcus's voice was gentler than Daniel had expected.

Daniel's head ached, and the back of his left shoulder stung when he moved. "I don't want your help."

"You need my help." He laid his hand on Daniel's shoulder. "I want you at my side. I want to teach you. Prepare you to stand at the head of New America. That position will be yours someday, if you're ready to accept it."

Daniel was no longer struggling, but his trembling kept him twitching against the weight of his father's hand. "I don't want to be part of what you're doing."

"You don't know *what* you want, and I'm out of time." Marcus drew his hand back. "I no longer have the luxury of giving you endless chances to recognize your foolishness. Beginning tomorrow, the nation will require my full attention."

Tomorrow. The word was a fist in Daniel's face. The Tremont birthday celebration. Ryce had seemed so sure Marcus wouldn't plan an attack on that day—that given his alleged devotion to Tremont's ideals, he wouldn't risk having followers who knew his identity see him desecrate a day devoted to Tremont.

"What's happening tomorrow?" Daniel asked.

"Are you interested? Didn't you tell me you want no part of what I'm doing?"

"Maybe the problem is that you've never been willing to *tell* me what you're doing. You worked behind my back, and then, when things hit a crisis point, you dropped everything on my head and I didn't know what to do with it."

"Are you admitting you made a mistake in betraying me?"

"I'm admitting the consequences aren't what I anticipated. Get these restraints off of me. I told Mother I was willing to talk to you. You don't have to tie me down to have that conversation."

"I wonder what kind of conversation you intended to have with me, Daniel." Marcus gestured at the countertop, and Daniel saw the stun square and syringe he'd been carrying around.

"Considering the things you've done in the past, I wanted to be able to defend myself in case you tried something like—this." Daniel kicked against the straps.

Marcus turned away and opened the brown leather briefcase he'd set on the counter—the briefcase he'd carried for years. The sight of it spread a disorienting film of unreality over the situation.

This was his father. He wouldn't—"Dad . . ."

Marcus pivoted toward Daniel. Ice filled Daniel's chest at the sight of the familiar vial in his father's hand.

Marcus couldn't do this. He was bluffing. Daniel had been certain, and Ryce had agreed, that Jocelyn would never permit Marcus to risk the life of her only son, no matter how much he might want to interrogate Daniel.

If Marcus put Daniel through Information Extraction now and asked about Ryce—wait—was there any hope Ryce was tracking—

Daniel lifted his head and looked at himself. He was wearing navy flannel pajama pants, a white T-shirt, and white socks—not the clothing he'd been wearing when he was kidnapped. Marcus would have scanned not only his clothes but also his person for any type of electronic device. The stinging in the back of his shoulder—had Marcus removed—

Marcus inserted a needle into the vial. "My only goal has always been to protect and strengthen New America." He tilted the vial and drew back on the plunger. "And you remain stuck in the childish self-centeredness that keeps you focused solely on your own needs. I hope you'll grow past that. You have the potential."

"Dad—"

"You wanted to talk to me." Marcus withdrew the needle and set the vial aside. "Let's talk. Let's discuss your friends and anything else rash you've been up to."

His friends. Even when Marcus found out where they were staying, it was unlikely he'd be able to reach them.

Not while Ryce was alive.

"You've lost your touch if you think I'll fall for a bluff," Daniel said coldly. "Mother would never let you give me something that could cause permanent damage . . . or prove fatal."

Marcus's voice was a razor sliding across Daniel's eardrums. "You betrayed your mother, drove her into hiding, and rejected her efforts to help you. Now, faced with the consequences of your actions, you try to cower behind her."

Familiar shame stirred in Daniel, but he refused to wallow in it. "I never wanted to hurt her. And she won't let you hurt me."

"A healthy young man with no prior exposure to Broc4 or to any drug that might alter his experience with Broc4." Marcus tore open an alcohol wipe. "What are the odds that he'll suffer complications?"

"Dad, don't do this."

Marcus walked to his side, the filled syringe in his hand. A hideous rush of empathy for the countless prisoners he'd helped the police interrogate left Daniel drenched in sweat. He'd never realized how it felt to lie there, unable to resist in any way, awaiting the administration of a drug that would eliminate his ability to control the words coming out of his mouth.

"What do think your mother would prefer?" Marcus asked. "That I leave you alone, assuring a 100 percent chance that you'll die at the hands of the police, or that I run a miniscule chance of complications by extracting the information necessary to clean up the mess you've made and protect you from your foolishness?"

Daniel's thoughts raced. "Whatever you think you'll accomplish tomorrow, it won't work. You can blow up a building, but if you think you can take over the government, the Council will never back you."

"What we need is a new Council. After tomorrow, we'll have one." Marcus reached for the tube extending from Daniel's forearm and swabbed an injection port.

Daniel felt as though he were looking at two people, the face of his father morphing into the face of Cadre killer Zero and back again. "Dad. *Please.*"

"You won't suffer, if that's what you're afraid of. We'll keep you comfortable during your recovery."

"Dad—"

"You're ill." Marcus's expression was soft now—traces of sadness, of tenderness, of affection. "I can help you but not until I've resolved the disaster you've created for yourself. For once, Son, trust me to do what's best for you."

He emptied the syringe into Daniel's IV port.

Chapter 28

THE BUZZ OF CONVERSATION FILLED the Executive Hall as Councilors and Council Assistants waited for the Tremont Birthday Commemoration to begin. Ryce looked out from the dais, scanning faces as apprehension gnawed at her composure.

The commemoration broadcast was set to begin in ten minutes, and Daniel Lansbury's reserved seat was empty. She'd known there was a high probability this would happen, though she'd hoped it wouldn't.

Sending the Lansbury boy home had been a poor option, but provoking his father by holding him was even more dangerous. Ryce hoped Daniel was naïve enough to believe the things she'd told him: that she wasn't planning to reveal his father's treason on the night of the birthday celebration, that she didn't yet have any backup plans for spreading the information if she couldn't broadcast over the national network, that she dared let Daniel go because she was sure his mother would never allow his father to chemically interrogate him. The more Daniel believed these fabrications, the more credibly he'd deliver them to his father if Marcus did decide to interrogate his son—which he probably had by now.

Astute Marcus wouldn't necessarily believe all of Daniel's report, but his contemptuous opinion of Ryce would warp his analysis. Marcus thought Ryce was weak, huddling in her office, stewing over her mortality and fearing to do anything that might endanger her life.

Unfortunately, he was mostly correct, or had been until Ryce had skydived into traitor-inspired insanity a few days ago. She *had* been cowardly for the past few years, her only semisurprising move a tacit endorsement of Brannigan's Constitutional Drive. She'd figured Brannigan's plans would pacify would-be revolutionaries, but she could ensure that no laws were made that significantly damaged her power.

Now, with the information from his son, Marcus would—if she was lucky—think her alleged intentions to procrastinate in revealing his treason grew from cowardice and that she hoped Daniel would capture Marcus for her, eliminating the need for her to risk her own power by exposing his crimes. The tracker Kelleher had implanted would feed this theory, and the fact that Daniel had been unaware of the monitoring would hopefully lead Marcus to assume his son was a pawn, deceived and manipulated by Ryce.

Not that she would have rejected the quiet capture of Marcus Lansbury as a solution to her problems if Daniel had managed it, but she'd known it wouldn't be that easy. Daniel's tracker was still transmitting from the Lansbury home, but her Guard reported that Daniel wasn't there—only the tiny, bloodied tracker, left on the garage floor.

It *would* have been helpful to have Daniel here tonight. His live, firsthand report of his experiences would create immediate sympathy and national outrage, followed by national awe when he told the people how he had saved his friends' lives. When he then endorsed Ryce and her stated goal of eliminating such deception from the way New America was governed, his endorsement would carry great influence.

No matter. Ryce's live speech and the recording of Daniel's and his friends' reports would be nearly as powerful. It would suffice.

Ryce caught Brannigan's gaze. He glanced significantly at Daniel's empty chair.

Ryce shook her head. Brannigan was savvy enough to know what had become of Daniel. Daniel hadn't run away; he wouldn't abandon Jill Roshek. If he wasn't here, his father was preventing it.

She touched a button on her phone and checked the readout. According to the trackers she'd had Kelleher implant in the Rosheks and Kent last night, along with the new ID chips, all three of them were still in Tremont, right where they were supposed to be.

A shudder chilled her. Trying to stay calm, she looked at the fifty velvet boxes stacked on a silver tray on the table in front of her. Once, she'd loved the idea of thrusting the medallions into the hands of both allies and enemies. As tradition dictated, they'd be expected to open the boxes and express their appreciation for the pleasure of a national audience and then later prominently display the gift in their homes. She'd delighted in the thought of her image gleaming permanently among their treasures, no matter how much most of them would rather have sold the gold.

It all seemed so ridiculous now. She could order that her own image be stamped on every scrap of metal in the nation, and it wouldn't matter. *Had* she wasted her life gathering power that, in the end, meant nothing? What a pathetic time to think such thoughts, right before she lit a fuse that might blow the nation—and herself—to dust.

But if she got killed in telling the nation the truth about a batch of religious believers, would she have *one* thing to offer to God after her death?

If she still existed? If God existed?

If the Rosheks, Alisa Kent, and Daniel Lansbury were right?

The word of four witnesses. How much was that worth?

Nothing?

Everything?

Ryce scanned the room, pausing on the face of each Councilor and Council Assistant. Who had already sworn their loyalty to Marcus? Who would stand with her? Who would reject them both and cling to the status quo?

She looked past the government leaders to the spectator seats, where two thousand fortunate citizens hoped the cameras might catch a glimpse of them for envious family and friends. She wasn't worried that one of them might be planning an attack here at the Executive Hall tonight. They'd been checked thoroughly before they'd entered; if any of them wanted to attack, they'd have to do so with their fingernails. As far as the police officers and Presidential Guard providing security within the hall, every one of them had been through a screening conducted by two of Ryce's Guard—captains whom Ryce had screened personally. The sensors used in preliminary screenings weren't foolproof, but they were accurate enough to show something as significant as an inclination to murder Ryce.

Though she hadn't been able to use the sensors to check the loyalty of the Council and Assistants, she *had* ordered her Guard to make sure none of them was armed. No one was going to assassinate her tonight. If Marcus did carry out a Cadre operation tonight—which he might do, despite what she'd told Daniel—he wouldn't strike here. He'd choose a less guarded target. Let him do it if he wanted to. It would only make him appear that much more of a monster when she told the nation the truth.

Her fingers were icy as she touched one of the velvet boxes. Her plan had been to welcome the nation as usual and present the Council and Assistants with their traditional gifts. By then, all the viewers—Marcus included—would be lulled into believing that the most exciting thing to happen this year was Ryce's scandalous decision to put her own image on the medallions. She would then strike with the truth, beginning with the revelation of Marcus's anarchist activities.

She glanced again at Daniel's empty chair, panic flaring. This was idiocy. Did she truly want to do something so risky? She *could* give the birthday speech her speechwriters had prepared. She could round up the religious anarchists she'd let loose on the city, kill them in secret, and leave the status quo unchanged.

And she could die at the hands of Marcus Lansbury.

Ryce shoved the tray of medallions away. If she was going to die soon, she wasn't going to die quaking in the shadows, nor would she ease into this by starting off with the medallions—that plan had been nothing more than contemptible stalling. The instant she stood at the podium, she would slam the nation with the truth. Gripping her cane, she rose to her feet. Three minutes to airtime.

"Madame President." Her media secretary was at her elbow, his face red. "Ma'am, we have a problem."

Ryce gripped his arm and escorted him off the dais, away from anyone who might overhear this conversation.

"What is it?" she whispered.

"The network is down," he said. "We can't figure out what's wrong. Everything was go until about five minutes ago. They're checking and rechecking everything, but for now, we can't broadcast."

Terror seared her, heat that cooled almost instantly. Hadn't she anticipated trouble? That's why crates of memory cards were already being transported to every city in the nation. That's why the Rosheks and Kent were on the streets of Tremont.

"The entire network is down?" she asked.

"No. Just the servers in the complex, including the emergency—"

"Fine." She couldn't delay her speech now. Marcus was already on the move. "Don't let word spread through the hall that we aren't broadcasting. We'll proceed with the program as planned."

He looked boggled. "Ma'am?"

"Act as though we're broadcasting. And fix the problem. Do whatever it takes. But do it quietly. Clear?"

"Yes, ma'am."

"Whatever portion of the broadcast the national audience misses will be rebroadcast the instant the network is up."

He nodded and hurried away.

Ryce reached for her phone.

* * *

It had felt strange enough walking around Jameston without being noticed when Ian had been *trying* to stay inconspicuous and speak to as few people as possible, but deliberately approaching dozens of people in Tremont without being recognized was surreal. Alisa had told Ian that the uniforms Ryce gave them would be intimidating enough to keep people from noticing their faces, and she was right: no one looked above his collar or below the brim of his hat to notice that the officer of the Presidential Guard marching into network branch stations was an anarchist who had been publicly executed three months earlier. When he scanned his new ID, the network managers were too intimidated to look above the level of his boots. Ian hadn't been called sir this many times since his first year teaching at the University of Tremont when he'd dealt with a freshman who thought groveling might make up for flunking the final.

The ID chip was a type Ian hadn't been familiar with. Instead of his name and other personal information, it contained only special temporary authorization from President Ryce to act in *her* name with full authority. Every network manager meekly accepted the memory card Ian gave him or her and fervently agreed to his instructions: if the birthday commemoration broadcast from the Executive Hall was interrupted or didn't begin on time, they were to broadcast the contents of the card immediately.

Ian hoped Alisa and Jill were having equal success. Last night he'd tried to convince them to stay in the relative safety of the Tremont Mansion and let him scatter the backup cards, which contained a recording of the speech Ryce planned to give, interviews with Daniel, Ian, Alisa, and Jill, and hundreds of pages of documentation. Both women had refused— Alisa calmly and Jill with a look that nearly electrocuted him. He'd tried one last time to get at least Alisa to remain behind lest a reversion put her at risk, but a Broc blocker patch Dr. Kelleher had provided reduced the danger that Alisa might have trouble on Ryce's errand.

Beneath his fear for Alisa and Jill, Ian knew they were right. The most vital thing at the moment was to spread this backup information as widely as possible. Nate and Rebecca weren't involved—they weren't young enough or spry enough to masquerade as Presidential Guard, and a civilian handing out the cards would get questioned by the police. Ryce hadn't dared enlist too many people lest they betray her intentions to Marcus, but Ian assumed she had a few more trusted people on the streets—Kelleher, maybe, and some of her Guard. He knew she'd ordered the overnight manufacture of many copies of the cards—thousands? Hundreds of thousands?—each stamped with the presidential seal, under cover of pretending they were commemorative copies of her personal memories of James Tremont, a surprise gift to the nation and supposedly the theme for her speech tonight.

On the surface, it seemed outright bizarre to Ian that Ryce would let her prisoners run around Tremont, but it did make sense. She knew there was nothing they wanted more than to get the truth out.

Ian touched the tender spot on his shoulder where Kelleher had inserted the tracker implant. Ryce had shown them how to access the encoded signal so they could keep tabs on each other, which he appreciated, though her explanation for why she'd given them access had been unnerving. She wanted them to keep an eye on each other's locations to ensure they were covering the vital points of their assigned areas, and if one of the tracker signals showed the owner out of area—or worse, no longer moving—there was trouble, and the others needed to compensate by hitting any critical locations the out-of-commission person had missed. Ian's pulse jolted every time he checked the tracker program, but so far, Alisa and Jill both seemed to be doing fine.

Ian parked the car Ryce had provided in front of the last branch station on his list and strode toward the building.

His phone beeped. Alarmed, Ian grabbed it off his belt. Ryce had ordered them to communicate only in an emergency.

Broadcast from Exec Hall blocked. Tell branches to broadcast immediately.

Ian sent a quick *Got it.* Not allowing himself time to think—and panic—he headed into the branch station, cornered a manager, and shoved the card at him with instructions to broadcast it immediately by order of President Ryce. Back in the car, he swiftly called all the stations he'd visited to give them Ryce's orders. They would broadcast it anyway when the transmission from the Executive Hall failed to begin, but he didn't want to take the chance of even a few minutes' delay.

Having completed his visits to branch stations, he sped toward his next destination, a nearby high school, where several chapters of the Neighborhood Security Watch had gathered in the auditorium to watch the commemoration broadcast. This was the third tier of Ryce's plan. If the broadcasts from the branch stations were silenced, then local Watch groups would already have the information in their hands. Ian hurried into the auditorium. The sight of Ryce's face on the pull-down screen brought a jolt of hope. She was talking about Marcus Lansbury, and the audience was so quiet that the sound of Ian's boots cracked like hammer blows against the tile. Two men and a woman—the Watch presidents— sprang up and came to meet him.

Ian handed cards to them and gave instructions: if the broadcast failed for any reason, they were to show their chapters of the Watch the information on the card. On the way out, he scattered a few handfuls of cards among the audience. He would have liked to give one to each adult in the room, but he didn't have either the time or the cards for that.

On to the next group. In the car, the radio blared Ryce's voice, now discussing the Council cover-up of Marcus's Liberty Cadre activities. Ian had never imagined he'd enjoy the sound of his own name being spoken over Tremont's network, and his apprehension dwindled, overpowered by determination and gratitude. This was going to work.

Ten minutes since the broadcast had begun, and Ryce's voice was still on the radio.

* * *

"It's a hoax!" Captain Whitney burst through the door of Colonel McLaughlin's office, his eyes crazed with rage. "An anarchist hoax! They've imitated her voice, computer-generated her image—"

"It's not a hoax!" Glenna McLaughlin snapped. "I have word straight from the Executive Hall. President Ryce is up there giving a speech exactly like the one going out over the network."

"That can't be! It's a lie! It's a recording made in her office, and it's coming from the branch stations. It's not coming from the Tremont Complex—"

"They can't broadcast from the Executive Building. They're trying to figure out why not. But I have dozens of eyewitness reports. Ryce *is* doing this. It appears the broadcasts from the branch stations are backups. Ryce must have anticipated interference."

"She's gone insane!"

McLaughlin's thoughts became agitated with a panic worse than any fear she'd experienced in all her years with the Tremont Police Service. Amanda Ryce *must* have gone mad. She was pouring out secrets that would not only destroy the reputation of Marcus Lansbury but also erode Council and police credibility so completely that New America might collapse. Was that what she wanted?

"She's a nut." Whitney swabbed his sweaty forehead. "We've all known it for years, but no one's had the guts to say it. I've sent teams to all the stations with orders to shut down the broadcasts. You need to get to a functioning station and tell the nation this was a hoax. They'll believe it if we act fast. We'll have to figure out a way to deal with the people who were present in the Exec Hall and heard her in person—we'll tell them the anarchists drugged her, threatened to destroy the nation if she didn't lie for them, *something*—"

Whitney was right. They had to shut this down immediately. Damage control would already be almost impossible. McLaughlin opened her mouth to confirm Whitney's words, but as she looked at Ryce's implacable face on the screen, fear burgeoned. "If we go up against the Presidential Guard, this will be a bloodbath. The stations report that the information was delivered by officers of the Guard with full authority from Ryce."

"Check the ID records at the station. Who are these people?"

"No names." McLaughlin threw a computer at Whitney. "Just special authorization from Ryce. If we come out in open defiance against her—" Her mouth slackened as she stared at the new image on the screen. Sitting on a couch in Ryce's office were four people: Ian Roshek, Alisa Kent, Jill Roshek, and Daniel Lansbury.

"They're still alive," Whitney said dazedly. "How is that possible—and Ryce is protecting them—"

"Call your teams back," McLaughlin ordered. "At least until we know what the army is going to do. General Davis won't stand for this, but General Bettencourt is Ryce's nephew—"

"You're *crazy*. We have to stop this!"

"You can't push a tidal wave back out to sea. Ryce may be crazy, but she's deadly. I'm not committing suicide by trying to fight her. Our job is to keep order until things settle down."

"You think selling out to that lunatic will let you keep your cushy position at the top?" Whitney's face distorted with fury. "What makes you think there'll be anything left for you in this wreck? You're one of the people Ryce is covering with mud."

"Shut up." McLaughlin slapped the button on her phone to contact Dispatch. "If you want to survive this, keep calm. I'm calling the teams back."

"I won't let that crazy old woman destroy us."

McLaughlin realized too late what was happening. Her hand moved toward her gun, but Whitney's gun was already aimed at her chest.

Rage erased her fear. "You're with Lansbury, aren't you? And now Ryce is blowing it for you. He's already lost, you fool. Drop your gun and save your own stupid neck."

Whitney pulled the trigger.

* * *

Hot and sweaty and out of breath, Jill knew she was no longer maintaining a demeanor appropriate to a member of the Presidential Guard, but the need for haste outweighed the need for authoritative dignity. Ian had called to warn her that the broadcasts were shutting down one by one. That meant interference from Marcus, which meant his people might intercept her at any moment. She needed to scatter as many cards as she could before that happened.

Fear flailed inside her, but she ignored it. Each Watch meeting was a blur, noisy with confusion when she arrived, silent as she fled to her next destination, leaving them with orders to play the recording on the card. Between Watch gatherings, she pulled over at random locations throughout the city and popped cards through mail slots or sprinkled them on the shelves in stores.

She threw open doors where lights indicated people had remained home to watch the birthday broadcast and threw cards at residents, panting out orders for them to share the information with as many people as possible. Back in the car, more Watch meetings, more scattering of cards.

242

Stephanie BlackStephanie Black

When the attitudes of the people she met began to darken from fear and respect to wariness and suspicion, Jill knew her time was almost up. She hadn't dared turn on her car radio for fear it would distract her, but she wouldn't be surprised if Zero's people were broadcasting warnings about imposters pretending to be members of the Presidential Guard.

In the distance, she heard sirens. She pulled over and sprinted into the library, where another Watch chapter had gathered. She flung a handful of cards into the audience, tossed a few at the Watch president, and raced out the door.

The sirens were deafening now, and two patrol cars were speeding toward the library. She tore across the lawn and down a side street. People were emerging from their houses, talking with neighbors and craning their necks to discern the source of the sirens. Jill hurled cards at anyone she passed.

Her phone rang. She snatched it and gasped a hello.

Alisa spoke urgently. "We're out of time. I'm coming to pick you up. Meet me behind the bank at Cameron Street and Ingraham Road."

"I'm on my way." Jill darted into a gas station, threw a couple of cards on the counter, and sped out again.

Sirens now blared from every direction. Jill ran behind the gas station and cut through the parking lot of the store next to it, heading for Cameron Street.

A dozen or so cards remained in the bag she carried. She eyed the nearest apartment building. She could detour toward the building, open the lobby doors, and toss her remaining cards inside so people would find them. It would only take ten or fifteen seconds; she hated letting any of the cards go to waste.

Before she could head toward the building, a car braked at the curb behind her, and she heard doors swing open. She whirled to face two police officers moving toward her with guns drawn.

Acting out of instinct and desperation, Jill steadied herself with boots flat on the sidewalk, and barked, "Stop!"

To her astonishment, it worked.

Out of breath, Jill infused her voice with all of the authority she could muster. "I'm here . . . by order of President . . . Ryce," she panted. "If you interfere with my work, you'll answer . . . to her. Check my . . . ID if you want to see . . . the official authorization."

The younger officer looked at his partner.

"We have orders to arrest you," the older one said, but Jill knew he was as confused as his partner. She'd been arrested before; by now, she ought to be flat on the ground, her arms pinned behind her back, not having a conversation.

"I'm here by . . . direct order of the president." Her shoulders heaved as she fought to catch her breath. "If whoever issued your orders outranks her, go ahead and arrest me."

"Put your hands in the air."

Jill didn't comply. "Shoot me. See what the president has to say to that."

It was so obvious that neither of them wanted to take responsibility for arresting her that Jill felt a rush of hope. They must have heard enough of the broadcast to generate doubt in the orders they'd been given.

"Captain Whitney's on his way," the older one said to his partner. "Let him deal with this."

"Then let me know when Captain Whitney arrives," Jill said. "I have presidential business to attend to." Her legs were cooked spaghetti as she walked away. Forget the apartment building. She'd head straight for her rendezvous with Alisa.

"Stop!"

She kept walking, light-headed with the fear that she was about to find out what it felt like to get shot.

She heard another car engine and a screech from too-fast braking. A man in a gray suit jumped out of a car, a gun in his hand. Whitney. As the head of the Sedition and Treason Division, he'd recognize her even if her interview with Ryce hadn't yet been broadcast. She couldn't stall or fool him.

"What are you waiting for?" he yelled. "Arrest her!"

As the officers hurried toward her, Jill snatched the phone off her belt and flung it through a nearby storm grate. She couldn't risk letting Whitney check the phone and use the tracking program to find Ian and Alisa.

From the distant splash below, she knew the phone wouldn't survive, even if Whitney sent a city maintenance crew to search the muddy water. Handcuffed, stripped of the remaining memory cards, Jill tried to stay calm as the officers marched her toward their patrol car.

"I'll take her in." Whitney nudged one of the officers aside and gripped Jill's arm.

"Yes, sir. We'll follow—"

"Go back to your duties. I'll handle this."

"Yes, sir." The officer sounded relieved. He and his partner hustled to their patrol car.

Whitney shoved Jill in the backseat of his unmarked car. Jill stared resolutely out the window as Whitney sped through Tremont. Was Whitney personally taking her to headquarters because he didn't trust his officers to handle the awkward, puzzling situation of a supposedly dead traitor masquerading as a member of the Presidential Guard and running around Tremont by order of President Ryce?

Or *was* he taking her to headquarters? He wasn't driving toward downtown.

Chapter 29

"MARCUS, LET'S GO." JOCELYN HATED how desperate she sounded, but she couldn't hide it. "We have Daniel. Let's go. This is falling apart."

Marcus's gaze remained on the TV screen. "We haven't lost."

"Darling." Jocelyn faced him, resting her hands on the taut muscles of his upper arms. Ryce's broadcast was completely off the network now, but it was likely only a matter of minutes before the Guard overruled the police and compelled at least a few of the branch stations to play her filthy report.

"That hag used Daniel," Jocelyn said. "She fed him partial information and lies and threw him out there for bait. Honey, we have no idea what else she's up to. Let's go. Please."

Marcus stroked Jocelyn's cheek. "Stay calm."

"Sweetheart, the *medallions*. She didn't hand out the medallions."

"I'm aware of that."

"Your enemies are alive. Rumors about you and the Cadre are spreading. The nation will be in an uproar."

"Only until I'm able to counteract these allegations." Marcus switched the channel to show the Executive Hall—images supplied by a hidden camera he'd had in place for years.

Jocelyn moaned. "Look at your people *sitting* there! If one of them would jump up and open a few of those boxes—the cowards—"

"Stay calm and trust me. New America needs us more than ever."

"Marcus." She took his face in her hands. "Darling, we need to give people time to calm down. The bombing at Newbold Bay is still so painful in memory. People hated Kent and Roshek for it—now they'll hate you. If you try to step in to bring peace, they'll turn against you."

Marcus lifted Jocelyn's hands from his face and kissed her fingers. "Trust me."

"Please." Tears ran down Jocelyn's face. "We'll go to the US or Canada and wait for things to settle down."

His phone rang. He answered it and listened. "Is she being tracked?" A pause. "Remove it and bring her here."

"What is it?" Jocelyn asked as he lowered the phone.

"Nick Whitney has arrested Jill Roshek."

"And you told him to bring her here? Marcus, *no*! Tell him to kill her. Don't bring her here!"

"She may be useful."

"*Please*. Let Nick take care of her. Daniel will never forgive you if—"

"Daniel will know nothing of what happens tonight unless I choose to tell him." He tapped the screen of his phone, checking something.

"Marcus, *please*—"

"If you can't let me concentrate, Jocelyn, leave the room."

It was so rare for him to speak to her like that that it stunned her. They'd passed the point where she could influence him, and by arguing with him, she was diverting his attention from where it needed to be—on defeating Amanda Ryce.

She *should* leave him alone to think, but she couldn't endure the idea of going to her room to wait. She curled up in a chair near the brick fireplace and closed her eyes, calming herself. Why was she losing confidence? Marcus knew what he was doing. He was stronger than Ryce. He'd win. He'd rule New America.

And he'd win Daniel's loyalty back for her.

* * *

At Alisa's warning that the police were attempting to detain or delay Guard members and confiscate memory cards, Ian abandoned the car. The police must have received hundreds of descriptions of it by now, and with Ryce showing Ian on her broadcast, thus reminding everyone of his name and face, the uniform would no longer be enough to distract people from recognizing him. If the police caught up with him, he'd get detained for sure.

In the alley between an Italian restaurant and a bar, he listened to the distant shriek of sirens and waited for Alisa. She had messaged a few minutes ago, saying she had a different vehicle, one the police weren't watching for, and she was coming to pick up Jill and him. They'd done all they could. It was time to return to the Tremont Mansion before they got trapped in the power struggle erupting between the police and the Presidential Guard.

Ian stared at his phone, watching Alisa's tracker dot move closer and praying frantically that Jill's dot would start moving as well. When he'd checked on Jill, he'd been horrified to see her on the east side of Tremont, out of her assigned territory, her dot motionless.

She was in trouble.

A car stopped at the end of the alley. Ian peeked out from around a garbage bin and saw Alisa in the driver's seat.

He hurried toward her and slid into the passenger seat. Alisa reversed out of the alley.

"Jill—" he began.

"I know." Her face was hard, her cheeks flushed. "Captain Whitney has her. I saw him arresting her. When her tracker dot stalled a block or so away from our rendezvous, I went to check things out. I got there a few moments too late."

Ian bent forward and braced his hands against the dashboard, fighting panic. "Whitney's a fool to go up against President Ryce. He won't be able to hold on to Jill for long."

"He took her alone and sent the other officers away. And he's not taking her to headquarters."

"The tracker shows her current location as—" Ian checked his phone and felt worse. Jill's dot was gone; a note had popped up saying *connection lost.* "Her signal is gone!"

Alisa braked at a stop sign, and Ian held his phone out. She glanced at the screen.

"I thought that might happen," she said, accelerating. "Whitney must have removed the tracker and destroyed it."

"*Removed* it?" Ian gripped his own shoulder where the tracker sat beneath the skin.

"It would be easy. A quick slice and it's out."

Ian pictured Whitney with a knife and blood streaming down Jill's arm. His hands shook as he zoomed in on Jill's last location. "Why would he—"

Alisa picked up her phone from where it lay on the dashboard and handed it to Ian. It showed a map and a moving red dot identified by letters and numbers that made no sense to Ian.

"That's Whitney's car," Alisa said. "Last night, I asked Ryce for access to police communications, and she authorized it. I can listen to all police chatter and track any police vehicle, including Whitney's."

"She's letting you *do* that?"

"Why wouldn't she? We're on *her* mission. She doesn't want us arrested or caught by surprise."

"Do you think Whitney is working for Zero?"

"It's the most likely explanation. If he's not working for Zero, why is he leaving the city?"

"Has he radioed in?"

"No. He's already given S and T instructions to stop the distribution of cards. But on the police frequencies, there's a lot of confusion and conflicting orders from different divisions. I don't know what Colonel McLaughlin is doing, but no one seems to be in charge."

"The Guard—"

"From what I can gather, even some of the Guard have been seen working to keep the broadcasts off the network and gather up the cards we scattered. But most of them are forcing the police to back down. No exchange of fire yet, but it will come."

"We need to get Jill back. *Now.* Do you think we should go to her last known location?"

"Whitney didn't destroy the tracker so he could leave her at the same spot. He took her with him. Watch where his car is going and guide me."

Ian focused on the moving red dot. "Where did you get this car?"

"I used my presidential authority to persuade a citizen to lend it to me."

"Good thinking." Ian wiped the phone on his pants; he was sweating all over it. He wanted to tell Alisa to drive faster, but if their speeding attracted police interest, they'd have another problem.

City to freeway. Freeway to countryside, until buildings and houses gave way to rolling farmland and tangled brown grape vines twined around fences. Sweat dampened Ian's shirt, and he kept pressing his foot against an imaginary accelerator. Whitney's dot had stopped moving ten miles south of Tremont and two miles east of the freeway, near an unpaved road.

"I'll do a search to see what's at that location," Ian said, but Alisa shook her head.

"*Don't.* If this is one of Lansbury's hideaways, he may have flagged it so he'll be notified if anyone investigates the location."

Ian was horrified at the possibility that he'd nearly alerted Jill's captors to their pursuit. "Next exit," he said.

Alisa swung off the freeway onto a road that ran between empty fields.

"On your right," Ian said. "Coming up . . . turn here."

Alisa turned onto a gravel road. Half a mile from the location where Whitney's car dot glowed on the map, Alisa pulled off the road and parked on a muddy shoulder covered in dead weeds. "We'd better not drive closer."

Ian nodded. With no streetlights and no traffic, it was so dark and quiet out here that it would be impossible to drive closer and go unnoticed. He opened the glove compartment in hopes of finding a flashlight. No luck. He checked the trunk and spotted a flashlight hanging in a bracket above a coil of jumper cables. Relieved, he grabbed it.

They jogged toward the location marked by Whitney's dot, Ian using the flashlight only when absolutely necessary. When they were near enough to see Whitney's car parked in the driveway of a white farmhouse, they left the road and circled to the back of the house. Standing in a copse of trees thick enough to hide them from view, they scanned the house.

Ian rested his hand against the trunk of a tree, memory wrenching him. Across the street from his apartment building in Tremont . . . crouching behind a tree . . . watching as Jill was arrested, helpless to save her.

Not this time.

The curtains were drawn, but light showed in some of the ground-floor rooms. A gardening or storage shed was located at the edge of the yard, not far from where Ian and Alisa hid.

"I'll go in and find her," Ian said. "Turn off the sound on your phone. I'll signal you every five minutes. If you don't hear from me—or if I don't say I'm all right—contact the Presidential Guard, the army, the police if you can trust any of them, anyone you can think of. Tell them we've found one of Marcus Lansbury's hideouts—we'll just assume we have—and if they hurry, they might be able to take one of his cronies, if not Zero himself. You'll inevitably end up contacting some of his people, but by then it won't matter."

"Because you'll already be dead," Alisa said. "No. You're not going in there alone. If we go in together, we have a better chance of—"

"Ending up trapped if something goes wrong. One of us needs to be free to act."

"Then let *me* go in. I have much more experience in—"

"But you also know much better than I do how to spread the word and summon help—if there *is* help to be summoned."

"Let me—"

"I'm going to check out that storage shed to see if there's anything there by way of a weapon. Then I'm heading in." Too bad Ryce hadn't given them sidearms along with the uniforms. *Wonder why she didn't want to hand loaded guns to a group of traitors.*

"Ian." Alisa gripped his elbow. "You are the person Zero would most like to kill. If he's there—"

"He'd kill you as happily as he'd kill me. Stay out of sight, and keep that phone ready. I'll feel a lot safer knowing you're out here to come to my rescue if I yell." He pulled his arm free and crept out of the trees toward the shed.

The shed door wasn't locked. In the black interior, he turned on his flashlight. Rakes, hoes, clippers, a shovel. Smaller tools hung on a pegboard. Ian chose a screwdriver, a file, pliers, and a small pair of garden clippers in hopes that one of the tools might come in handy. Matches— sure. He shoved the items into the various pockets of his uniform.

As far as weapons, none of the tools looked remotely likely to defeat Whitney's gun. Ian finally grabbed a crowbar. Swung at an enemy's skull, it might prove useful.

Mouthing a prayer, he stepped out of the shed. Branches rattled in the wind. Alisa was nowhere in sight. Grateful that she'd given up her protests and remained concealed among the trees, Ian darted across the yard to the door that opened onto a screened-in patio. If it was locked, he'd rip through a screen.

Unlocked. He inched the door open and stepped onto the patio. The curtains on the door that led to the house were open, and the room beyond was dark. He squinted through the glass. The kitchen.

Ian reached for the doorknob. It turned under his hand, bringing both relief and wariness. Shouldn't Whitney—or whoever had been here before Whitney arrived—have been careful enough to lock the back door?

Maybe not. They didn't expect anyone to look for them here. They knew Jill wasn't trackable, and Whitney would have no idea Alisa had seen him and could track his car.

Ian edged the door open and slipped into the kitchen, then eased the door shut behind him and stood listening.

A clock ticked on the wall.

Afraid to breathe, Ian inched through the kitchen toward the hallway, crowbar ready, ears straining for any sound that might indicate where Jill was being held. The only sound he could hear was President Ryce speaking from somewhere in the house. A television.

Please let Jill be all right. Ian crept along the darkened hallway, poked his head into a deserted living room, and crept up a flight of stairs.

Along the upstairs hallway, doors stood ajar. Ian flicked the flashlight beam around the rooms. A bedroom with twin beds covered with matching patchwork quilts. A master bedroom. A bathroom with towels hung on racks and a bowl of potpourri on the counter. It all looked so normal that Ian started to wonder if, far from being Zero's hideout, this was an ordinary farmhouse where he was about to scare someone's grandma into heart failure.

But Whitney's car was here.

He texted Alisa that he was okay and sneaked down the stairs, heading for the hallway door he'd passed that he assumed led to the basement. He'd search down there next, hoping Whitney might have locked Jill up and left her alone while he consulted Marcus.

The central room in the basement was empty, except for a few cardboard boxes. A hallway led off to the left. Ian moved along the corridor as quietly as he could manage in his Guard boots. The first door he tried led to a room that had the feel of an infirmary, with a hospital bed and cabinets along one wall.

The second door was locked.

His heartbeat accelerated. If Jill was behind that door, he had a good chance of slipping her out. So far, no one seemed to have noticed him.

Ready to do whatever it took to break into the room, he shone the flashlight on the lock and smiled in relief. It was a dead bolt lock installed on the outside of the door, intended to keep a prisoner trapped inside the room, not to keep intruders out. Jill *must* be here.

Ian drew back the bolt and pulled the door open. He flashed his light around the room and stared in surprise.

The captive wasn't Jill. It was Daniel. He lay on a pad in the middle of an empty room, a blanket draped over him. His eyes were closed, and his face so still and colorless that Ian hastily shone the light on his rib cage to see if he was breathing. He was.

Ian closed the door and moved to Daniel's side. "Daniel," he whispered.

No response. He jiggled Daniel's shoulder. Daniel didn't stir. Dismayed, Ian shook Daniel harder, as if jostling could counteract whatever drug was keeping him unconscious. Ian had assumed Daniel was at the Executive Building with Ryce, participating in the live speeches. Ryce hadn't told them he'd been kidnapped.

When she'd sent him home, she'd seemed confident that Marcus wouldn't come after him immediately—and Daniel had been certain that no matter how much his father wanted to know what he'd been doing at the Tremont Mansion, Jocelyn wouldn't let Marcus interrogate him.

From the way Daniel looked now, Ian suspected Daniel had been wrong. Marcus probably *had* used Broc4 to get information, then—his concession to Jocelyn—had knocked Daniel out so he wouldn't have to suffer through the brutal hallucinatory aftermath. No wonder Marcus had been ready to block the live broadcast tonight. At least Ryce had only briefed them on the details of her plans *after* she'd sent Daniel home, so Marcus could have learned only a fraction of her strategy from Daniel.

Now what? Ian had to get Daniel out of here, but he doubted his ability to hoist all six feet four inches of Daniel over his shoulder and carry him up the stairs. If he tried dragging Daniel, the scrapes and thuds involved in getting him out of the house would alert Whitney, get Jill and Ian shot, and land Daniel back in his cell.

Frustrated, Ian slipped out of Daniel's cell, leaving the door unlocked. Once Jill was safe, he'd figure out how to get Daniel out of here. At least Daniel's life—unlike Jill's—wasn't in imminent danger.

He signaled again to tell Alisa he was all right and proceeded to check the rest of the basement. No sign of Jill. She must be in the one part of the house he hadn't checked—the part with lights, television noise, and armed captors.

He crept back up the stairs. He needed a way to distract the occupants of the house while he rescued Jill.

In the hallway, the ghostly shape of a smoke detector on the ceiling gave him an idea. He sneaked to the bathroom on the second floor, took the trash basket, and filled it with a dry towel and a dozen handfuls of wadded tissue. He lit several matches and dropped them into the basket. A couple of them fizzled out without creating much smoke, but the rest caught hold. He lit another towel on fire, then ignited the curtains at the window. Whitney would be able to put the fires out before they threatened Daniel's safety, but it would take him a few minutes to bring everything under control.

Ian retreated down the stairs and crept along the hallway leading toward the television noise. Only one door was closed, with light showing under the door. Ian slipped into a room across the hall—another bathroom—and watched the hallway.

The smoke detector upstairs started wailing. The door swung open, and Captain Whitney rushed out. As soon as Whitney was out of sight, Ian crossed the hall and crept toward the television room, keeping himself pressed against the wall so anyone remaining in the room wouldn't see him approaching. Gripping the crowbar, he peeked into the room.

Jill lay on her side on the rug in front of a brick fireplace. Her hands were shackled behind her back, and her ankles were tied. Her left sleeve had been cut away, and a gauze square reddened by seeping blood showed where Whitney had removed the tracker. Ian couldn't see anyone else in the room.

No longer worried about being quiet—Whitney wouldn't hear him over the din of the smoke detector—he darted into the room. He set the crowbar aside, snatched the garden clippers from his pocket, and bent to cut the rope around Jill's ankles.

"Time to get out of here," he whispered.

Unable to speak through the tape covering her mouth, Jill shot him a frenzied look of fear.

Behind him, the door thudded shut.

Chapter 30

As she watched the house and waited for any hint that Ian needed help, Alisa struggled to employ the skills she'd honed as a police officer. Vigilance, concentration, the ability to cope rationally with a dangerous situation—the skills were still there, but terror for Ian muddled them.

Her phone vibrated silently in her hand. She checked the display and saw two letters: *OK.* Ian's signal. It would be another excruciating five minutes before she heard from him again.

If she heard from him.

The snapping of twigs jerked her attention from the house to the trees behind her. Underbrush rustled. Coming from the left—the right—angling toward her, getting faster, and now the blaze of two flashlights.

Instinctively, Alisa jumped behind a tree to avoid the beams of the flashlights and heard a pop accompanied by the crack of wood splintering.

Another pop. A gun fitted with a sound suppressor. Alisa tore across the lawn and headed for the fields, zigzagging erratically to make herself a difficult target.

Her boots sank into the mud as she ran, slowing her. She glanced over her shoulder. The flashlights were moving closer. Desperately, she wove to the right, then left again. Her lungs burned. She was out of shape, weakened by her imprisonment and months of hiding.

Ahead, she could see the silhouettes of farm equipment—a trailer, a tractor, other dark shapes she couldn't identify in the dim moonlight. She had to reach the trailer. She could shield herself behind it for a few seconds, maybe long enough to summon help for Ian and Jill—but no help could reach them quickly enough. If Lansbury's people knew she was in the yard, they knew Ian was in the house. Ian had assuredly already been captured. He might already be dead.

Please spare their lives. She darted behind the trailer, stumbling over a pile of rocks, wrenching her ankle. Knowing it would be only seconds before the gunmen caught up with her, she snatched her phone and tapped the screen with frantic speed. A distraction—something to give Ian even a tiny advantage—

The beam of one flashlight came around the end of the trailer. Alisa dropped to the ground and slid beneath the trailer. Her fingers touched a chunk of stone.

Where was the second flashlight? Her pursuers must have split up to search around the farm equipment. Good. She'd never be able to defeat two armed attackers together, but one on one, she might have a chance.

She watched as the light came closer to her hiding place. Gripping the rock, she waited.

The beam of light came under the trailer, sweeping along the ground, and Alisa could see the faint silhouette of the gunman where he stood bent over, looking under the trailer.

The flashlight beam settled on Alisa.

Alisa hurled the rock. It struck the gunman's face, and he reeled backward, his flashlight dropping into the mud.

Alisa shot out from under the trailer. The man lay on the ground; she couldn't see where his gun had landed. She grabbed his flashlight and felt something slam into her arm. A second bullet hit the trailer behind her.

Alisa dove back under the trailer, rolled, and emerged on the other side. Staggering, she made it to her feet and sped into the darkness, trying to concentrate on keeping her footing and not on the blood flowing down her arm.

* * *

Ian grabbed the crowbar and spun around. Fear scorched every nerve in his body.

"Dr. Roshek," Marcus Lansbury said mildly. "You may drop that ridiculous crowbar."

Ian eyed the gun aimed at him and dropped the crowbar. Behind Marcus, Jocelyn hurried out of the room.

Marcus touched the screen of his phone, turning off the television. "The rest of your motley collection of tools can go as well, along with your phone and the matches."

Stoically, Ian dropped the items on the carpet.

"Your stupidity is astounding." Marcus started toward him. "Didn't you stop to think how unlikely it was that we'd leave the house so accessible—unless we wanted you to enter? Or did you suppose God was magically unlocking each door as you came to it?"

Ian would have ignored Marcus's mockery, but he was desperate to prolong this conversation. His only hope now was to stall and pray that the people Alisa summoned would arrive in time—and that not everyone who answered her call would be on Marcus's side.

"I figured you're overconfident enough to make mistakes, as you've shown in the past," Ian said. "You're certainly overconfident now if you were willing to waste time standing around while I wandered into your trap. Don't you have something better to do?"

"I've made good use of my time while you blundered around the house. The situation downtown is under control." Marcus picked up Ian's phone.

It surprised Ian how irritated and idiotic he felt at the way Marcus had toyed with him. What did it matter now? He was going to die regardless of whether Marcus sent his minions to ambush Ian the moment he set foot on the property or waited, smug and amused, for Ian to locate Jill so Marcus could personally destroy him the moment Ian thought he'd succeeded.

"You won't win this time," Ian said. "No matter what you do, you can't call back the truth."

Marcus now stood only a few feet from Jill's head. Ian wanted to fling himself on top of her in the futile hope that his body could shield her from Marcus's bullets.

"Let Amanda Ryce trumpet her scandals." Marcus tapped the screen on Ian's phone with his thumb, the gun steady in his other hand. "She's destroyed herself. The government will wallow in chaos for a few weeks. The people will riot and rebel—if they need a little push to get things moving, I'll see to that. There will be unrest, confusion, and bloodshed on the streets and the same in the chambers of the Council, starting with the death of Ryce. It won't take long before the nation is desperate for a strong leader to restore peace."

"That won't be you. The people will hang you before they'll let the bomber of Newbold Bay lead them."

"People believe what they want to believe, whatever brings them personal gain. As a historian, you know that's true. I'll ensure that it's to their advantage to believe whatever I say. Ryce's accusations will crumble."

"Tell it to the Presidential Guard. They're on their way."

"Neither you nor Lieutenant Kent has contacted the Guard."

"You can't be sure she hasn't." Ian tried not to show how disheartened he was at Marcus's reference to Alisa. He'd hoped Marcus didn't know she'd accompanied him. Had he already sent Whitney after her, or was she momentarily safe while Whitney was upstairs fighting the fire? The blare of the smoke detector had stopped.

Marcus chuckled. "If she had attempted to contact the Guard—or the police—to give them this location, I'd know it."

Ian glanced at the clock on the wall. It was three minutes past the time when he should have signaled Alisa. She would call for help if she could, but if Marcus had conspirators who would alert him to that call, did his people also have the power to intercept her message completely?

"Whether or not we've called the Guard, they'll find us," Ian said. "We're all carrying tracker implants."

"I'm aware of that. But who do you think will pay attention to your signals tonight? The fact that Amanda Ryce would employ your services in the first place indicates extraordinary paranoia. She has almost no one she can trust, and anyone she *can* trust to that degree is completely occupied with protecting her. At a time of crisis, Ryce's only priority will be her own life. If you think she would divert scarce resources to check on you, you are afflicted with delusions of grandeur. You are tools to Ryce, disposable."

"Tools who might lead her to you."

Marcus shrugged. "By the time she has a chance to consider that, it won't matter. We're leaving here as soon as I deal with you. We won't use this location again. But if it will comfort you to communicate with her—" He touched the phone screen, and Ian heard the beep he'd heard several times tonight when he'd recorded messages to be sent in text form.

Marcus lifted the phone to his mouth. "The police are after us. We can't make it back to the Mansion. We had to leave the city. Jill's tracker is offline. We can't find her. Need help." He glanced at the screen, checking to make sure the phone had transcribed his words correctly. "Send."

Ian grimaced. Marcus had no doubt sent that message to the number Ryce had been using to issue orders. Nice touch, to have Ian whining about his missing sister and wanting Ryce to send a rescue party, even though the city was in turmoil and she had no manpower to spare. If Ryce did see the message soon, which she probably wouldn't, it would annoy her, not cause her to dispatch Guard in his direction.

"If you think she's not a danger to you, you're a fool," Ian said.

Marcus set the phone aside. "Lie on the ground, Dr. Roshek. Put your hands behind you."

"I'll stand, thanks," Ian said.

Marcus's voice was as sleek as his silk tie. "If you're stalling in hopes that Lieutenant Kent will be able to help you, I advise you to think of a new strategy. Two of my men were waiting behind the house while you and Kent separated. A few minutes after you came inside, they went after her. She's dead by now."

This confirmation of his fears hit him so viciously that he felt disoriented, unable to think past the image of Alisa lying dead.

"Get on the ground." Marcus drew handcuffs from his pocket.

Ian forced himself to focus. "You're going to kill us no matter what. I don't see any reason to make it convenient for you."

Marcus took a step closer to Jill. "If you'd like a reason—"

"*No.*" Fury at his helplessness engulfed him. Jill's face was ashen, her teary eyes blank. She looked as though she'd succumbed to fear so completely that she wouldn't be able to move even if Marcus freed her. Marcus gave her a glance of contempt before returning his gaze to Ian. He used the gun to gesture toward the floor.

Numbly, Ian sank to his knees. *Please let Jill faint. Let her remain unconscious. Don't let her know what's happening.*

In a flash of movement so sudden that it blurred in Ian's vision, Jill yanked her legs up, whirled her body around, and slammed her feet into Marcus's legs. Marcus fired, but the bullet hit the floor; he was reeling, struggling to keep his balance.

Ian sprang to his feet and lunged toward Marcus. Marcus fired at him and missed; Ian landed on top of him and knocked him to the ground, Marcus's head barely missing the edge of the brick hearth. The gun had fallen out of his hand, and Ian scrambled to grab it. Marcus pushed to his knees and struck Ian in the side of the head with a blow that wrenched his neck muscles. The door slammed, but Ian was facing the wrong way to see who had entered. He rammed his fist into Marcus's gut, and Marcus doubled over, the gun still on the carpet.

Ian grabbed the weapon, but a blow across his spine sent him sprawling facedown. A hand—not Marcus's—tore the gun out of his grasp. Captain Whitney stood over him, Marcus's gun in one hand, his own weapon in the other.

Marcus stumbled to his feet, his face white. He snatched his gun from Whitney.

"Cuff him and tie his feet," Marcus gasped, still hunched in pain as he backed away from Ian. "Then get out. I'll deal with him."

Ian tensed his muscles, readying himself for the last battle. Marcus would have no mercy on Jill now no matter what Ian did, and to die fighting was far preferable to what was going to happen to both of them if he let Whitney render him helpless.

As Whitney picked up the handcuffs Marcus had dropped, Ian jammed his hands against the floor and, with all the speed he could rally, heaved himself upright.

The lights went out.

In the blackness, Ian couldn't even see Whitney next to him. He threw himself back to the floor as a gunshot nearly deafened him. More shots. A weight thudded onto Ian's legs. He struggled to free himself from Whitney and realized Whitney wasn't fighting back. He had collapsed, struck by Marcus's bullets. Ian scrabbled frantically on the floor around Whitney's body. Where was his gun?

Marcus fired again. Ian army crawled away from Whitney, feeling along the carpet for the gun. How far could Whitney have flung it? Ian expected at any instant to feel bullets tearing into his body, but nothing happened.

In the silence, the friction between his elbows and the carpet made a swishing noise. Ian froze. Marcus was awaiting sounds of movement to help him aim. A beep came from a phone, but Ian didn't know if it was from his phone, Marcus's, or Whitney's. He couldn't see any screen light up.

Rapid footsteps came from the hallway, and light flickered in the crack under the door. A flashlight.

"Marcus?" Jocelyn's shaky voice. "What happened to the power?"

Marcus didn't respond, and Ian knew he didn't want to give away his position in case Ian had Whitney's gun.

"Are you all right? *Marcus!*" She hammered on the door. Whitney wouldn't have had time to lock it. Maybe Marcus had ordered Jocelyn not to enter until he was finished.

Hoping any sounds he made would be camouflaged by Jocelyn's noise, Ian pulled his knee to his chest and unlaced his boot. He worked the boot off and hurled it across the room. A crash—the boot had knocked something to the floor.

Marcus fired several bullets in that direction. The sight of the muzzle flash made Ian realize he was closer to Marcus than he'd thought. Instantly, he launched himself forward in the darkness. His outstretched hands slammed into Marcus's legs. Marcus hurtled backward. There was a heavy thud, and Marcus lay still.

Ian crawled on top of him and patted the ground around Marcus's right hand. His fingers touched the warm metal of the gun.

"Marcus!" Jocelyn cried.

Ian shoved the gun in his pocket, fumbled around Marcus's neck, and tugged his necktie loose. He rolled Marcus onto his stomach, drew his arms behind his back, and knotted the necktie around his wrists. He could feel the motion of Marcus's breathing. He was alive. Ian searched him for additional weapons and found only a phone and a set of keys.

Guided by the flicker of light under the door, Ian moved across the dark room, stepping cautiously to avoid colliding with furniture or stomping on someone. He drew the gun and swung the door open.

Jocelyn screamed.

Ian pressed the gun to her ribs. "Stay quiet and stay still. I don't want to hurt you." Quickly, embarrassed despite the circumstances, he searched her for weapons and took her flashlight.

"What did you do to him?" Jocelyn shrieked.

Frantic to find out if Jill was all right, Ian used the barrel of the gun to nudge Jocelyn ahead of him into the room and flashed the light over the carpet. When the light reached Marcus, Jocelyn moaned.

"He's alive," Ian said. "He hit his head on the hearth." Ian turned the flashlight toward a rustling noise and saw Jill rolling out from under the desk. He shone the light over her body. No blood, except for the stained bandage on her shoulder. Gratitude overwhelmed him.

Whitney's gun. He'd better find it. Keeping Jocelyn next to him, he walked to where Whitney lay and swept the light in a circle around him. *There* was his gun, near the wall. Holding the flashlight under his arm, Ian picked up the second gun and slid it in his pocket. What about the handcuffs Whitney had dropped? He took the flashlight back in his hand and located them near Jocelyn's feet.

"Pick up those handcuffs," he said. She picked them up and offered them to him. Ian took them with two fingers of the hand already holding the flashlight.

"Go grab those cutters." He aimed the light at the spot on the rug where he'd dropped his tools.

She brought him the cutters. "Let me go to him. Please."

"Cut the rope off Jill's ankles. Cut it next to the knot, then unwind it. And take that tape off her mouth."

While Jocelyn worked to free Jill, Ian risked setting the gun on the table next to him so he could pull Marcus's keys out of his pocket to see if they included the key to the handcuffs. A small key looked like a possibility. He tossed the keys at Jocelyn's feet.

"Get the handcuffs off of her. Then lie on your stomach."

Jocelyn complied. As she lay on the carpet, she started to cry in quiet sobs, and Ian had to forcibly remind himself he was dealing with Zero's wife and accomplice, not an innocent woman drawn into a nasty situation. He handcuffed her, then took the rope and tied her ankles.

Across the room, he could hear Marcus starting to stir. He hastened to snap the other set of handcuffs on Marcus. Steel seemed a safer restraint than a necktie.

"There are—at least two more out there." Jill's voice choked, and Ian knew she was thinking of Alisa.

"You cover the window, and I'll cover the door." Ian shone the flashlight on the pile of tools, grabbed the other flashlight, and gave it to Jill, along with Marcus's gun. "Can you stand up?" He gripped her elbow and drew her to her feet.

She winced. "Circulation's coming back." She wobbled toward the window.

"Keep to the side, out of the way, in case they start shooting through the glass," Ian said.

"I know. I am."

Ian hurried to lock the door, but he was starting to feel nauseated and dizzy. His head, neck, and back hurt so much from his fight with Marcus and Whitney that he wondered if bones were cracked or muscles torn. *You don't have time to think about it.* He picked up his phone and called Ryce. No answer, of course. He tried three more times and sent several messages, hoping the repeated signals would get her attention. She must be done speaking by now. Maybe she'd have a moment to notice his desperate contacts.

Considering the number of shots fired and the lack of communication from Marcus or Whitney, the Cadre thugs outside had to know something was wrong. Would they call in reinforcements? Ian would have to summon the Presidential Guard, even if it alerted more of Marcus's people. He couldn't just stand here rubbing the bruise on his head and waiting for the siege to start.

The phone beeped in his pocket. Marcus's phone. Ian pulled it out and read the message from an unidentified contact: *Your location given to Watch groups. People on their way. Evacuate immediately.*

Ian stared. What was this? He swiftly accessed the news network. Two channels were back online. One channel was playing Ryce's video of Daniel's interview; the other showed a chaotic auditorium with people hurrying past in the background and a man shouting at the camera that the anarchist Marcus Lansbury had been found. Watch groups were being asked to surround his hideout to make sure he couldn't run.

"*What* did that say?" Jill asked. "Turn it up!"

Ian turned up the volume on the phone. At the sound of the location of the farmhouse being shouted over the network, he directed his flashlight toward Jocelyn and saw shock on her face. She wriggled until she was on her knees, and Ian didn't stop her as she scooted toward Marcus. Marcus rolled clumsily onto his side and looked at her.

"Alisa—must have had time to call for help after all," Ian said, unable to keep his voice steady when speaking her name. "If this information is going out on the network, then the police and Guard must be—"

Marcus's phone beeped again, and Ian looked at the screen to see another message similar to the first, warning Marcus to flee. Should he answer the message, pretend to be Marcus, and claim he had left the farmhouse so Marcus's people would think—

A chime sounded from Marcus's phone, and a picture popped up on the screen showing a car on a dark road. "What's this?" Ian asked sharply, holding the phone where Marcus and Jocelyn could see it.

"It . . . it's from the sensor that signals when a . . . a car has turned onto the road that leads to the house," Jocelyn said.

"Off the main road onto the gravel lane, you mean? A couple of miles away?"

"Yes."

No wonder Marcus had known to expect Ian and Alisa. Two more chimes sounded. A fourth, a fifth. Ian tapped the screen, zeroing in on each car, seeing pictures of license plates and the occupants of the vehicles. None of the photos helped him—he didn't know if the people were Marcus's allies or Ryce's. Most likely, the procession included both. A police car . . . more civilian cars . . . a Guard jeep . . .

"Jill, get ready," he said. "No matter who's coming, they're not taking the Lansburys unless I have word directly from President Ryce."

"You won't be able to hold us," Jocelyn said. "Our people are coming."

She sounded composed now, but in the beam of the flashlight, her face was bloodless, and she arched over Marcus as though protecting him.

The chimes continued. Ian's heart pounded. He couldn't imagine that secretive, careful Marcus had recruited a large group of civilians. He'd recruited a few crucial people and used them to manipulate the rest. But if even a handful of Marcus's people were out there mixing with Watch group citizens who had come to trap an anarchist, how many would they kill in an attempt to protect their leader? From outside, he could hear voices—talking, yelling, cheering. How many people were out there?

"I'm opening the blinds," Jill said. "We need to know what's happening."

Ian wanted to protest, but she was right. They couldn't hide in here for long. Soon, the Watch groups or Marcus's people would storm the house. They needed to assess the situation and try to take control. *Not a problem, right?*

Ian clicked his flashlight off; Jill did the same. With the room darkened, she pulled the blinds up, then darted to the side. Ian dropped to the ground, out of the line of fire.

No gunshots. No shattering glass. Blue lights from a patrol car flashed against the glass. Voices mixed with the rumble of car engines and the clap of slamming doors. Were Alisa's killers there with the growing crowd?

Jill risked a peek through the window. "It's hard to see what exactly . . . but there's a bunch of people . . . they're spreading out across the lawn. Cars are parking all along the road . . . there are a bunch of headlights approaching. . . . Okay, this might be a problem . . . "

"What?" Ian asked.

"Police officers *and* Guard—are both going to try to assert control? . . . But there are a bunch of people with them . . . Whose side are they—"

"Surround the house!" an electronically augmented voice boomed out.

"Okay, maybe they're on our side," Jill said.

Or they're faking it so they don't get mobbed, Ian thought. But at least no one was shooting yet.

The chimes continued relentlessly. Ian called Ryce again. No answer. He tapped the phone screen, finding a map of the area that would show traffic.

"Jill, look at this." Keeping to the side of the window, Ian approached Jill. She glanced at the phone, where red lines indicated streams of heavy traffic flooding the freeway leading to the farmhouse in both directions.

"There are a *lot* of people heading this way," Jill said.

Ian showed Marcus and Jocelyn the phone screen. "You've lost," he said. "People know the truth about you. They won't let you escape. It doesn't matter what lies you tell now or what your people do. You've lost."

He returned to the window and reached to unlatch it.

"What are you doing?" Jill seized his arm.

"Trying to keep them from tearing the house down." Ian watched the shadows edging closer. "I'll tell them we have the Lansburys—"

At the distant throbbing of helicopter rotors, Ian lowered his hand from the window and gave Jill a *good news or bad news?* look.

"Um . . . any word from President Ryce yet?" Jill asked.

"Nope." Ian reached again for the window latch. "I'll tell them we have the Lansburys at gunpoint and that they should stay put until I get orders from President Ryce."

"Let me. They'll be more likely to listen to me. I'm less controversial." Jill pushed him aside.

"We're both—"

Jill slid the window open. "*Hey!*" she hollered. "This is Jill Roshek. We have Marcus Lansbury at gunpoint, and we're getting instructions from President Ryce. Surround the house and stay put!"

Rumbling, chattering voices. The noise spread, growing to a cacophony of yelling. Ian expected to hear more orders from police or Guard officers, but either they didn't want to try to take control for fear of being accused of supporting Marcus, or they were willing to let the people run with this.

A few shadows resumed moving toward the house. More shadows. Earsplitting cheers and clapping.

"We can't keep them out," Jill said. "There are already tons of people, and there must be thousands coming. We need to—"

"Marcus, *no!*" Jocelyn's cry startled Ian. "Daniel's here—you can't—no, *don't—*"

Alarmed, Ian clicked his flashlight on and aimed the beam at Marcus. Jocelyn threw herself on top of her husband, knocking him onto his back. He rolled to the side, and she twisted wildly, grabbing at his hands, her efforts hampered by the handcuffs that bound her wrists. Marcus looked up at Ian and in the glare of the flashlight, Ian saw pure hatred.

And victory.

Knowledge flared. "Jill, *go!*" Ian screamed. "Out the window! *Now!* Get away from the house!"

Jill popped the screen out and jumped. Ian threw himself after her and thrashed through the bushes. "Get back! Get back! There's a bomb!"

In smudges of motion, people whirled and fled. Ian hurtled across the lawn.

A roar shook the ground. Ian flung himself on top of Jill, shielding his head with his arms as heat blasted over him.

When he felt safe sitting up, he turned to look at the house. One corner of it had collapsed. Flames jabbed the sky.

"Are you all right?" Jill cried.

"Yes." He snatched the flashlight he'd dropped in the grass and jumped to his feet. "Stay here. I'm going after Daniel."

"*Daniel?*" Jill chased him as he sprinted toward the house. "Where is he?"

"In the basement. Unconscious." Ian chose a window far from the flames, smashed it with the base of the flashlight, and reached in to unlatch it. "Stay back." He raised the window. "I don't want you to—"

"If he's unconscious, you'll need help getting him out of there." Jill shoved herself in front of Ian and vaulted through the window. Knowing it was useless to try to force her to remain behind, Ian followed her into the darkened living room.

"This way," he said, picturing the layout of the house. The smoke filling the living room made him cough. Bending low, he hurried toward the hallway, his footsteps thumping awkwardly, one sock foot, one boot. If Daniel's prison was directly beneath the study, the blast would have buried him in flaming debris.

Don't waste time panicking. Go!

Flames consumed the end of the hallway near the study, and Ian saw a flash of night sky where the ceiling and upper level used to be. Coughing, he opened the door to the basement and sped down the stairs.

The ceiling had collapsed at the end of the corridor, and flames were demolishing the rubble and spreading along the walls. Ian couldn't remember the distance between Daniel's cell and the end of—

"Which room?" Jill yelled.

"Second door." Smoke wafted out from under the door, but the door itself was cool under his palm. Ian yanked it open.

The ceiling near the far wall had buckled, and the carpet in the corner was burning, but Daniel lay untouched.

Praying Daniel hadn't already succumbed to the smoke filling the room, Ian sprang forward, ripped the blanket off of Daniel, and grabbed him under the arms.

Coughing spasmodically, Jill lifted Daniel's feet. She staggered for an instant to gain her balance, then charged through the doorway.

A crash sounded behind Ian, and bits of burning debris pelted his back. He lurched into the corridor, nearly losing his grip on Daniel.

"The ceiling," Jill gasped.

"I *know*. Move," he croaked, though Jill was already hurrying toward the stairs as fast as she could go, her arms curled around Daniel's ankles.

Sweat poured down Ian's face, and smoke singed his lungs. Coughing, he stumbled up the stairs, hoping the exit wasn't blocked.

In the upstairs hallway, smoke and darkness made it impossible to see, and Ian didn't have a hand free for his flashlight. The only light glowed from the flames at the end of the corridor.

He heard a thud as Jill collided with the wall. "Get down on the floor," he said, his eyes streaming tears. "Let go of Daniel and crawl. I'll drag him."

"I've got him; I'm all right."

Ian felt a tug on Daniel as Jill started moving again. He shuffled closer to the wall and bumped it with his shoulder every few steps so he'd know when he reached the doorway to the living room. When his shoulder bumped empty space, he stopped.

"Right here," he yelled.

They staggered into the living room. "Push Daniel . . . through first . . . the bushes will cushion his fall," Ian gasped between coughs.

Jill hoisted Daniel's feet onto the windowsill, and Ian shoved him through. Jill climbed out the window, and Ian followed.

A cluster of people had already moved in, lifting Daniel, carrying him away from the house. Battling dizziness, Ian stumbled after them. His throat burned, and his breath came in strangled rasps.

Where had Jill gone? Ian tried to look around for her, but coughing knotted his muscles, and his knees gave out. The dampness of grass cooled his face. Grass, still dormant from winter but ready for new spring growth. His mind wandered to thoughts of grass fully green, the trees covered with leaves. Soon it would be summer. But Alisa wouldn't be here to see it . . .

Hands lifted him. He couldn't muster the energy to figure out if he was in the custody of friends or foes . . . If he could just get some air into his lungs . . .

Alisa.

At first, Ian thought he was hallucinating, his mind clouded by smoke. She was walking toward him, smiling, her face lit by the headlights of a nearby car. Mud smeared her uniform, and blood soaked one sleeve.

He tried to call her name, but his throat produced a parched, inaudible whisper. He flopped an arm between two of the arms carrying him and reached for her. Her fingers closed around his.

Chapter 31

"ABOUT TIME, HUH?" IAN JOKED to Jill as they followed President Ryce's secretary toward the elevator that would take them to Ryce's office. "It's almost like she had other priorities than chatting with us."

"Imagine that." Jill's eyes showed the same blend of relief and apprehension that was making Ian sweat. A few days under guard in the hospital, followed by an additional ten days imprisoned with Alisa and Jill in a house somewhere outside of Tremont—with no access to current information—had frustrated and frightened all of them. What was happening in Tremont? Was the nation at peace or falling into chaos? If Ryce *had* maintained order, what changes did she plan to implement—or, now that Marcus was dead, would she try to back away from implementing change at all? And what did she plan to do with the traitors-cum-allies who had helped her defeat her enemy?

Ian glanced at Alisa walking beside him and found it so hard to look away that he nearly crashed into a hall table. She wore an emerald green dress she'd found in the closet at the house, and her black hair was styled with the front pulled back in an intricate braided twist and the rest shimmering over her shoulders. Jill had created the style for her—Alisa had difficulty using her injured arm, and with absolutely nothing else to do, Jill had passed time fixing Alisa's hair. Ian would have teased them about reverting to age thirteen and asked when the toenail-painting party would begin, but he conceded that experimenting with braids was better than the only activity he'd come up with: roaming the house and staring out the windows at a landscape that consisted of a fenced yard, endless trees beyond that, and occasional glimpses of the Presidential Guard.

"I suppose it's a sign of stability that the Mansion is still standing," Alisa said under her breath.

"Or a sign that the Guard has confiscated all battering rams," Ian whispered back, resisting the urge to take her hand.

The secretary touched her ID chip to the elevator controls and gestured for her guests to do the same. Ian followed Jill and Alisa, his forearm still tender from yesterday's removal of the Guard chips followed by the insertion of his own IDs. The two Guard officers who had escorted them to the Mansion followed.

Daniel and Dr. Kelleher were waiting in a reception area outside Ryce's office. Daniel quickly rose to his feet. Jill flew to meet him. Ian would have expected circumspect Jill to worry about the etiquette of kissing Daniel when awaiting an audience with the president, but from the length of the kiss, neither she nor Daniel cared. Ryce's secretary frowned, and Ian wondered if she would tap Daniel on the shoulder and demand appropriate protocol.

Daniel finally released Jill and stepped forward to embrace Ian. "I don't know what to say. *Thank you* sounds ridiculously inadequate."

"Now you know how I felt trying to thank *you*. Sorry about throwing you in the bushes." Ian waved at the nearly healed scratches on Daniel's face.

Daniel chuckled. "Yes, next time you and Jill are rescuing me, would you please throw me onto the grass?" He turned toward Alisa and hugged her gently, not touching the sling on her left arm. "How are you feeling? Dr. Kelleher told me what happened."

"Healing well. The injury wasn't severe."

"How's the pain?"

"Manageable. How are *you* doing?"

"I'm fine, fully recovered. Dr. Kelleher has cleared me to go back with you today."

Alisa didn't speak for a few seconds but held Daniel's gaze. "I'm sorry," she said softly.

Grief mixed with the joy in Daniel's face. "It's . . . surprising that losing them can hurt this much when it's . . . what needed to happen."

"I imagine that makes the pain worse," Alisa said.

Daniel smiled slightly and touched her shoulder. "Maybe so."

"Come in, come in." Ryce stood in the door of her office, waving them inside. "Sit down, let's get to this."

They walked into the office, and she closed the door. "As you might imagine, I'm very busy, but I suppose I owe you a report."

To hear Ryce say she "owed" them struck Ian as a positive sign. The fact that armed guards hadn't followed them into the room was another positive sign, though Ian figured Ryce's men could stampede into the room in a heartbeat if any of her guests made a threatening move.

Ryce seated herself on the couch next to Kelleher, and Ian and the rest chose seats.

"First," Ryce said, "I've read your reports and am amazed any of you survived. I suppose you feel your escape was due to God's assistance?"

"Yes," Ian said flatly.

Ryce's gaze shifted to Alisa. "Impeccable timing on your order to the power company to cut service to the area."

"I didn't know if it would help or not," Alisa said. "But I was short on ideas and extremely short on time."

"The blackout *did* keep Jill and me from being murdered, so I'd say it helped." Ian grinned at Alisa. She smiled back, a mesmerizing look that made Ian feel his smoke-damaged lungs had suffered a relapse.

"And to notify the central Watch committee of Marcus Lansbury's whereabouts and ask them to spread the message was brilliant strategy," Ryce said. "I compliment you."

"Thank you," Alisa said, but she looked troubled. "The people seemed like a better resource than either the police or the Guard, both of which Councilor Lansbury had infiltrated. I doubted he had significant numbers of citizens as allies, so large numbers of people would—I hoped—tilt the balance in our favor. But it was risky. Police and Guard—including Lansbury's people—would inevitably answer the summons as well, and I didn't know what the consequences . . . possible casualties . . ."

"There were no other deaths at the farmhouse that night, if that is your concern," Ryce said. "There were a few minor injuries from debris from the explosion."

"It was an effective way to prove to Zero that he'd lost," Ian said. "Up until that point, he was convinced he could spin everything you'd done to his advantage."

"Arrogant," Ryce muttered. "As to the explosion, we've confirmed beyond question that Marcus and Jocelyn Lansbury are dead. You may think it ridiculous that we'd wonder, but with Zero, it never pays to make assumptions, as I learned the hard way. DNA testing—double-verified by comparison with Daniel—has made it certain."

"How did he set off the explosion?" Despite Daniel's even tone, Ian knew the question was painful for him.

"My investigators are still analyzing the details of the scene. The explosive is one they have never encountered before. Your father or one of his network must have created it. Very compact, powerful, and insensible to heat, friction, and impact. It would have taken only a small amount to create the blast at the farmhouse, and it appears the explosive was concealed in two places. The first was between layers of fabric, probably in his suit jacket. The second was in his briefcase. As to how he detonated the explosives at the desired moment—or rather a few moments too late—my investigators are still working on that one."

Remembering the way Jocelyn had grabbed at Marcus's hands, Ian figured the trigger must have been there, concealed in a watch, a ring, or even a subcutaneous implant.

"I knew he'd never allow himself to be arrested." Daniel's face was flinty.

"Daniel," Ian said. "Your mother's last concern was for you."

Daniel turned sharply toward Ian. "What did she say?"

"She must have realized your father was about to set off the explosives, and she was fighting to stop him. She threw herself on top of him, yelling about how he couldn't do it, that you were in the house. That's what alerted us to the danger and gave us time to get out of there. Otherwise . . ."

"Thank you." Daniel reached for Jill's hand. "I appreciate knowing that."

"As to penetrating your father's inner circle, we've had an interesting source of information," Ryce said. "A young police officer by the name of Rae Pulansky contacted us and offered a bargain—information on Lansbury's inner circle in exchange for amnesty."

"An intrepid move," Alisa remarked.

"Lansbury had sensitized Pulansky to Broc4 as he had Patrick Haines, so we couldn't put her through Information Extraction. But it *was* brave, considering there are plenty of other ways we could go after the information she holds. Pulansky is an extraordinarily bright young woman, as is evidenced by the fact that she was one of the few Lansbury admitted into his inner circle. She liked the rewards he offered her, so she joined him. Now that he's gone, she's not going to cower, waiting for us to find her. She prefers to offer her services to us and take the consequences. I like her. She has guts."

"Did you accept her bargain?" Ian asked.

"A modified version of it. We didn't offer her amnesty, but we did offer to spare her life, which is generous. Lieutenant Kent, it may interest you to know that the assailant whose skull you fractured with a rock was Grant Winston, a Council Clerk. His compatriot—the one who shot you—was Richard Montoya, the Councilor who disappeared not long ago."

"They were working for my father?" Daniel asked.

"Yes. Zero had pulled Montoya from his position because he needed active assistance in preparing for what should have been his day of triumph. We've arrested both Montoya and Winston. One thing is very clear: this organization was all about Marcus Lansbury. There is no heir. Whether or not we manage to find every one of his coconspirators, the Cadre is dead."

"What about Nadia Sears?" Daniel asked.

"Kidnapped, to clear the way for your appointment to the position of Council Assistant. Pulansky told us where to find her, along with a kidnapped police officer, Lieutenant Blake Peale."

"Peale, huh?" Ian grinned at Jill. "Hope the experience improved his personality."

Jill laughed.

"According to Pulansky, the inner circle was principally Council Assistants," Ryce said. "People poised to step into the places of their chiefs after the mass assassination that should have taken place at the Tremont Birthday Celebration."

"Mass assassination?" Ian asked in surprise.

"Yes. I had some gold medallions I was planning to distribute—this year's gift to the Council and Assistants. Zero had arranged for the individual boxes to be rigged with packets containing a neurotoxin. If the boxes had been opened at the commemoration—as they should have been; it's traditional—the toxin would have been released into the air. Within an hour, at least 75 percent of the people in that hall would have been dead, including me."

Ian stared in horror. "I thought you said Zero had his own people there too."

"Inoculated against the toxin. They would have been among the few to survive and to participate in the rebuilding of our government under Lansbury's direction. Apparently, he was planning to blame this attack on religious anarchists—perhaps as a personal thank you for the way you corrupted his son, Dr. Roshek."

"I'm flattered," Ian said acidly. "How did you learn about this in time to avoid handing out the medallions? Or had you never intended to distribute them?"

"I didn't learn of this until Pulansky told us later. I *did* intend to hand them out, to lull Lansbury and everyone else into thinking this broadcast was the usual pomp and nonsense—and perhaps, still wanting to feed my vanity. But at the last minute, I changed my mind."

"A timely change of heart," Alisa said.

"Timely indeed. Now, I assume you want to know what's happening nationwide. My broadcast has been repeated multiple times and is available on the national network, along with supporting documentation. I guarantee there is not one man or woman in New America who has not begun to gain an accurate picture of both Lansbury's Liberty Cadre activities and the same tactics indulged in by our government."

"What has been the overall reaction?" Alisa asked.

"Anger, naturally, but mingled with hope and a thirst to learn more. Millions of people have examined the documents I've offered. I've held several news conferences and have encouraged the press to ask questions, all of which I've answered candidly. As far as peace and order, things have remained mostly quiet. There have been a number of violent incidents— damage to the police station in Paxton, for instance—but nothing in the way of large-scale rioting. Each chapter of the Watch has held a meeting, as ordered, to give people an organized opportunity to discuss these revelations. Next week, the Watch will hold a second meeting and leaders will report back on the national temperament."

"How is the Council reacting?" Daniel asked.

"At first they were furious. They thought I was a lunatic old lady who had doomed all of us to death by mob violence. Now, with the people backing me, the majority figure it's safer to support me than to fight me." Ryce's eyes gleamed. "As for the Tremont Police Service, there is still confusion there. Colonel McLaughlin is dead—shot by Nicholas Whitney— and we haven't yet named her successor, since I want to make sure I trust the new appointee. Basic policing functions continue to ensure public safety, and I've announced that anyone caught venting anger on a police or Guard officer will be dealt with harshly. I will not allow chaos to take hold."

Ian wasn't sure what to say. It was amazing that things were as stable as they were. But did that stability come mostly from Ryce's increasingly powerful grip on the nation? Did both leaders and populace see her as safety, thus giving her *more* power than she'd had before this shake-up?

Ryce's gaze met Ian's. Neither of them spoke, and he sensed she was trying to search as deeply into his mind as he was trying to search hers.

"You're worried," she said. "You think all you've helped me accomplish is to strengthen my power. My strongest enemy is dead, and a nervous population clings to me as the person promising them justice and truth— whether or not I intend to deliver. Why would I yield up any control or do anything more than pretend to listen to dissenting viewpoints?"

"Why *would* you?" Ian asked.

Ryce rose stiffly to her feet and took her cane from where it leaned against the arm of the couch. "I am ninety-four years old," she said. "Given the consistent failure of our life-extension projects, I'm not likely to live for more than five or ten years—probably fewer. If I amass more power in that time, what will it gain me? Another dozen pages in the history books? A larger mausoleum, leafed in gold, that I will never see?"

"Is there anything else to be gained?" Ian asked.

"You claim there is."

"Yes."

"That's priceless knowledge." Ryce walked across the carpet and stopped in front of him. "If it's true."

He looked up into her knife-sharp eyes. "How much would it be worth to you to know it's true?"

"What would it cost me?"

"If it cost a kingdom, would you pay it?"

She laughed softly, white eyebrows lifting. "The same offer made by a king of old, isn't it?"

Ian's heart pounded. "You've been reading."

Her hand closed on his shoulder, and she bent over him, fingers sinking into his flesh. "I would pay it," she said. "To know that life continues—I would pay it."

"Then ask the question, and pay whatever it costs to get the answer."

She released him and stepped back. "There *will* be changes," she said, and from the way her voice rose, she was ending her dialogue with Ian and engaging all of her visitors again. "Councilor Brannigan is still leading the drive to create a written constitution. We'll study and compile the feedback we receive from the nation before determining exactly how to go about creating a written charter. That is a crucial first step."

Brannigan was still on the Council after what he'd done?

Before Ian could ask the question, Alisa spoke. "You say the majority are backing you. What about the remainder? I assume you are facing some dangerous opposition."

"Naturally. I always have enemies, Lieutenant. Open enemies and secret enemies, and yes, there have been a few who have tried to move against me in the past two weeks. If you want a guarantee that I'll succeed, that there will be change in New America, I can't give you that promise. But I *will* fight for it, and I'll make sure the people know that."

Alisa scrutinized Ryce, making Ian wonder if she—like Ian—questioned how much Ryce's focus on the people grew from her desire to treat them justly and how much grew from a desire to make herself so beloved that popular support would help protect her from enemies on the Council.

But Ryce *had* been allowing Brannigan to go forward with his Constitutional Drive for months now. Her motives were unquestionably mixed, but her willingness to consider change was not entirely new.

"What are your goals?" Alisa asked.

"My only answer there is a weak one I wouldn't give publicly: namely, they're a work in progress. I don't feel any loyalty to James Tremont's prescription for stability, but neither am I sure what ought to replace it." She rubbed the hand she'd used to grip Ian's shoulder as though she'd strained the joints. "But at the moment, we must do something with the four of you. You're an awkward problem. You are traitors, and I'd rather not hold up your treason as a model for the citizenry to emulate. Orderly change is what I seek—not brazen defiance. But given the amount of information I've shared about you, many view you as heroes—flawed, possibly insane heroes, but heroes still—for the courage you showed in defeating the bomber of Newbold Bay. Twice."

"You've released the details of what took place at the farmhouse?" Alisa asked.

"Yes, of course. I wouldn't have a lot of credibility in promising to eliminate lies if I started off by attempting to conceal your role in thwarting Zero."

"That beats the press we got last time," Ian said dryly.

"I'm grateful for your service," Ryce said. "But I can't simply grant you amnesty and release you. You're too controversial. Whether you wanted it or not, you would attract radicals who seek revolution and assume you would sympathize, troubled citizens who want to share their own pain over government actions, traditionalists who still idolize Tremont and would hate and hurt you for defying him, and a horde of other unstable people who'd want to worship you, use you, or punish you. Whether you're viewed as heroes or villains, you'd be a disruption at a critical time, and I won't risk that."

Ian glanced at Jill. She sat gripping Daniel's hand, and from the tightness in her face, she was bracing herself for whatever sentence Ryce was about to pronounce.

"So are we prisoners, or are we dead?" Ian asked.

"I don't want you dead." Ryce returned to her seat. "Yes, you'll remain prisoners—or let's say you'll remain in seclusion—until the situation is more stable, but you'll be comfortable. You'll be at an estate near the north border. Nathan and Rebecca Halbrook will be there as well, and you'll be working for me. You'll have access to whatever sources you request, and you'll conduct research and provide insights relevant to governmental reform. You all have valuable and relevant areas of expertise—history, medicine, local and national security, even the arts." She gave a half smile. "Religion. No topic is off-limits at the moment, official bans notwithstanding."

"Will this be dangerous for you, keeping us alive?" Alisa asked. "Using us as a resource?

"Yes. But if I executed you or threw you into prison, my enemies would use *that* against me as well—cruel treatment for the heroes who defeated Zero. Therefore, I'll do what I feel is best."

"What about Spencer Brannigan?" Daniel asked. "You've allowed him to remain on the Council?"

"Spencer is less problematic—guilty solely of turning a blind eye to your refusal to condone what is now viewed as the scandalous Cadre cover-up. Without other treasonous acts to complicate things, and given his position, which makes it difficult for potential troublemakers to access him and attempt to use him in creating unrest, it was not difficult to persuade the Council to grant him amnesty."

"I assume his pardon also serves as an olive branch to the people," Alisa said.

"Yes, Lieutenant. Follow-through on my admission that covering for Marcus Lansbury was a mistake. The people seem pleased that Spencer and I can shake hands and work together on the reform movement." Ryce pointed her cane at the door. "Go. You'll get additional instructions later. Dr. Kelleher now requires you to accompany him to his office so he can nag you regarding your health."

* * *

Kelleher's office turned out to be part of a hospital wing at the Tremont Mansion. Apparently, Ryce liked to stay home when she needed medical care, Ian noted. After examining Ian and Jill to verify that they were fully recovering from the skirmish and fire at the farmhouse, Kelleher called in Alisa and Daniel together. Whatever they were doing took so long that Ian and Jill finally gave up on an uncomfortable effort to chat under the eye of their Guard escort. Too drained to stay alert while sitting silently, Ian leaned his head against the wall and dozed, wondering sleepily how long it would be until Ryce transferred them up north.

It was evening before they were escorted back to the house in the wooded area outside Tremont. After a freeze-dried meal, Jill and Daniel settled in the living room, Daniel's arm around Jill. Ian declined Jill's invitation to join them; they needed time alone.

At loose ends, he wandered over to the glass door at the back of the kitchen and scanned the backyard. Alisa stood at a cupboard, doing a one-handed inventory of the remaining pouches of food as though hoping to find something appetizing to look forward to for breakfast.

"Want to go on a walk?" Ian asked.

"Circle the backyard, you mean?" She closed the cupboard.

"Yep. But only if you're feeling up to it."

"Let me get a jacket," she said.

The fresh breeze, the buds of new leaves, the vivid yellow of forsythia bushes—it was a beautiful spring evening, and Ian was intensely grateful they weren't locked inside. He couldn't see any of the Guard around. He'd seen one on the front porch and assumed more patrolled nearby. Security devices probably ringed the yard as well, set to trip if they stepped over the perimeter. But being outside was always a relief, even if they weren't permitted to walk more than a few dozen yards from the house.

"What was Kelleher up to?" he asked, taking the jacket from Alisa's hands so he could help her put it on.

"Tests," she said, slipping her right arm into the sleeve. "Brain scans, blood work. Endless questions. Consultation with Daniel. They're determined to eradicate the very last of my reversions."

"That's fantastic." Ian carefully draped the jacket around her injured arm. "I'm impressed Ryce would let him spend his time on us."

"I get the impression Dr. Kelleher does what he wants, and Ryce trusts him enough to let him have that autonomy."

"What do you think of all this?" Ian asked as they stepped off the back porch. "The things President Ryce said today?"

She looked pensive. "I'm hopeful. It's significant that she's made at least outward peace with Councilor Brannigan. That's not something she would have done in the past—let people know he defied her and she not only didn't punish him but allowed him to maintain his power."

"True," Ian said. "I've seen enough miracles lately to believe more are coming—maybe through Ryce."

"I agree."

Ian picked up a small evergreen branch that had fallen into the bed of tulips near the porch. "I had no idea what she'd do with the rest of us, but I didn't expect to get hired."

Alisa smiled. "I'm not surprised she wants your insights. You'll be a tremendous help. You are . . . one of the most remarkable people I've ever known."

Ian felt himself turning red. He picked a few needles off the branch. "I . . . hope you don't mind being stuck with my company for a while longer."

"I don't mind."

Looking at Alisa, Ian had trouble remembering or caring that Presidential Guard and security cameras lurked nearby. He focused on a budding tree. "Do you want to march around the yard clockwise or counterclockwise?" he joked, hoping Alisa wouldn't notice how nervous he sounded.

"A difficult decision."

"We specialize in hard decisions." Ian looked at her, and her eyes met his. Tender, inquisitive eyes. He broke eye contact and pulled a few more needles off the branch in his hands. Alisa had never treated him as more than a friend or a brother, and he knew he had to be careful not to hint at his feelings. Thanks to Ryce's decision, his and Alisa's lives would remain intertwined for an indefinite period, and he didn't want that proximity to include embarrassment and Alisa's wishing she could request a transfer to a cell in the Detention Annex to get away from him.

Alisa stepped so they were standing face-to-face. "I hope you don't mind being stuck with *my* company."

"No, are you kidding? It's great that . . . great that . . . I mean, I enjoy . . . I'm glad that . . ." He held up the branch. "Uh, so is this pine or spruce?"

She rested her hand on his arm. "Why don't you tell me what you're really thinking?"

His pulse raced. Alisa was smiling at him, the setting sun casting clear, bright light over her face.

"Okay," he said. "I'm thinking . . . do you mind if I kiss you?"

She stepped closer to him, put her hand on the back of his neck, and drew his head down to meet hers.

He figured that counted as an answer.

About the Author

STEPHANIE BLACK HAS LOVED BOOKS since she was old enough to grab the pages and has enjoyed creating make-believe adventures since she and her sisters were inventing long Barbie games filled with intrigue and danger or running around pretending to be detectives. She is a four-time Whitney Award winner for Best Mystery/Suspense, most recently for *Rearview Mirror* (2011).

Stephanie was born in Utah and has lived in various places, including Arizona; Massachusetts; New York; and Limerick, Ireland. She currently lives in Northern California and enjoys spending time with her husband, Brian, and their five children. She is a fan of chocolate, cheesecake, and her husband's homemade bread.

Stephanie enjoys hearing from readers. You can contact her via e-mail at info@covenant-lds.com or by mail, care of Covenant Communications, P.O. Box 416, American Fork, UT 84003-0416. Visit her website at www.stephanieblack.net and her blog, *Black Ink*, at www.stephanieblackink.blogspot.com.